BE PREPARED

VERA BROSGOL

COLOR BY
ALEC LONGSTRETH

W9-BLK-303

:01

First Second
NEW YORK

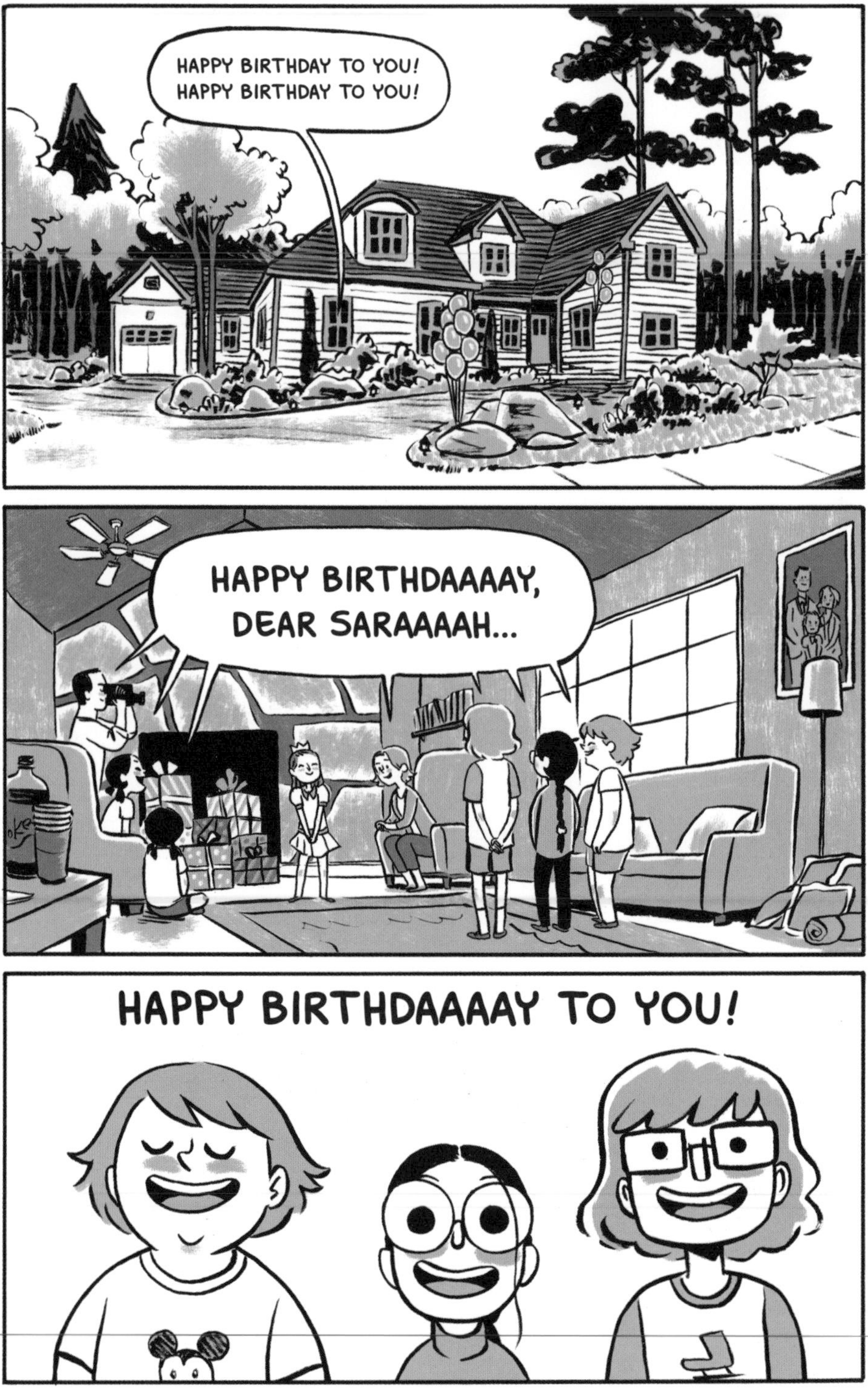
HAPPY BIRTHDAY TO YOU!
HAPPY BIRTHDAY TO YOU!
HAPPY BIRTHDAAAAY,
DEAR SARAAAAH...
HAPPY BIRTHDAAAAY TO YOU!

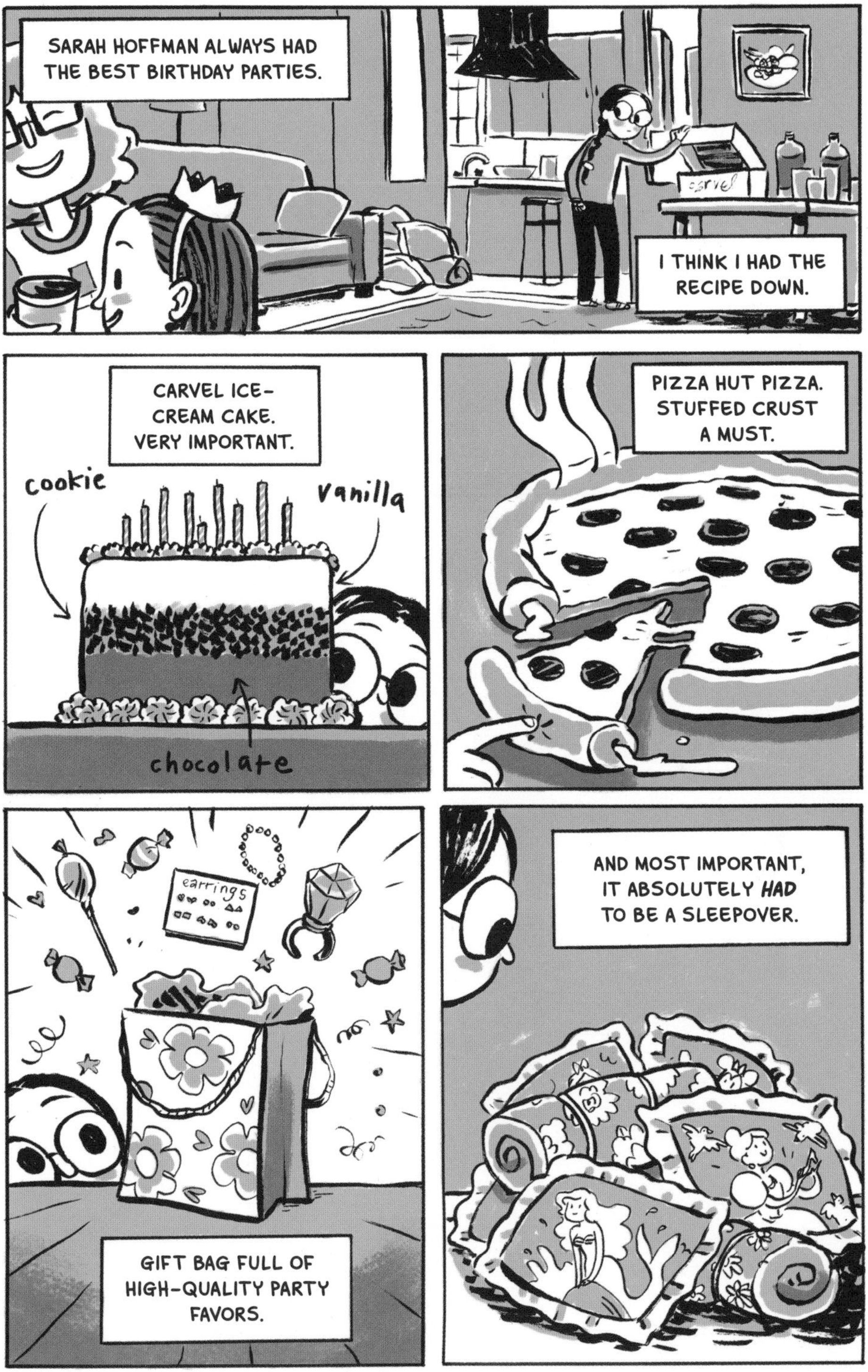
SARAH HOFFMAN ALWAYS HAD THE BEST BIRTHDAY PARTIES.
I THINK I HAD THE RECIPE DOWN.
CARVEL ICE-CREAM CAKE. VERY IMPORTANT.
cookie
vanilla
chocolate
PIZZA HUT PIZZA. STUFFED CRUST A MUST.
earrings
GIFT BAG FULL OF HIGH-QUALITY PARTY FAVORS.
AND MOST IMPORTANT, IT ABSOLUTELY *HAD* TO BE A SLEEPOVER.

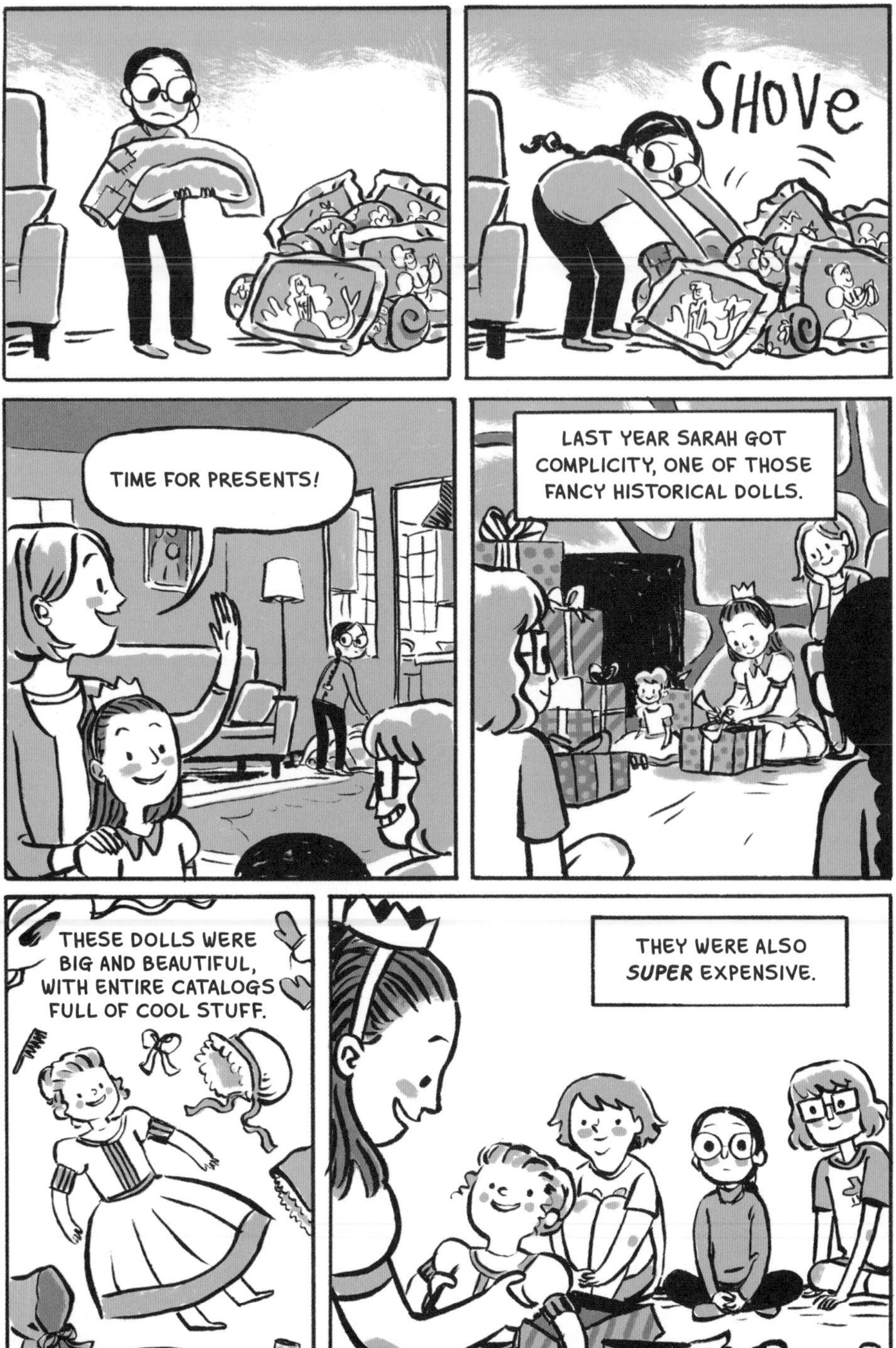
SHOVE
TIME FOR PRESENTS!
LAST YEAR SARAH GOT COMPLICITY, ONE OF THOSE FANCY HISTORICAL DOLLS.
THESE DOLLS WERE BIG AND BEAUTIFUL, WITH ENTIRE CATALOGS FULL OF COOL STUFF.
THEY WERE ALSO *SUPER* EXPENSIVE.

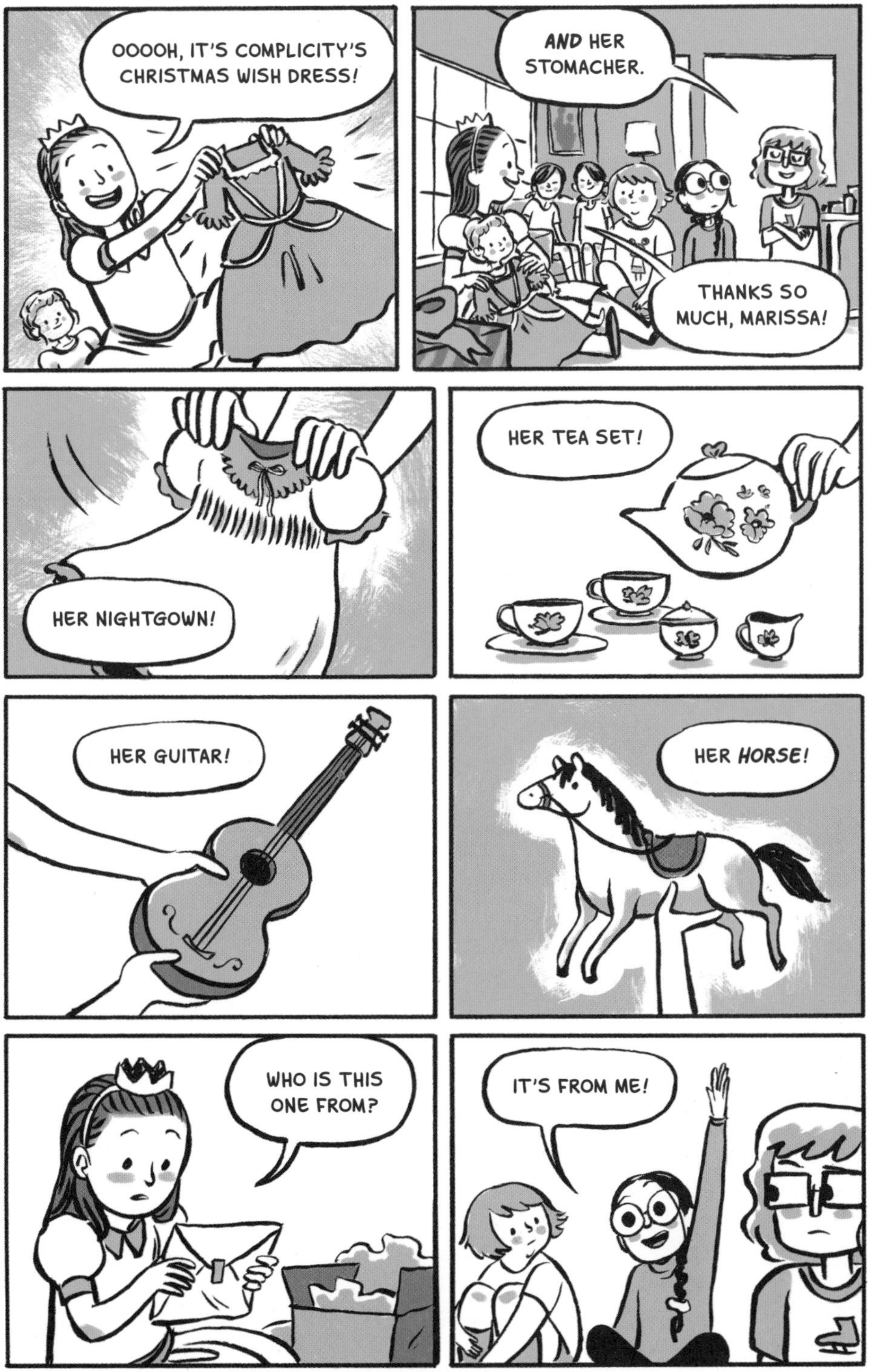
OOOOH, IT'S COMPLICITY'S CHRISTMAS WISH DRESS!
AND HER STOMACHER.
THANKS SO MUCH, MARISSA!
HER NIGHTGOWN!
HER TEA SET!
HER GUITAR!
HER HORSE!
WHO IS THIS ONE FROM?
IT'S FROM ME!

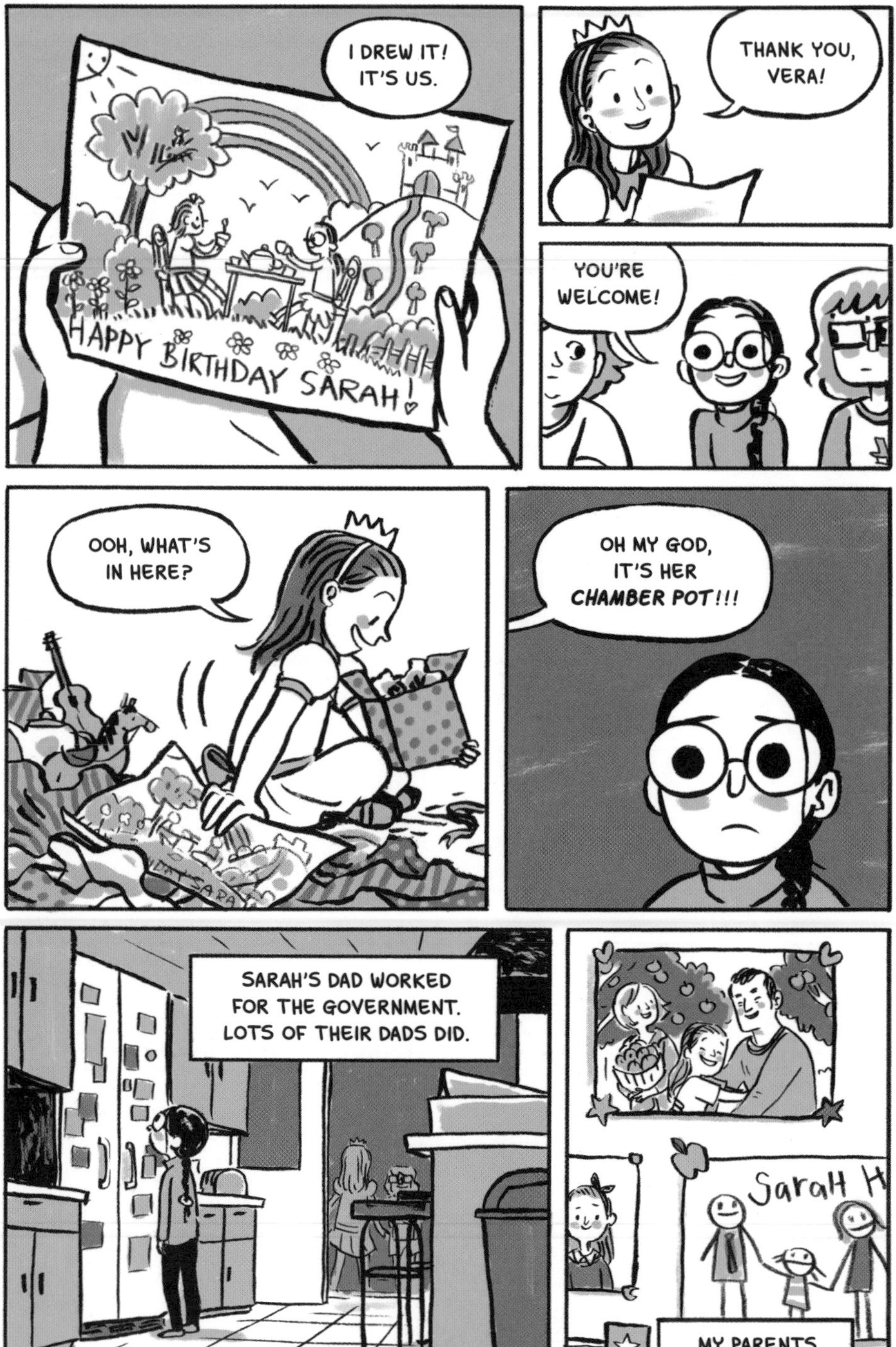
HAPPY BIRTHDAY SARAH!
I DREW IT! IT'S US.
THANK YOU, VERA!
YOU'RE WELCOME!
OOH, WHAT'S IN HERE?
OH MY GOD, IT'S HER CHAMBER POT!!!
SARAH'S DAD WORKED FOR THE GOVERNMENT. LOTS OF THEIR DADS DID.
Sarah H
MY PARENTS WERE DIVORCED.

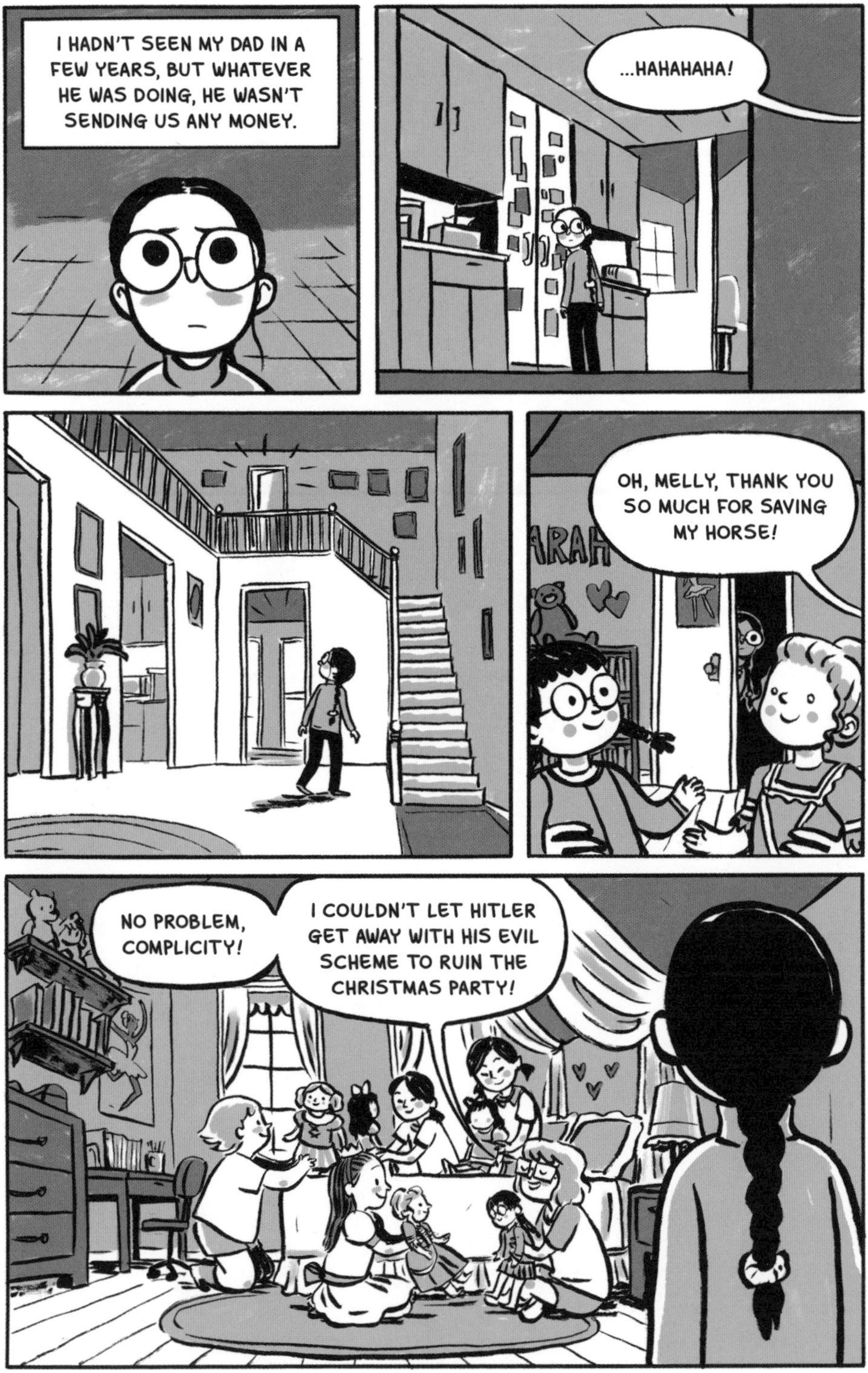
I HADN'T SEEN MY DAD IN A FEW YEARS, BUT WHATEVER HE WAS DOING, HE WASN'T SENDING US ANY MONEY.
...HAHAHAHA!
OH, MELLY, THANK YOU SO MUCH FOR SAVING MY HORSE!
NO PROBLEM, COMPLICITY!
I COULDN'T LET HITLER GET AWAY WITH HIS EVIL SCHEME TO RUIN THE CHRISTMAS PARTY!

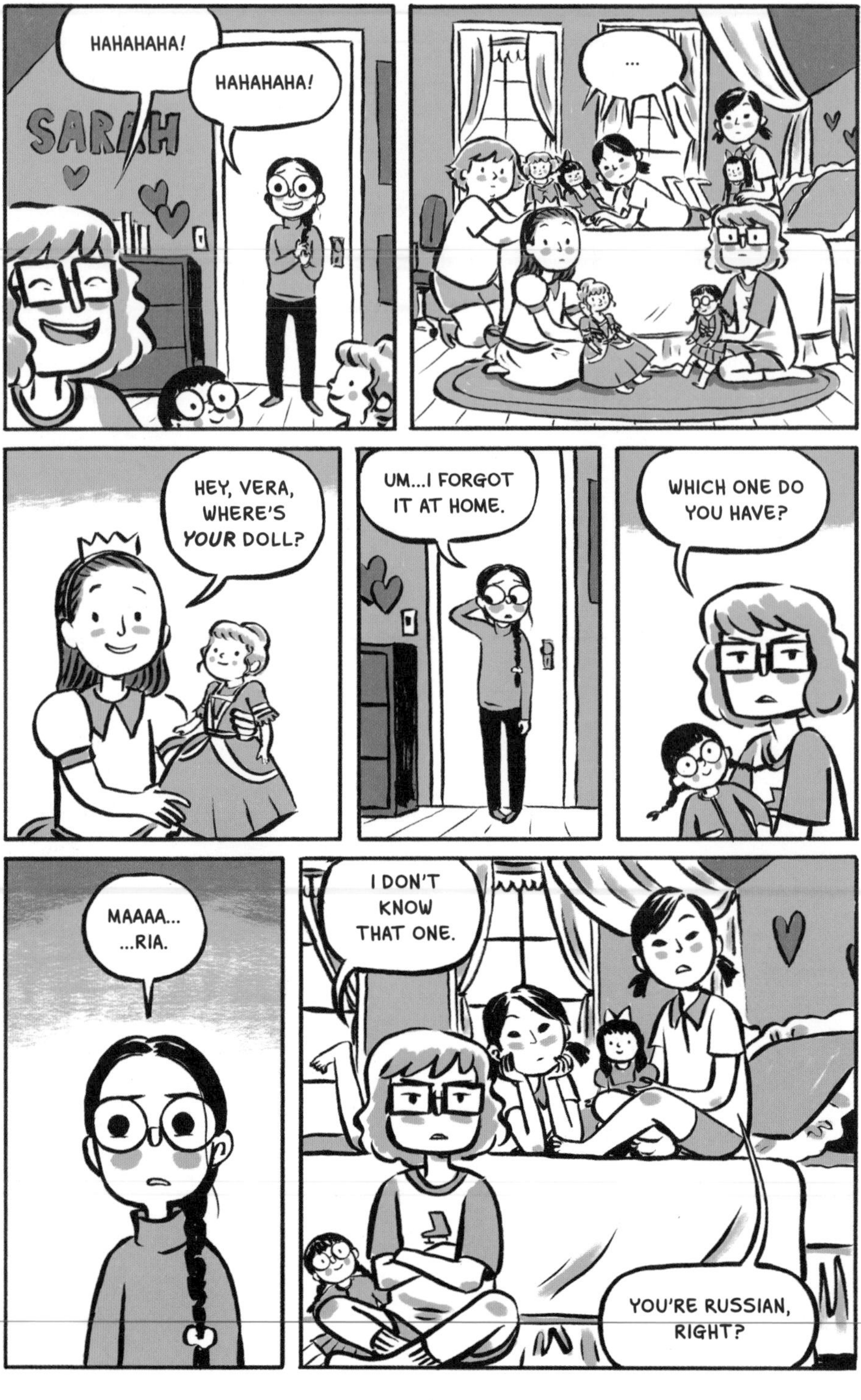

HAHAHAHA!
HAHAHAHA!
SARAH
...
HEY, VERA, WHERE'S *YOUR* DOLL?
UM...I FORGOT IT AT HOME.
WHICH ONE DO YOU HAVE?
MAAAA... ...RIA.
I DON'T KNOW THAT ONE.
YOU'RE RUSSIAN, RIGHT?

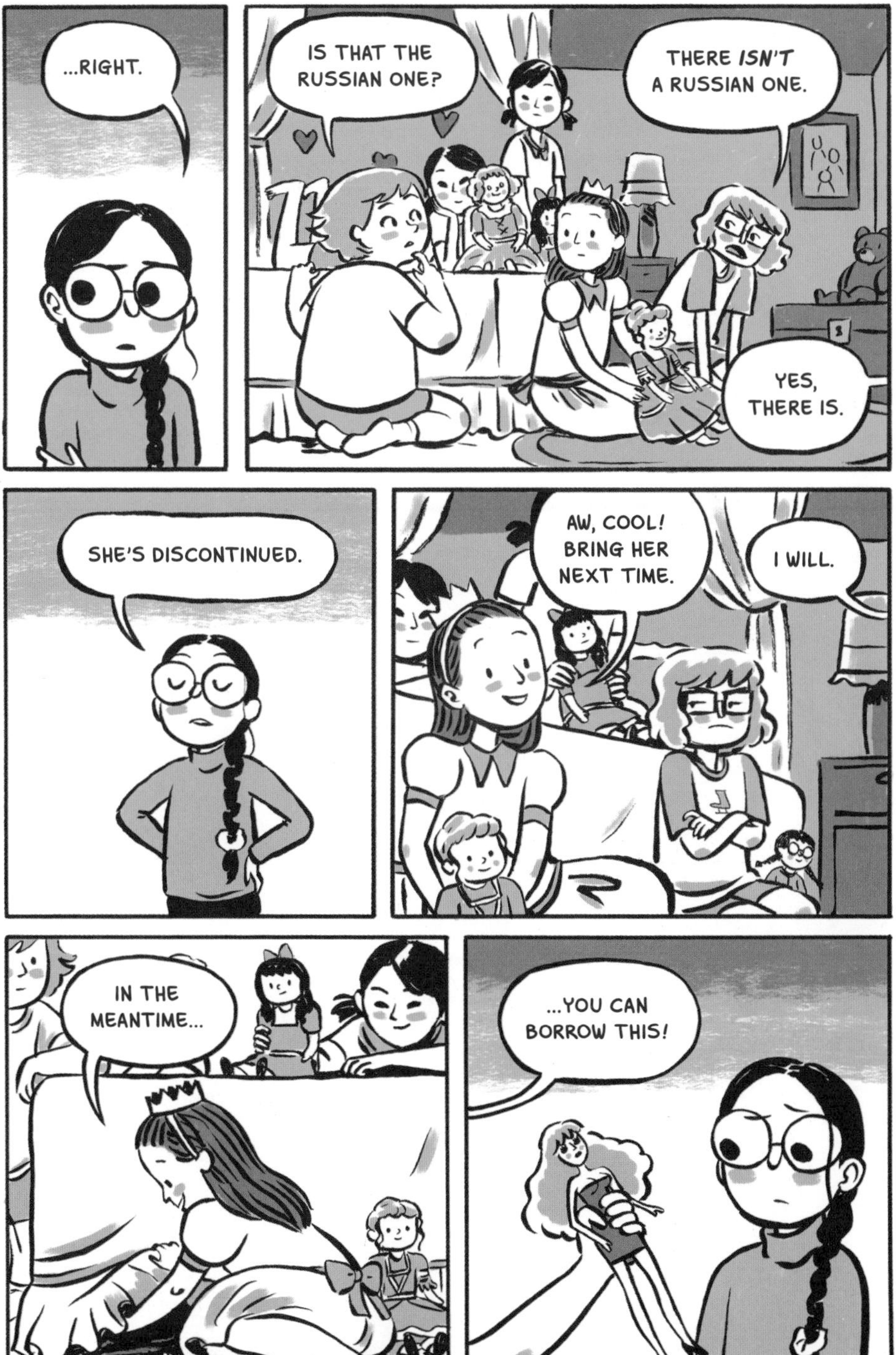
...RIGHT.
IS THAT THE RUSSIAN ONE?
THERE *ISN'T* A RUSSIAN ONE.
YES, THERE IS.
SHE'S DISCONTINUED.
AW, COOL! BRING HER NEXT TIME.
I WILL.
IN THE MEANTIME...
...YOU CAN BORROW THIS!

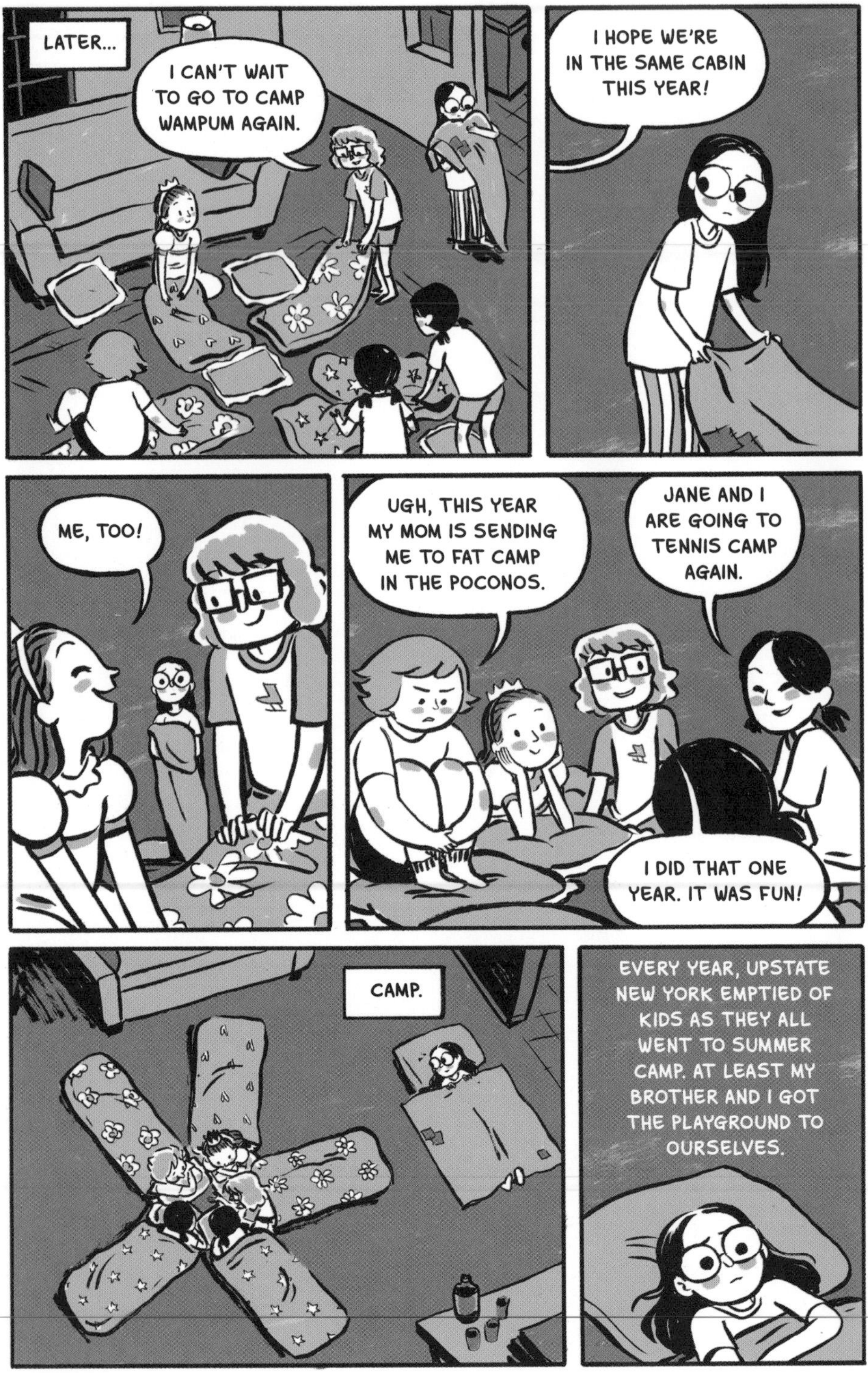
LATER...
I CAN'T WAIT TO GO TO CAMP WAMPUM AGAIN.
I HOPE WE'RE IN THE SAME CABIN THIS YEAR!
ME, TOO!
UGH, THIS YEAR MY MOM IS SENDING ME TO FAT CAMP IN THE POCONOS.
JANE AND I ARE GOING TO TENNIS CAMP AGAIN.
I DID THAT ONE YEAR. IT WAS FUN!
CAMP.
EVERY YEAR, UPSTATE NEW YORK EMPTIED OF KIDS AS THEY ALL WENT TO SUMMER CAMP. AT LEAST MY BROTHER AND I GOT THE PLAYGROUND TO OURSELVES.

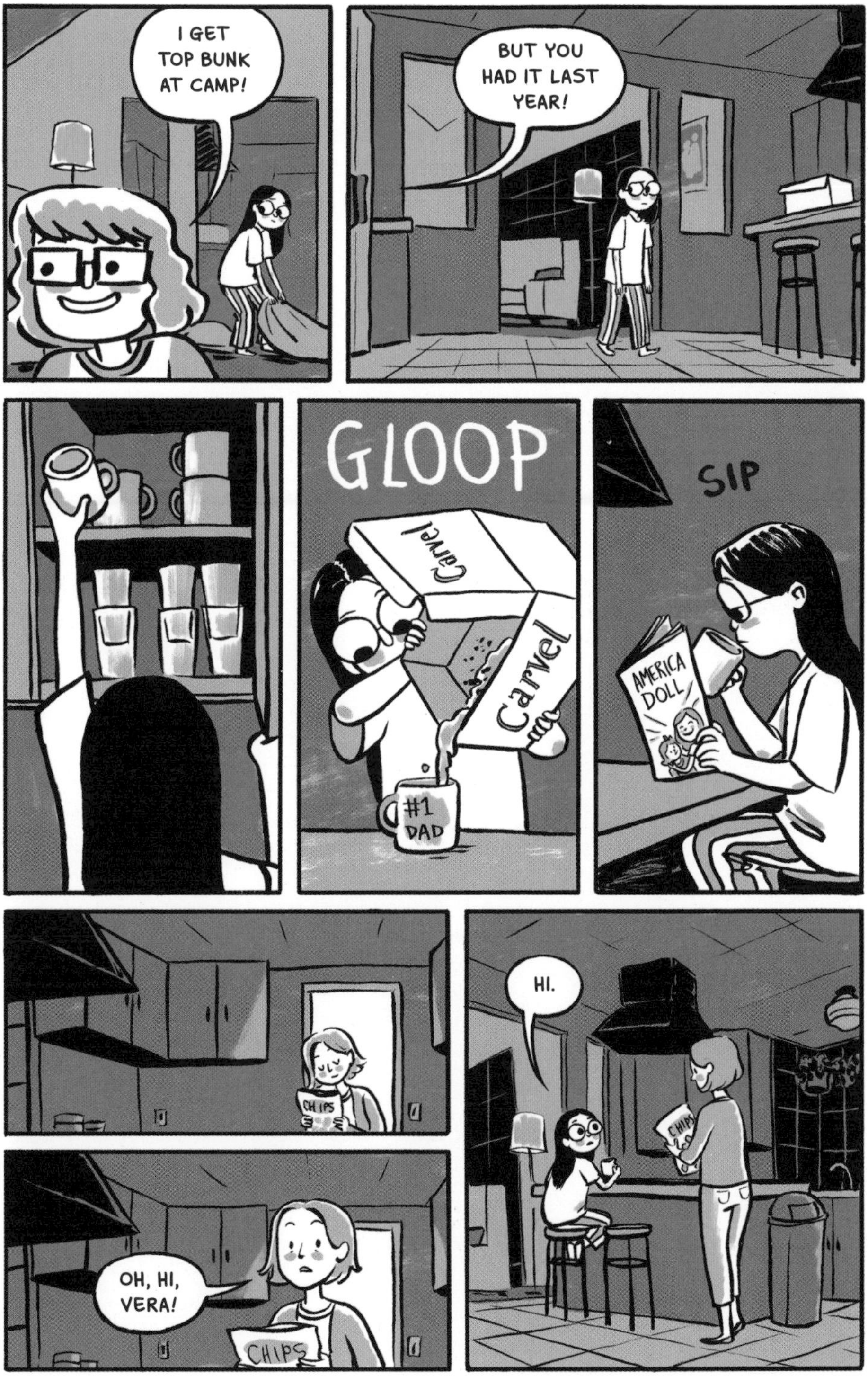
I GET TOP BUNK AT CAMP!
BUT YOU HAD IT LAST YEAR!
GLOOP
Carvel
Carvel
#1 DAD
SIP
AMERICA DOLL
CHIPS
HI.
CHIPS
OH, HI, VERA!
CHIPS

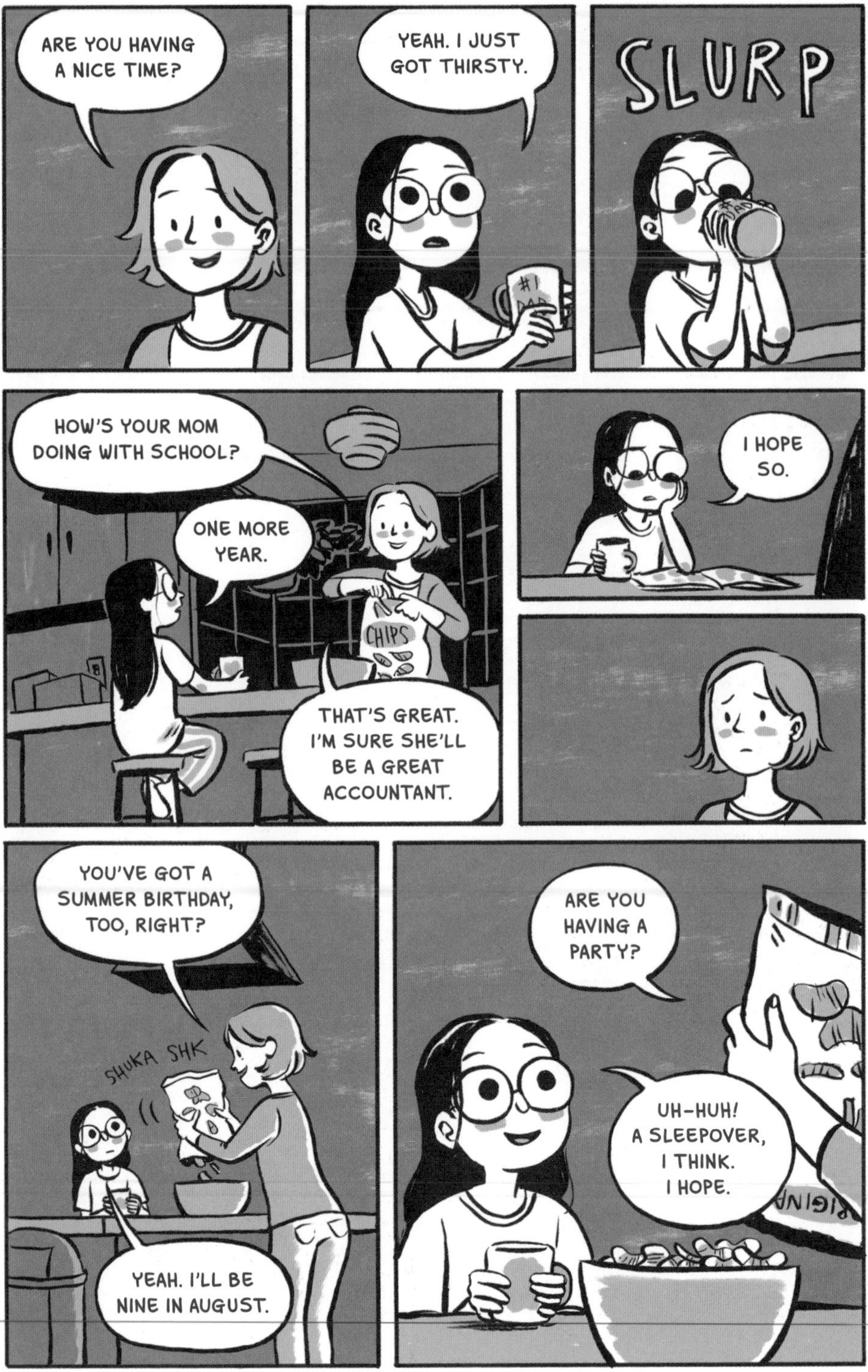
ARE YOU HAVING A NICE TIME?
YEAH. I JUST GOT THIRSTY.
#1 DAD
SLURP
HOW'S YOUR MOM DOING WITH SCHOOL?
ONE MORE YEAR.
CHIPS
THAT'S GREAT. I'M SURE SHE'LL BE A GREAT ACCOUNTANT.
I HOPE SO.
YOU'VE GOT A SUMMER BIRTHDAY, TOO, RIGHT?
SHUKA SHK
YEAH. I'LL BE NINE IN AUGUST.
ARE YOU HAVING A PARTY?
UH-HUH! A SLEEPOVER, I THINK. I HOPE.

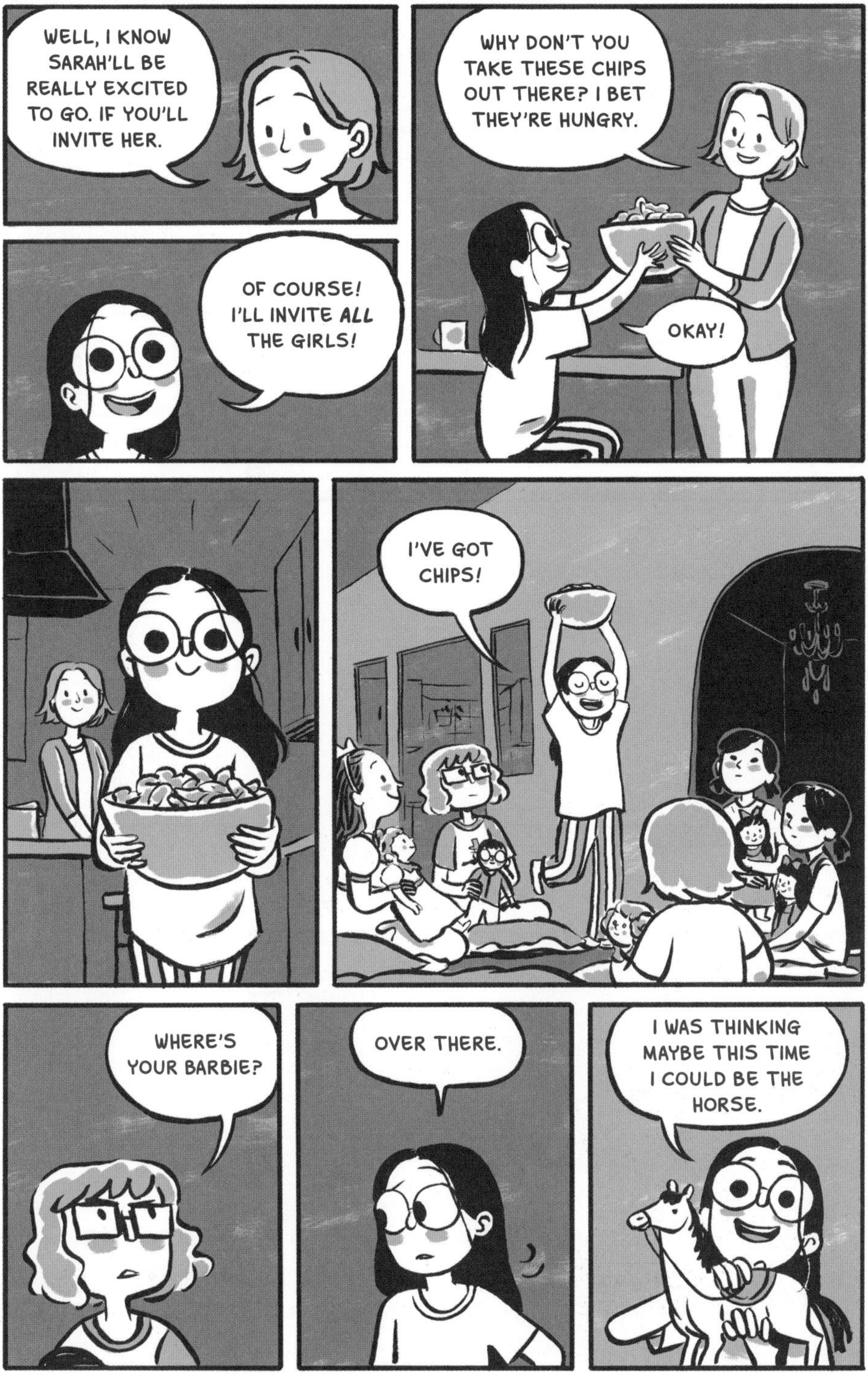
WELL, I KNOW SARAH'LL BE REALLY EXCITED TO GO. IF YOU'LL INVITE HER.
OF COURSE! I'LL INVITE ALL THE GIRLS!
WHY DON'T YOU TAKE THESE CHIPS OUT THERE? I BET THEY'RE HUNGRY.
OKAY!
I'VE GOT CHIPS!
WHERE'S YOUR BARBIE?
OVER THERE.
I WAS THINKING MAYBE THIS TIME I COULD BE THE HORSE.

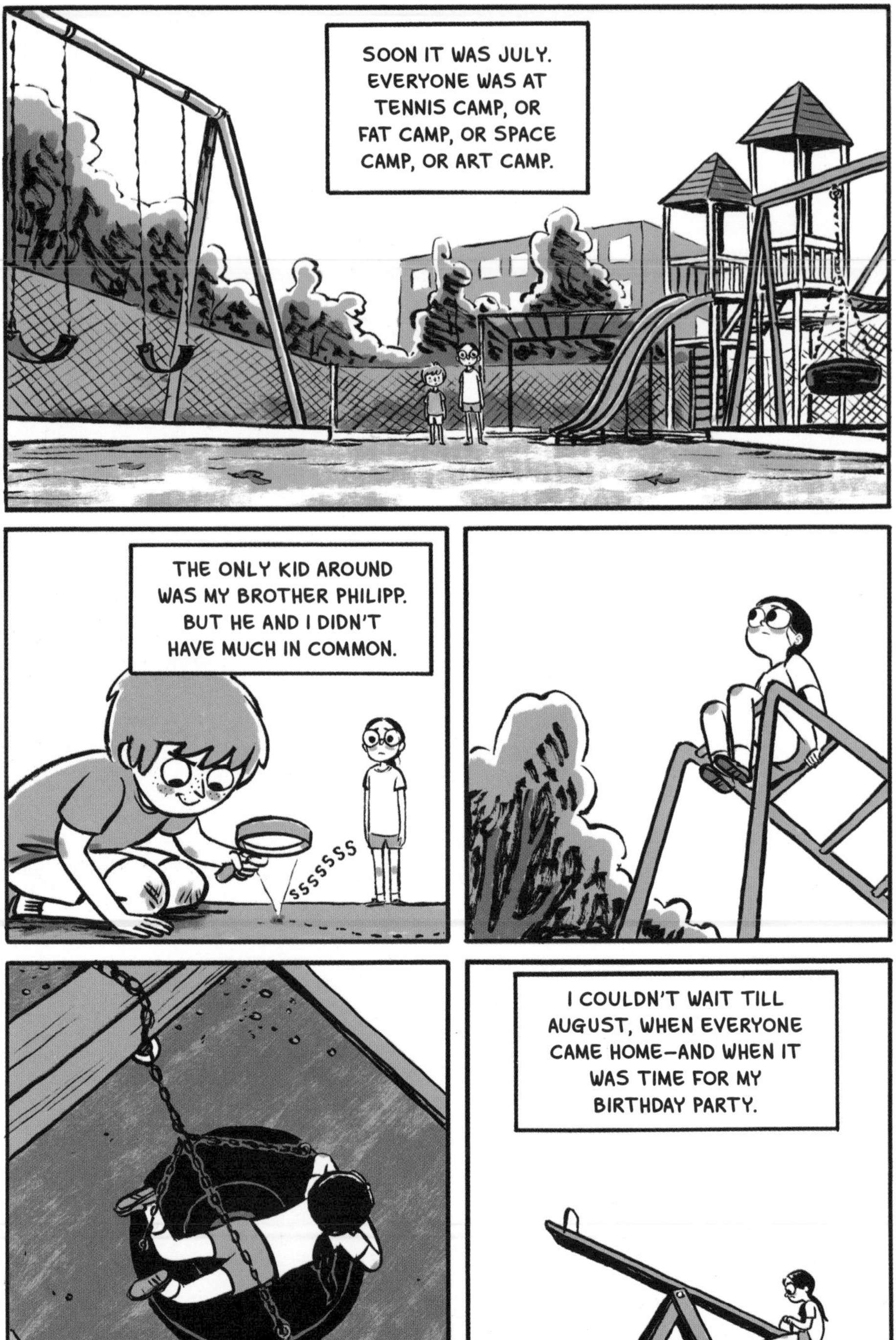
SOON IT WAS JULY. EVERYONE WAS AT TENNIS CAMP, OR FAT CAMP, OR SPACE CAMP, OR ART CAMP.
THE ONLY KID AROUND WAS MY BROTHER PHILIPP. BUT HE AND I DIDN'T HAVE MUCH IN COMMON.
SSSSSSS
I COULDN'T WAIT TILL AUGUST, WHEN EVERYONE CAME HOME—AND WHEN IT WAS TIME FOR MY BIRTHDAY PARTY.

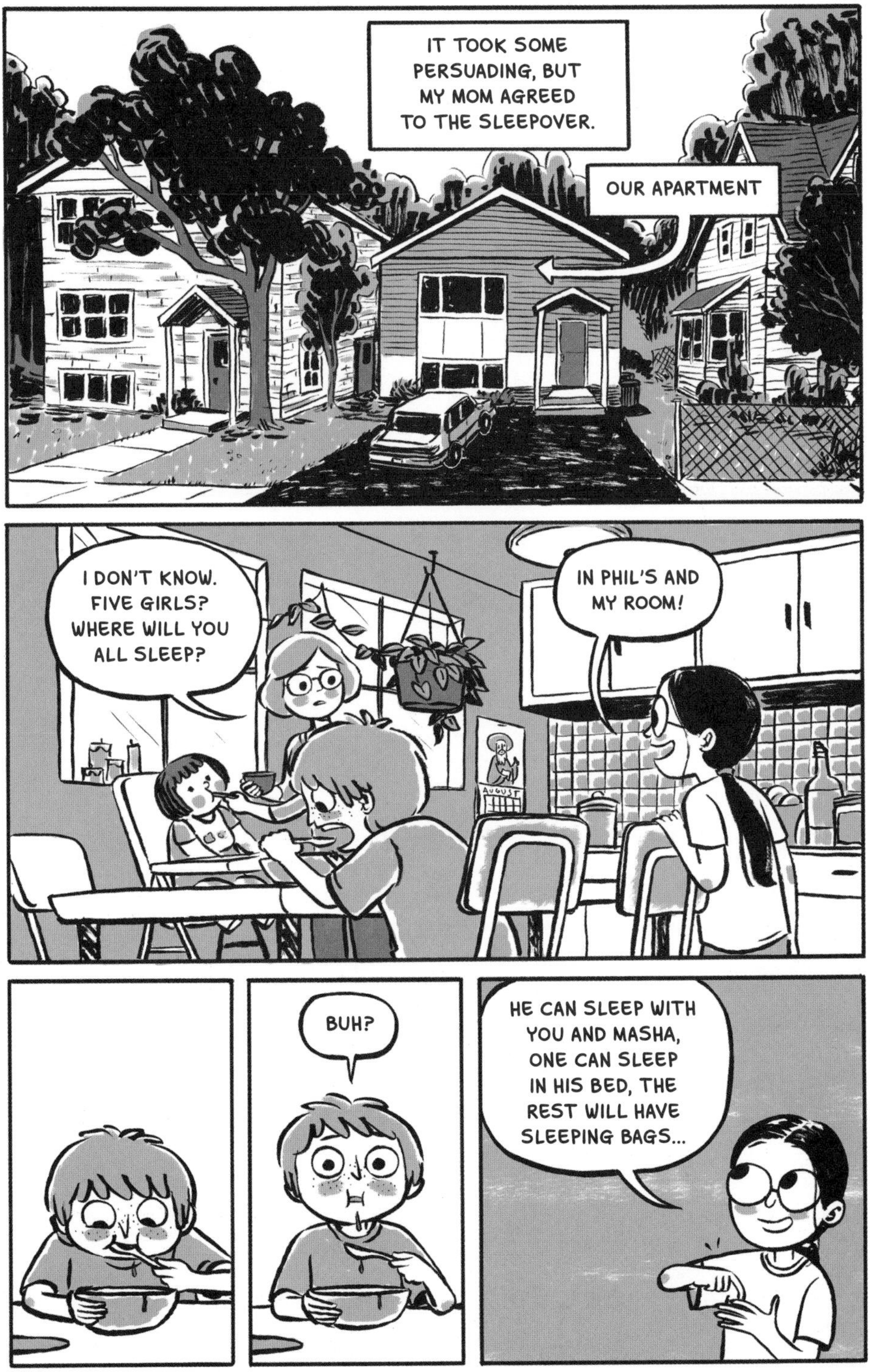
IT TOOK SOME PERSUADING, BUT MY MOM AGREED TO THE SLEEPOVER.
OUR APARTMENT
I DON'T KNOW. FIVE GIRLS? WHERE WILL YOU ALL SLEEP?
IN PHIL'S AND MY ROOM!
AUGUST
BUH?
HE CAN SLEEP WITH YOU AND MASHA, ONE CAN SLEEP IN HIS BED, THE REST WILL HAVE SLEEPING BAGS...

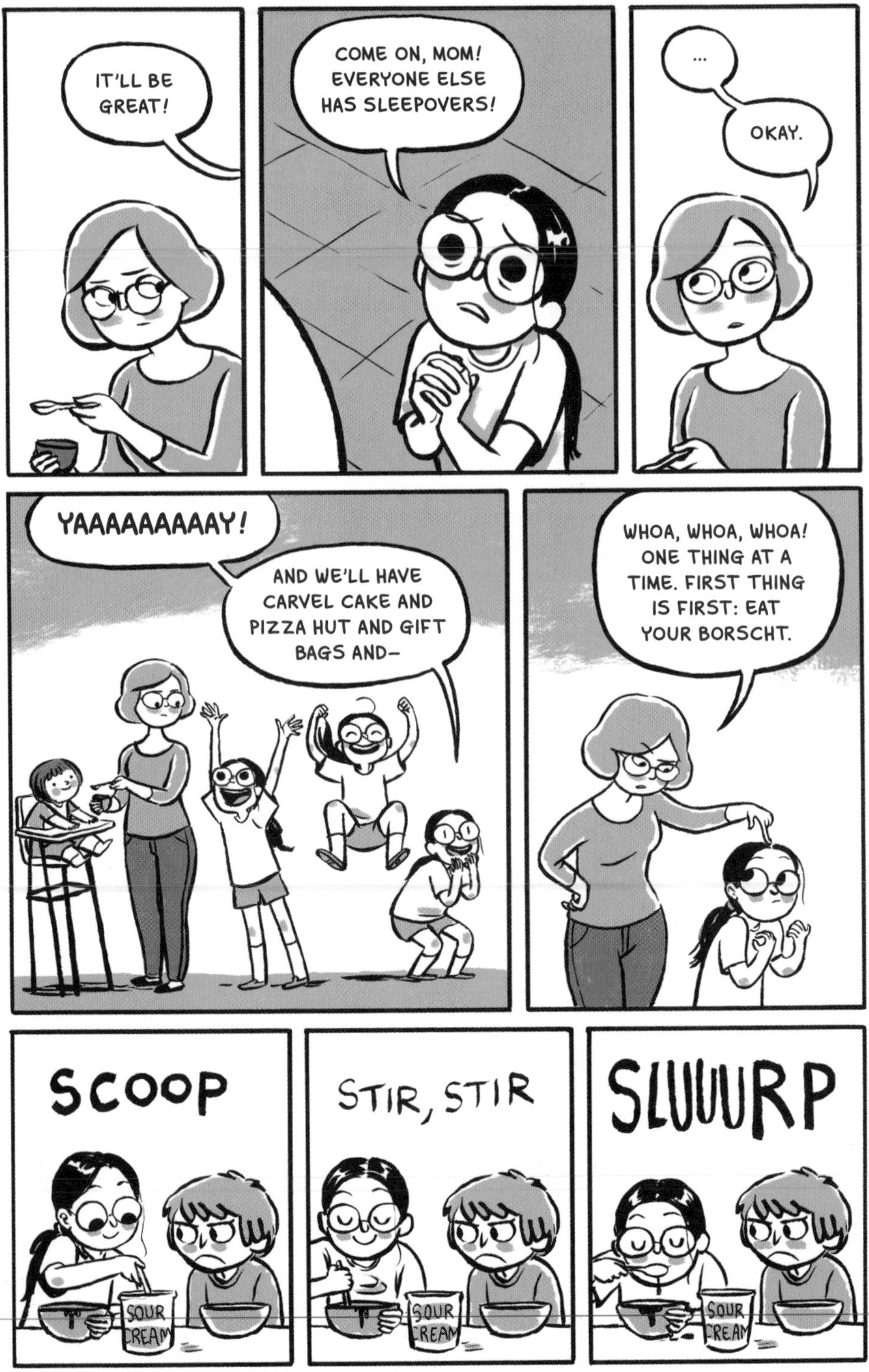
IT'LL BE GREAT!
COME ON, MOM! EVERYONE ELSE HAS SLEEPOVERS!
...
OKAY.
YAAAAAAAAAY!
AND WE'LL HAVE CARVEL CAKE AND PIZZA HUT AND GIFT BAGS AND—
WHOA, WHOA, WHOA! ONE THING AT A TIME. FIRST THING IS FIRST: EAT YOUR BORSCHT.
SCOOP
SOUR CREAM
STIR, STIR
SOUR CREAM
SLUUURP
SOUR CREAM

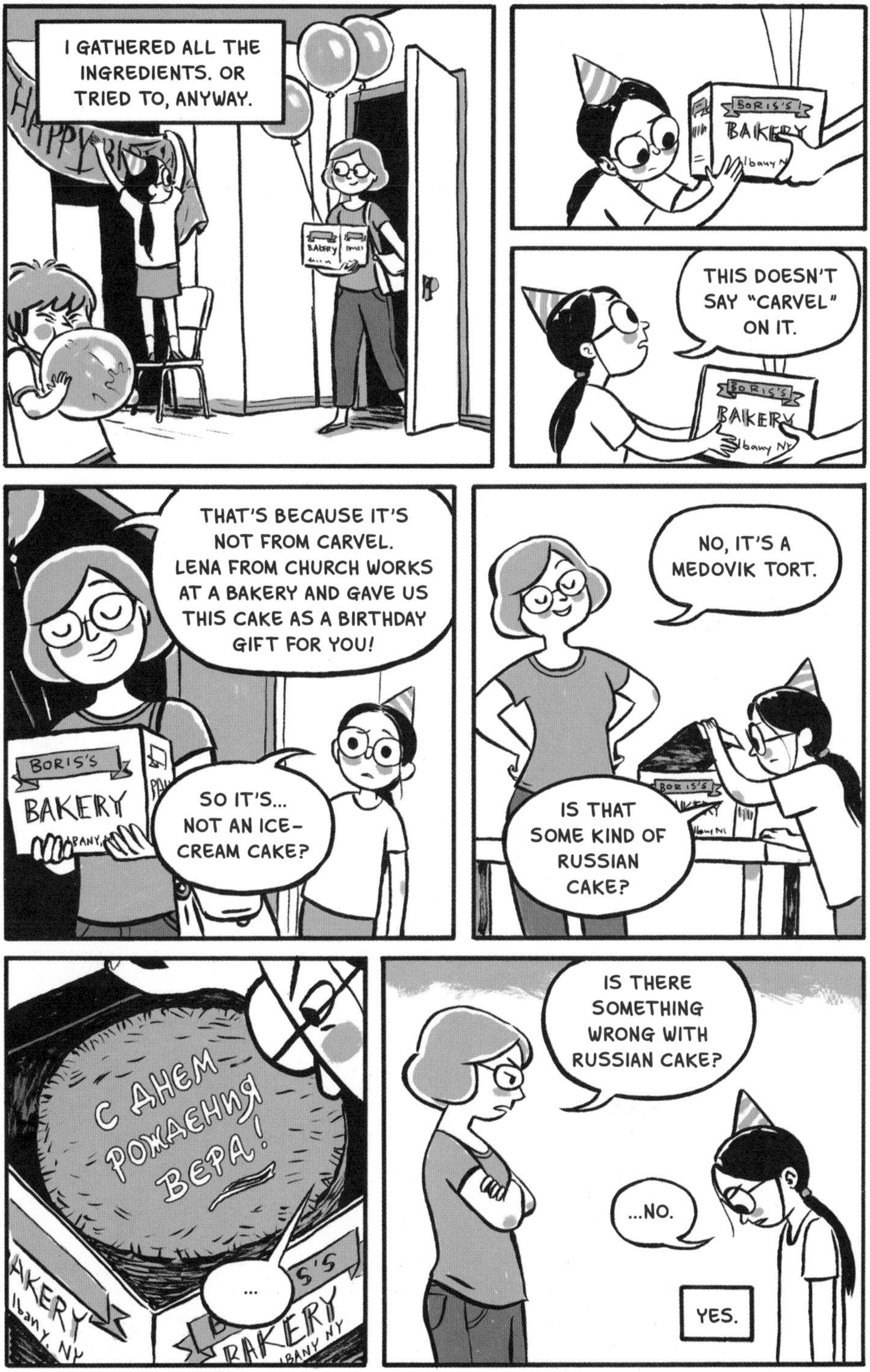
I GATHERED ALL THE INGREDIENTS. OR TRIED TO, ANYWAY.
HAPPY BIRT
BORIS'S BAKERY
BORIS'S BAKERY Albany NY
THIS DOESN'T SAY "CARVEL" ON IT.
BORIS'S BAKERY lbany NY
THAT'S BECAUSE IT'S NOT FROM CARVEL. LENA FROM CHURCH WORKS AT A BAKERY AND GAVE US THIS CAKE AS A BIRTHDAY GIFT FOR YOU!
BORIS'S BAKERY ALBANY, NY
SO IT'S... NOT AN ICE-CREAM CAKE?
NO, IT'S A MEDOVIK TORT.
IS THAT SOME KIND OF RUSSIAN CAKE?
С ДНЕМ РОЖДЕНИЯ ВЕРА!
...
IS THERE SOMETHING WRONG WITH RUSSIAN CAKE?
...NO.
YES.

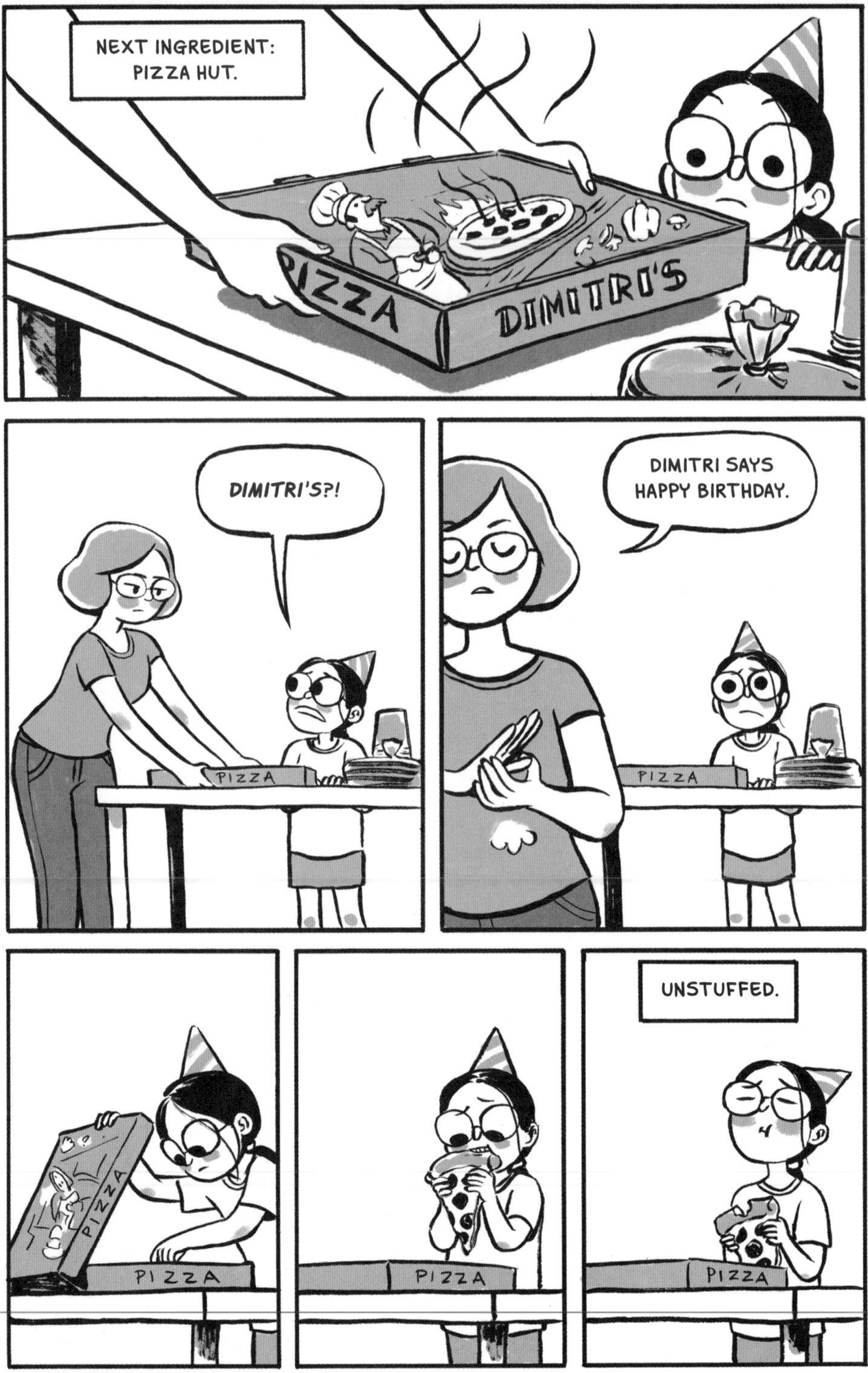
NEXT INGREDIENT: PIZZA HUT.
PIZZA
DIMITRI'S
DIMITRI'S?!
PIZZA
DIMITRI SAYS HAPPY BIRTHDAY.
PIZZA
PIZZA
PIZZA
PIZZA
UNSTUFFED.
PIZZA

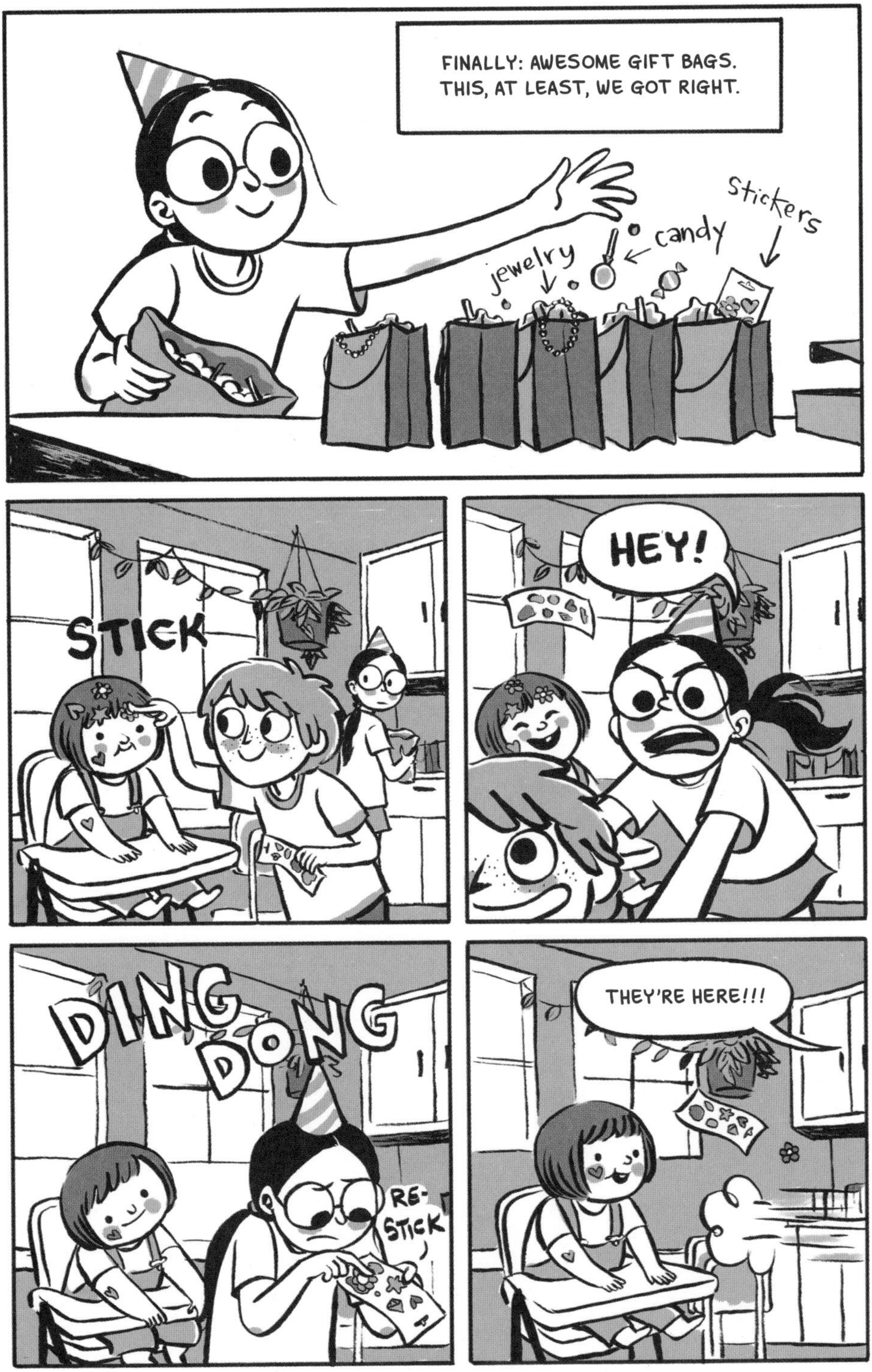
FINALLY: AWESOME GIFT BAGS.
THIS, AT LEAST, WE GOT RIGHT.
stickers
candy
jewelry
STICK
HEY!
DING
DONG
RE-
STICK
THEY'RE HERE!!!

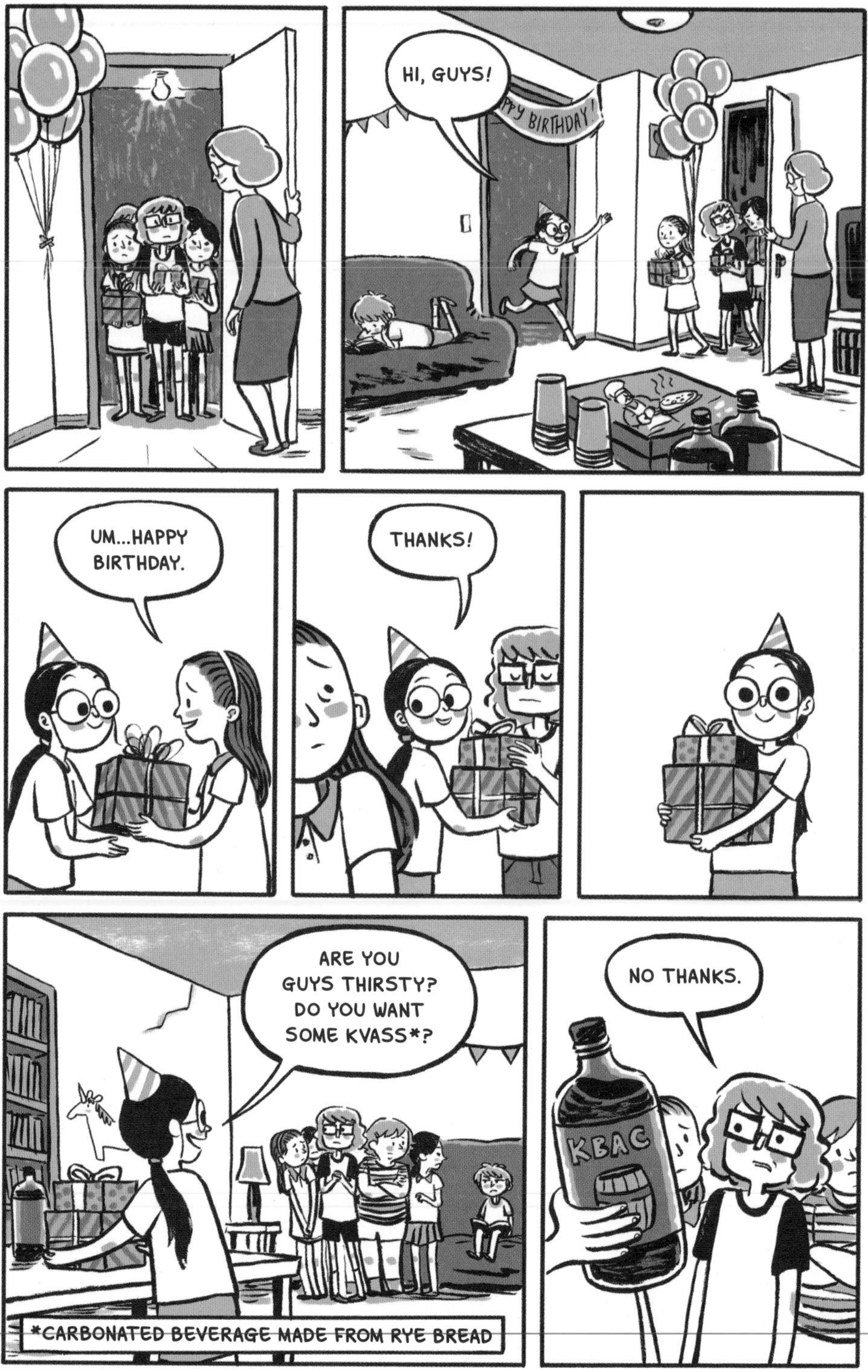
HI, GUYS!
HAPPY BIRTHDAY!
UM...HAPPY BIRTHDAY.
THANKS!
ARE YOU GUYS THIRSTY? DO YOU WANT SOME KVASS*?
*CARBONATED BEVERAGE MADE FROM RYE BREAD
NO THANKS.
KBAC

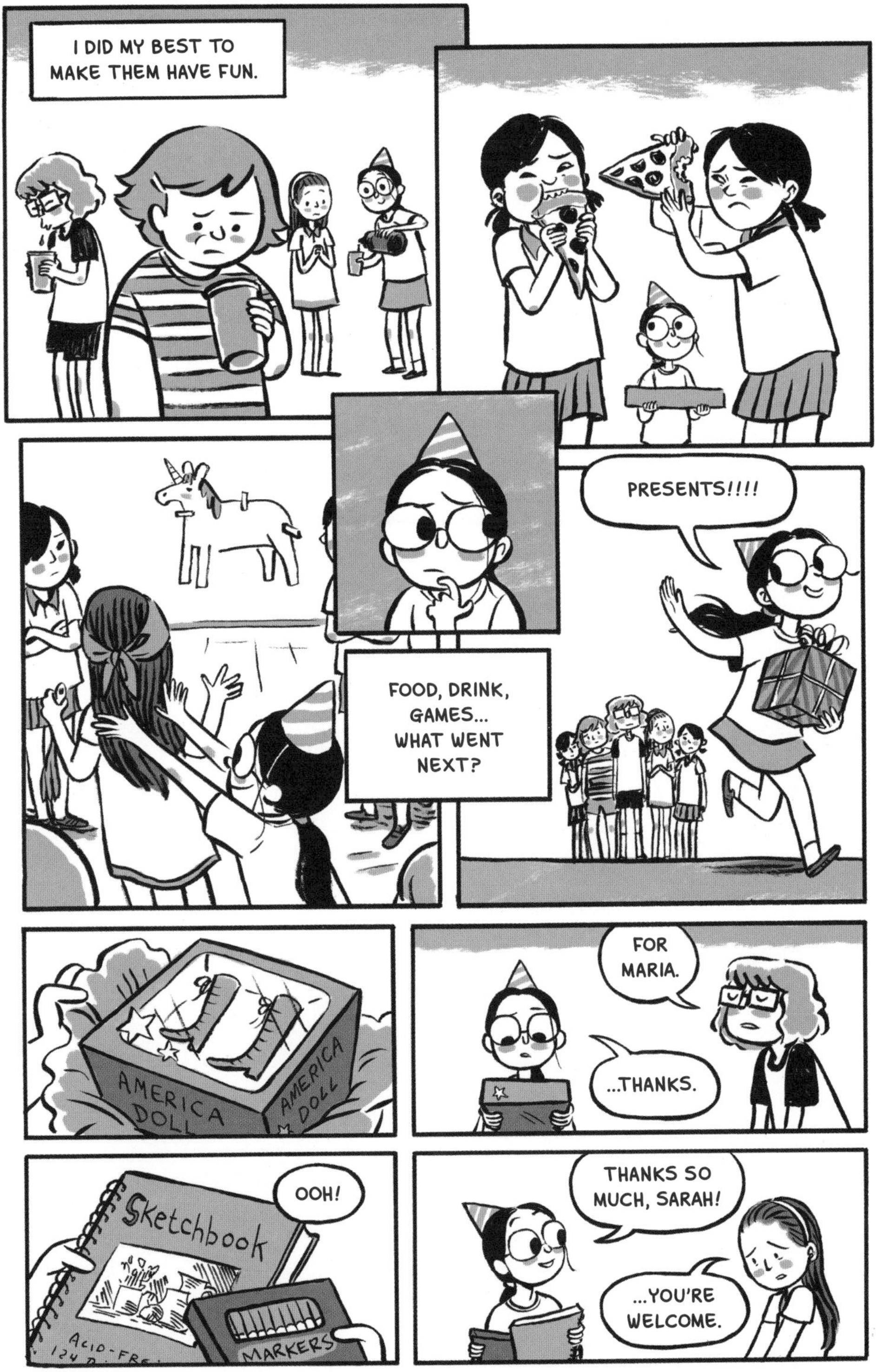
I DID MY BEST TO MAKE THEM HAVE FUN.
FOOD, DRINK, GAMES... WHAT WENT NEXT?
PRESENTS!!!!
AMERICA DOLL
AMERICA DOLL
FOR MARIA.
...THANKS.
Sketchbook
OOH!
MARKERS
THANKS SO MUCH, SARAH!
...YOU'RE WELCOME.

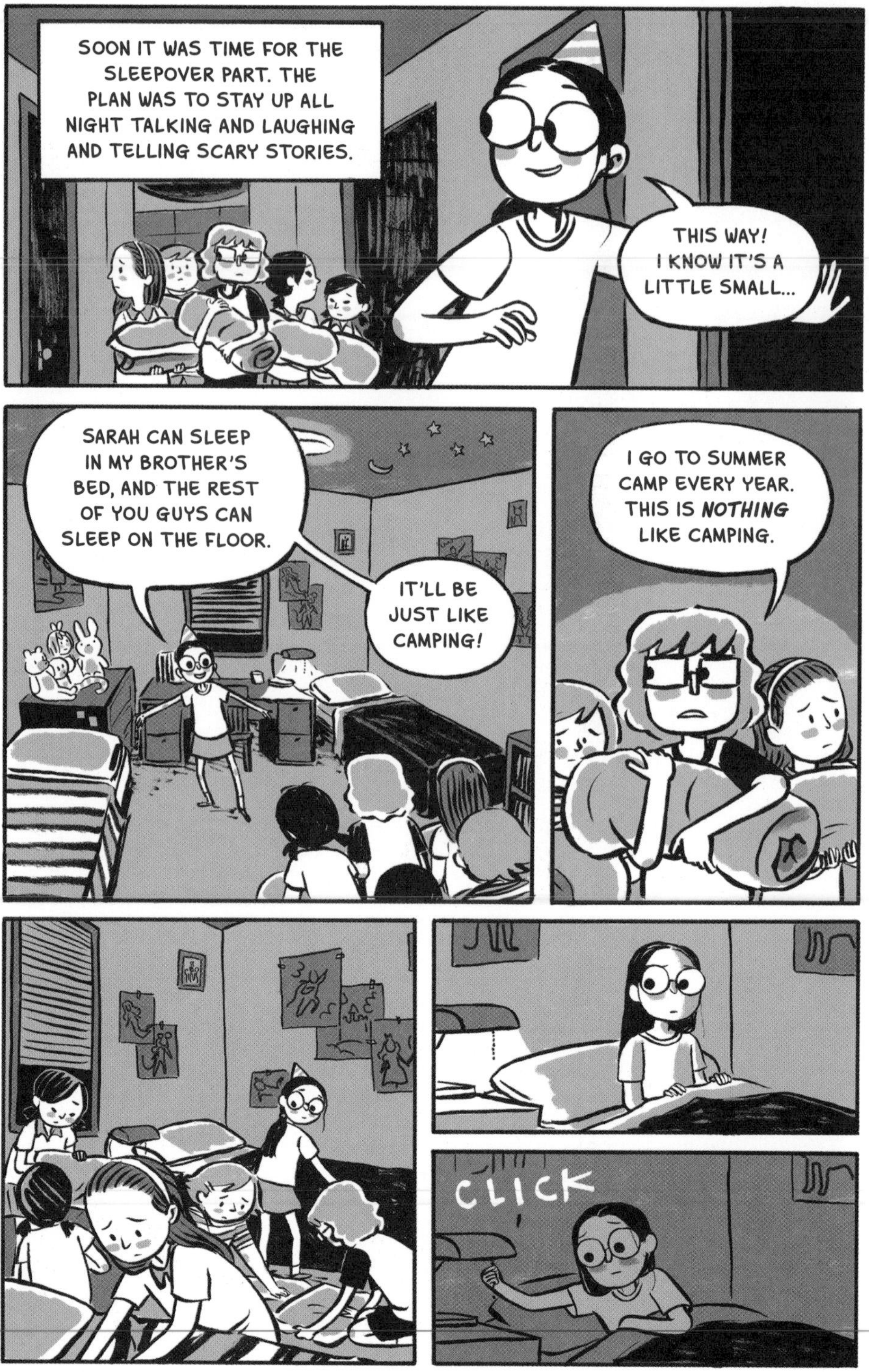
SOON IT WAS TIME FOR THE SLEEPOVER PART. THE PLAN WAS TO STAY UP ALL NIGHT TALKING AND LAUGHING AND TELLING SCARY STORIES.
THIS WAY! I KNOW IT'S A LITTLE SMALL...
SARAH CAN SLEEP IN MY BROTHER'S BED, AND THE REST OF YOU GUYS CAN SLEEP ON THE FLOOR.
IT'LL BE JUST LIKE CAMPING!
I GO TO SUMMER CAMP EVERY YEAR. THIS IS *NOTHING* LIKE CAMPING.
CLICK

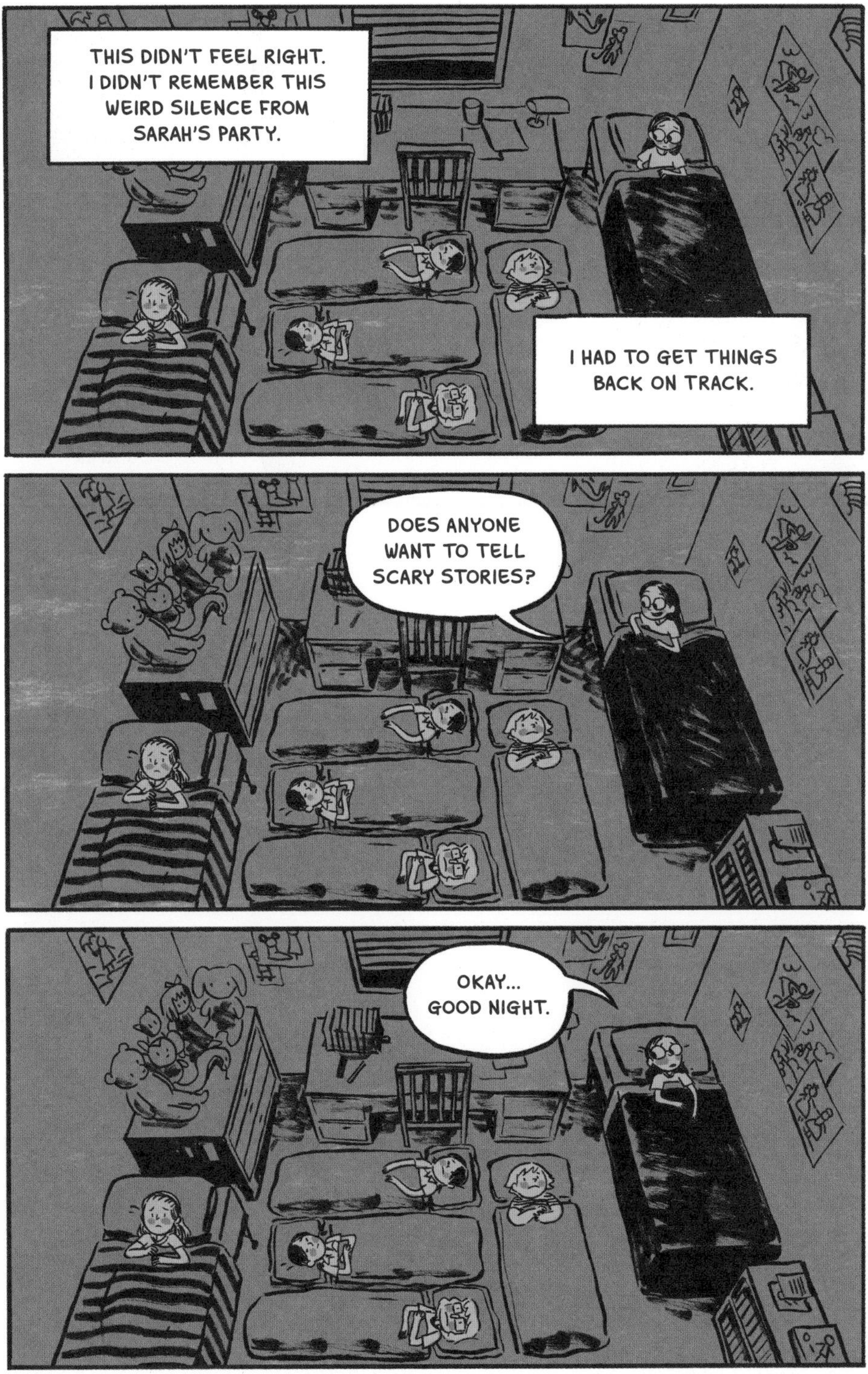
THIS DIDN'T FEEL RIGHT. I DIDN'T REMEMBER THIS WEIRD SILENCE FROM SARAH'S PARTY.
I HAD TO GET THINGS BACK ON TRACK.
DOES ANYONE WANT TO TELL SCARY STORIES?
OKAY... GOOD NIGHT.

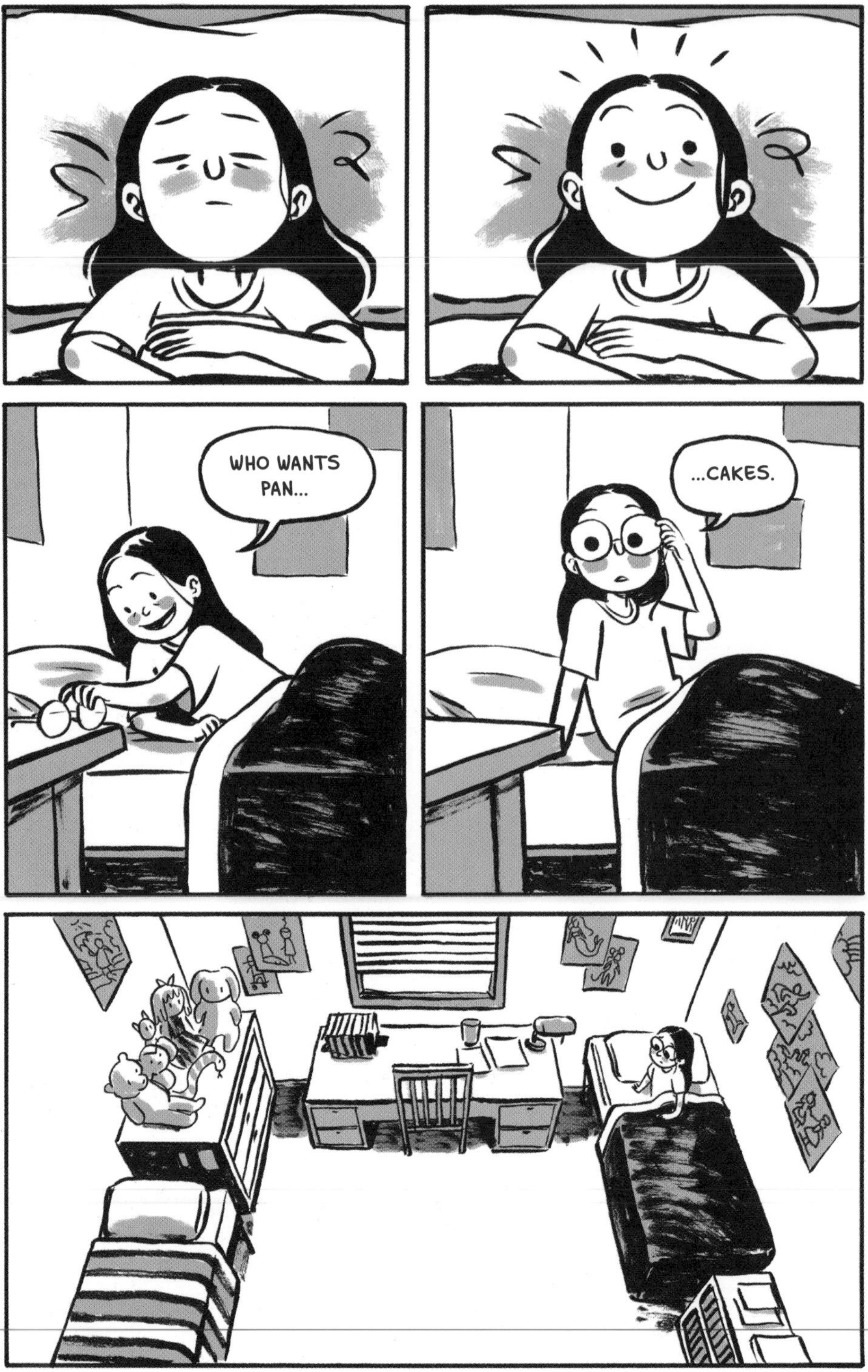
WHO WANTS PAN...
...CAKES.

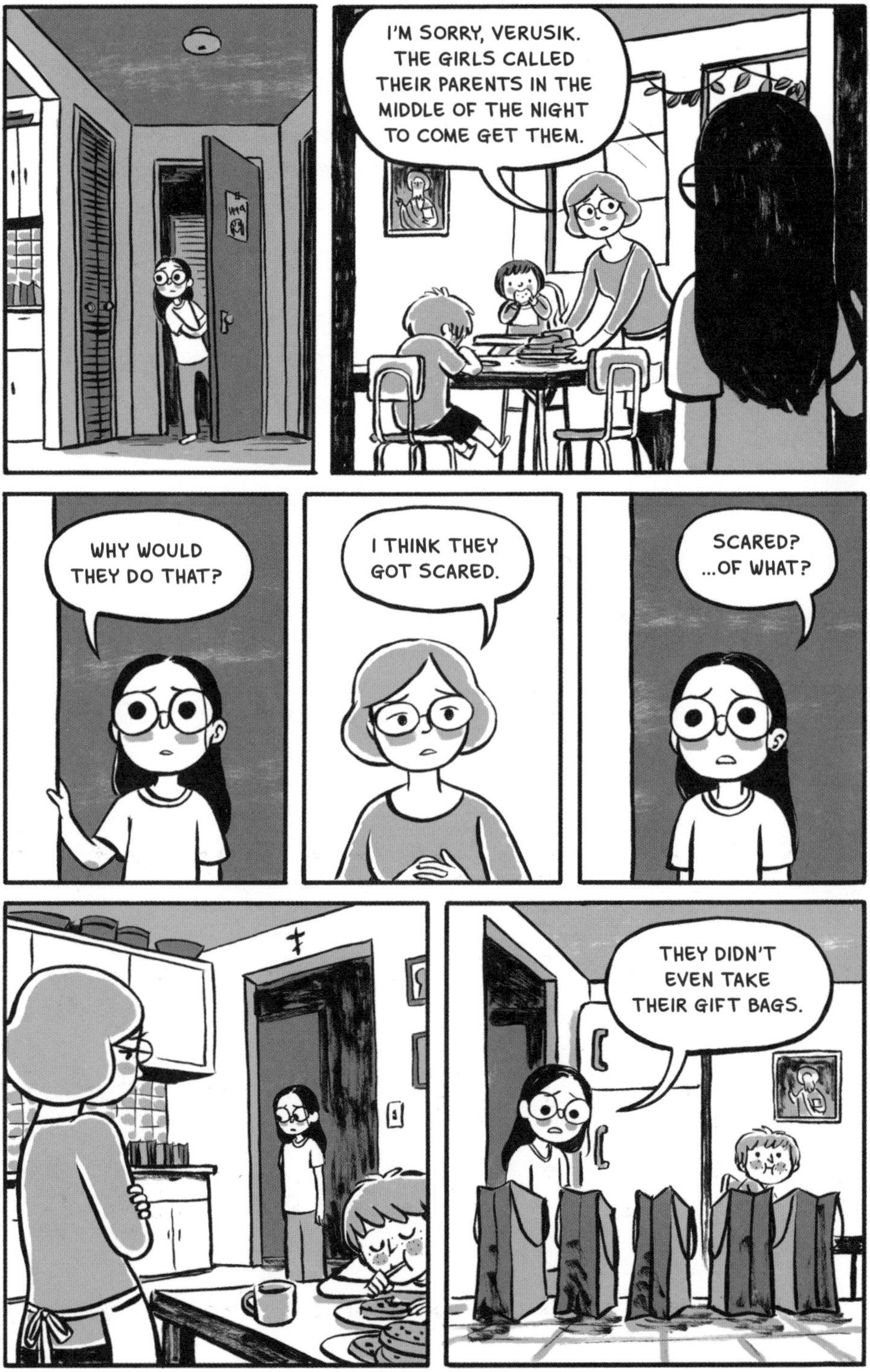
I'M SORRY, VERUSIK. THE GIRLS CALLED THEIR PARENTS IN THE MIDDLE OF THE NIGHT TO COME GET THEM.
WHY WOULD THEY DO THAT?
I THINK THEY GOT SCARED.
SCARED? ...OF WHAT?
THEY DIDN'T EVEN TAKE THEIR GIFT BAGS.

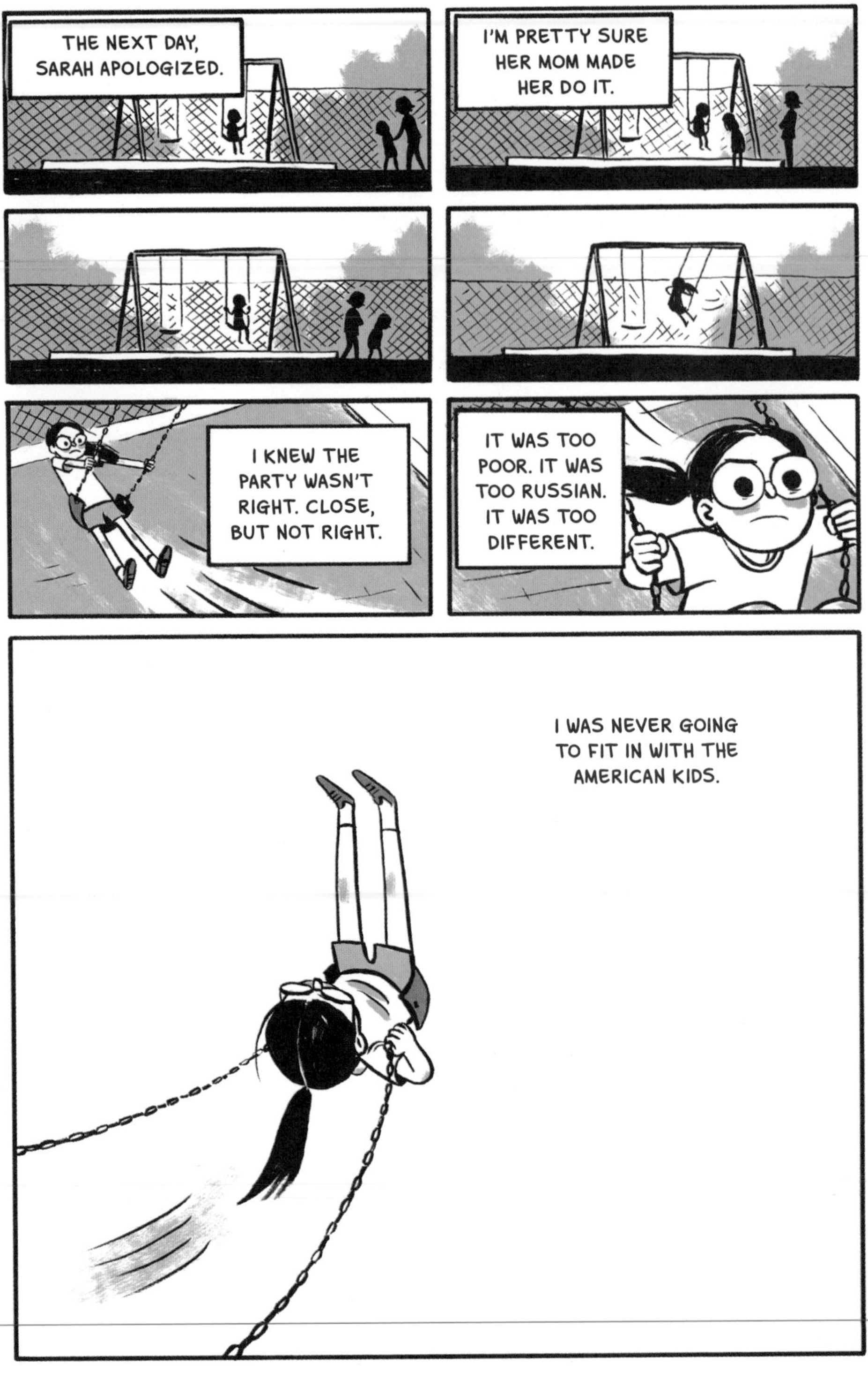
THE NEXT DAY, SARAH APOLOGIZED.
I'M PRETTY SURE HER MOM MADE HER DO IT.
I KNEW THE PARTY WASN'T RIGHT. CLOSE, BUT NOT RIGHT.
IT WAS TOO POOR. IT WAS TOO RUSSIAN. IT WAS TOO DIFFERENT.
I WAS NEVER GOING TO FIT IN WITH THE AMERICAN KIDS.

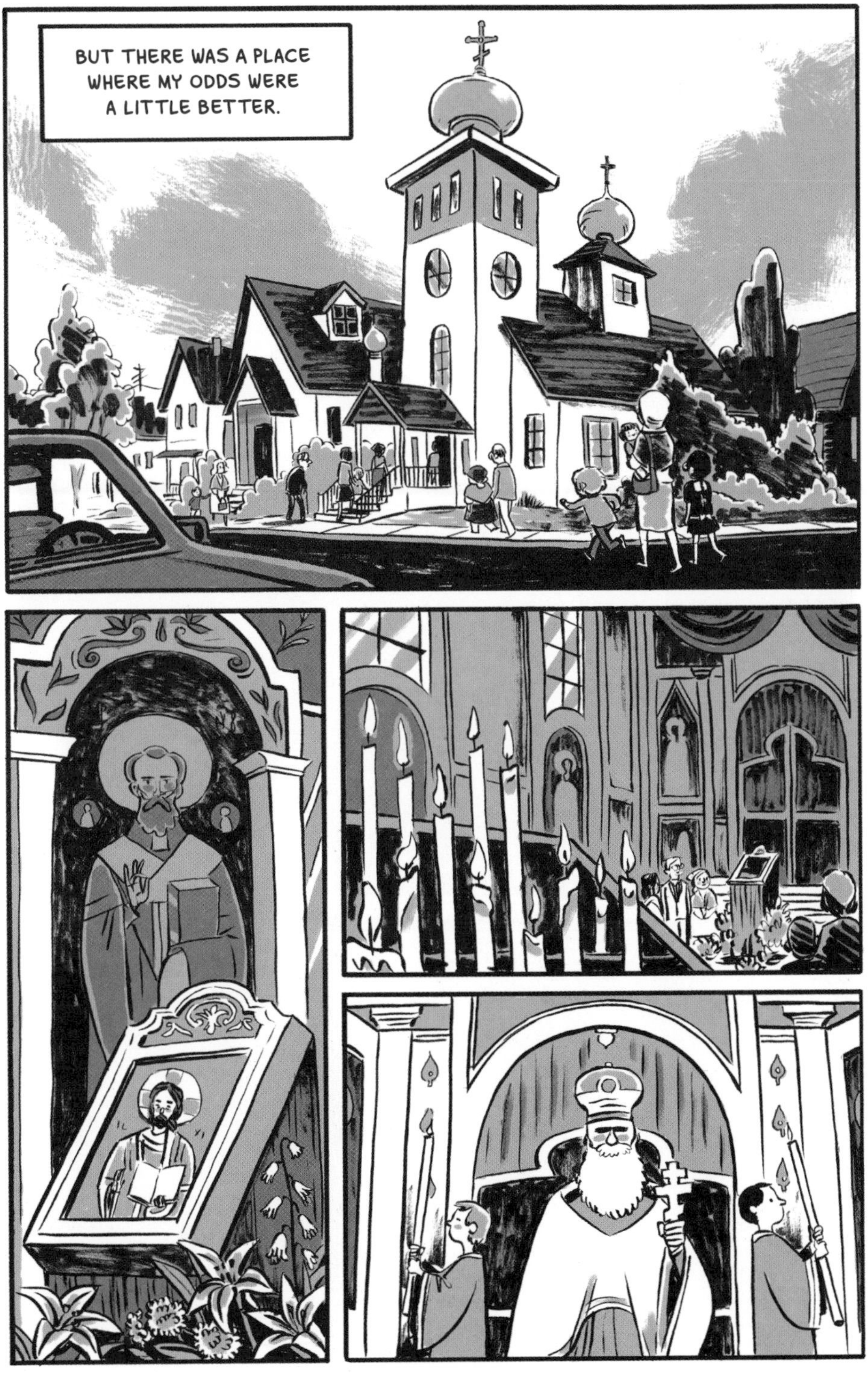
BUT THERE WAS A PLACE WHERE MY ODDS WERE A LITTLE BETTER.

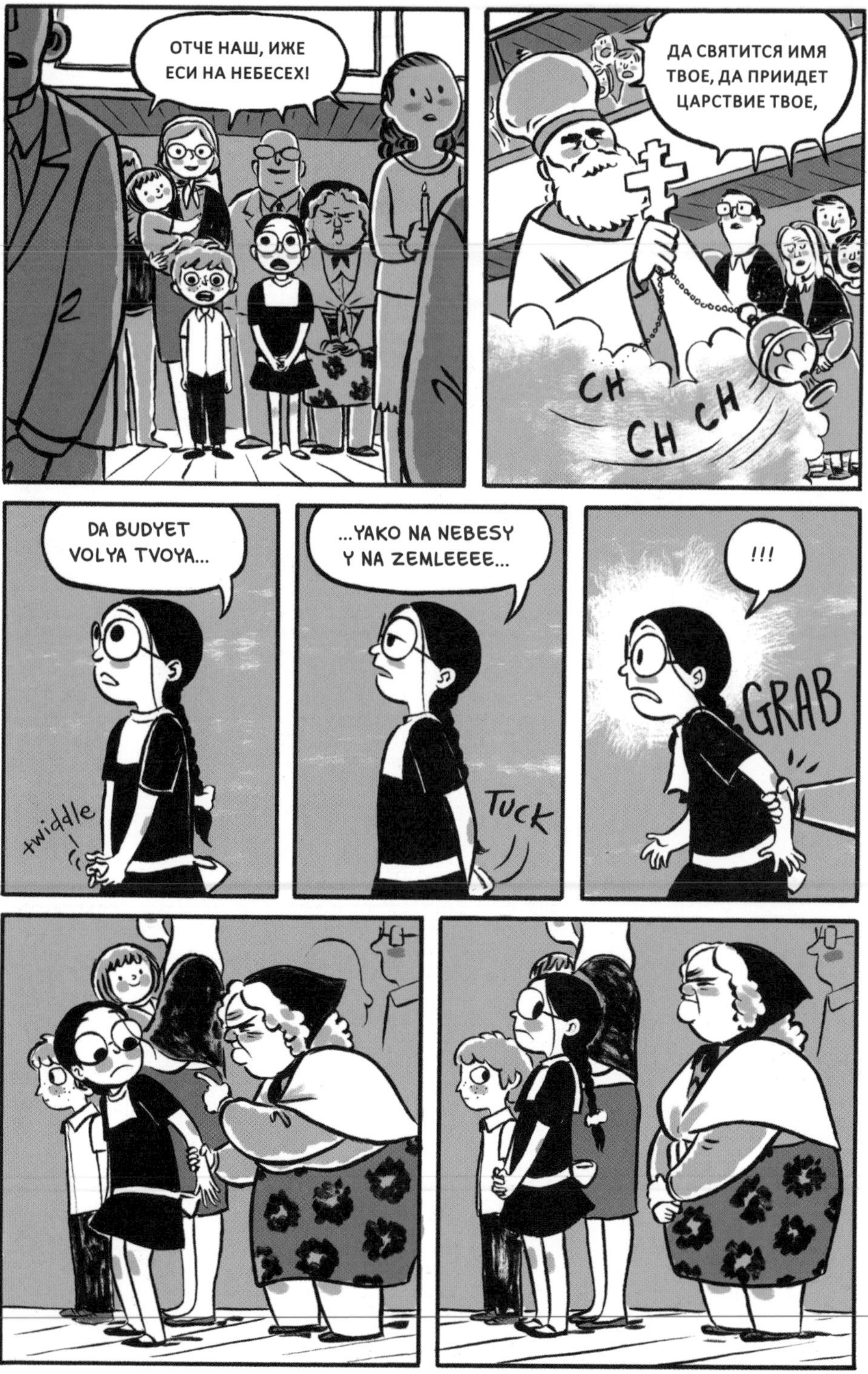
ОТЧЕ НАШ, ИЖЕ ЕСИ НА НЕБЕСЕХ!
ДА СВЯТИТСЯ ИМЯ ТВОЕ, ДА ПРИИДЕТ ЦАРСТВИЕ ТВОЕ,
CH
CH CH
DA BUDYET VOLYA TVOYA...
twiddle
...YAKO NA NEBESY Y NA ZEMLEEEE...
TUCK
!!!
GRAB

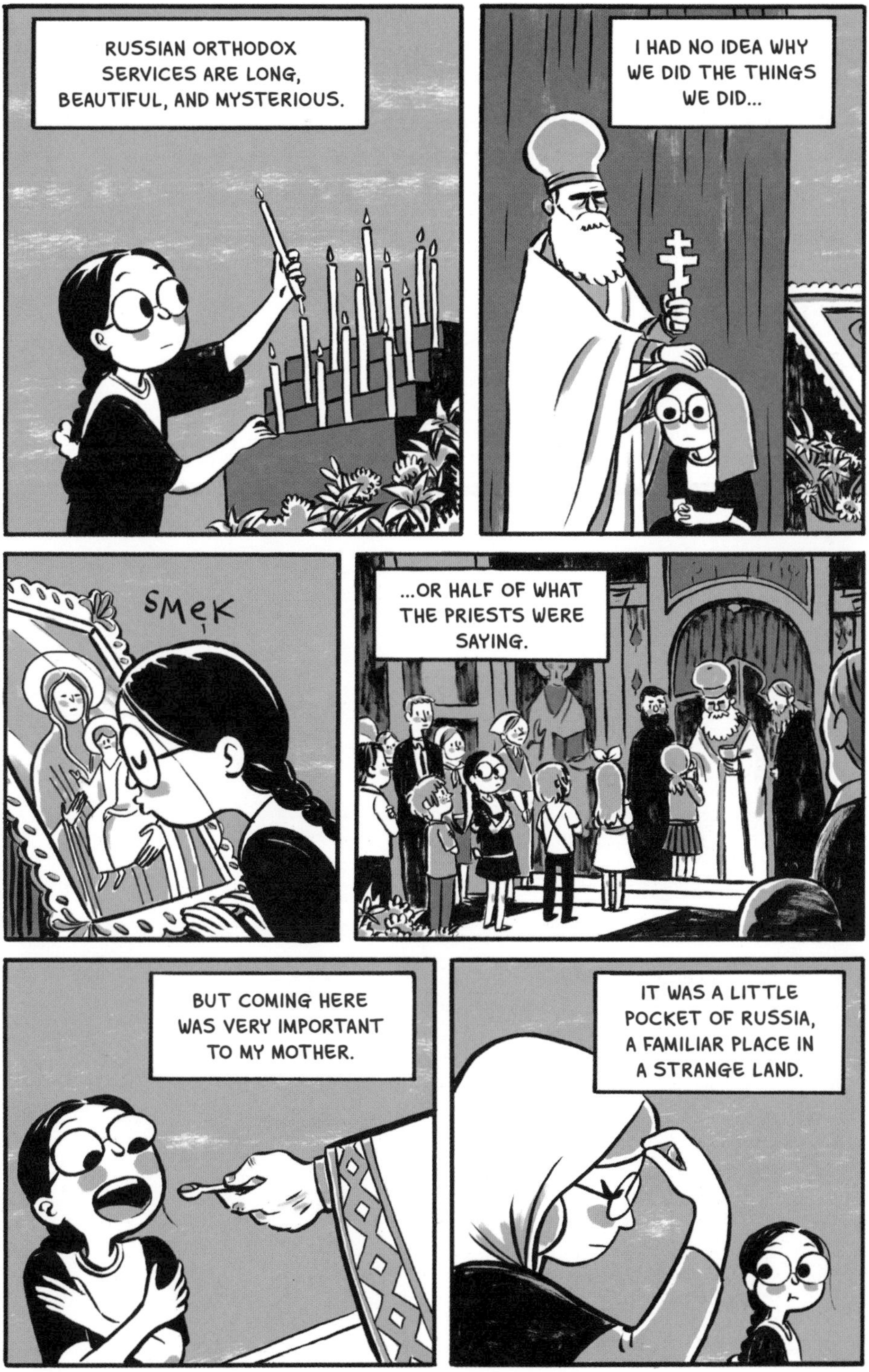
RUSSIAN ORTHODOX SERVICES ARE LONG, BEAUTIFUL, AND MYSTERIOUS.
I HAD NO IDEA WHY WE DID THE THINGS WE DID...
SMEK
...OR HALF OF WHAT THE PRIESTS WERE SAYING.
BUT COMING HERE WAS VERY IMPORTANT TO MY MOTHER.
IT WAS A LITTLE POCKET OF RUSSIA, A FAMILIAR PLACE IN A STRANGE LAND.

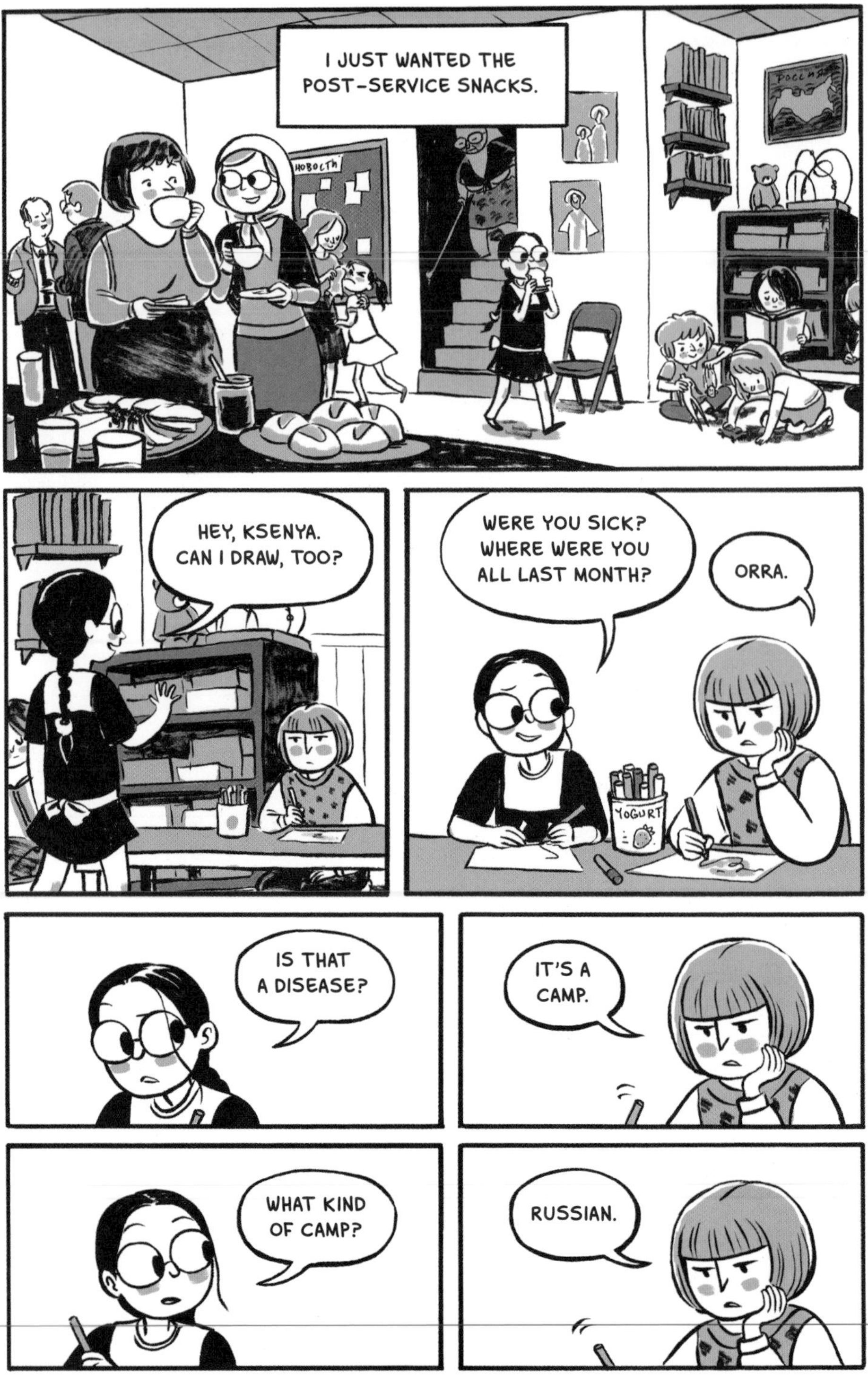
I JUST WANTED THE POST-SERVICE SNACKS.
HEY, KSENYA. CAN I DRAW, TOO?
WERE YOU SICK? WHERE WERE YOU ALL LAST MONTH?
ORRA.
YOGURT
IS THAT A DISEASE?
IT'S A CAMP.
WHAT KIND OF CAMP?
RUSSIAN.

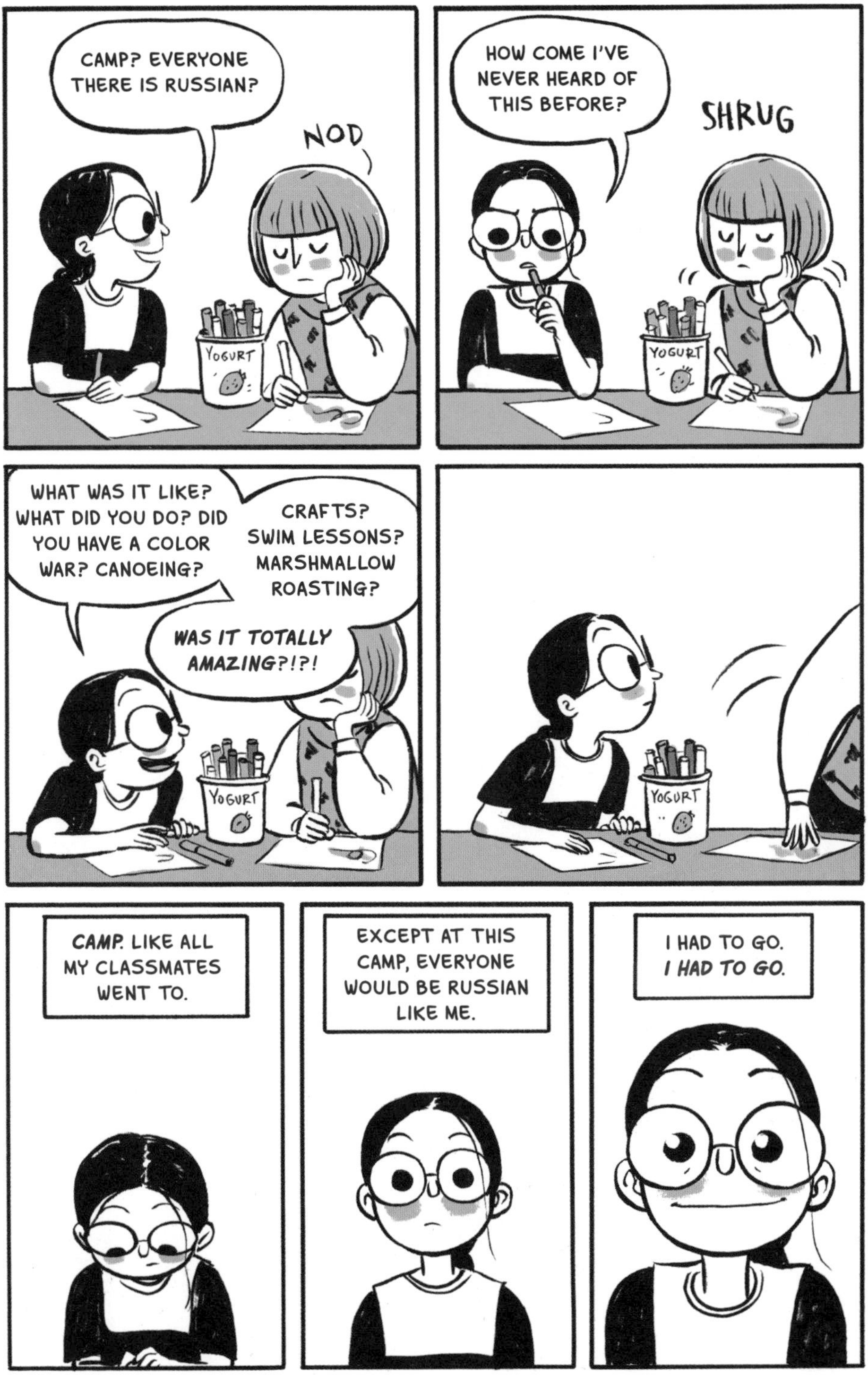
CAMP? EVERYONE THERE IS RUSSIAN?
NOD
YOGURT
HOW COME I'VE NEVER HEARD OF THIS BEFORE?
SHRUG
YOGURT
WHAT WAS IT LIKE? WHAT DID YOU DO? DID YOU HAVE A COLOR WAR? CANOEING?
CRAFTS? SWIM LESSONS? MARSHMALLOW ROASTING?
WAS IT TOTALLY AMAZING?!?!
YOGURT
YOGURT
CAMP. LIKE ALL MY CLASSMATES WENT TO.
EXCEPT AT THIS CAMP, EVERYONE WOULD BE RUSSIAN LIKE ME.
I HAD TO GO.
I HAD TO GO.

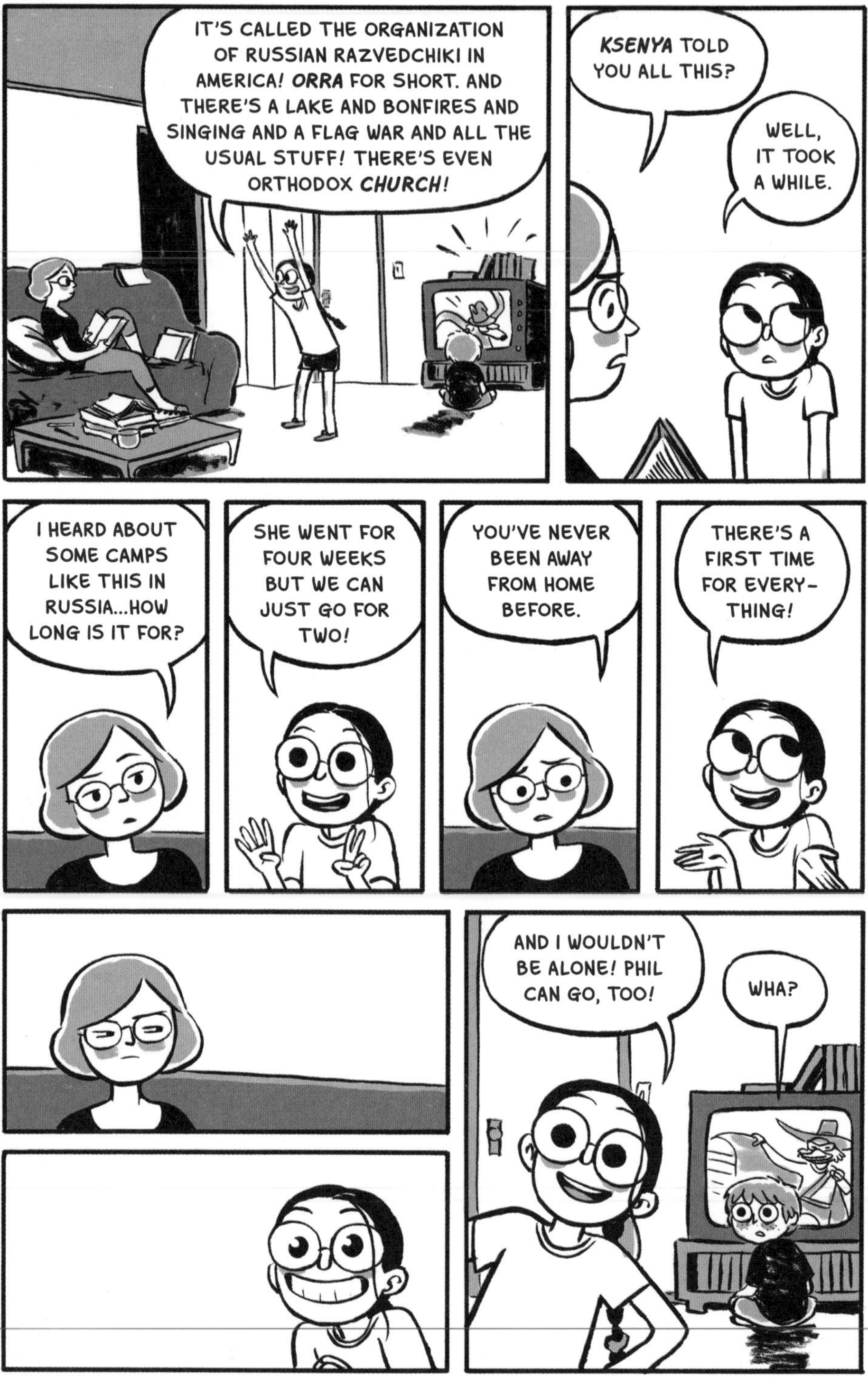
IT'S CALLED THE ORGANIZATION OF RUSSIAN RAZVEDCHIKI IN AMERICA! ORRA FOR SHORT. AND THERE'S A LAKE AND BONFIRES AND SINGING AND A FLAG WAR AND ALL THE USUAL STUFF! THERE'S EVEN ORTHODOX CHURCH!
KSENYA TOLD YOU ALL THIS?
WELL, IT TOOK A WHILE.
I HEARD ABOUT SOME CAMPS LIKE THIS IN RUSSIA...HOW LONG IS IT FOR?
SHE WENT FOR FOUR WEEKS BUT WE CAN JUST GO FOR TWO!
YOU'VE NEVER BEEN AWAY FROM HOME BEFORE.
THERE'S A FIRST TIME FOR EVERY-THING!
AND I WOULDN'T BE ALONE! PHIL CAN GO, TOO!
WHA?

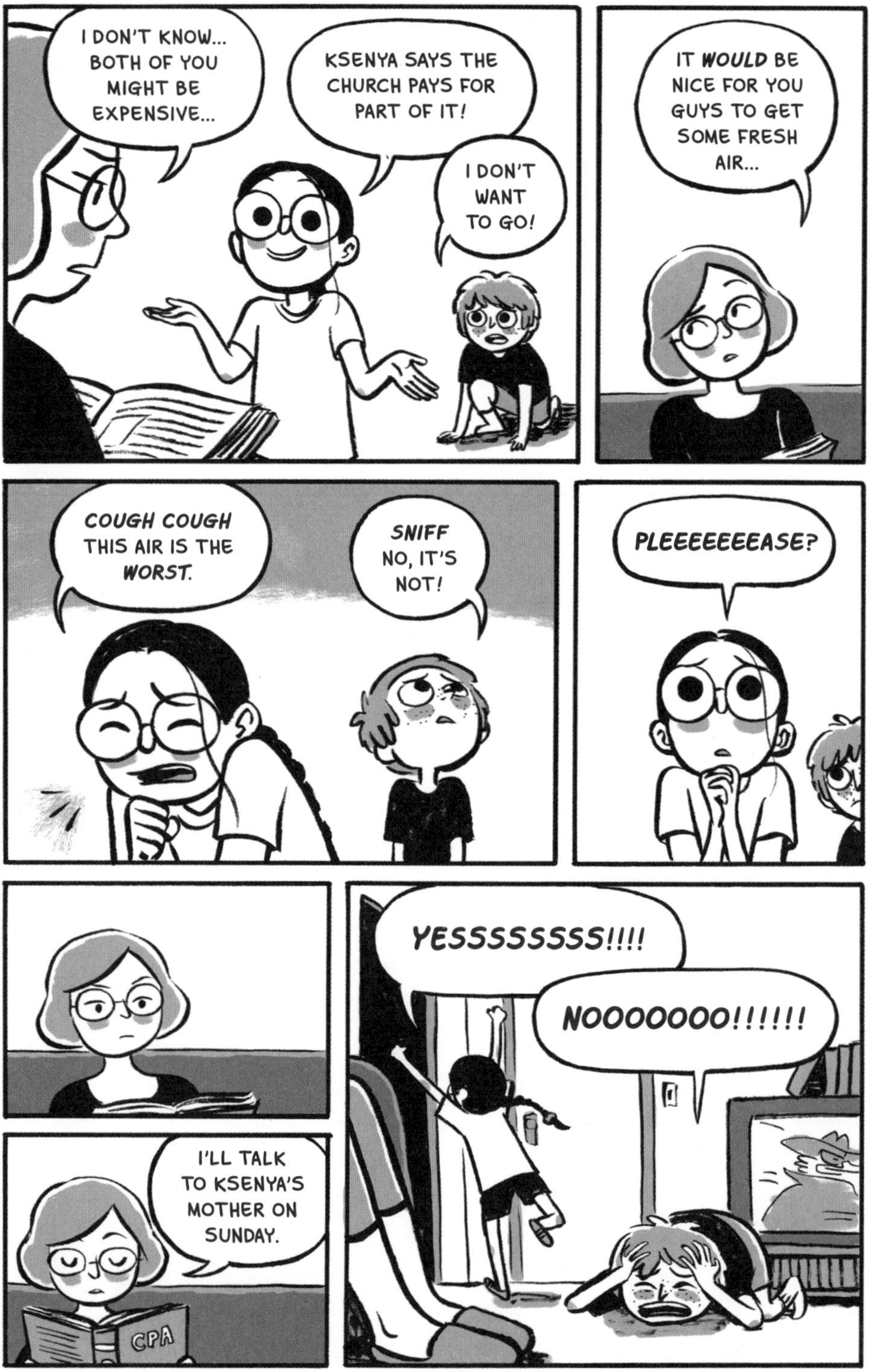
I DON'T KNOW... BOTH OF YOU MIGHT BE EXPENSIVE...
KSENYA SAYS THE CHURCH PAYS FOR PART OF IT!
I DON'T WANT TO GO!
IT WOULD BE NICE FOR YOU GUYS TO GET SOME FRESH AIR...
COUGH COUGH THIS AIR IS THE WORST.
SNIFF NO, IT'S NOT!
PLEEEEEEEEASE?
I'LL TALK TO KSENYA'S MOTHER ON SUNDAY.
CPA
YESSSSSSSS!!!!
NOOOOOOO!!!!!!

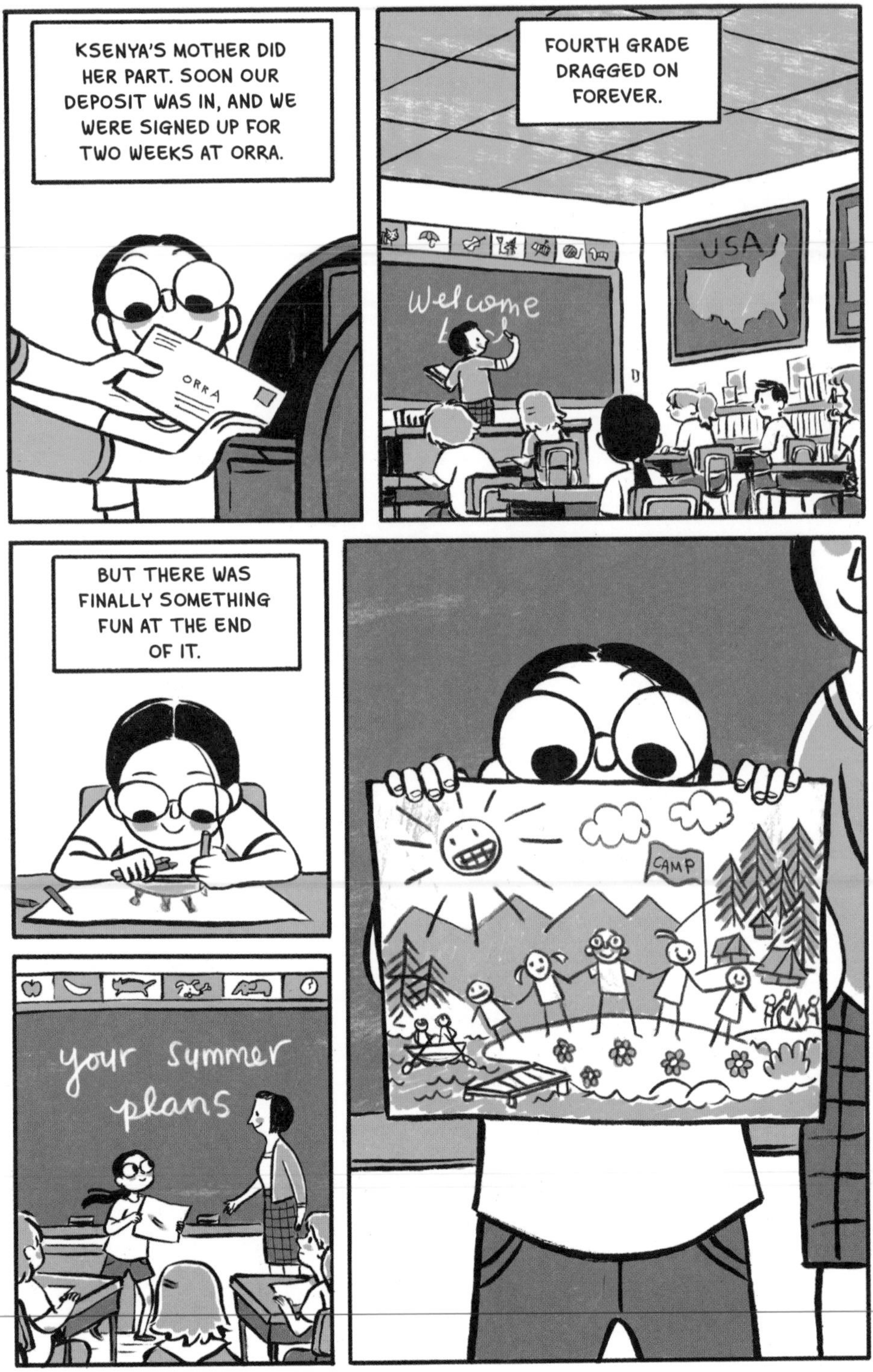
KSENYA'S MOTHER DID HER PART. SOON OUR DEPOSIT WAS IN, AND WE WERE SIGNED UP FOR TWO WEEKS AT ORRA.
ORRA
FOURTH GRADE DRAGGED ON FOREVER.
Welcome
USA
BUT THERE WAS FINALLY SOMETHING FUN AT THE END OF IT.
your summer plans
CAMP

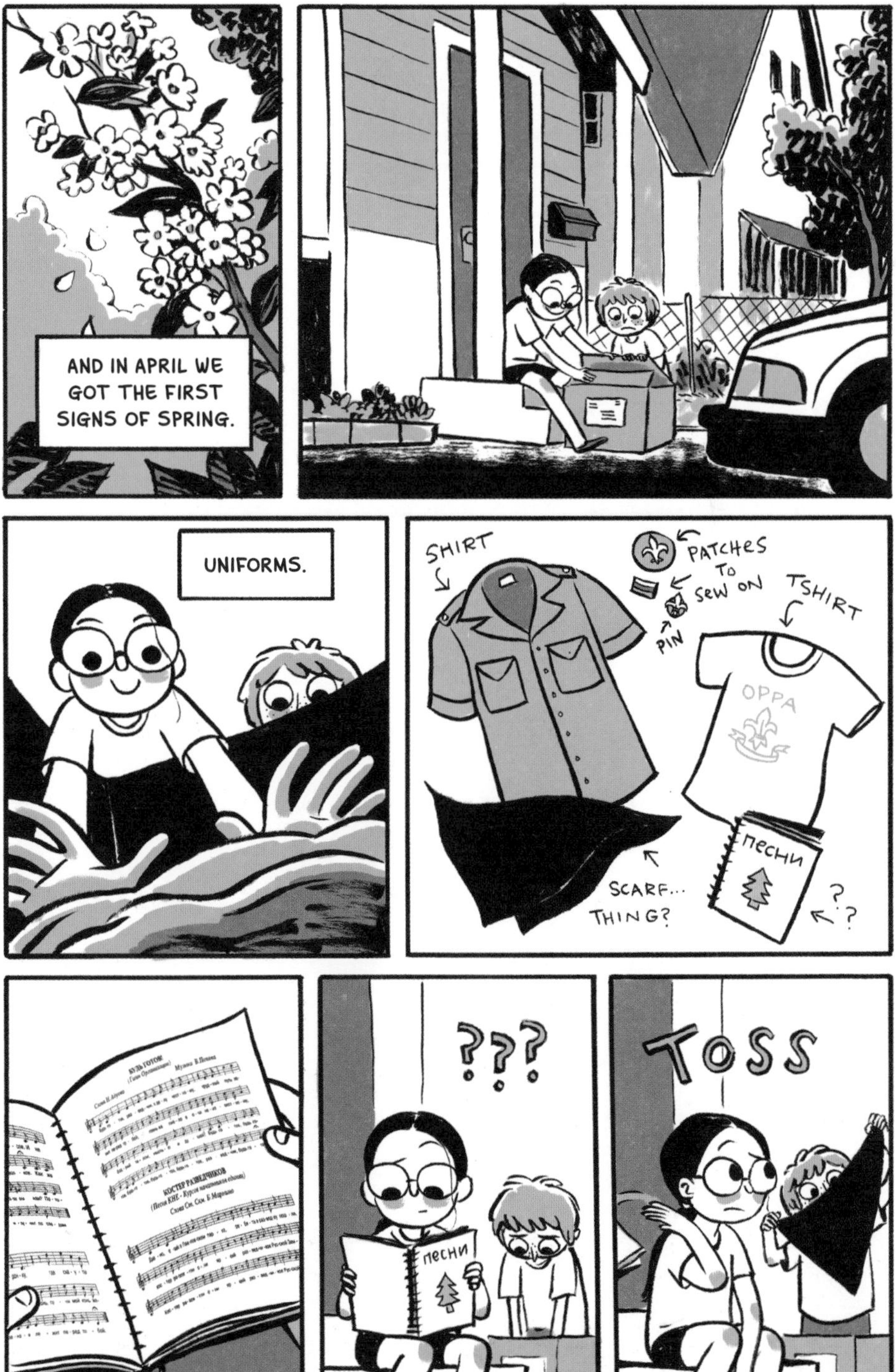

AND IN APRIL WE GOT THE FIRST SIGNS OF SPRING.
UNIFORMS.
SHIRT
PATCHES TO SEW ON
PIN
TSHIRT
OPPA
ПЕСНИ
SCARF... THING?
??
???
ПЕСНИ
TOSS

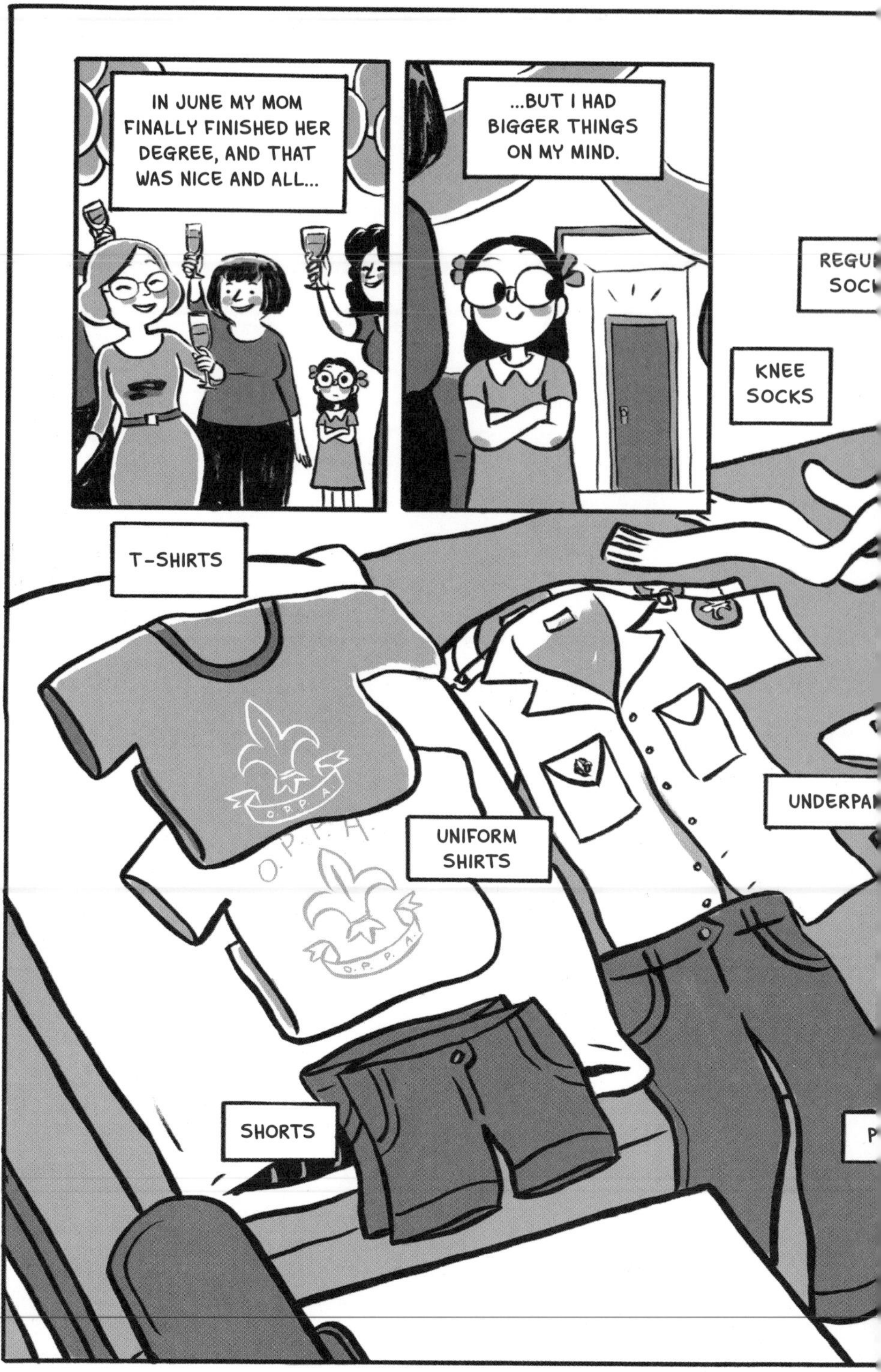
IN JUNE MY MOM FINALLY FINISHED HER DEGREE, AND THAT WAS NICE AND ALL...
...BUT I HAD BIGGER THINGS ON MY MIND.
REGU
SOC
KNEE SOCKS
T-SHIRTS
O.P.P.A.
UNIFORM SHIRTS
UNDERPA
SHORTS

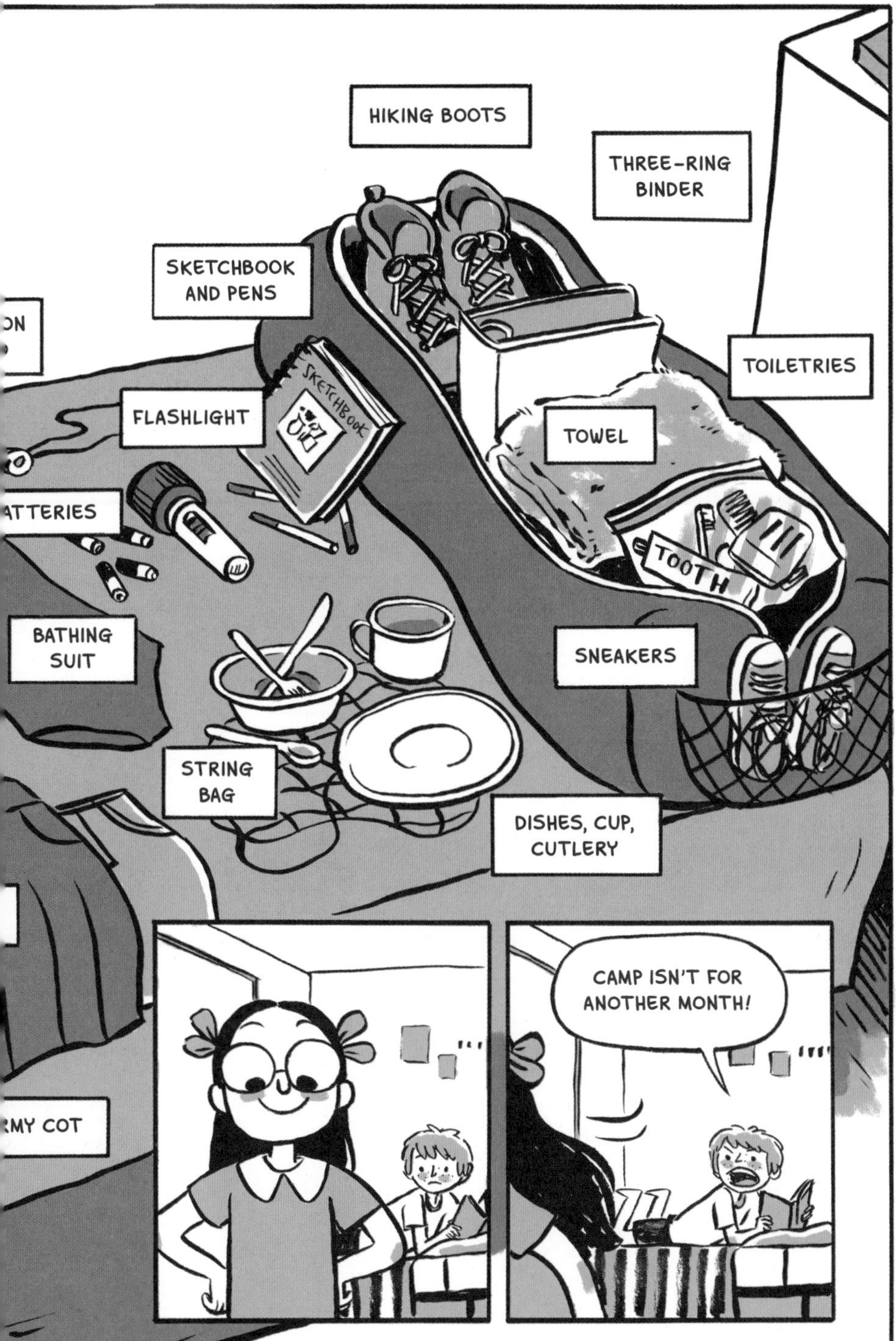
HIKING BOOTS
THREE-RING BINDER
SKETCHBOOK AND PENS
TOILETRIES
FLASHLIGHT
TOWEL
SKETCHBOOK
TOOTH
BATHING SUIT
SNEAKERS
STRING BAG
DISHES, CUP, CUTLERY
CAMP ISN'T FOR ANOTHER MONTH!

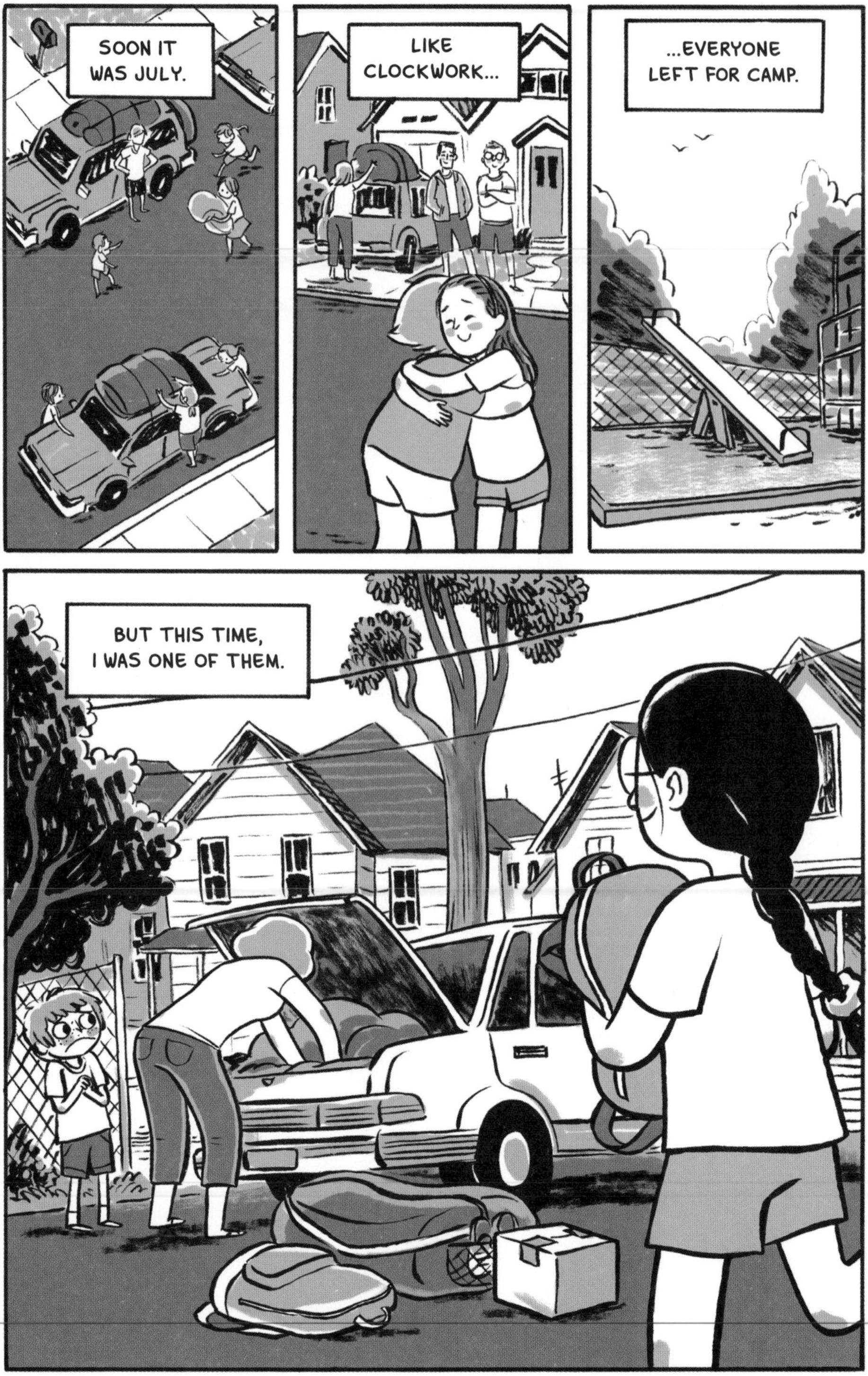
SOON IT WAS JULY.
LIKE CLOCKWORK...
...EVERYONE LEFT FOR CAMP.
BUT THIS TIME, I WAS ONE OF THEM.

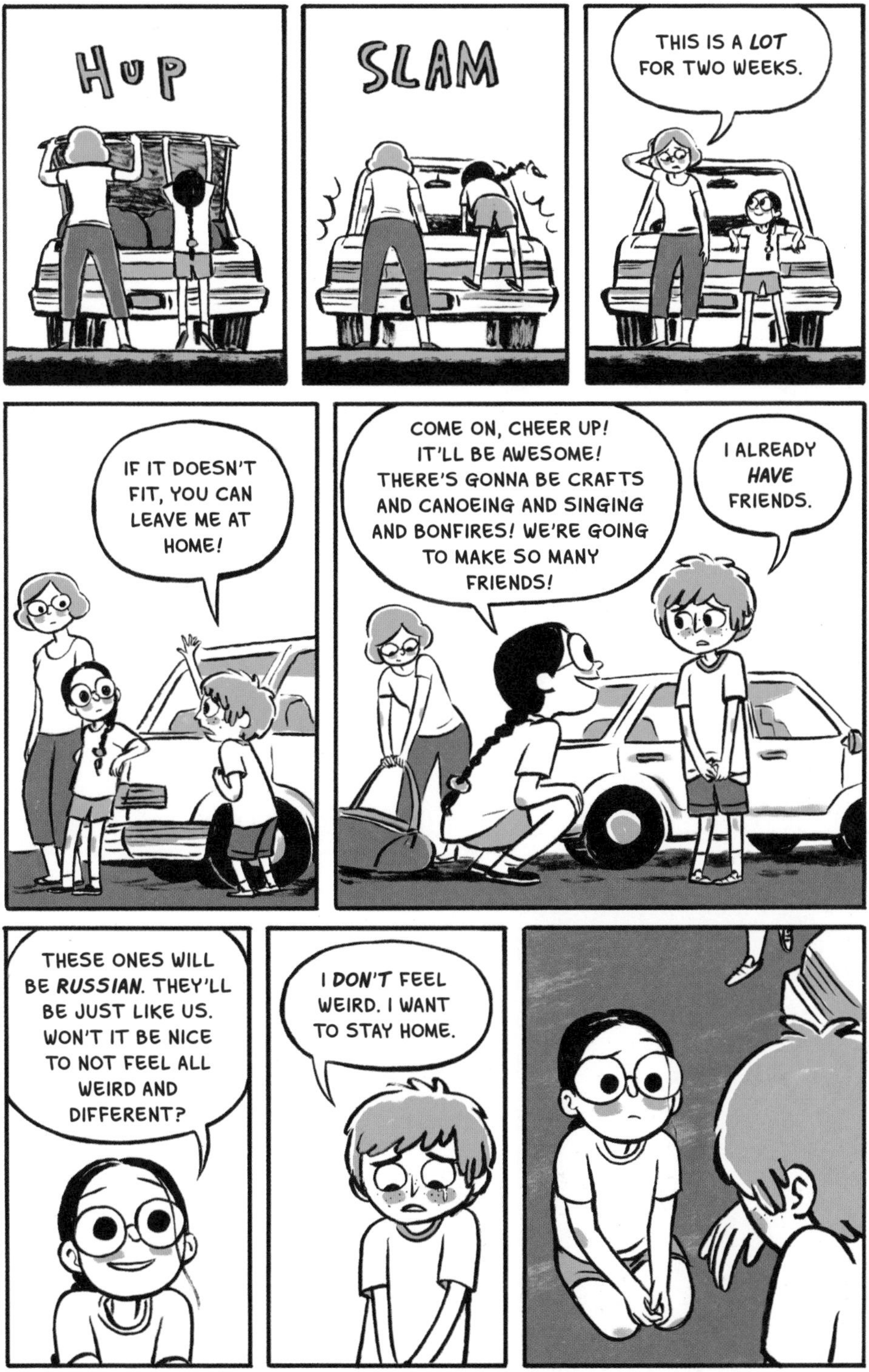
HUP
SLAM
THIS IS A *LOT* FOR TWO WEEKS.
IF IT DOESN'T FIT, YOU CAN LEAVE ME AT HOME!
COME ON, CHEER UP! IT'LL BE AWESOME! THERE'S GONNA BE CRAFTS AND CANOEING AND SINGING AND BONFIRES! WE'RE GOING TO MAKE SO MANY FRIENDS!
I ALREADY *HAVE* FRIENDS.
THESE ONES WILL BE ***RUSSIAN***. THEY'LL BE JUST LIKE US. WON'T IT BE NICE TO NOT FEEL ALL WEIRD AND DIFFERENT?
I *DON'T* FEEL WEIRD. I WANT TO STAY HOME.

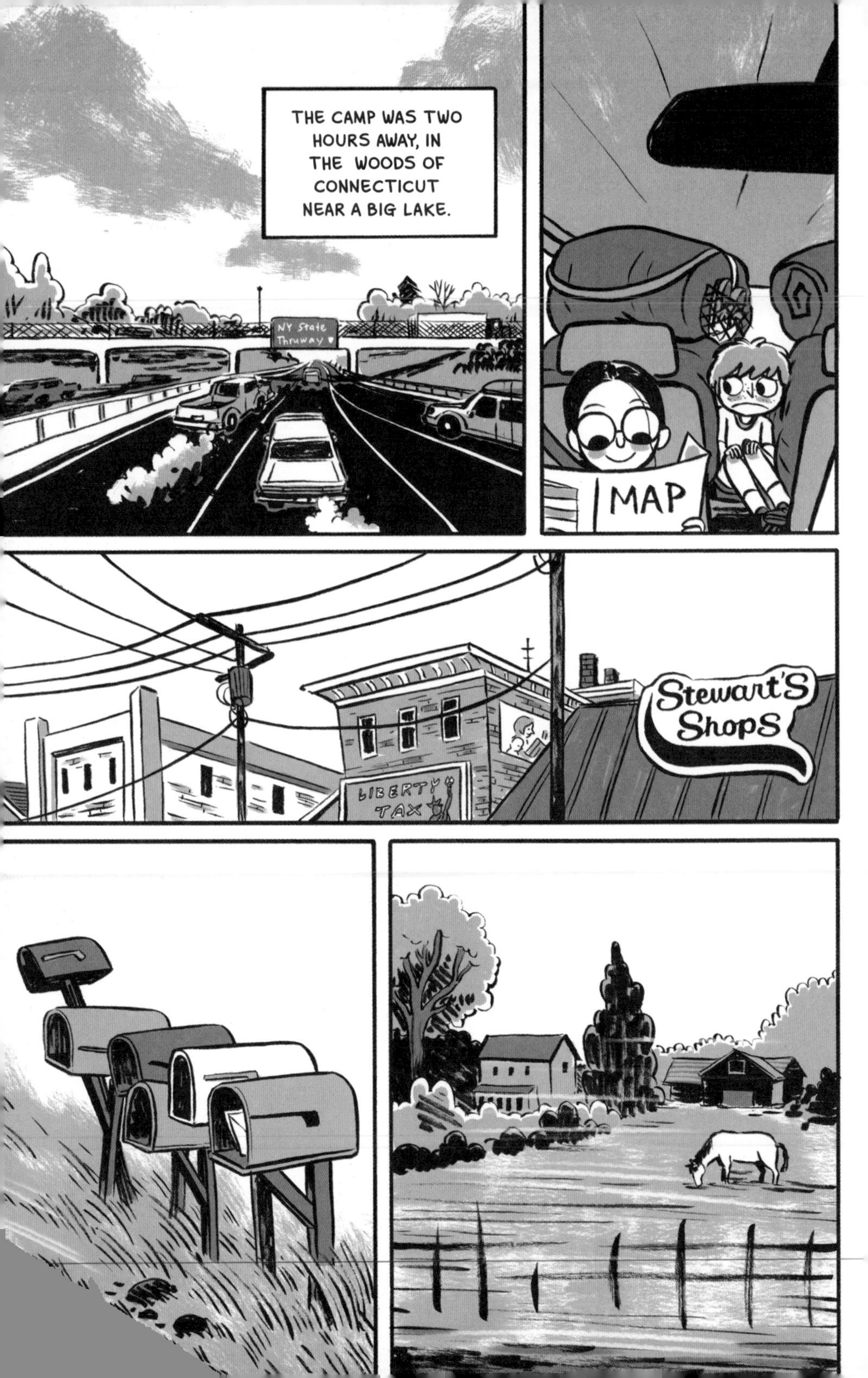
THE CAMP WAS TWO HOURS AWAY, IN THE WOODS OF CONNECTICUT NEAR A BIG LAKE.
NY State Thruway
MAP
LIBERTY TAX
Stewart's Shops

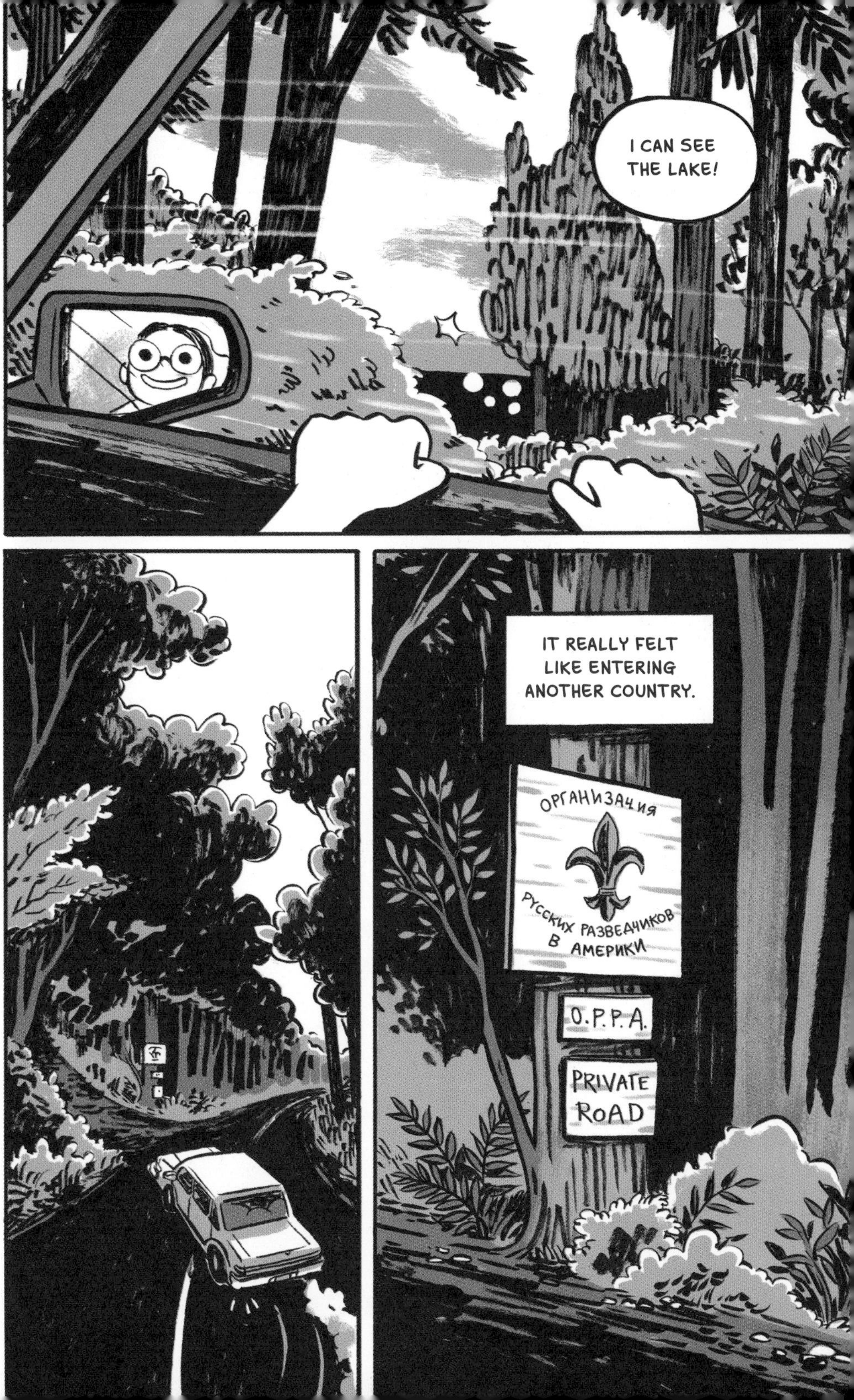

I CAN SEE THE LAKE!
IT REALLY FELT LIKE ENTERING ANOTHER COUNTRY.
ОРГАНИЗАЦИЯ
РУССКИХ РАЗВЕДЧИКОВ В АМЕРИКИ
О.Р.Р.А.
PRIVATE ROAD

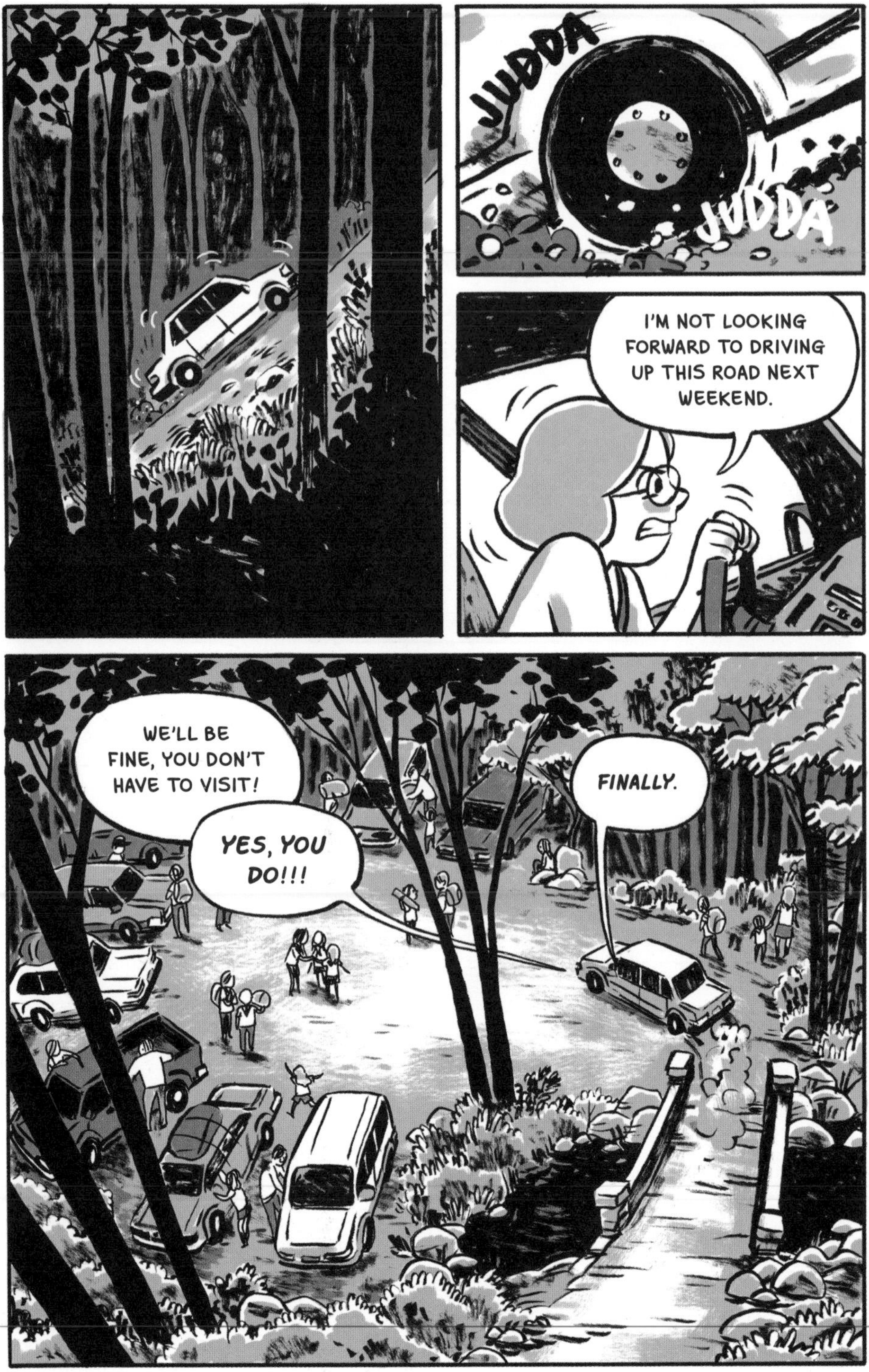
JUDDA
JUDDA
I'M NOT LOOKING FORWARD TO DRIVING UP THIS ROAD NEXT WEEKEND.
WE'LL BE FINE, YOU DON'T HAVE TO VISIT!
YES, YOU DO!!!
FINALLY.

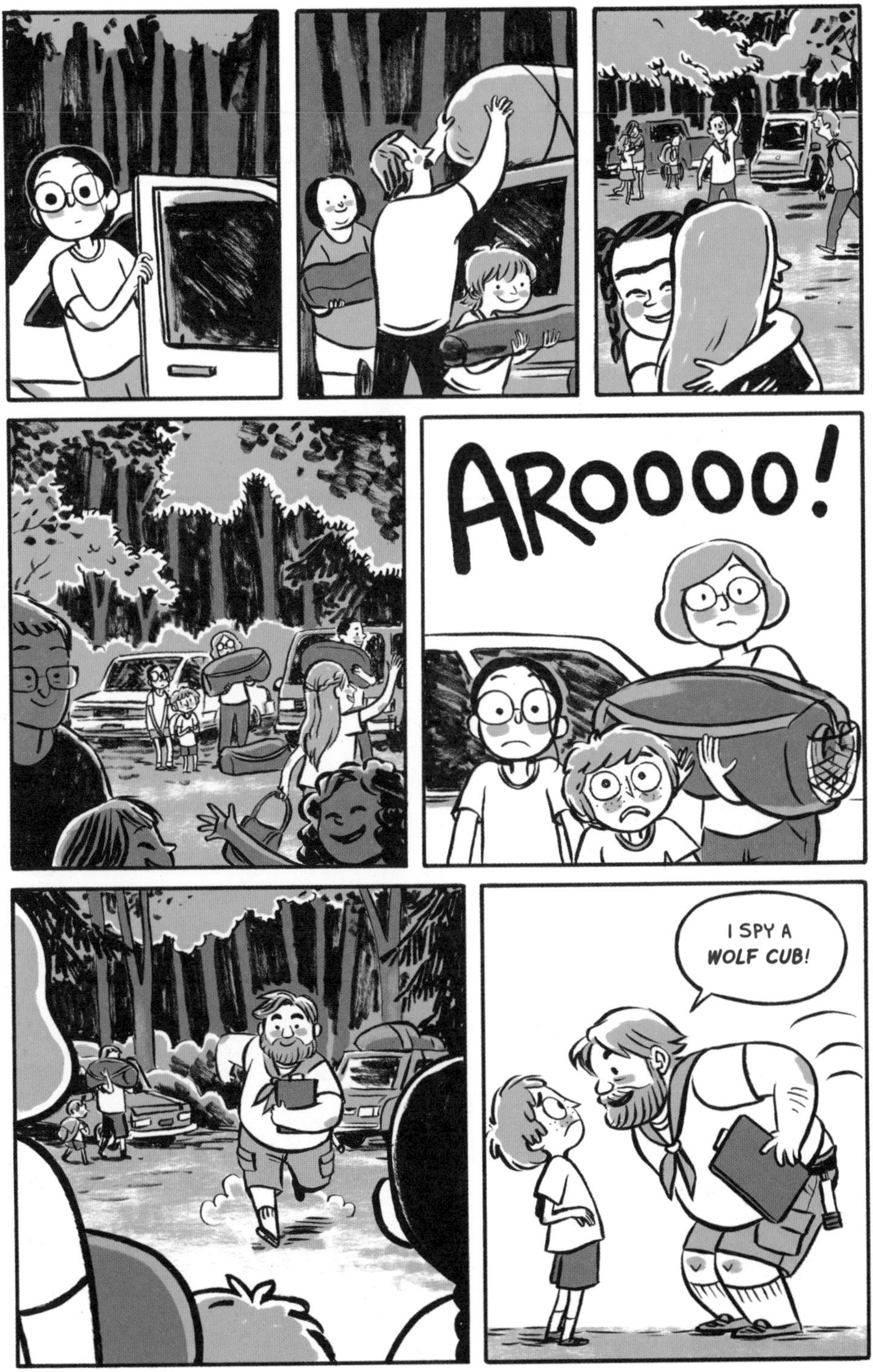
AROOOO!
I SPY A WOLF CUB!

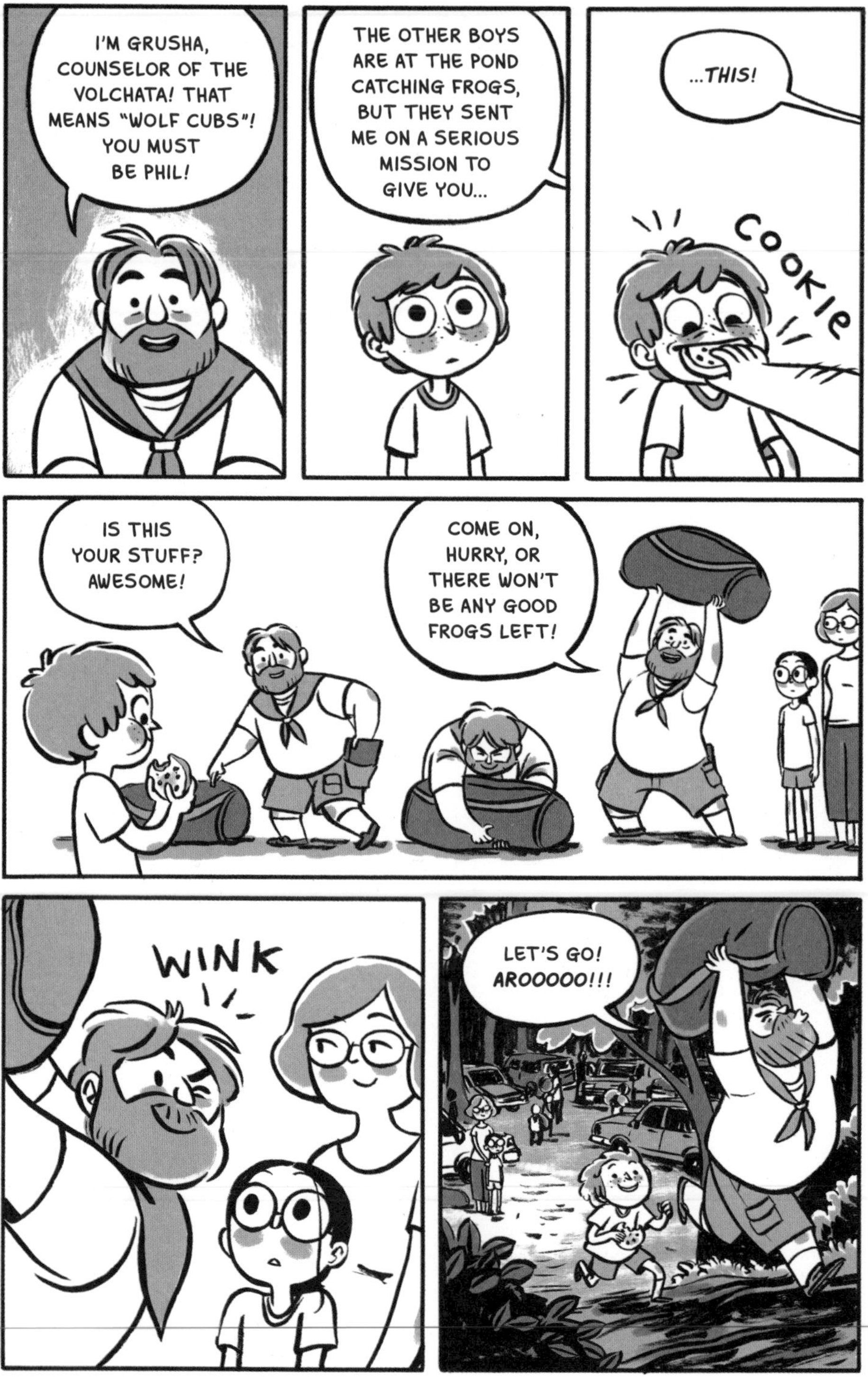
I'M GRUSHA, COUNSELOR OF THE VOLCHATA! THAT MEANS "WOLF CUBS"! YOU MUST BE PHIL!
THE OTHER BOYS ARE AT THE POND CATCHING FROGS, BUT THEY SENT ME ON A SERIOUS MISSION TO GIVE YOU...
...THIS!
COOKIE
IS THIS YOUR STUFF? AWESOME!
COME ON, HURRY, OR THERE WON'T BE ANY GOOD FROGS LEFT!
WINK
LET'S GO! AROOOOO!!!

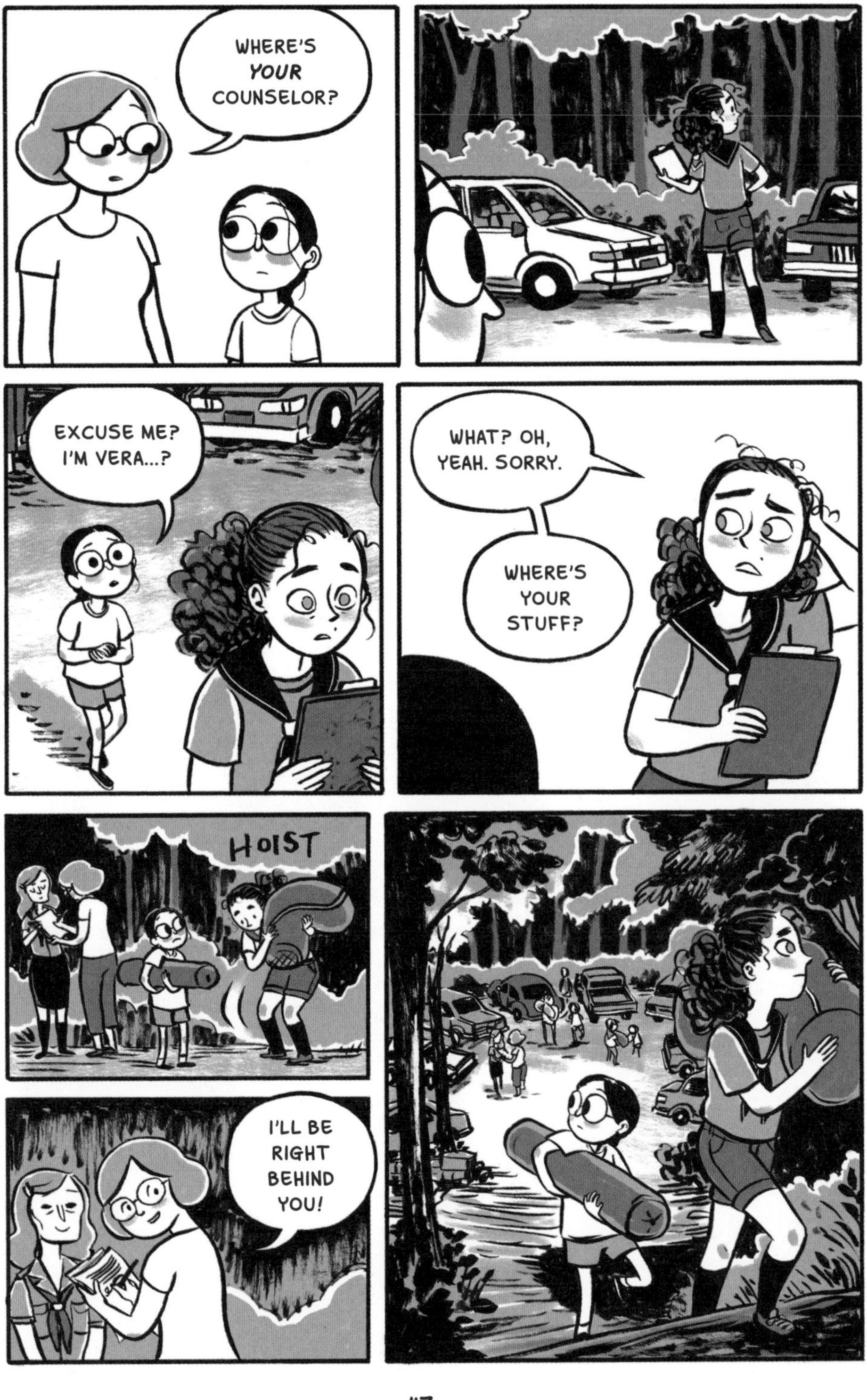
WHERE'S *YOUR* COUNSELOR?
EXCUSE ME? I'M VERA...?
WHAT? OH, YEAH. SORRY.
WHERE'S YOUR STUFF?
HOIST
I'LL BE RIGHT BEHIND YOU!

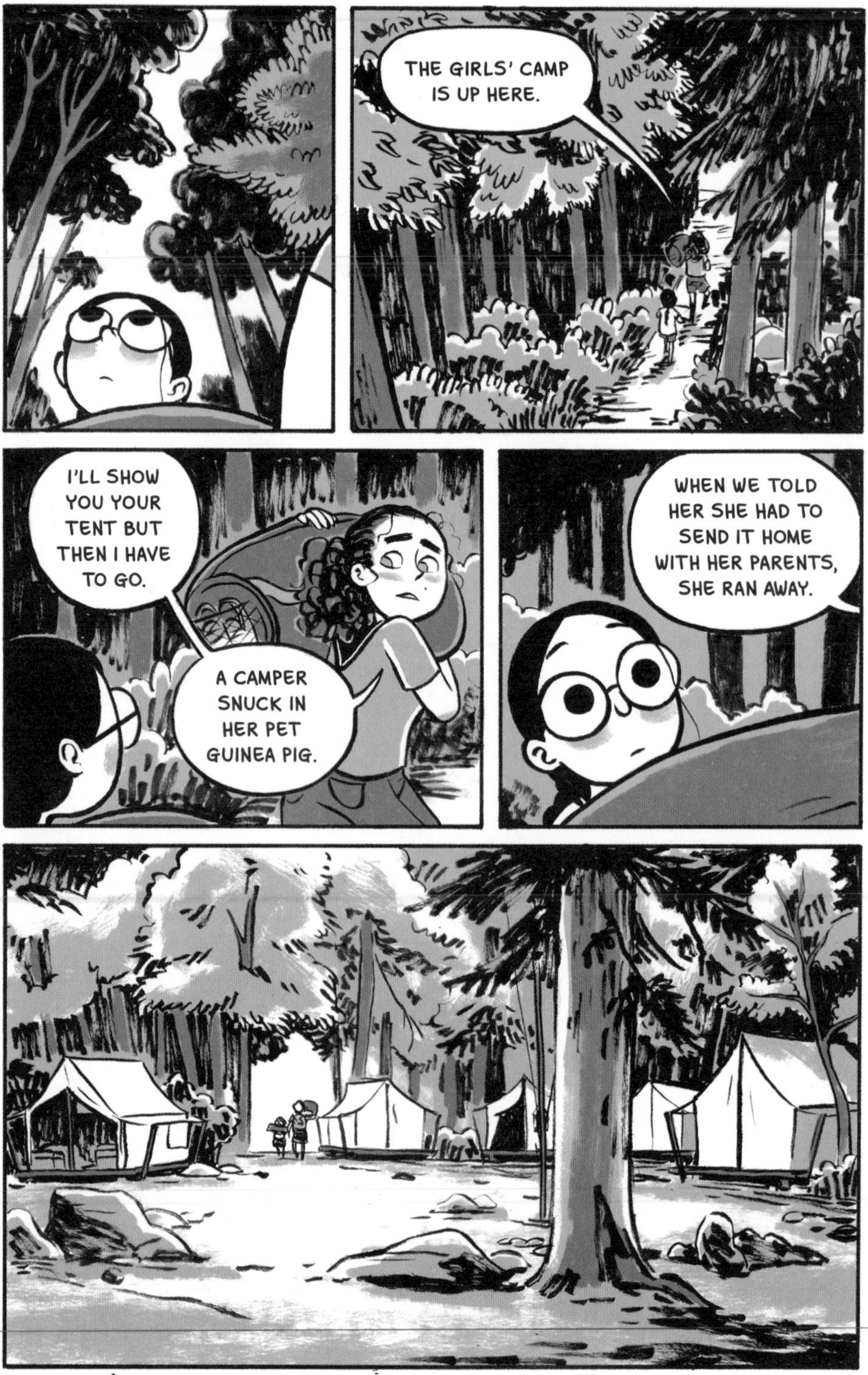
THE GIRLS' CAMP IS UP HERE.
I'LL SHOW YOU YOUR TENT BUT THEN I HAVE TO GO.
A CAMPER SNUCK IN HER PET GUINEA PIG.
WHEN WE TOLD HER SHE HAD TO SEND IT HOME WITH HER PARENTS, SHE RAN AWAY.

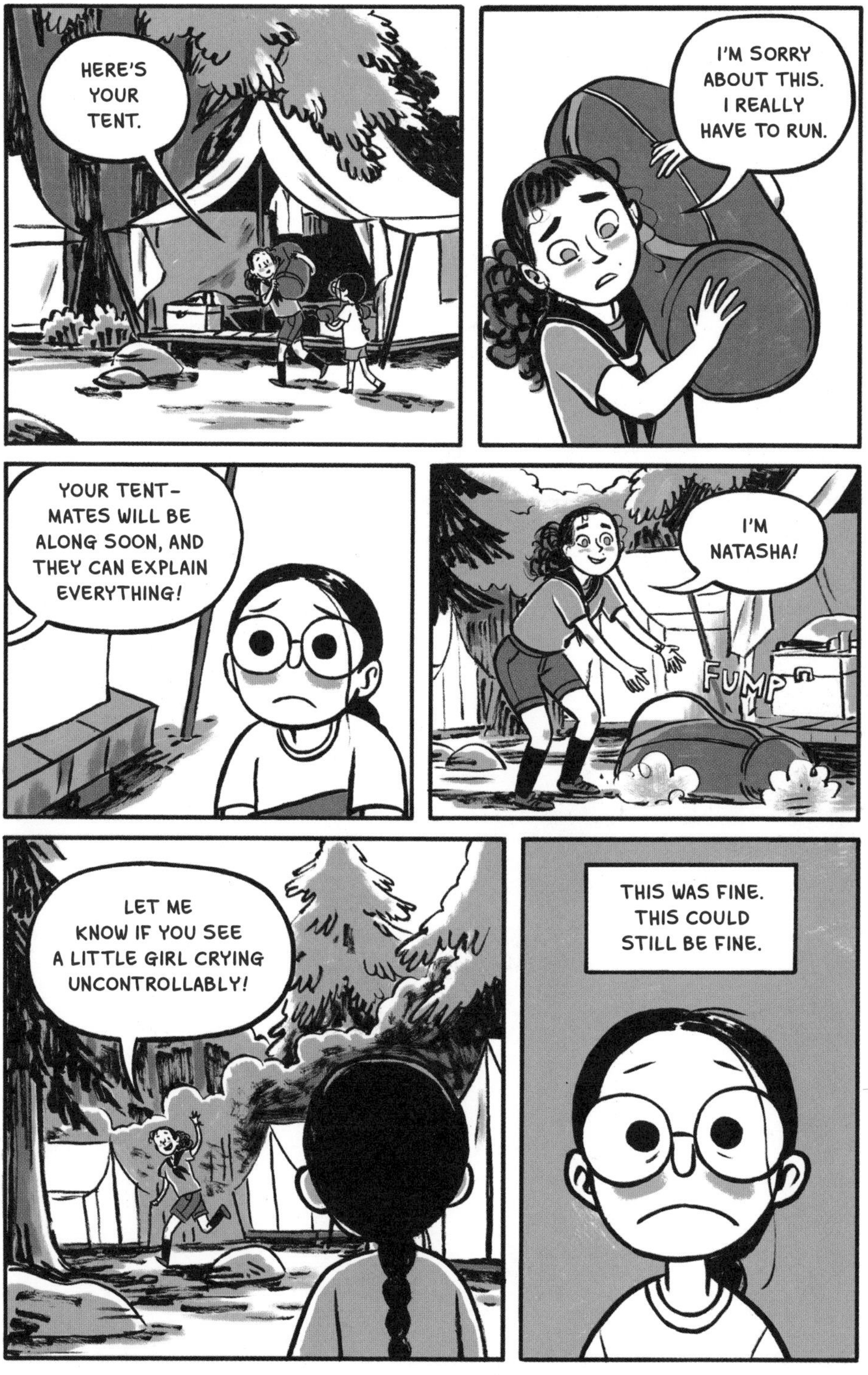
HERE'S YOUR TENT.
I'M SORRY ABOUT THIS. I REALLY HAVE TO RUN.
YOUR TENT-MATES WILL BE ALONG SOON, AND THEY CAN EXPLAIN EVERYTHING!
I'M NATASHA!
FUMP
LET ME KNOW IF YOU SEE A LITTLE GIRL CRYING UNCONTROLLABLY!
THIS WAS FINE. THIS COULD STILL BE FINE.

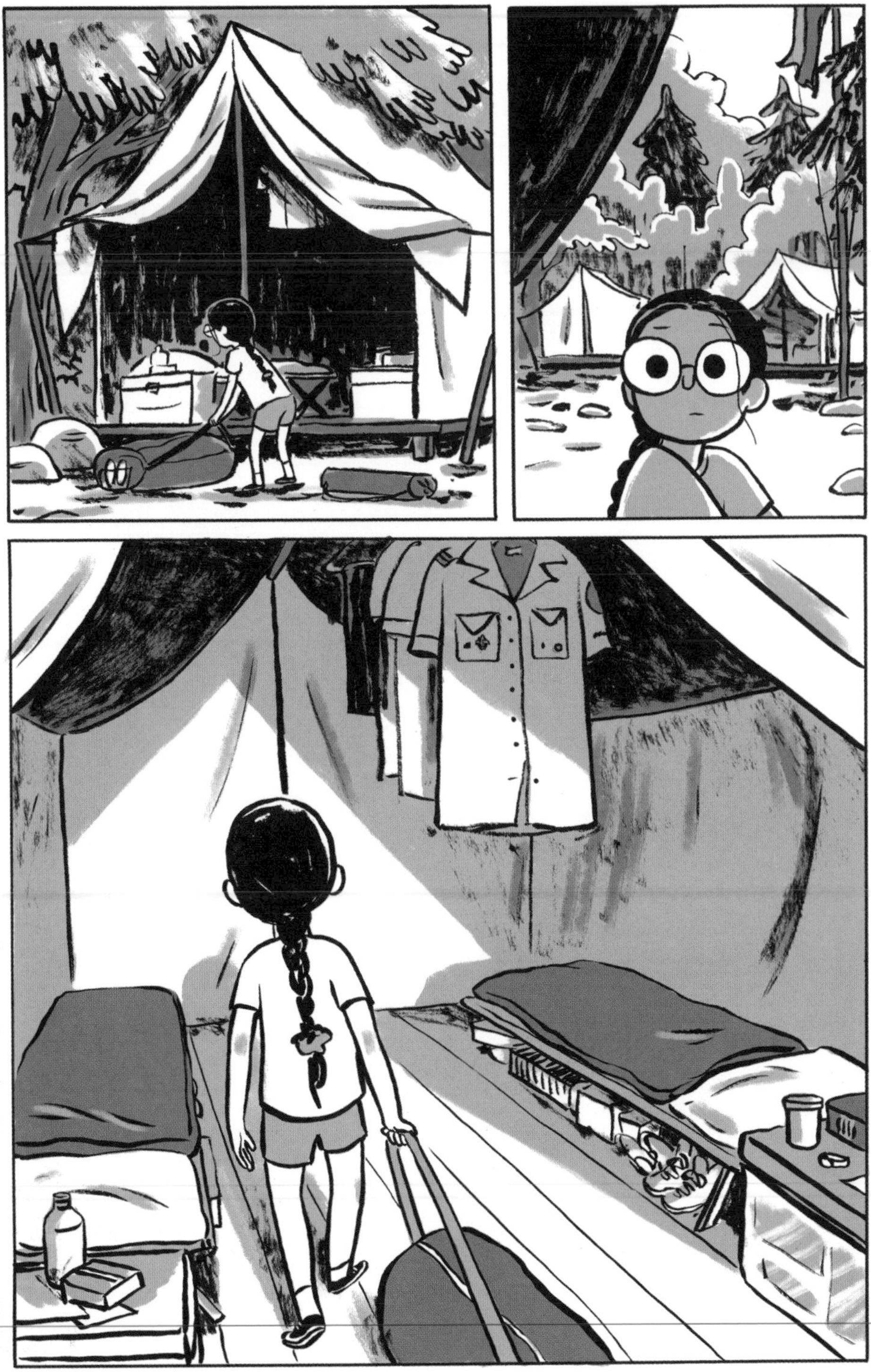

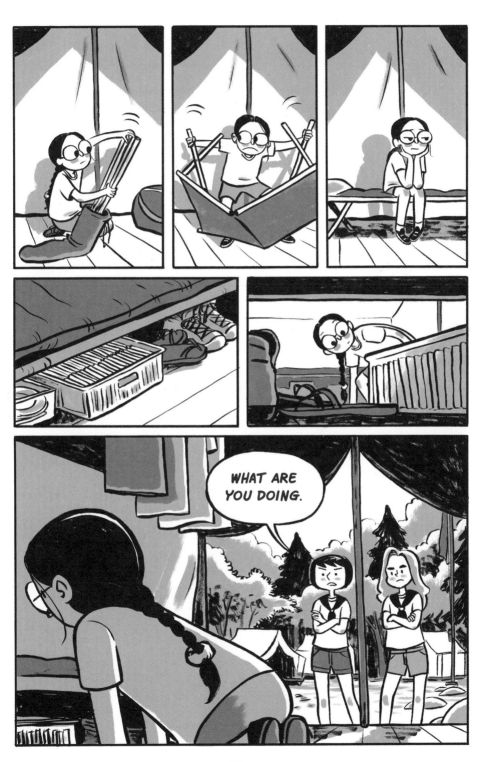

WHAT ARE
YOU DOING.

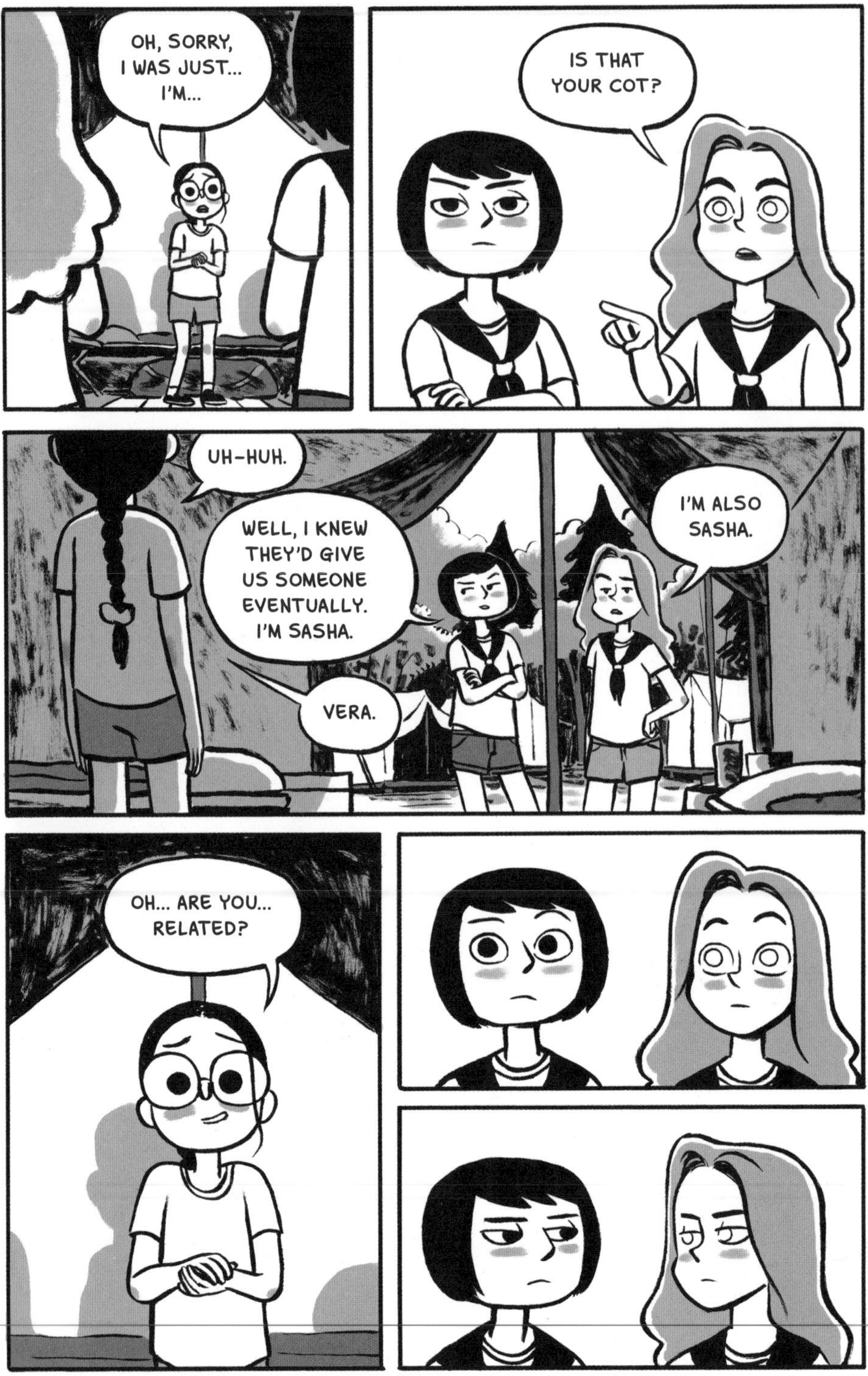
OH, SORRY, I WAS JUST... I'M...
IS THAT YOUR COT?
UH-HUH.
WELL, I KNEW THEY'D GIVE US SOMEONE EVENTUALLY. I'M SASHA.
I'M ALSO SASHA.
VERA.
OH... ARE YOU... RELATED?

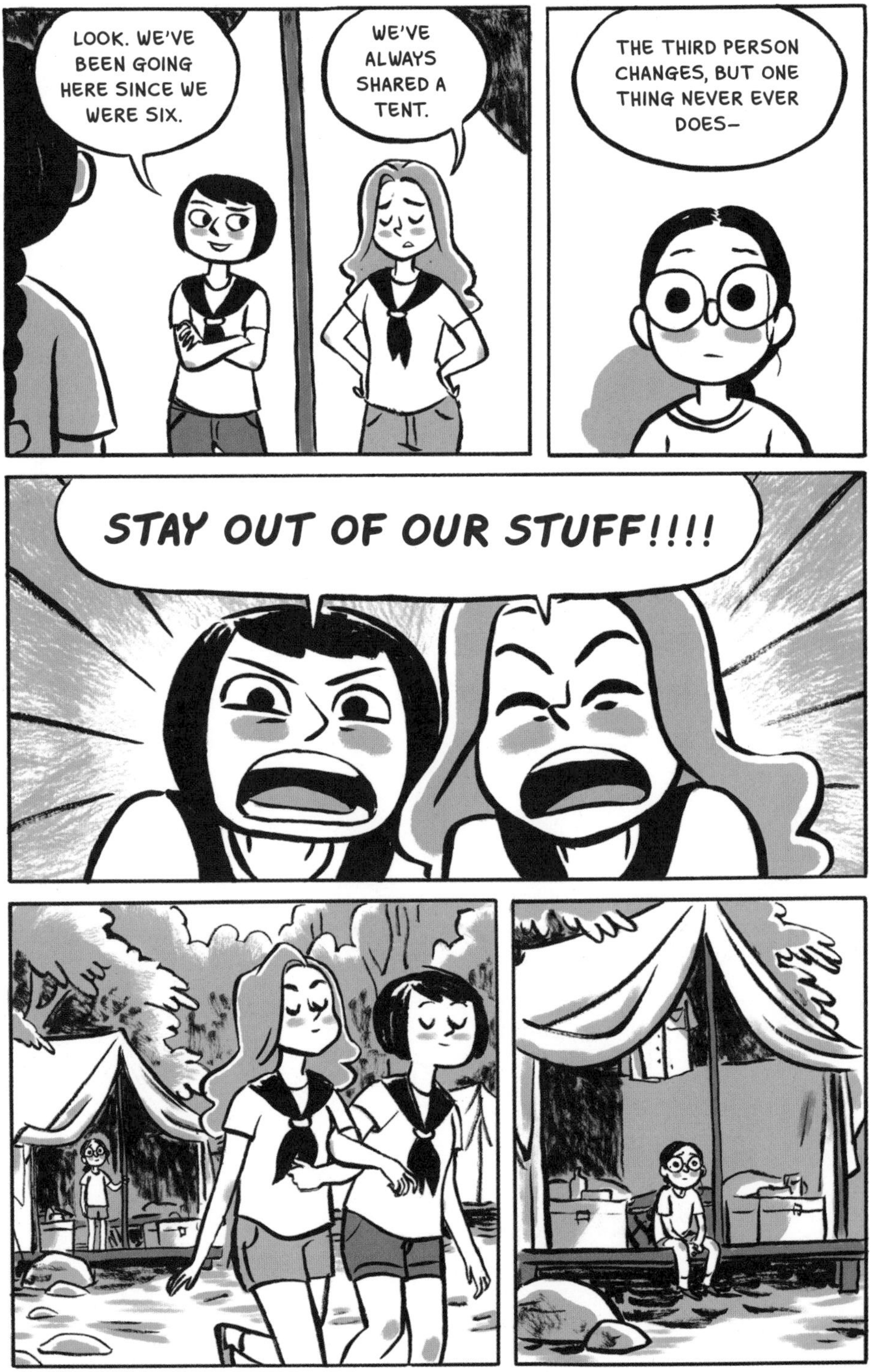
LOOK. WE'VE BEEN GOING HERE SINCE WE WERE SIX.
WE'VE ALWAYS SHARED A TENT.
THE THIRD PERSON CHANGES, BUT ONE THING NEVER EVER DOES–
STAY OUT OF OUR STUFF!!!!

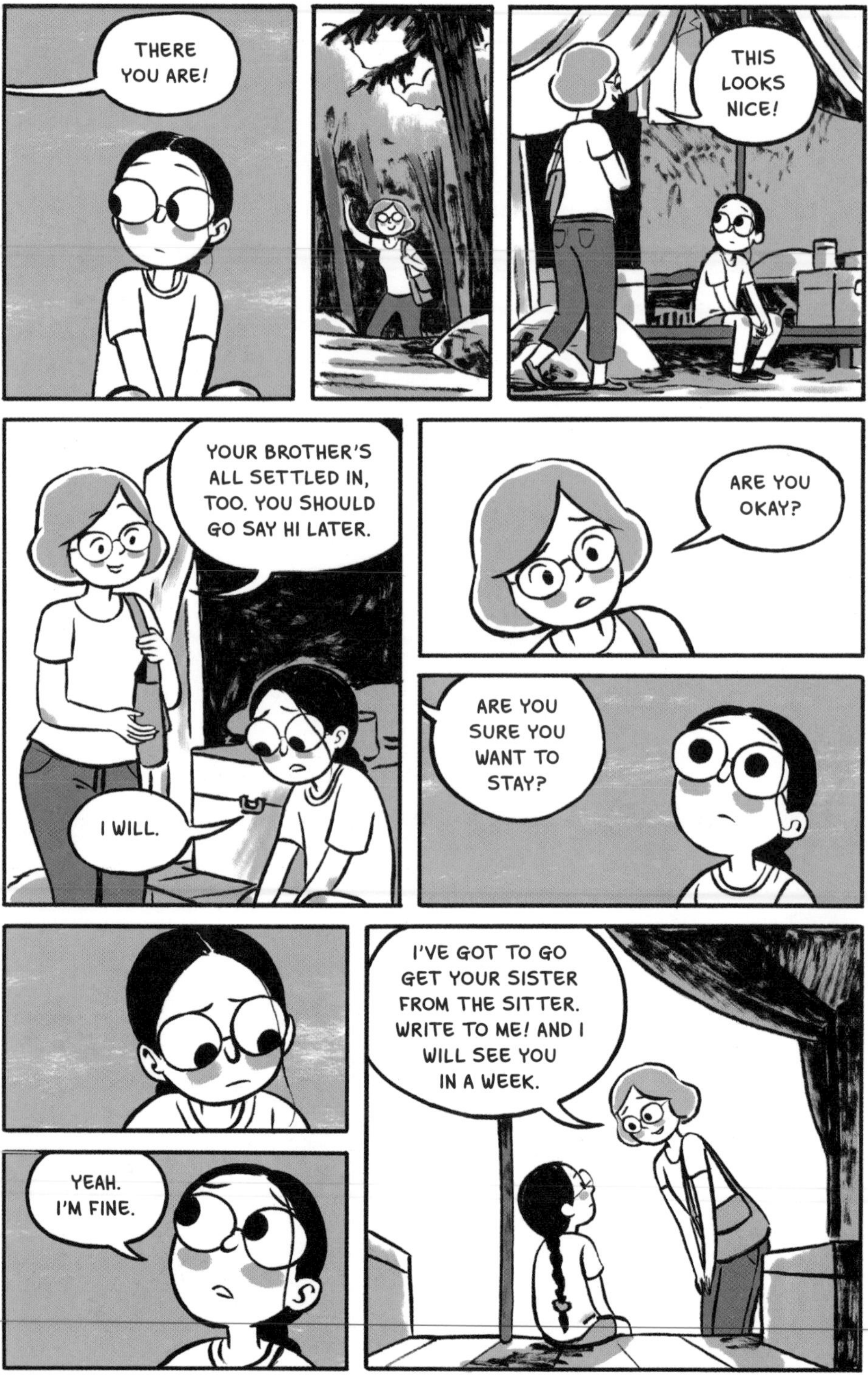
THERE YOU ARE!
THIS LOOKS NICE!
YOUR BROTHER'S ALL SETTLED IN, TOO. YOU SHOULD GO SAY HI LATER.
I WILL.
ARE YOU OKAY?
ARE YOU SURE YOU WANT TO STAY?
YEAH. I'M FINE.
I'VE GOT TO GO GET YOUR SISTER FROM THE SITTER. WRITE TO ME! AND I WILL SEE YOU IN A WEEK.

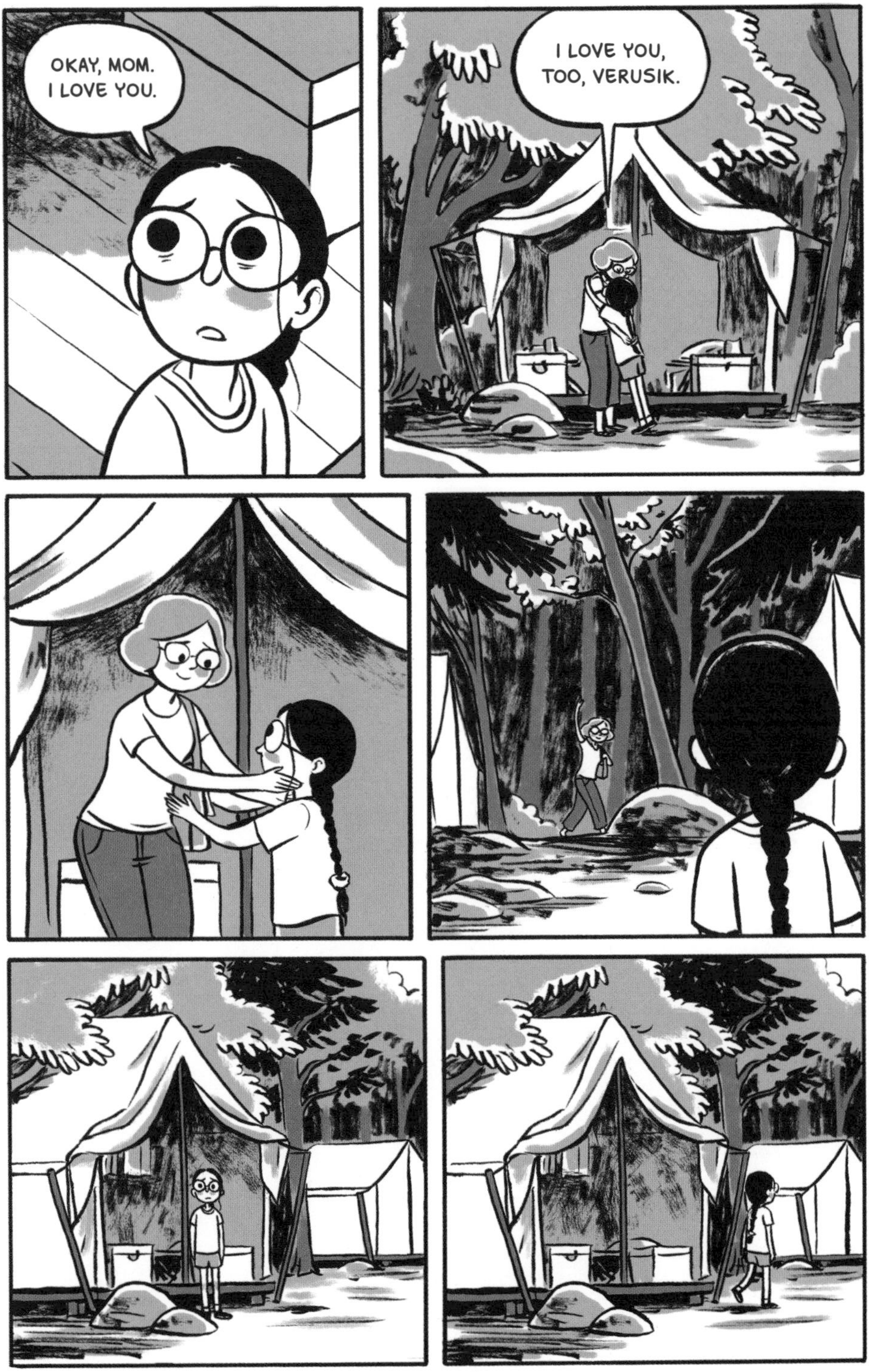
OKAY, MOM.
I LOVE YOU.
I LOVE YOU,
TOO, VERUSIK.

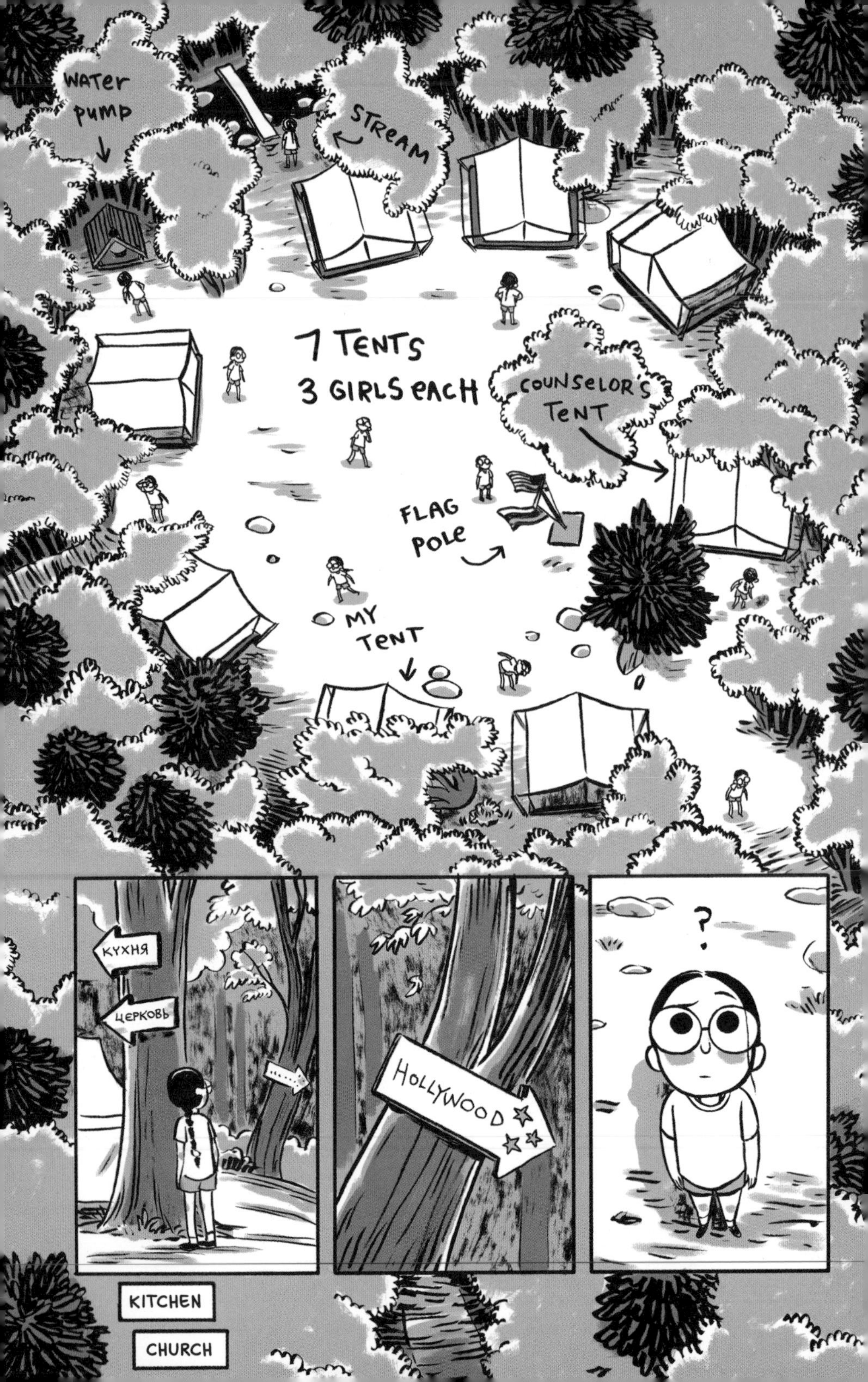

WATER PUMP
STREAM
7 TENTS
3 GIRLS EACH
COUNSELOR'S TENT
FLAG POLE
MY TENT
КУХНЯ
ЦЕРКОВЬ
HOLLYWOOD
?
KITCHEN
CHURCH

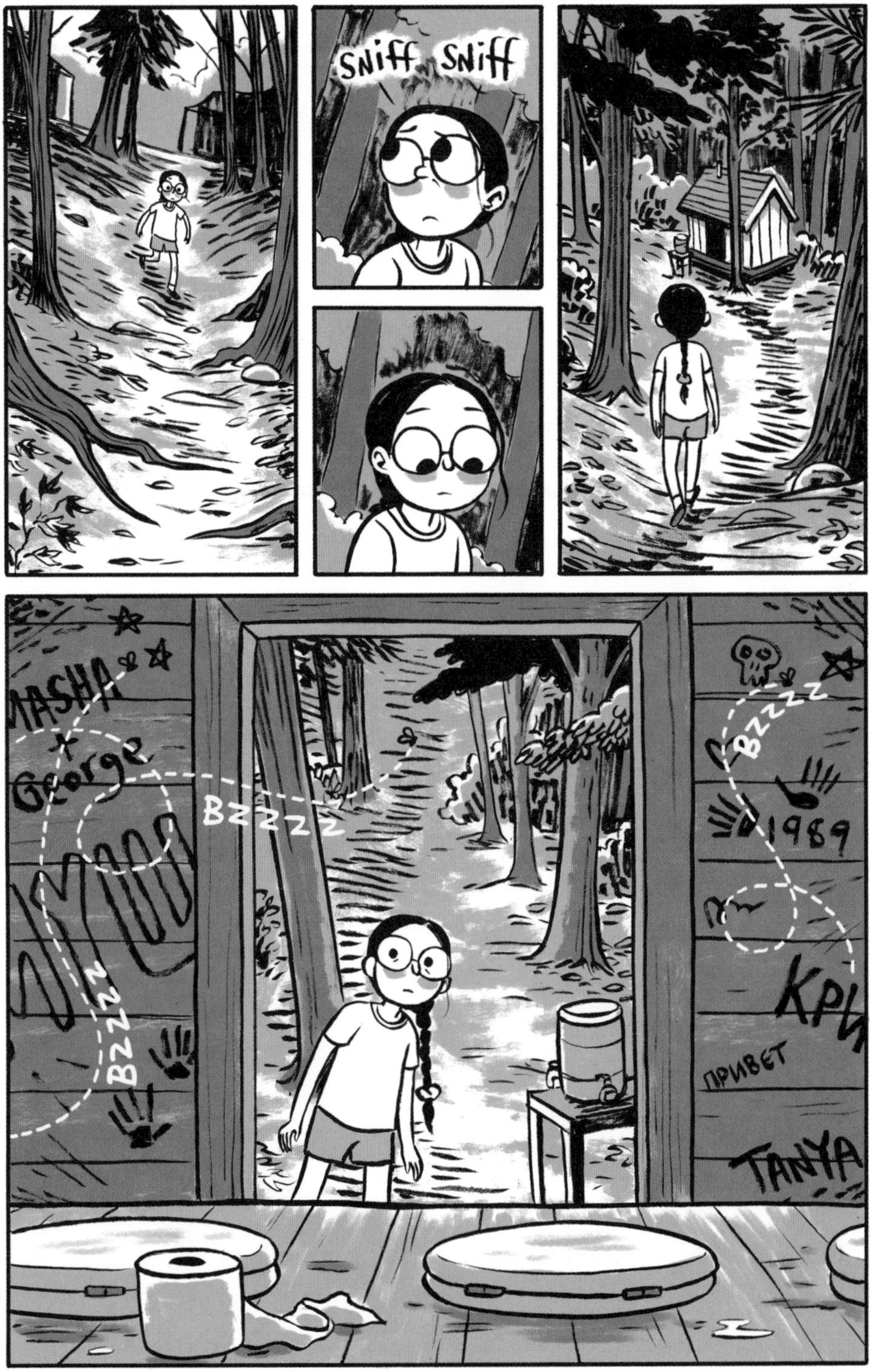
SNIFF SNIFF
MASHA
+
George
BZZZZZ
BZZZZ
BZZZZ
1989
ПРИВЕТ
TANYA

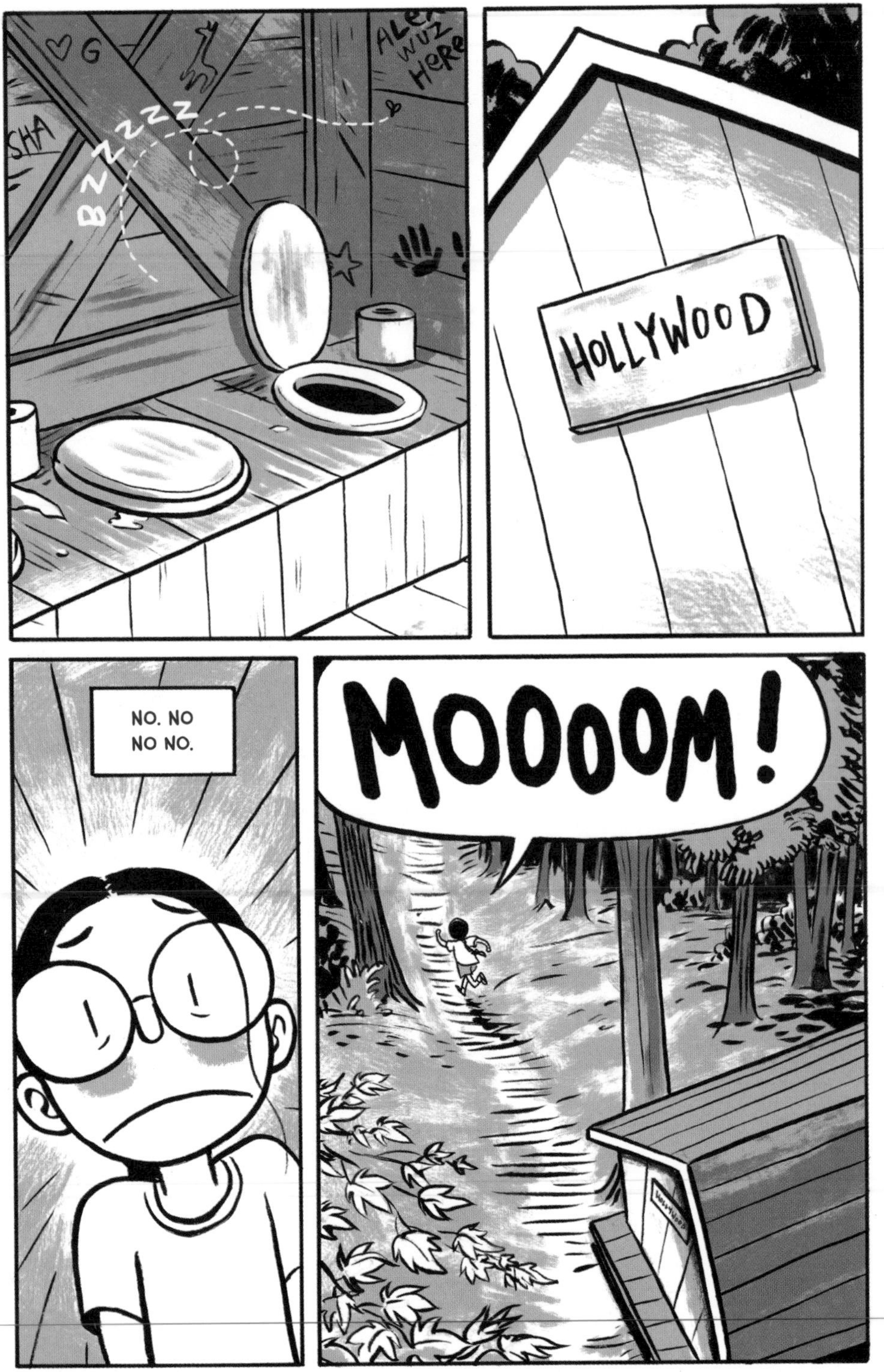
SHA
G
ALEX WUZ HERE
BZZZZZZ
HOLLYWOOD
NO. NO
NO NO.
MOOOOM!

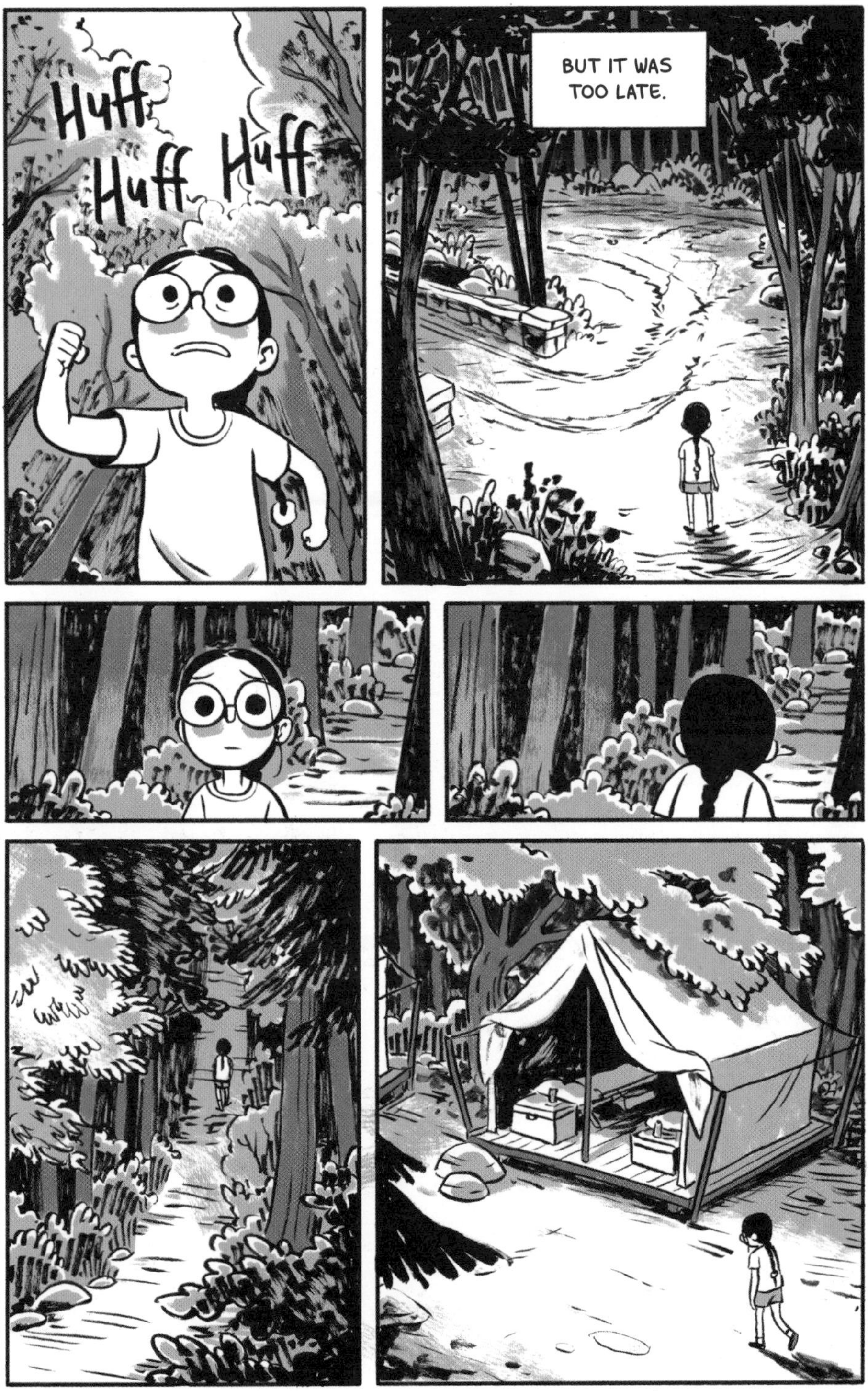
Huff
Huff Huff
BUT IT WAS TOO LATE.

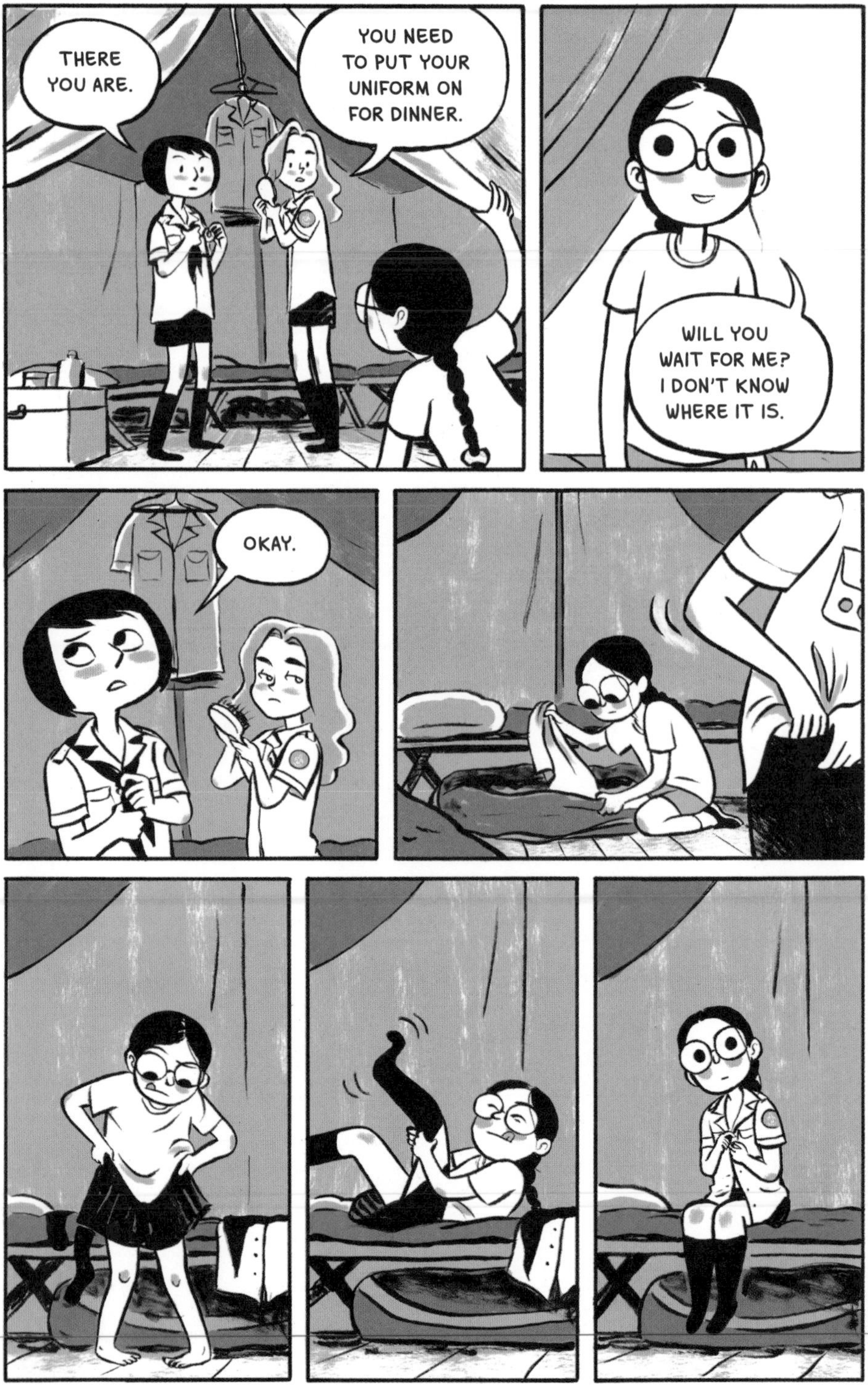
THERE YOU ARE.
YOU NEED TO PUT YOUR UNIFORM ON FOR DINNER.
WILL YOU WAIT FOR ME? I DON'T KNOW WHERE IT IS.
OKAY.

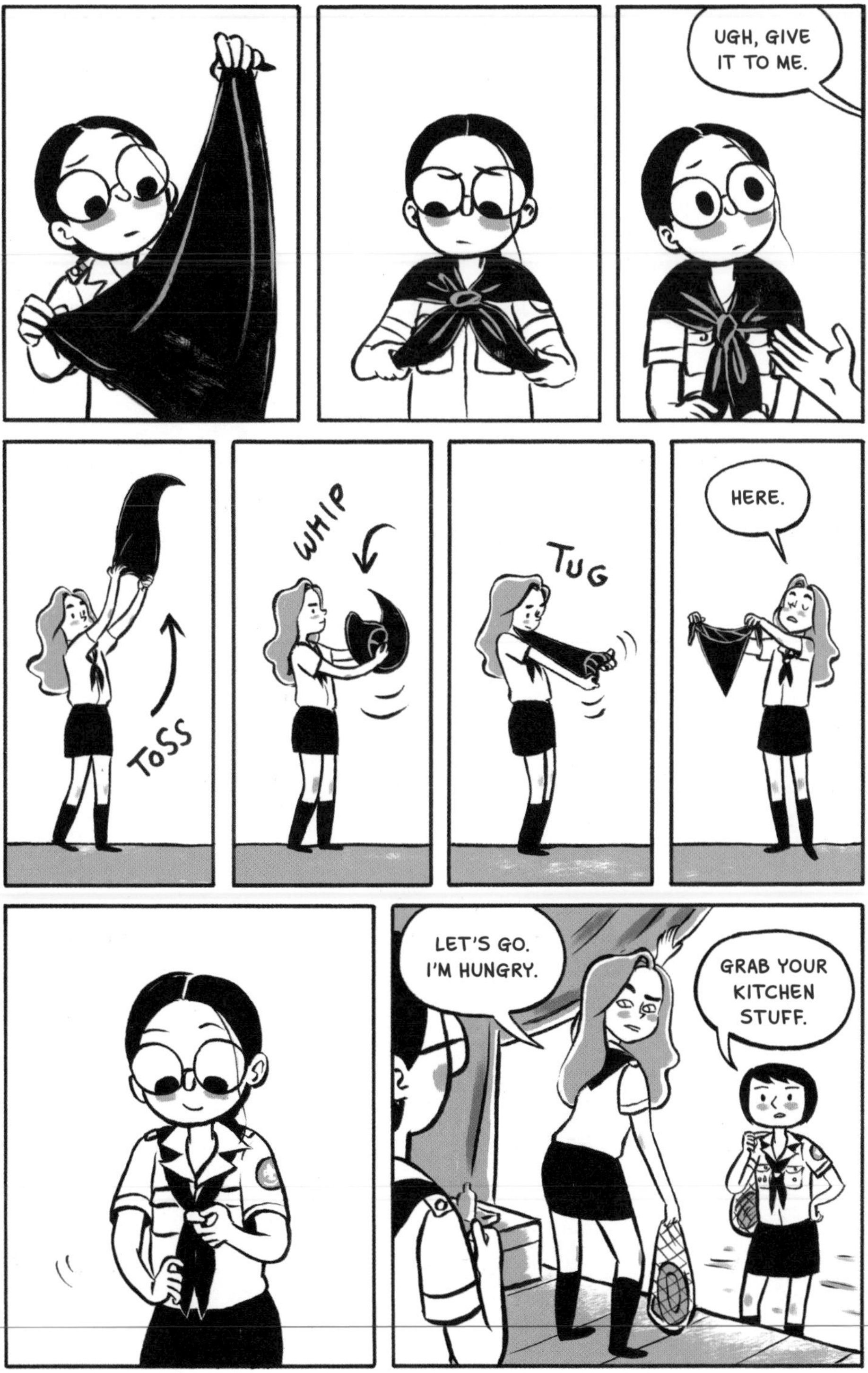
UGH, GIVE IT TO ME.
TOSS
WHIP
TUG
HERE.
LET'S GO. I'M HUNGRY.
GRAB YOUR KITCHEN STUFF.

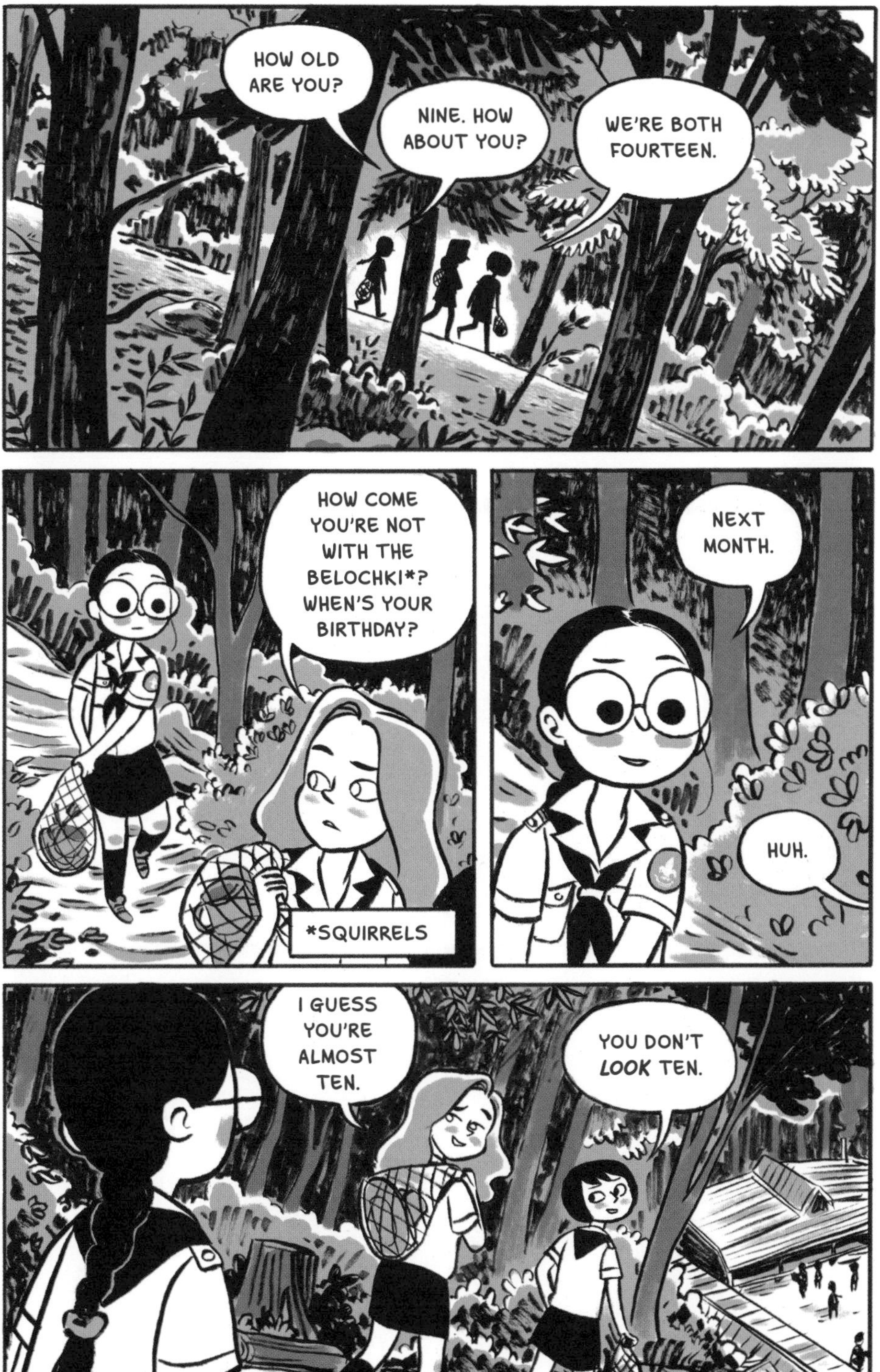
HOW OLD ARE YOU?
NINE. HOW ABOUT YOU?
WE'RE BOTH FOURTEEN.
HOW COME YOU'RE NOT WITH THE BELOCHKI*? WHEN'S YOUR BIRTHDAY?
*SQUIRRELS
NEXT MONTH.
HUH.
I GUESS YOU'RE ALMOST TEN.
YOU DON'T *LOOK* TEN.

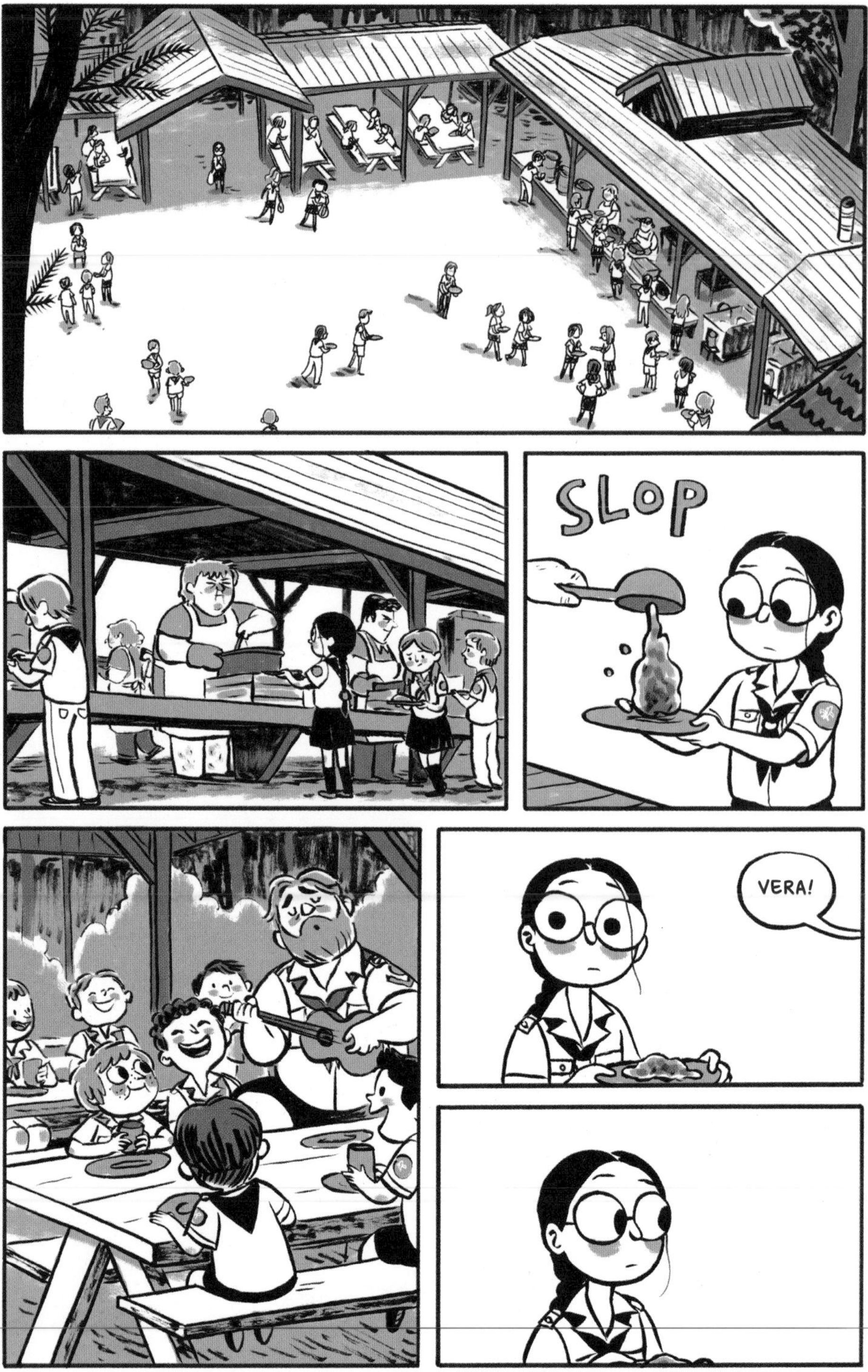
SLOP
VERA!

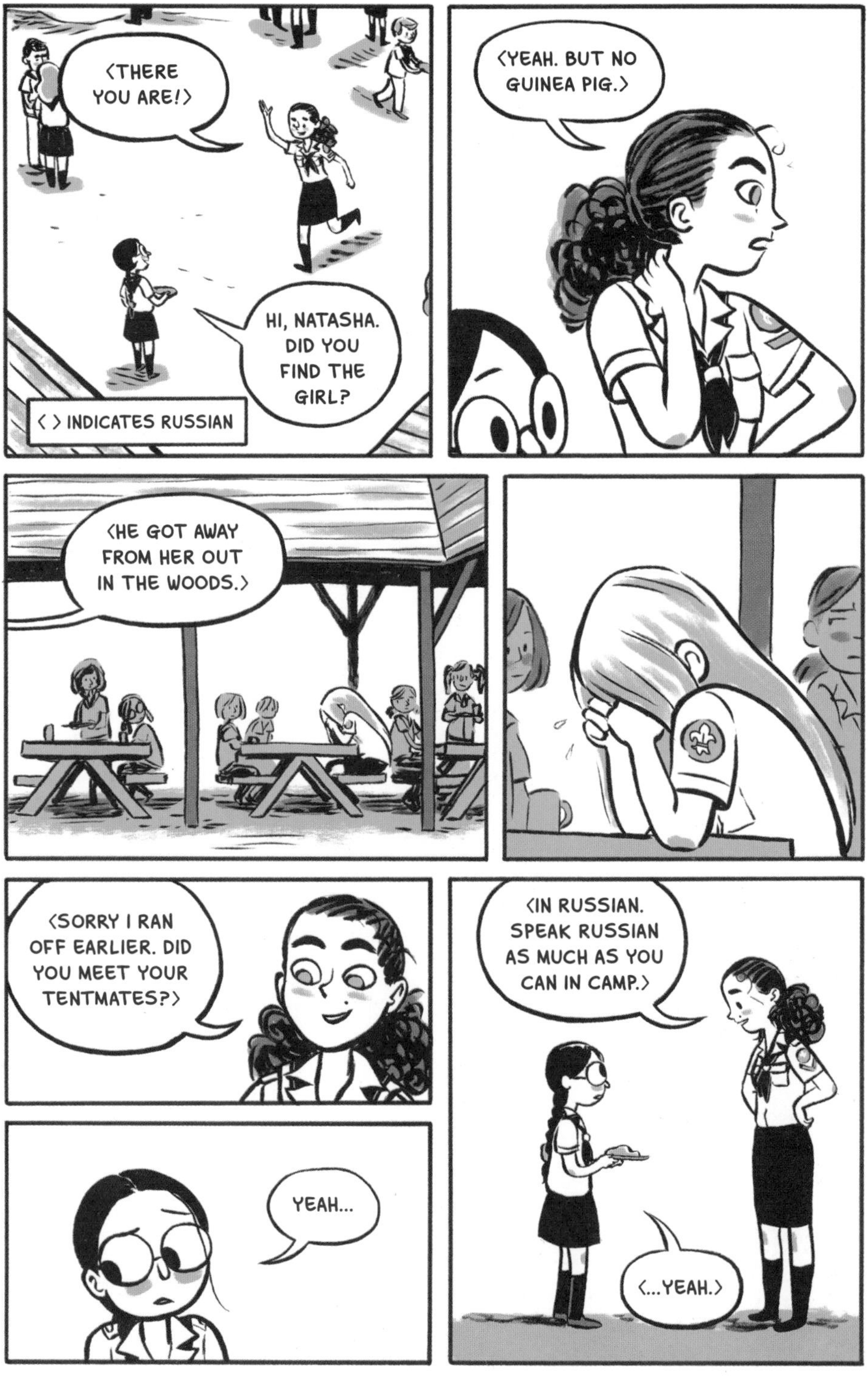

⟨THERE YOU ARE!⟩
HI, NATASHA. DID YOU FIND THE GIRL?
⟨ ⟩ INDICATES RUSSIAN
⟨YEAH. BUT NO GUINEA PIG.⟩
⟨HE GOT AWAY FROM HER OUT IN THE WOODS.⟩
⟨SORRY I RAN OFF EARLIER. DID YOU MEET YOUR TENTMATES?⟩
YEAH...
⟨IN RUSSIAN. SPEAK RUSSIAN AS MUCH AS YOU CAN IN CAMP.⟩
⟨...YEAH.⟩

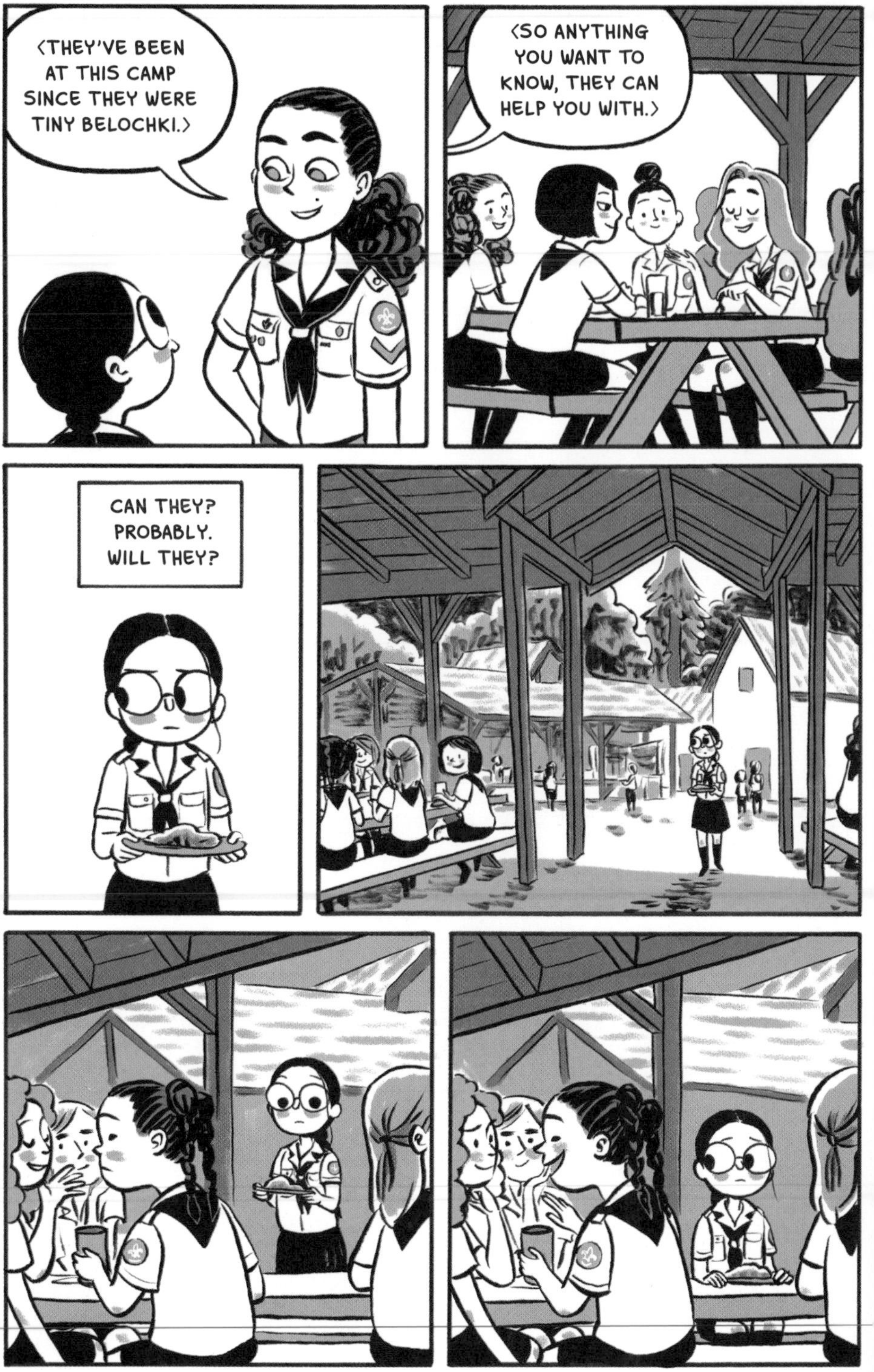

<THEY'VE BEEN AT THIS CAMP SINCE THEY WERE TINY BELOCHKI.>
<SO ANYTHING YOU WANT TO KNOW, THEY CAN HELP YOU WITH.>
CAN THEY? PROBABLY. WILL THEY?

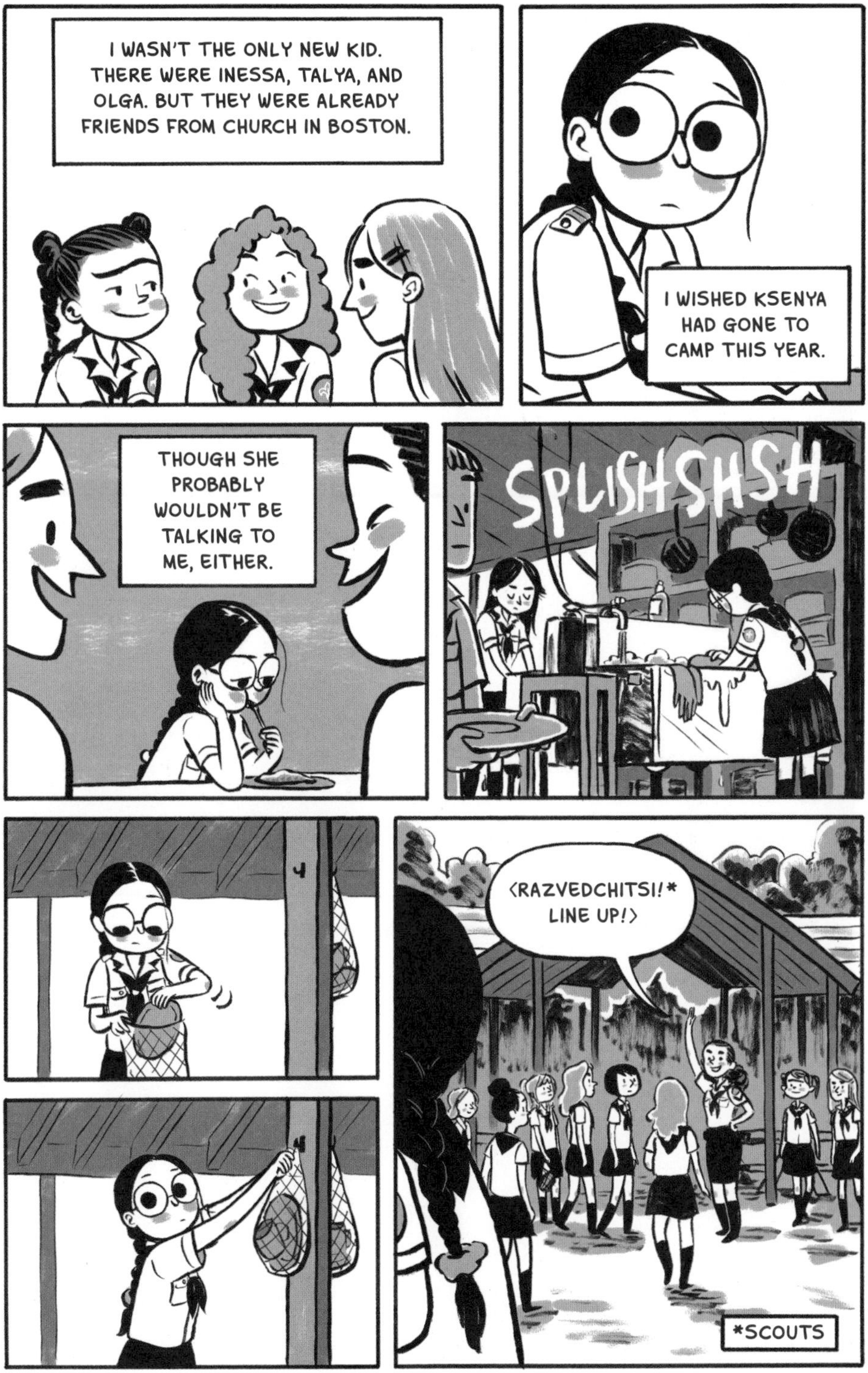
I WASN'T THE ONLY NEW KID. THERE WERE INESSA, TALYA, AND OLGA. BUT THEY WERE ALREADY FRIENDS FROM CHURCH IN BOSTON.
I WISHED KSENYA HAD GONE TO CAMP THIS YEAR.
THOUGH SHE PROBABLY WOULDN'T BE TALKING TO ME, EITHER.
SPLISHSHSH
4
<RAZVEDCHITSI!* LINE UP!>
*SCOUTS

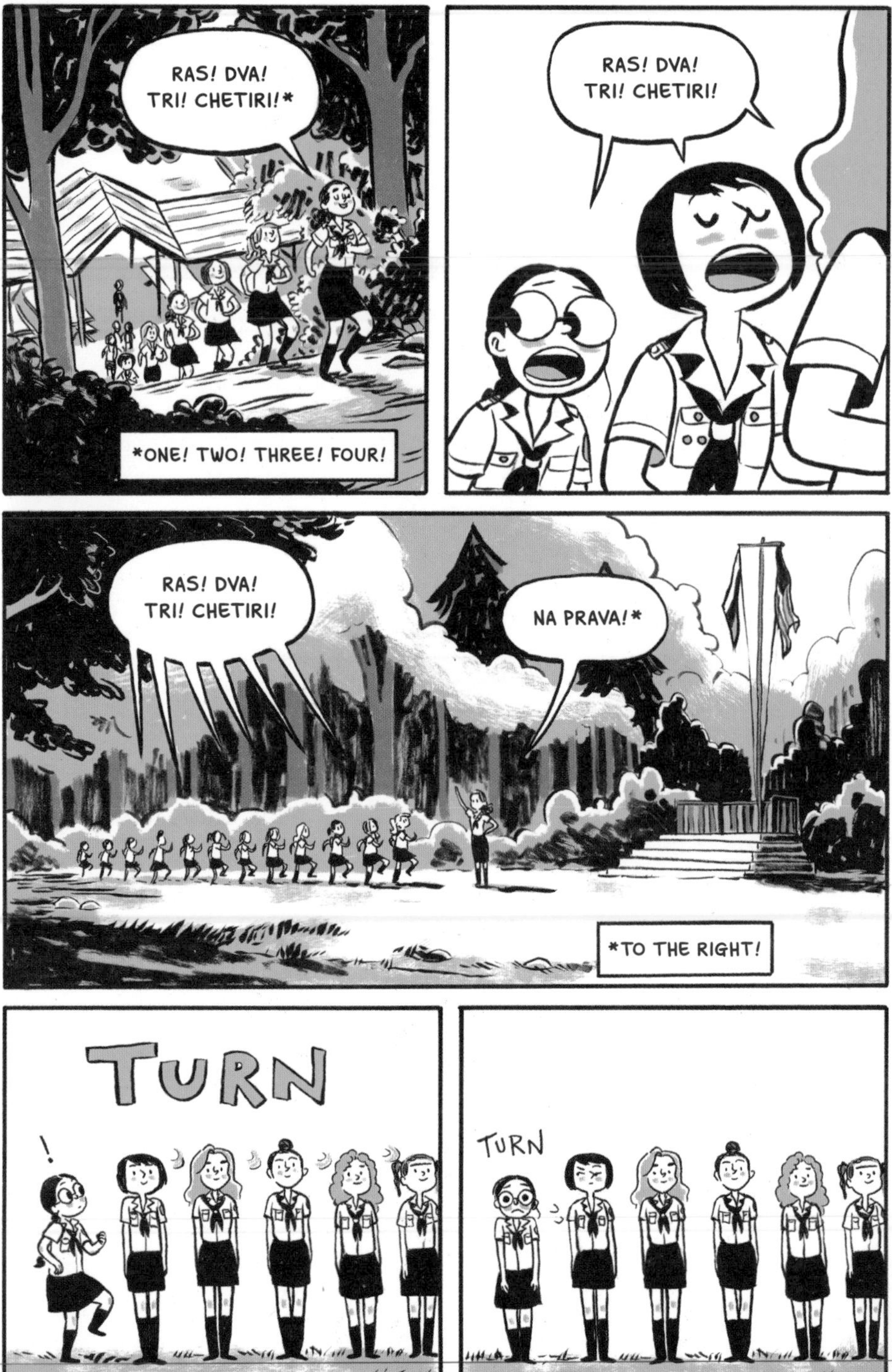
RAS! DVA! TRI! CHETIRI!*
*ONE! TWO! THREE! FOUR!
RAS! DVA! TRI! CHETIRI!
RAS! DVA! TRI! CHETIRI!
NA PRAVA!*
*TO THE RIGHT!
TURN
!
TURN

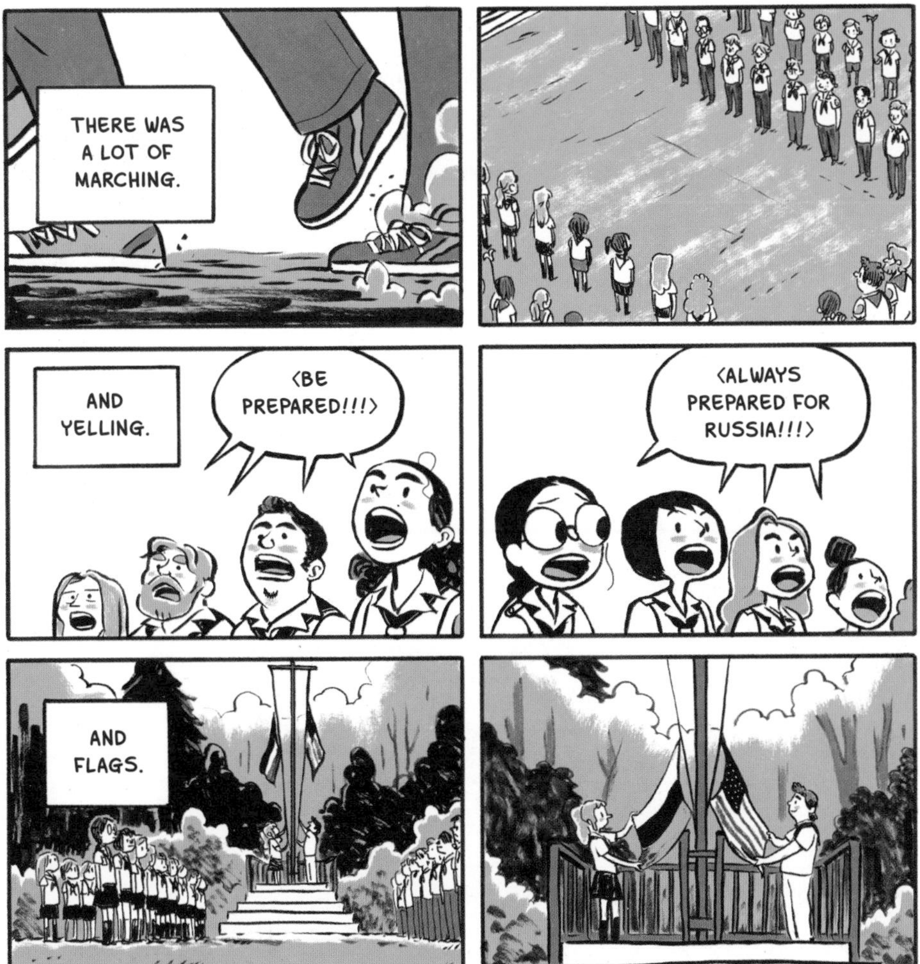
THERE WAS A LOT OF MARCHING.
AND YELLING.
<BE PREPARED!!!>
<ALWAYS PREPARED FOR RUSSIA!!!>
AND FLAGS.
WHEN HAD EVERYONE LEARNED ALL THIS STUFF?

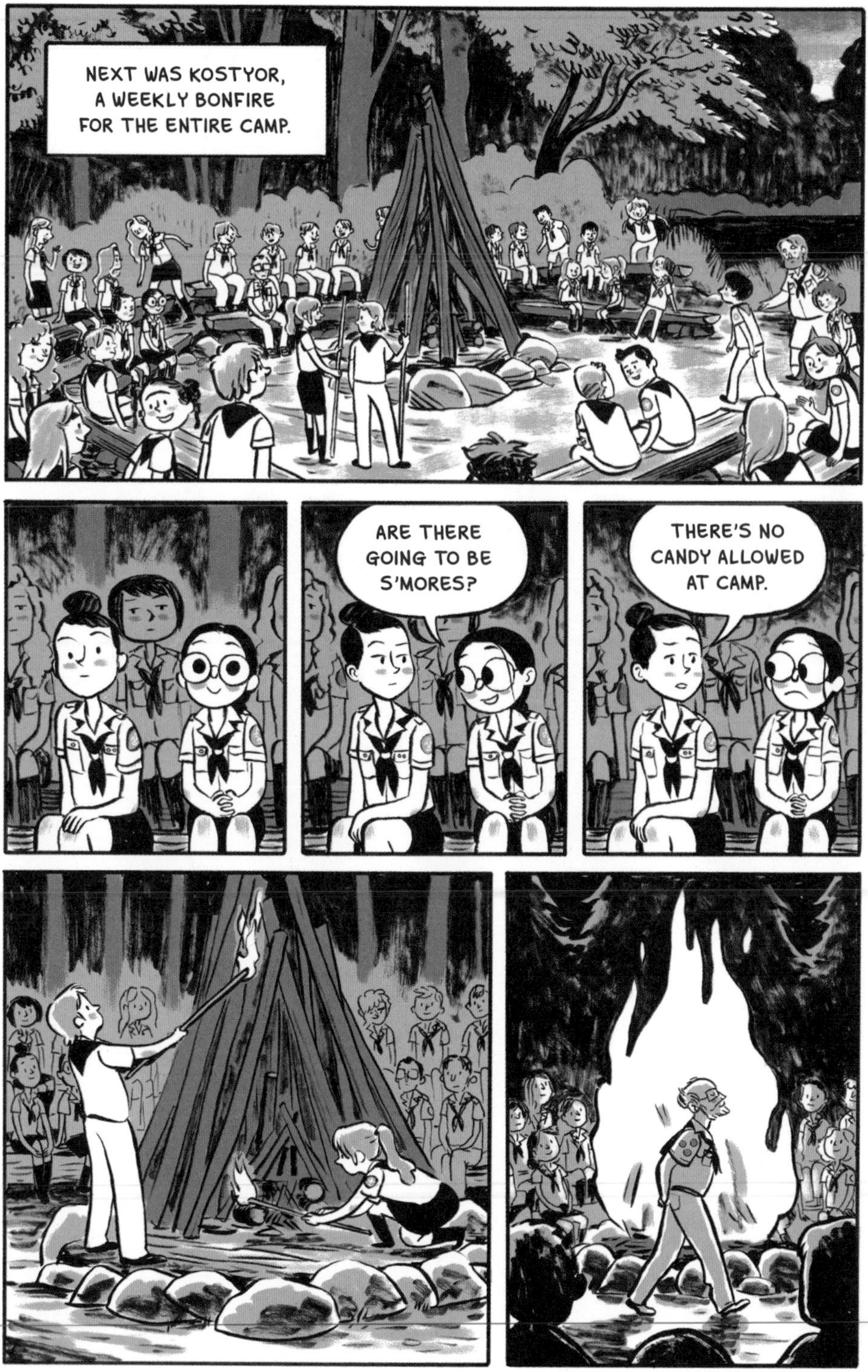
NEXT WAS KOSTYOR, A WEEKLY BONFIRE FOR THE ENTIRE CAMP.
ARE THERE GOING TO BE S'MORES?
THERE'S NO CANDY ALLOWED AT CAMP.

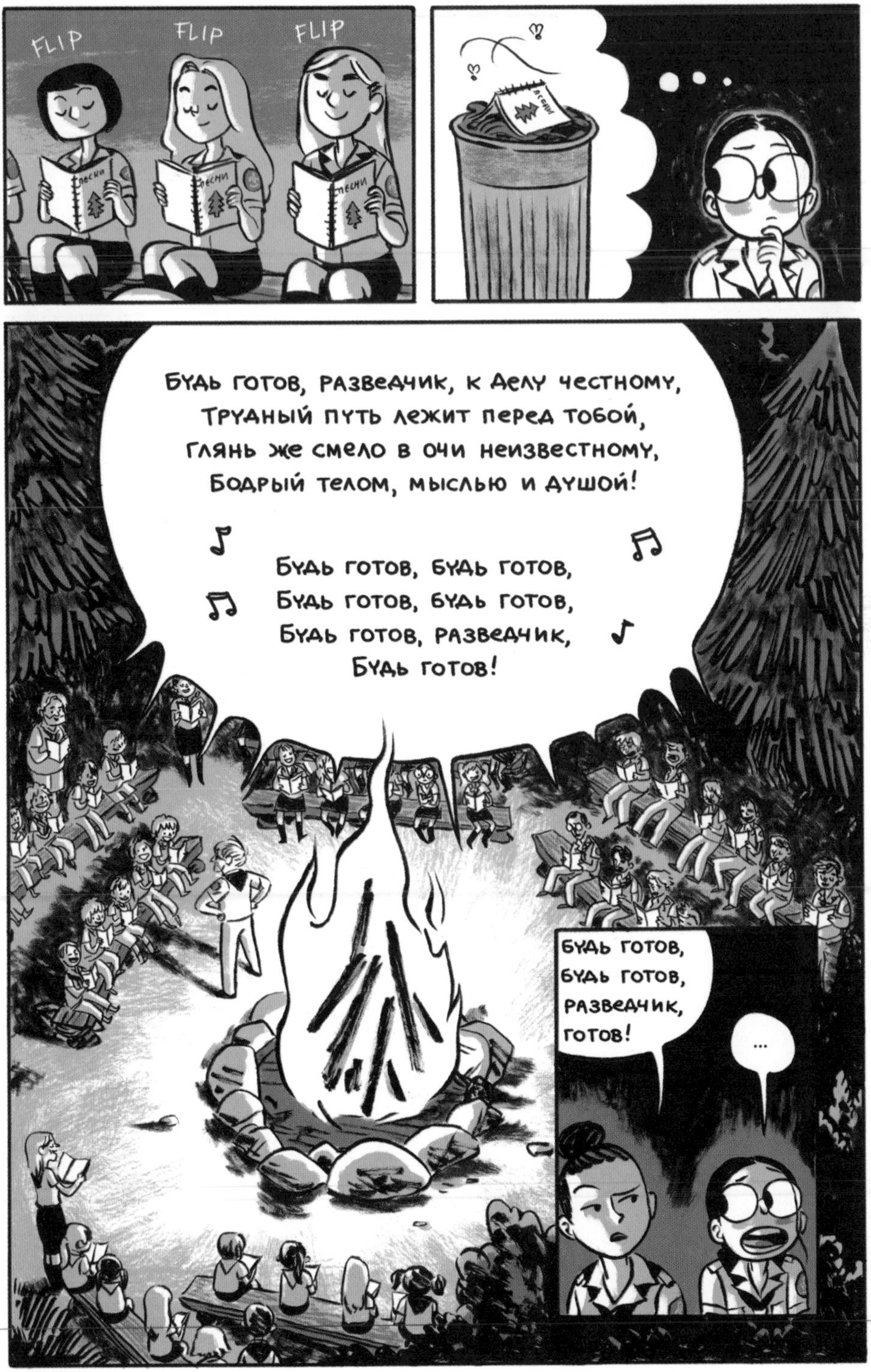
FLIP
FLIP
FLIP
ПЕСНИ
ПЕСНИ
ПЕСНИ
ПЕСНИ
Будь готов, разведчик, к делу честному,
Трудный путь лежит перед тобой,
Глянь же смело в очи неизвестному,
Бодрый телом, мыслью и душой!
Будь готов, будь готов,
Будь готов, будь готов,
Будь готов, разведчик,
Будь готов!
Будь готов,
будь готов,
разведчик,
готов!
...

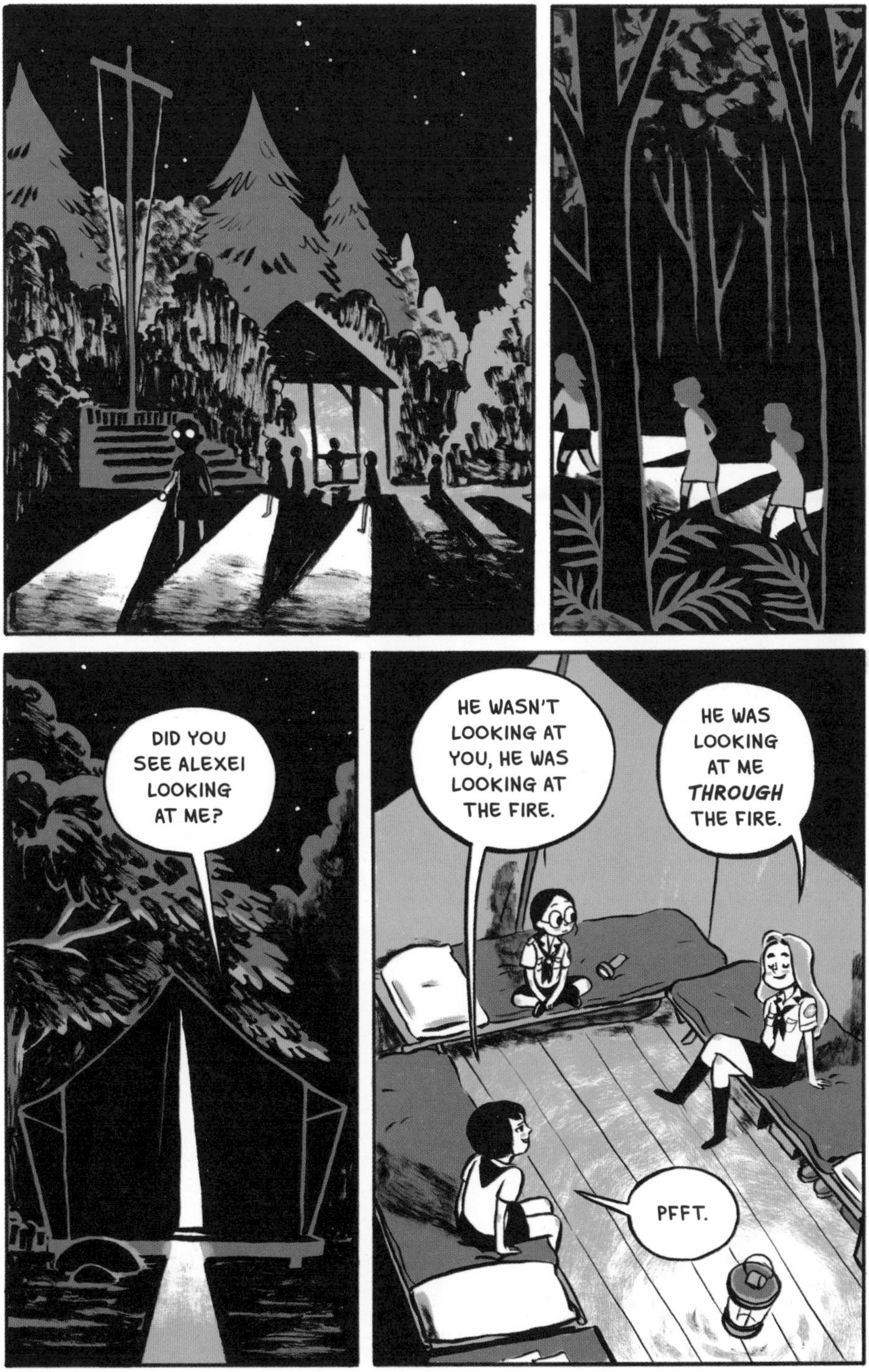
DID YOU SEE ALEXEI LOOKING AT ME?
HE WASN'T LOOKING AT YOU, HE WAS LOOKING AT THE FIRE.
HE WAS LOOKING AT ME *THROUGH* THE FIRE.
PFFT.

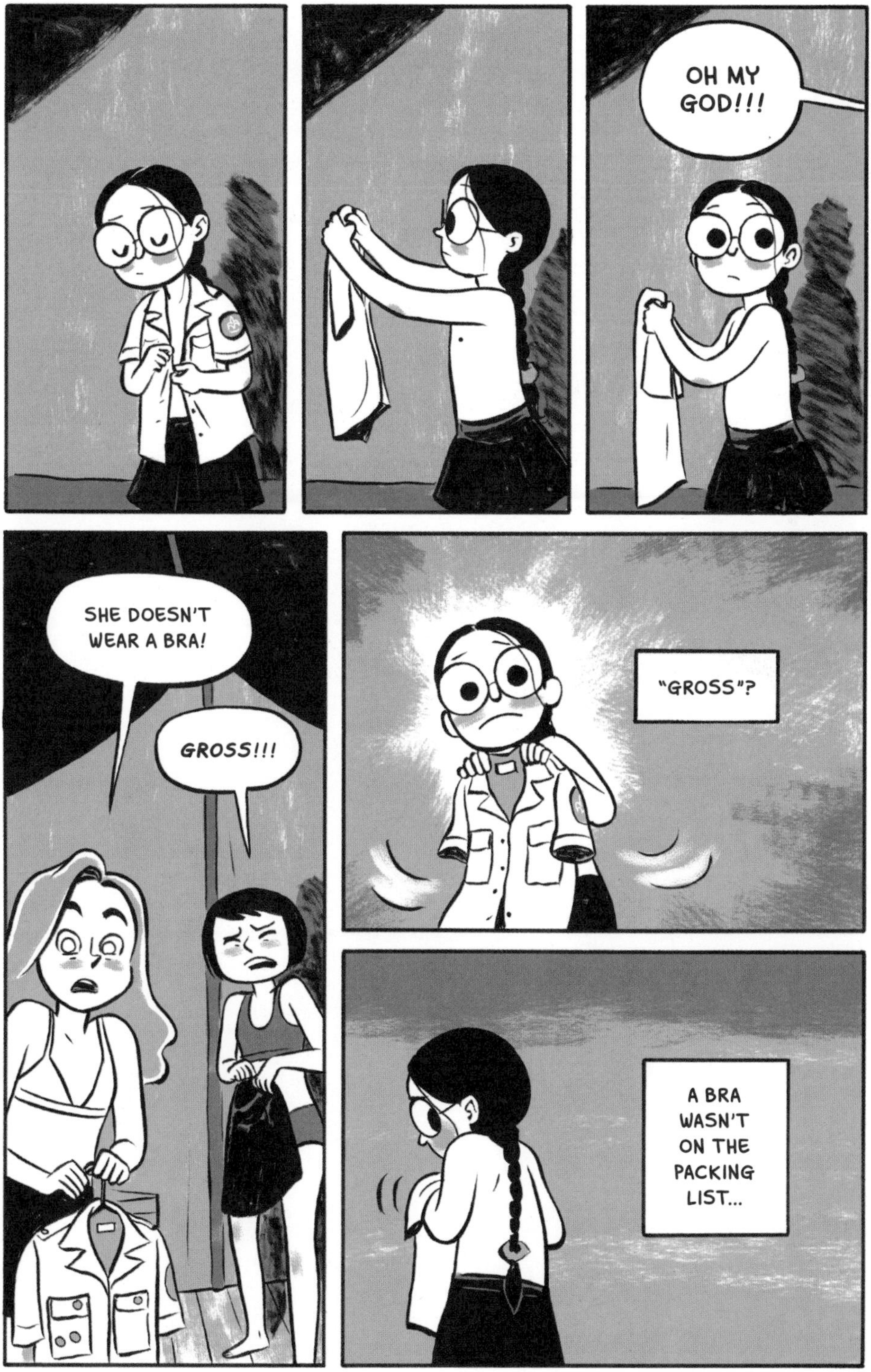
OH MY GOD!!!
SHE DOESN'T WEAR A BRA!
GROSS!!!
"GROSS"?
A BRA WASN'T ON THE PACKING LIST...

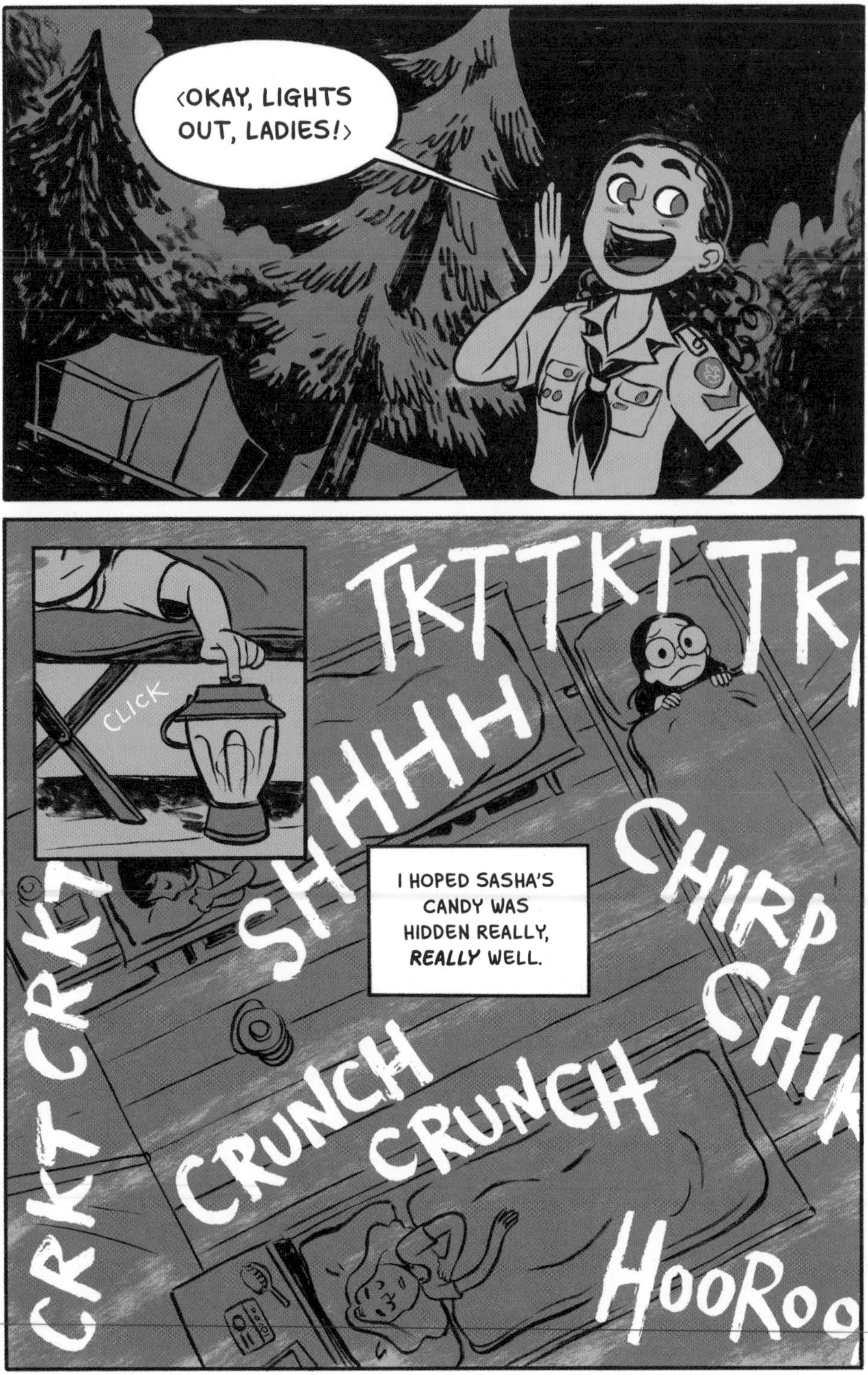

‹OKAY, LIGHTS OUT, LADIES!›
CLICK
TKTTKT TK
SHHHH
I HOPED SASHA'S CANDY WAS HIDDEN REALLY, *REALLY* WELL.
CHIRP CHIR
CRKT CRKT
CRUNCH CRUNCH
HOOROO

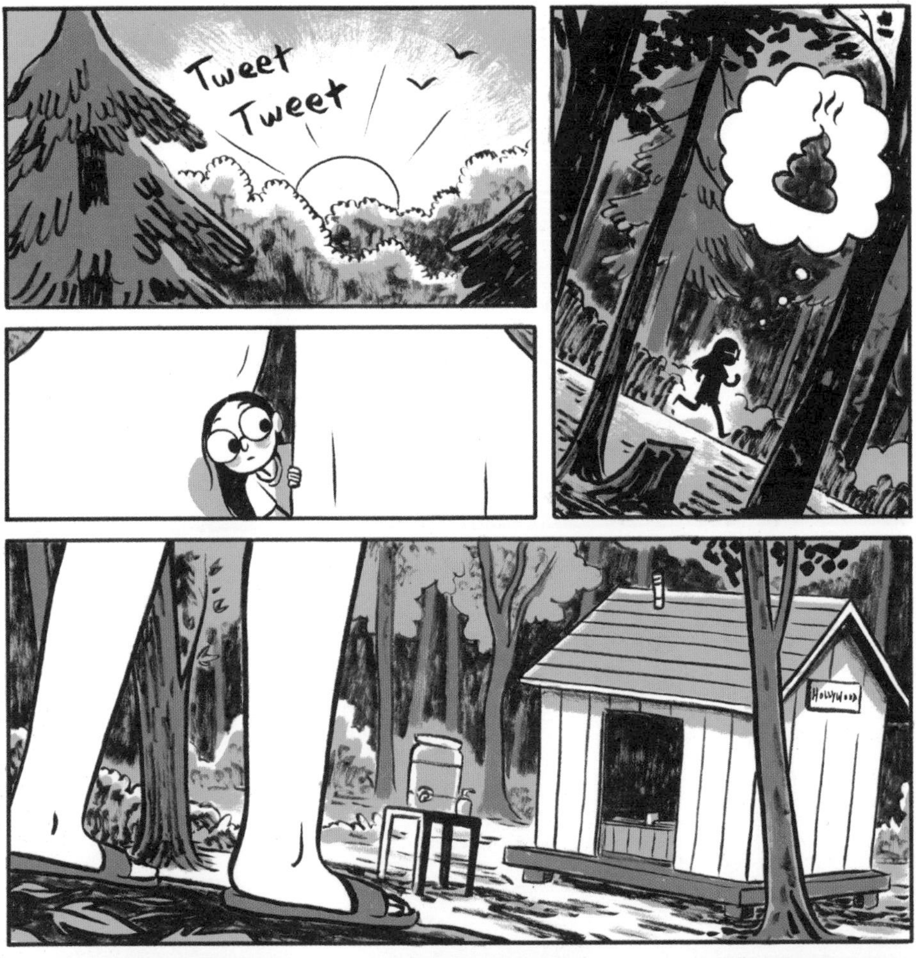
Tweet
Tweet

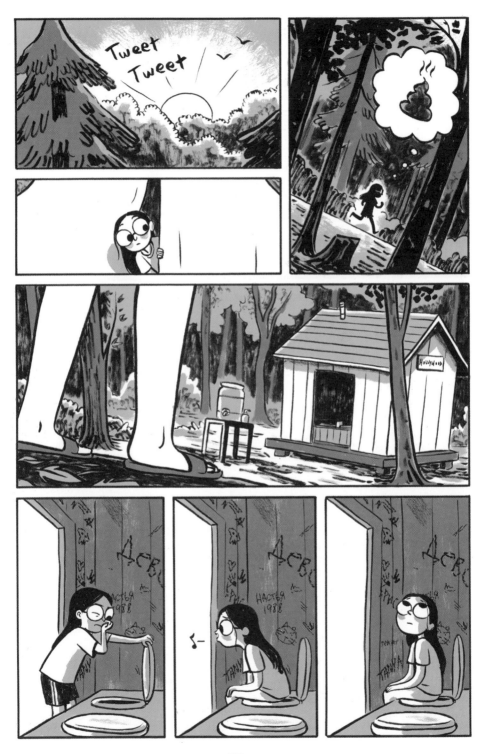

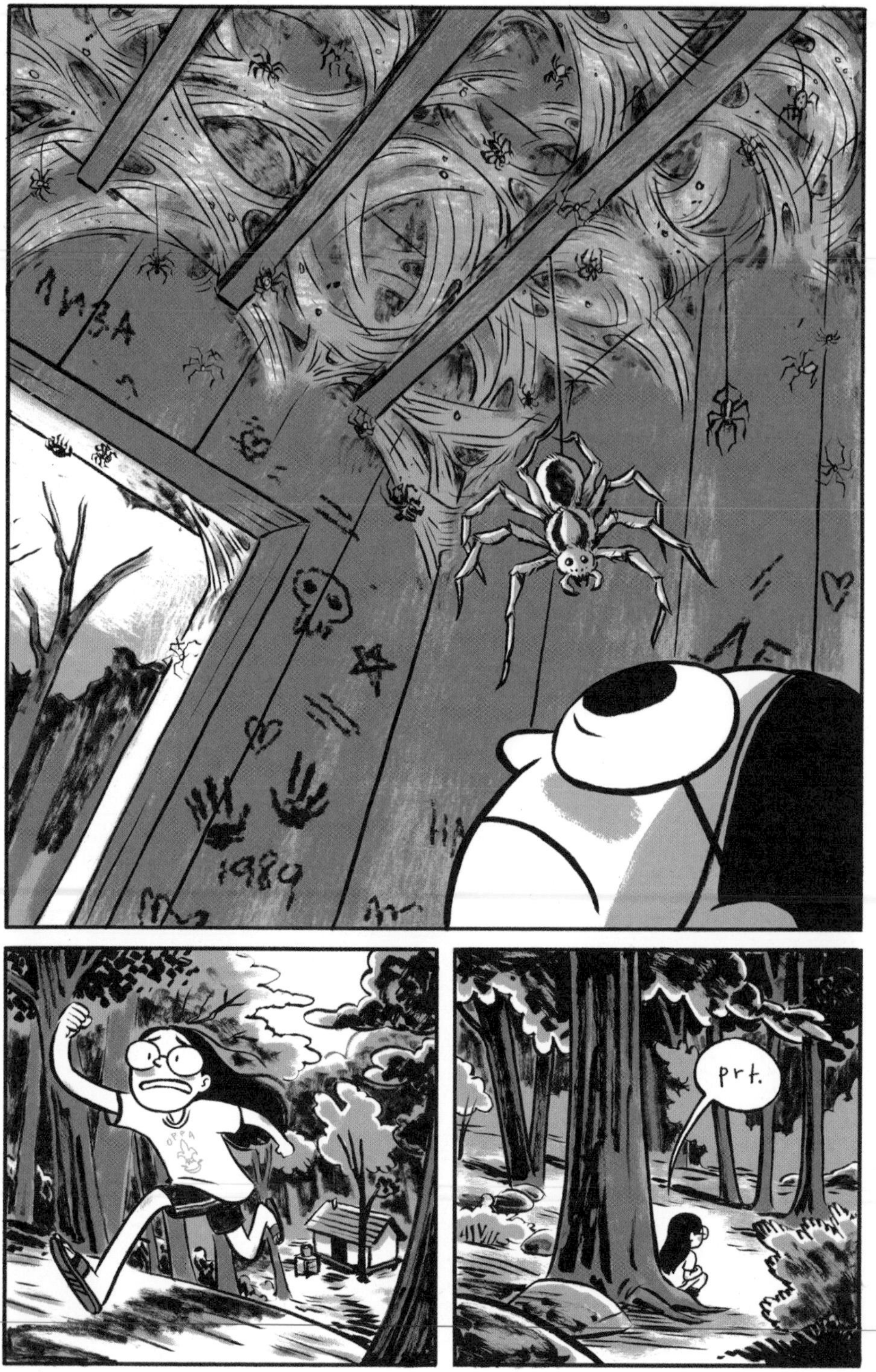
1989
prt.

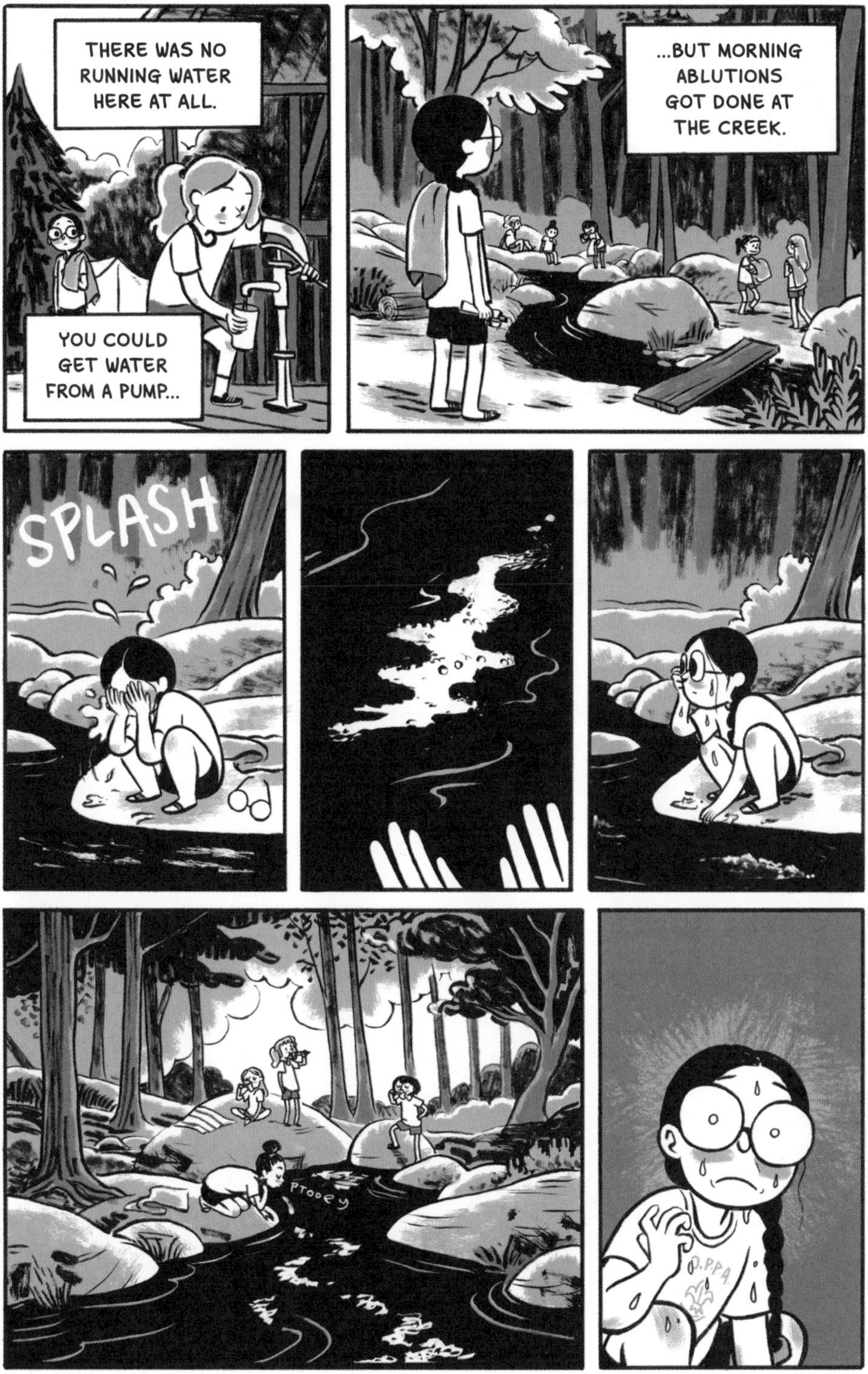
THERE WAS NO RUNNING WATER HERE AT ALL.
YOU COULD GET WATER FROM A PUMP...
...BUT MORNING ABLUTIONS GOT DONE AT THE CREEK.
SPLASH
PTOOEY
O.P.P.A.

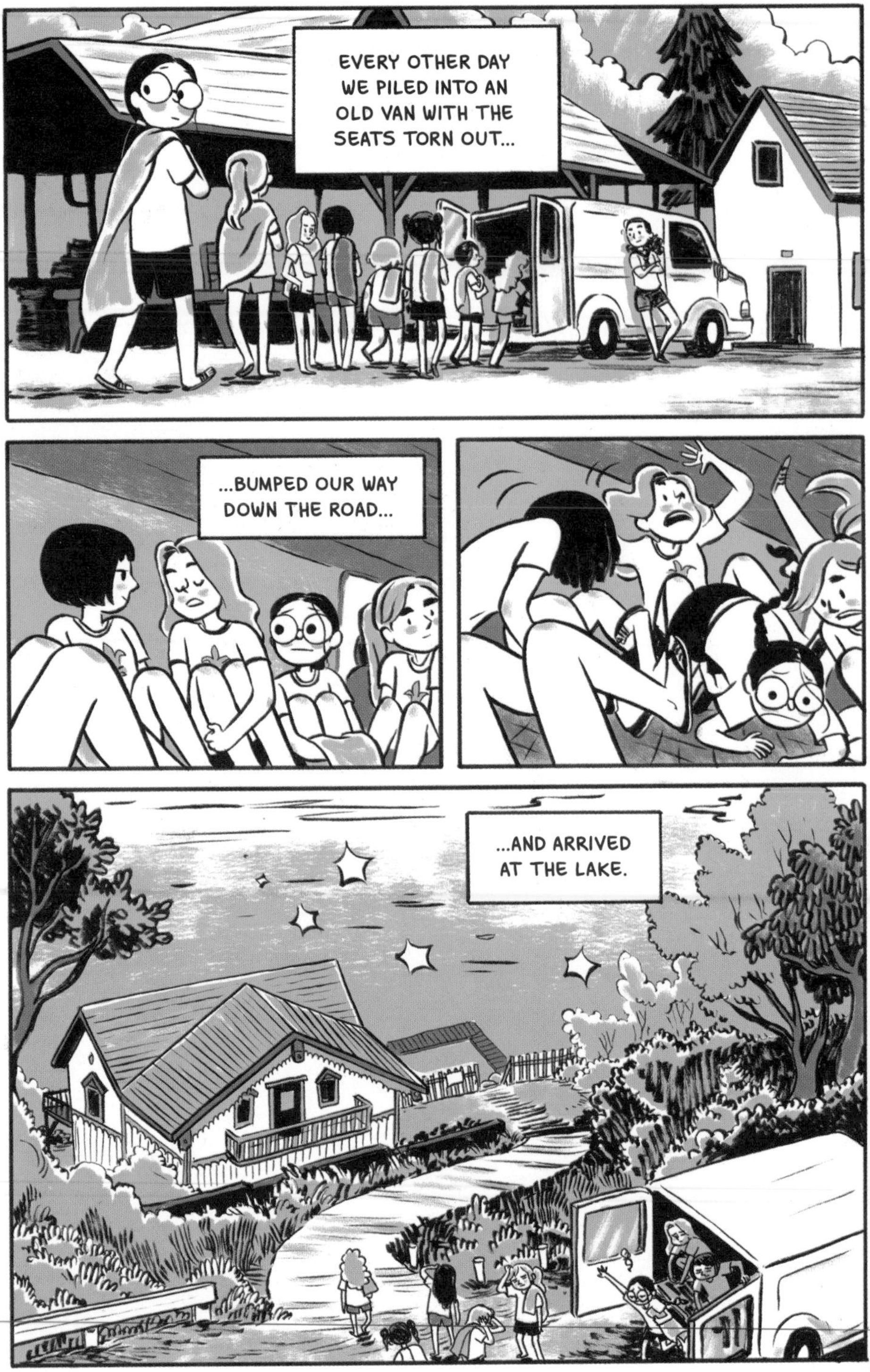
EVERY OTHER DAY WE PILED INTO AN OLD VAN WITH THE SEATS TORN OUT...
...BUMPED OUR WAY DOWN THE ROAD...
...AND ARRIVED AT THE LAKE.

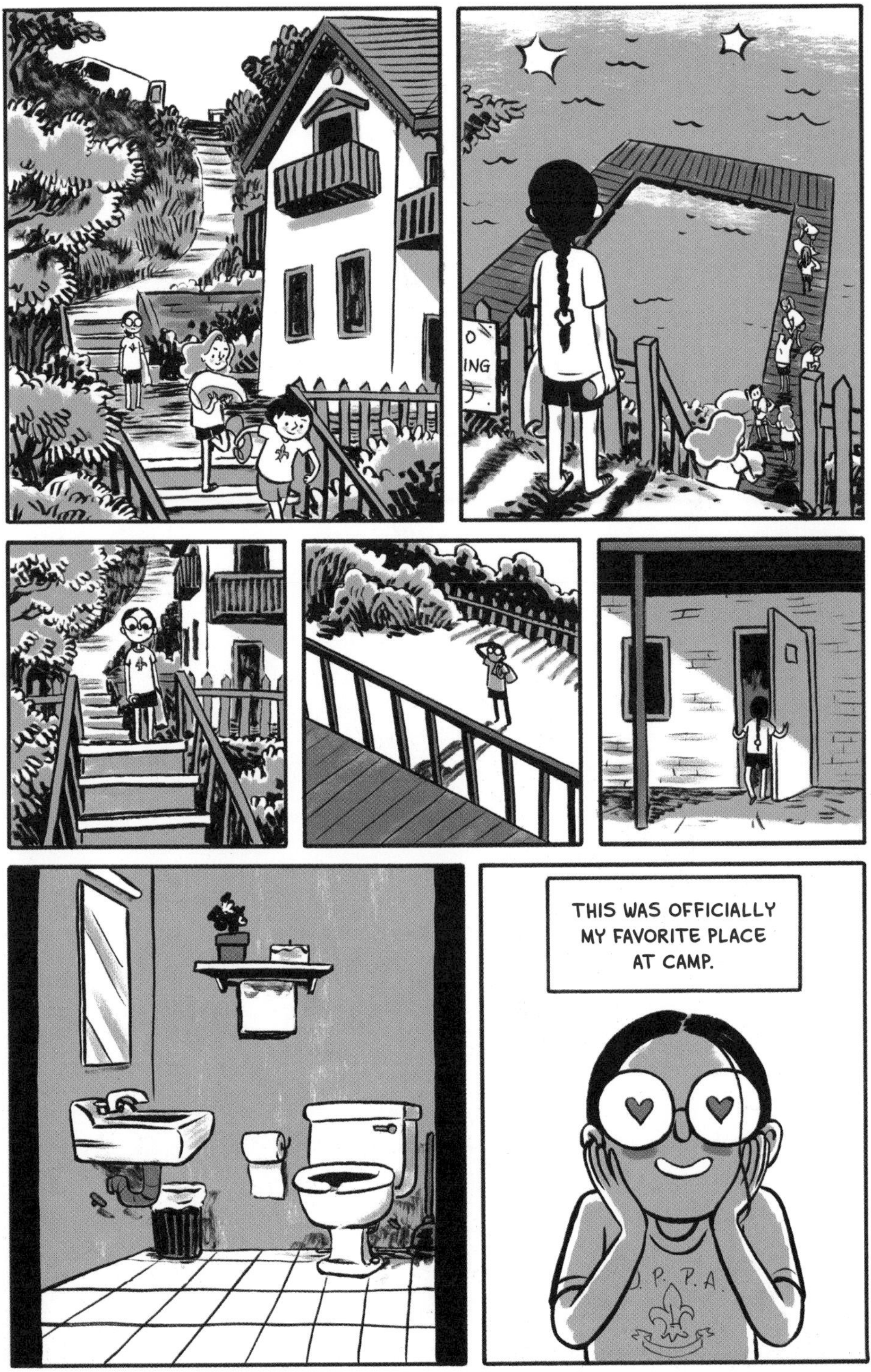
THIS WAS OFFICIALLY MY FAVORITE PLACE AT CAMP.

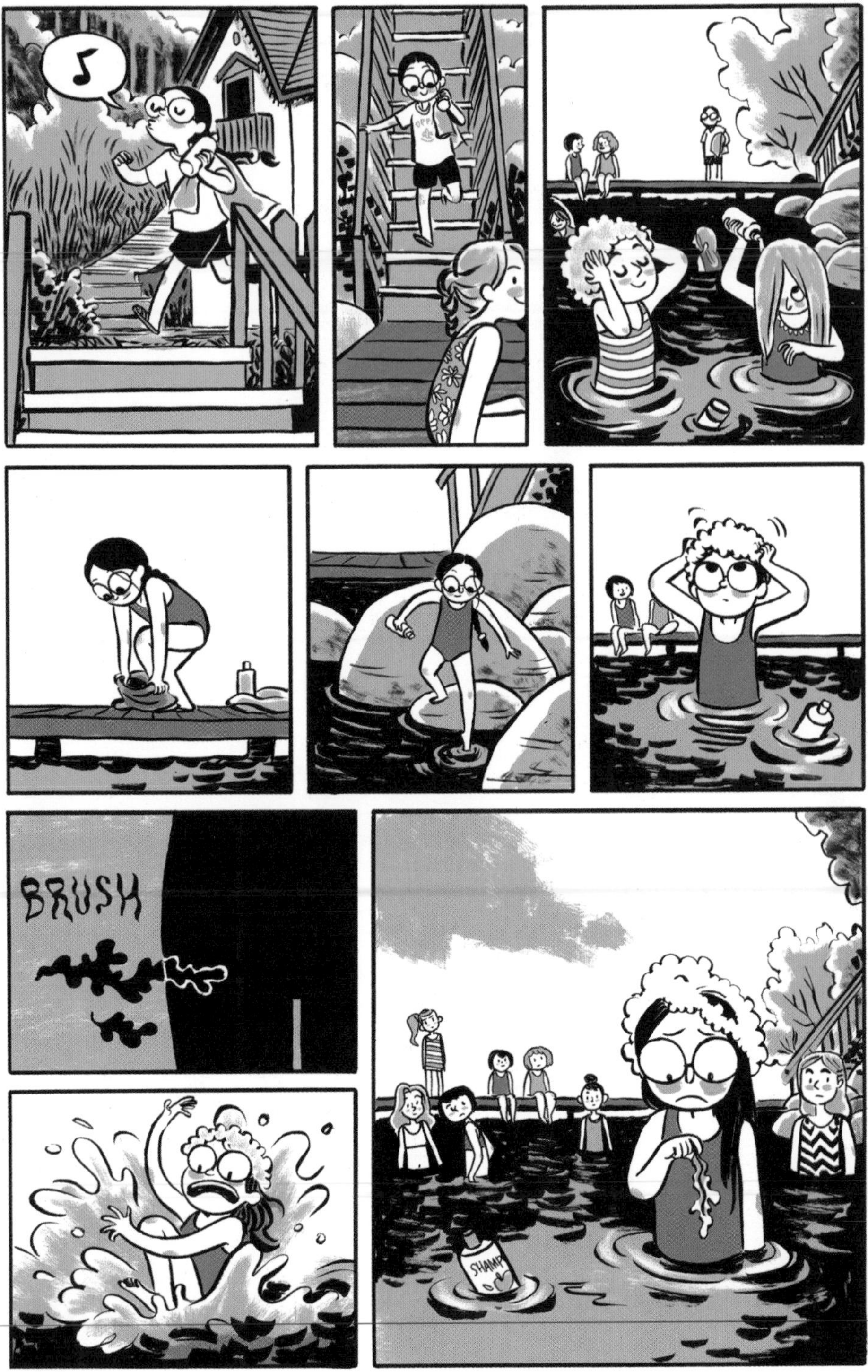
BRUSH
SHAMP

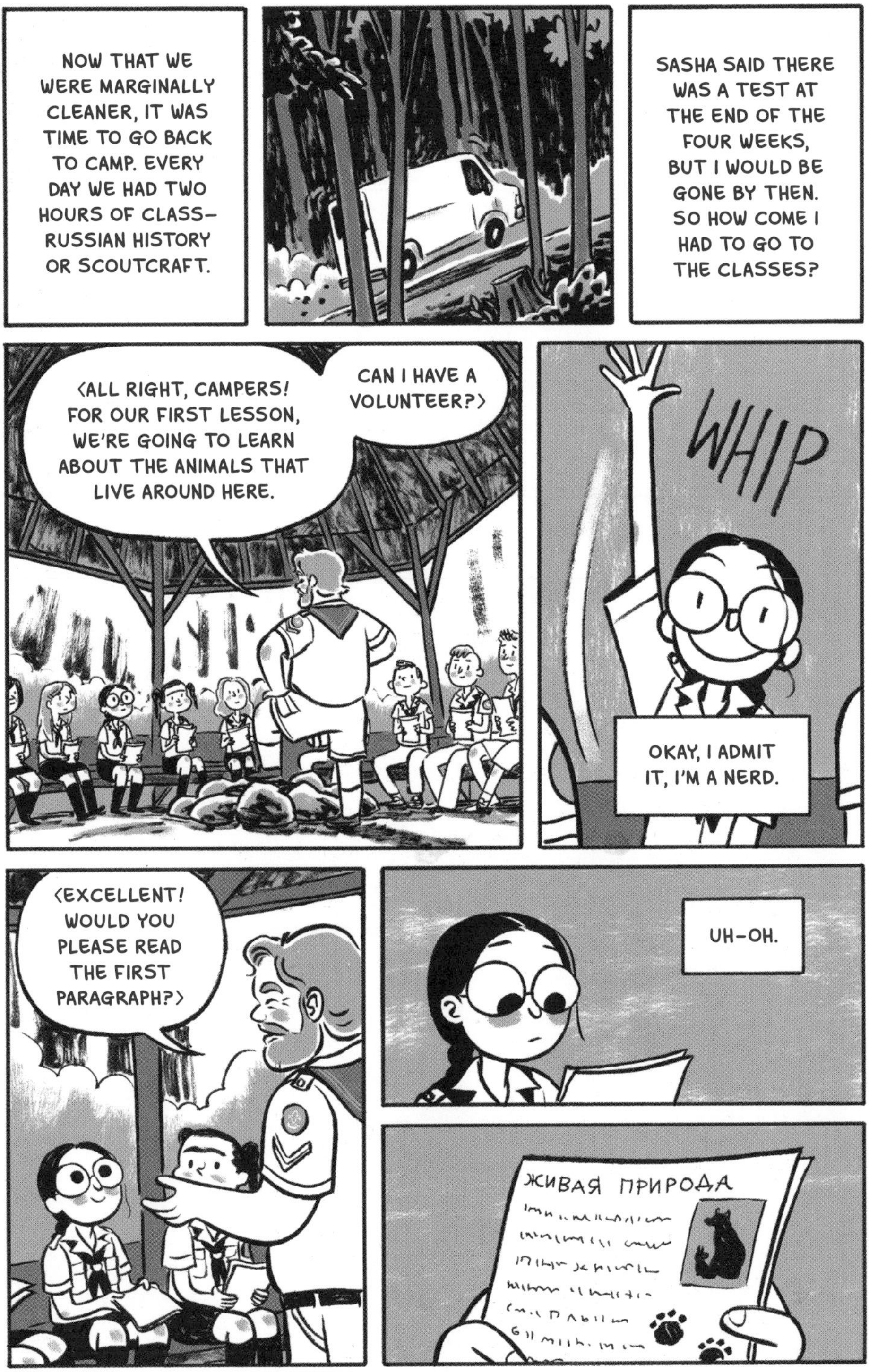
NOW THAT WE WERE MARGINALLY CLEANER, IT WAS TIME TO GO BACK TO CAMP. EVERY DAY WE HAD TWO HOURS OF CLASS—RUSSIAN HISTORY OR SCOUTCRAFT.
SASHA SAID THERE WAS A TEST AT THE END OF THE FOUR WEEKS, BUT I WOULD BE GONE BY THEN. SO HOW COME I HAD TO GO TO THE CLASSES?
<ALL RIGHT, CAMPERS! FOR OUR FIRST LESSON, WE'RE GOING TO LEARN ABOUT THE ANIMALS THAT LIVE AROUND HERE.
CAN I HAVE A VOLUNTEER?>
WHIP
OKAY, I ADMIT IT, I'M A NERD.
<EXCELLENT! WOULD YOU PLEASE READ THE FIRST PARAGRAPH?>
UH-OH.
ЖИВАЯ ПРИРОДА

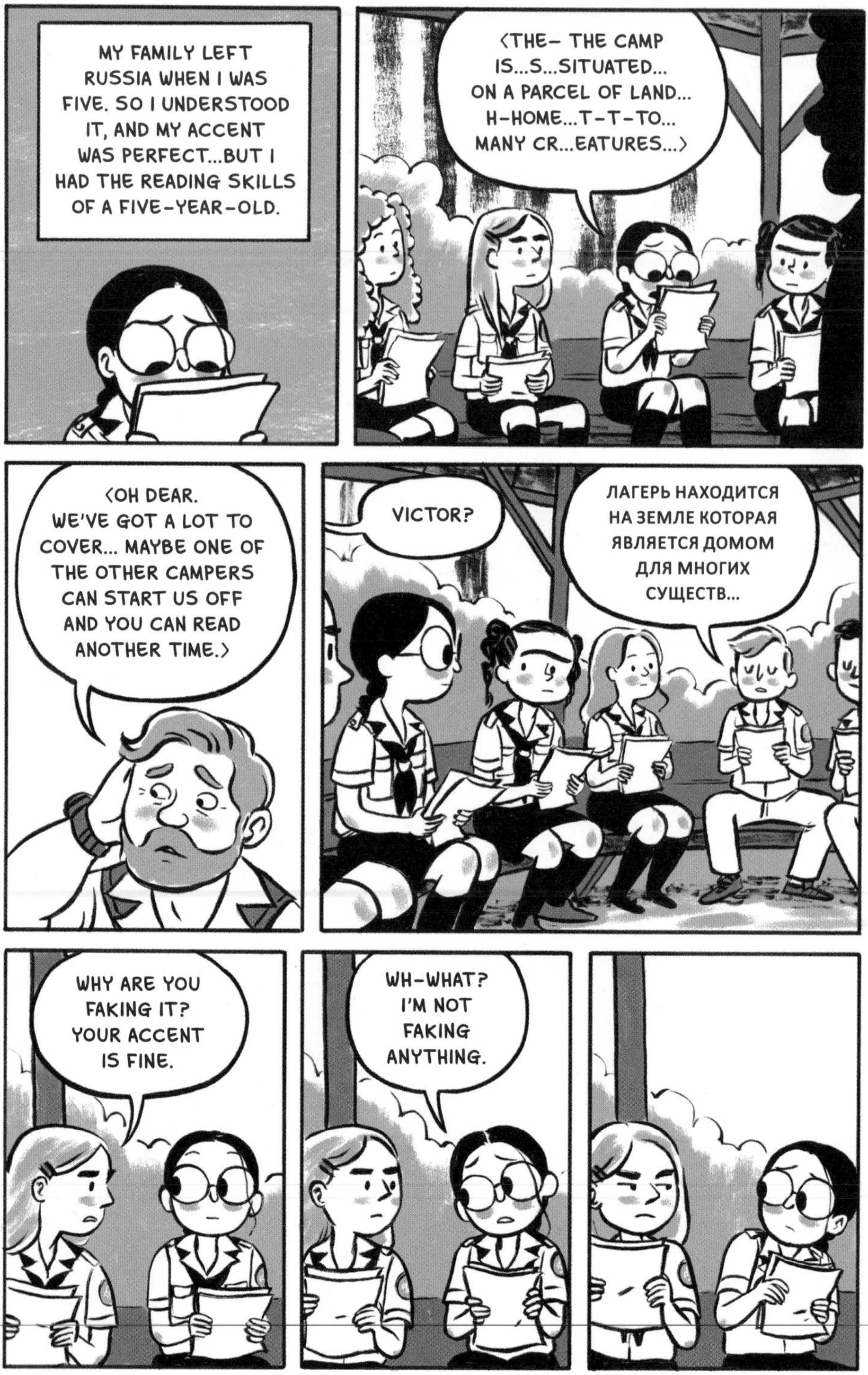
MY FAMILY LEFT RUSSIA WHEN I WAS FIVE. SO I UNDERSTOOD IT, AND MY ACCENT WAS PERFECT...BUT I HAD THE READING SKILLS OF A FIVE-YEAR-OLD.
<THE- THE CAMP IS...S...SITUATED... ON A PARCEL OF LAND... H-HOME...T-T-TO... MANY CR...EATURES...>
<OH DEAR. WE'VE GOT A LOT TO COVER... MAYBE ONE OF THE OTHER CAMPERS CAN START US OFF AND YOU CAN READ ANOTHER TIME.>
VICTOR?
ЛАГЕРЬ НАХОДИТСЯ НА ЗЕМЛЕ КОТОРАЯ ЯВЛЯЕТСЯ ДОМОМ ДЛЯ МНОГИХ СУЩЕСТВ...
WHY ARE YOU FAKING IT? YOUR ACCENT IS FINE.
WH-WHAT? I'M NOT FAKING ANYTHING.

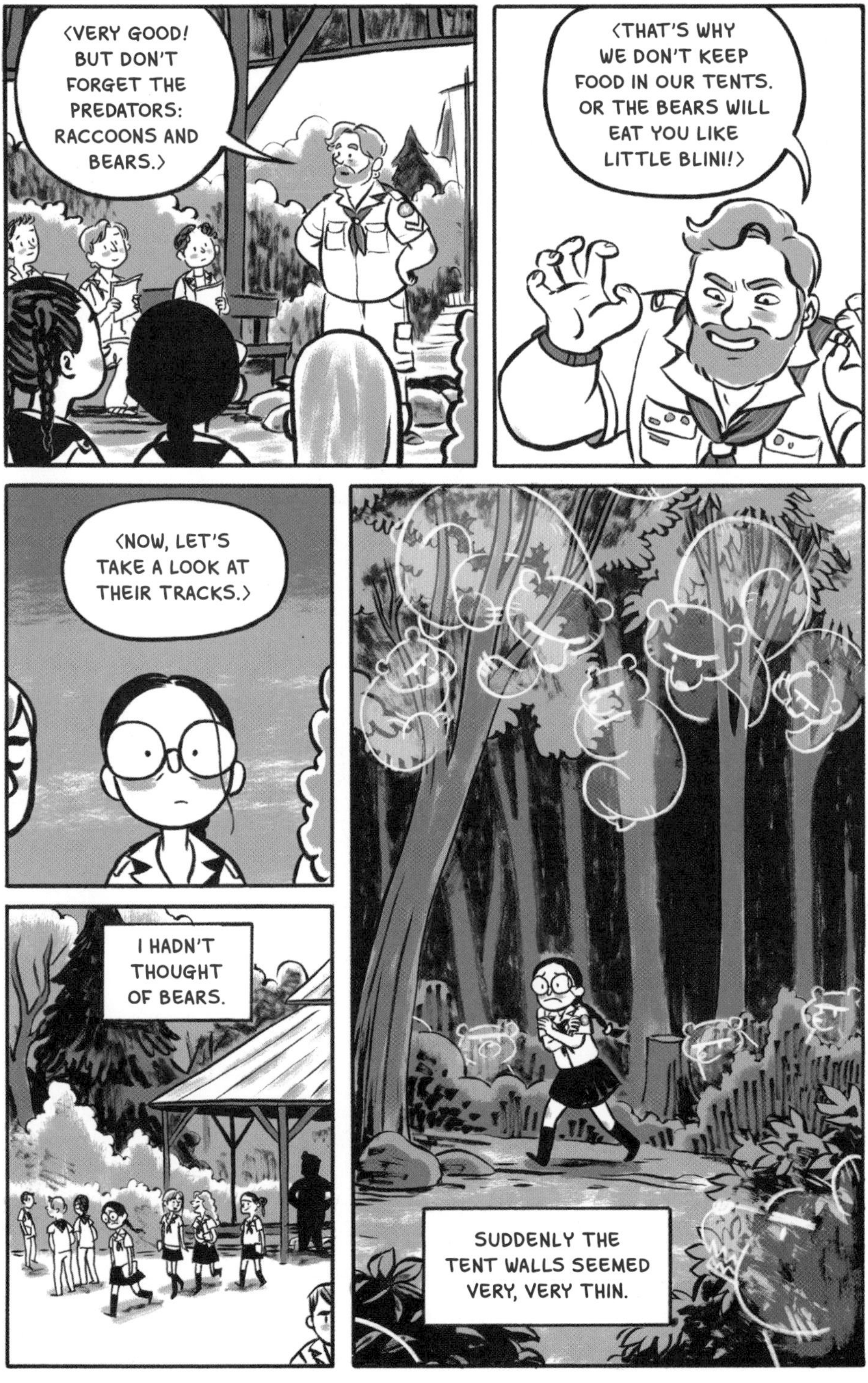
‹VERY GOOD! BUT DON'T FORGET THE PREDATORS: RACCOONS AND BEARS.›
‹THAT'S WHY WE DON'T KEEP FOOD IN OUR TENTS. OR THE BEARS WILL EAT YOU LIKE LITTLE BLINI!›
‹NOW, LET'S TAKE A LOOK AT THEIR TRACKS.›
I HADN'T THOUGHT OF BEARS.
SUDDENLY THE TENT WALLS SEEMED VERY, VERY THIN.

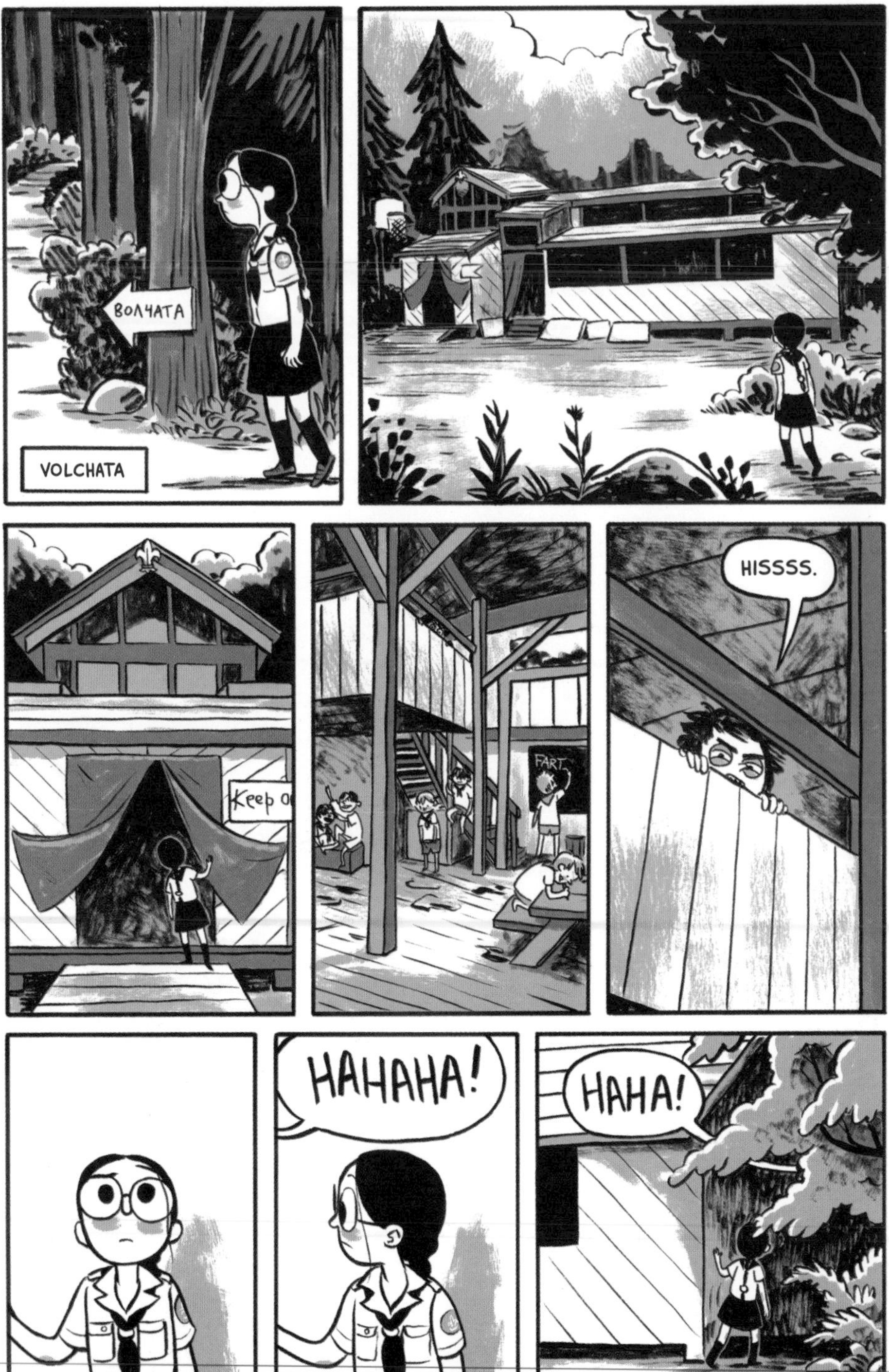
ВОЛЧАТА
VOLCHATA
Keep o
FART
HISSSS.
HAHAHA!
HAHA!

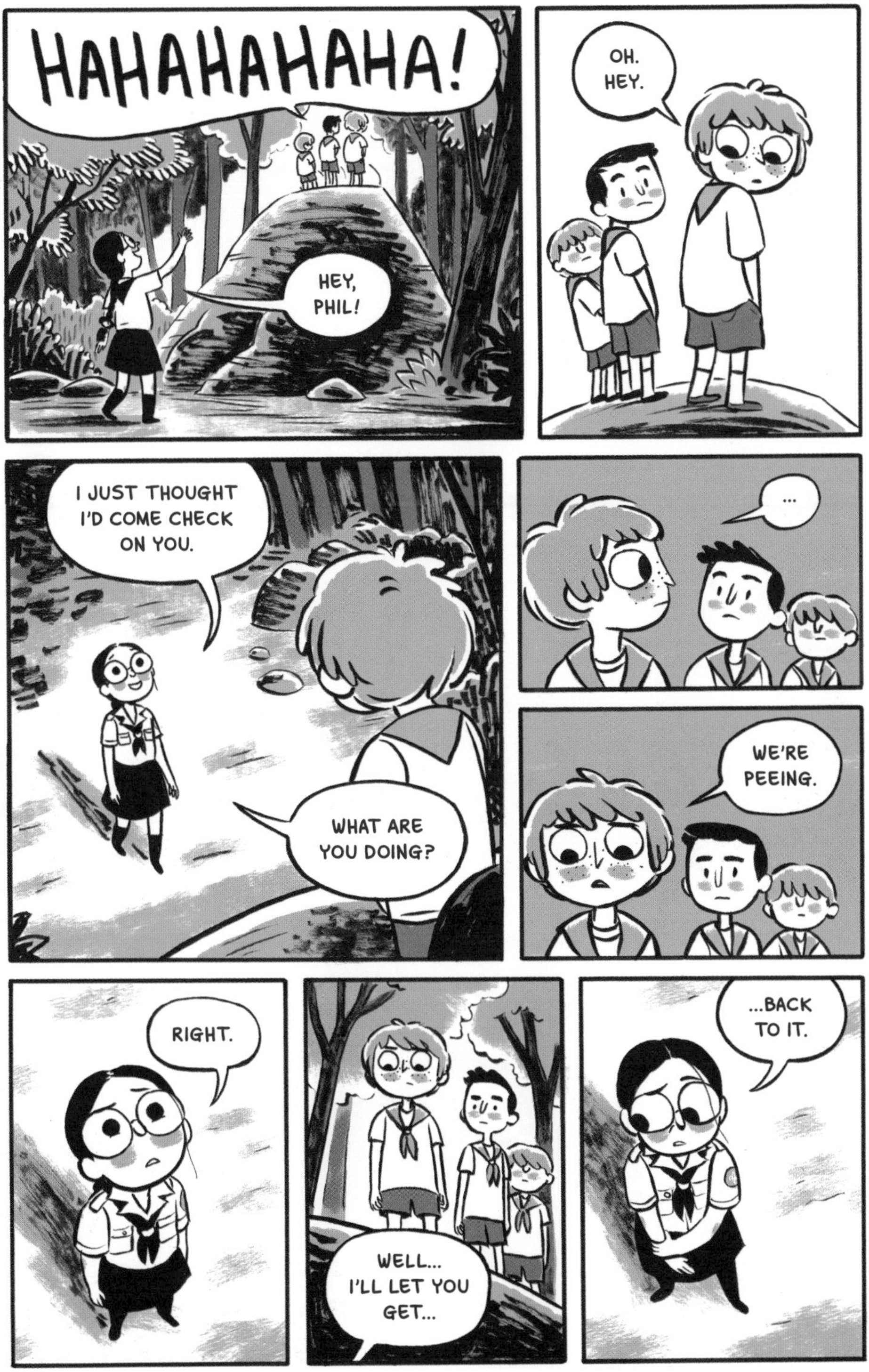
HAHAHAHAHA!
HEY, PHIL!
OH. HEY.
I JUST THOUGHT I'D COME CHECK ON YOU.
WHAT ARE YOU DOING?
...
WE'RE PEEING.
RIGHT.
WELL... I'LL LET YOU GET...
...BACK TO IT.

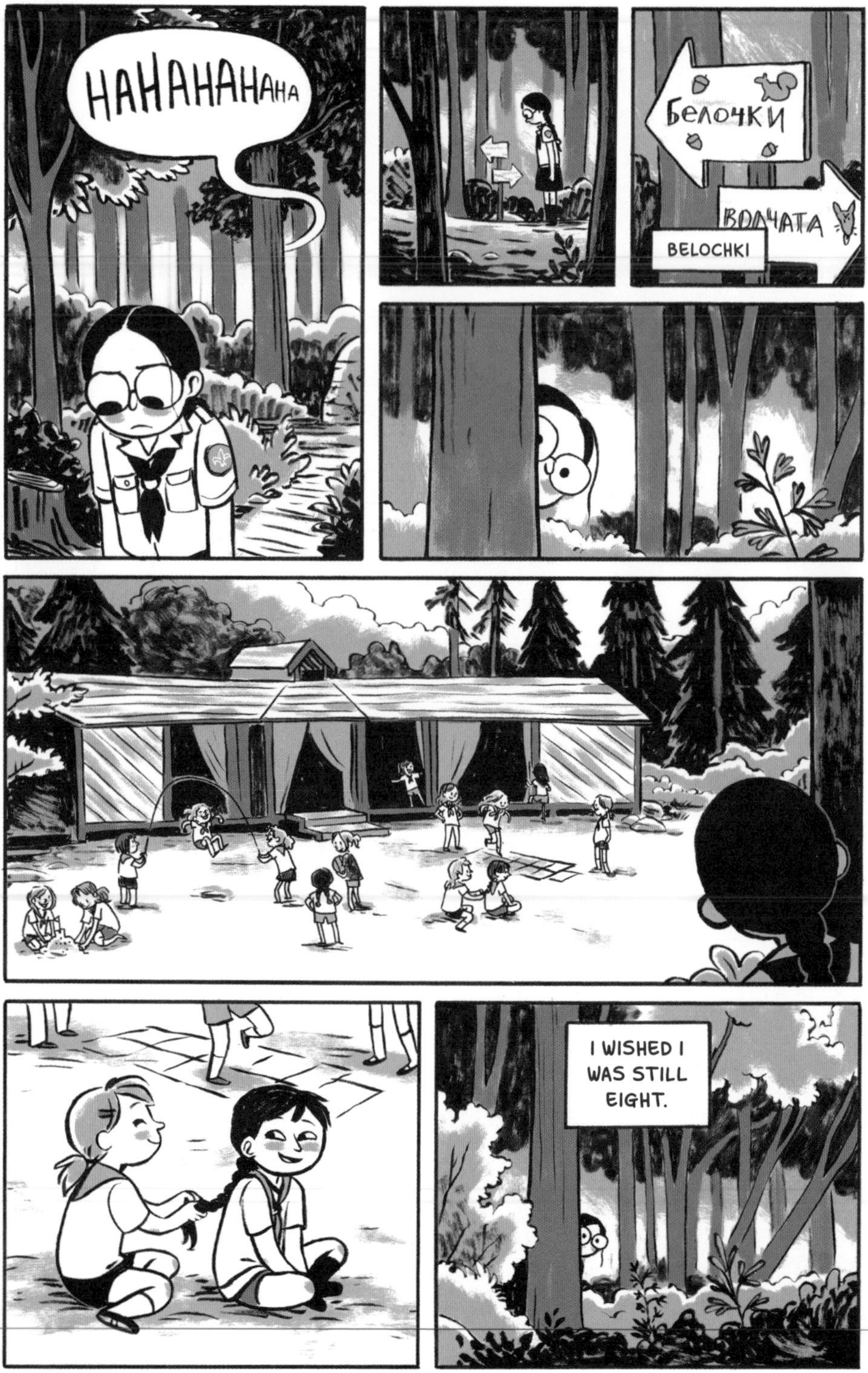
HAHAHAHAHAHA
Белочки
Волчата
BELOCHKI
I WISHED I WAS STILL EIGHT.

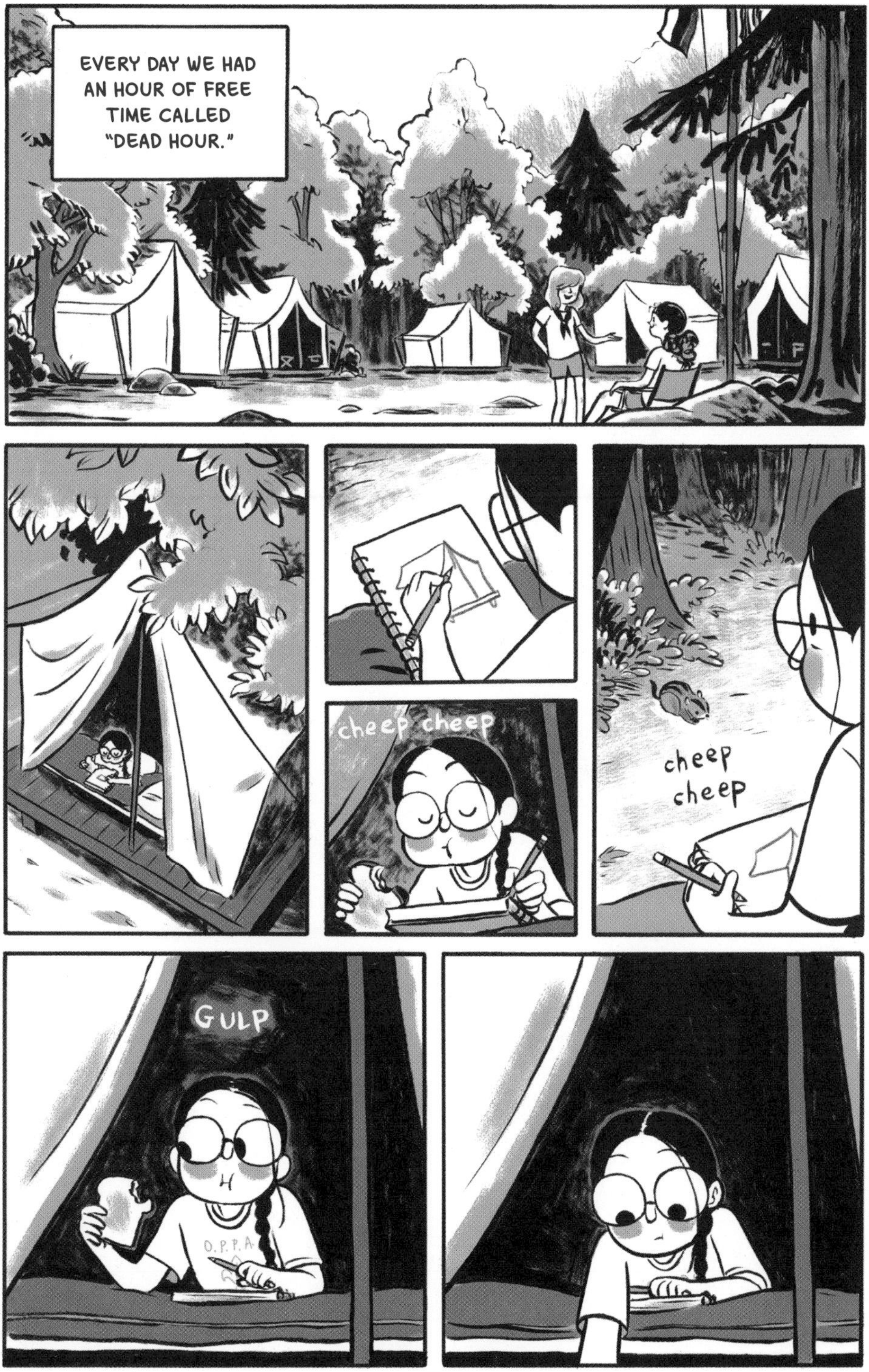
EVERY DAY WE HAD AN HOUR OF FREE TIME CALLED "DEAD HOUR."
cheep cheep
cheep cheep
GULP
O.P.P.A.

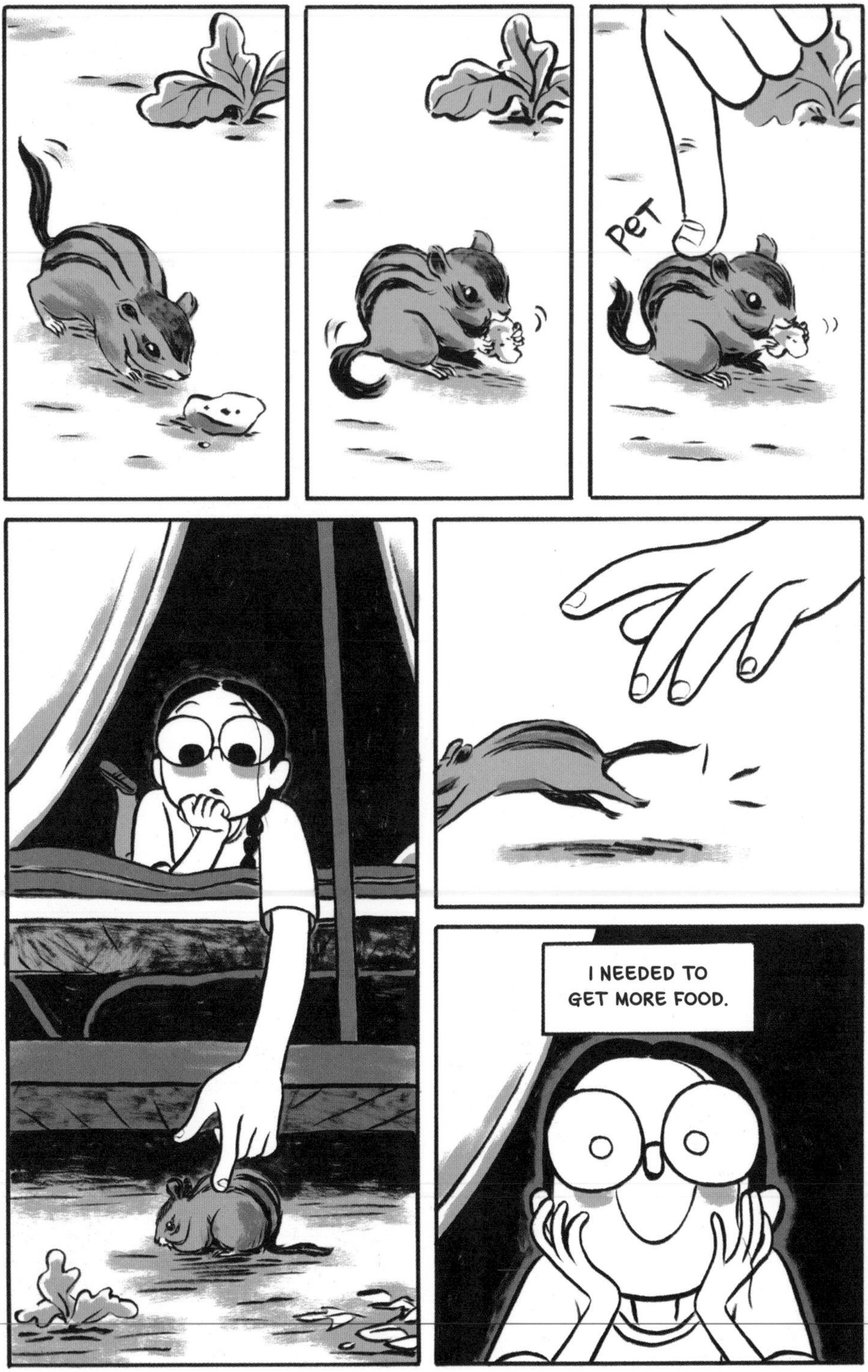
PET
I NEEDED TO
GET MORE FOOD.

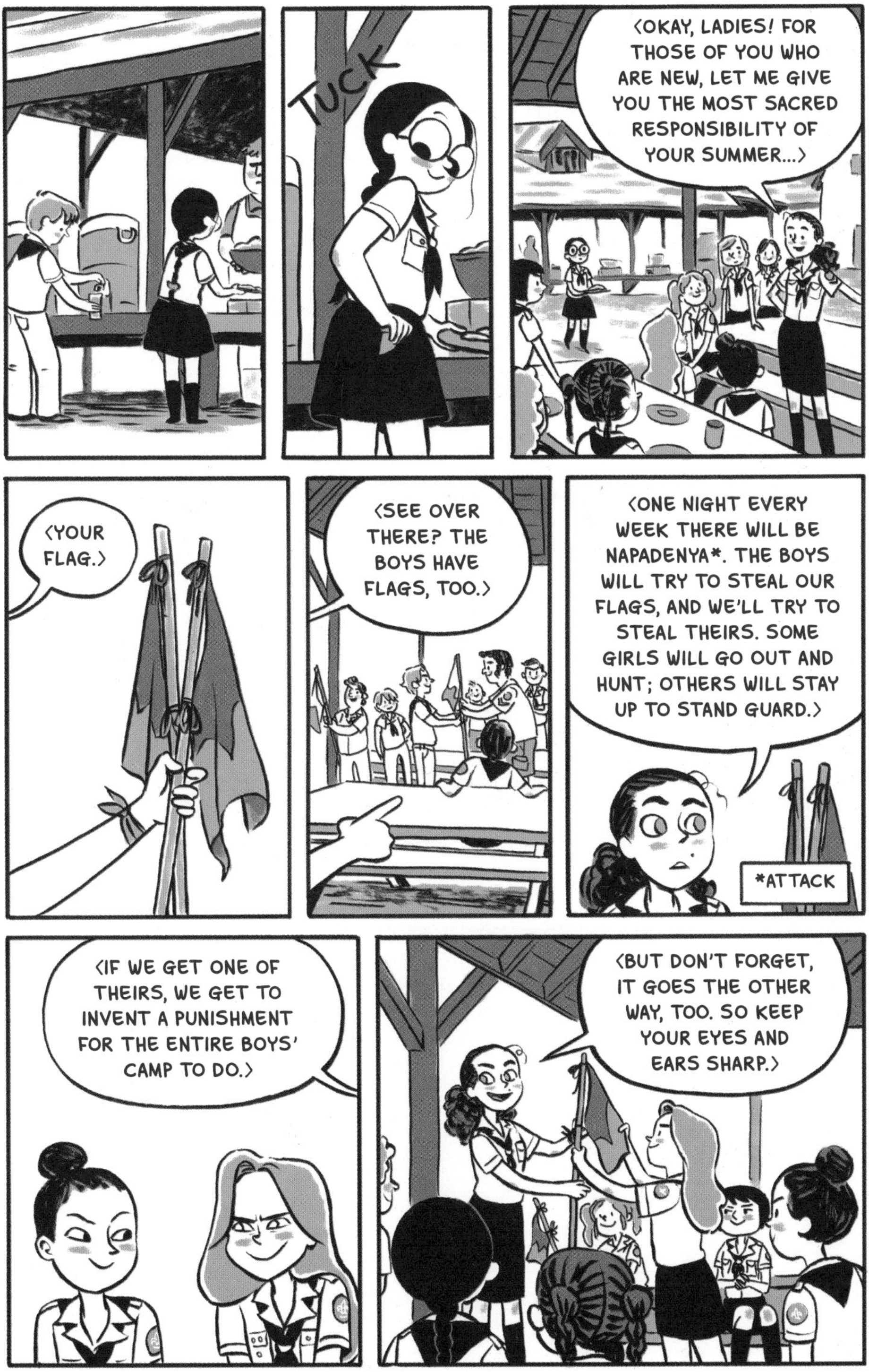
TUCK
<OKAY, LADIES! FOR THOSE OF YOU WHO ARE NEW, LET ME GIVE YOU THE MOST SACRED RESPONSIBILITY OF YOUR SUMMER...>
<YOUR FLAG.>
<SEE OVER THERE? THE BOYS HAVE FLAGS, TOO.>
<ONE NIGHT EVERY WEEK THERE WILL BE NAPADENYA*. THE BOYS WILL TRY TO STEAL OUR FLAGS, AND WE'LL TRY TO STEAL THEIRS. SOME GIRLS WILL GO OUT AND HUNT; OTHERS WILL STAY UP TO STAND GUARD.>
*ATTACK
<IF WE GET ONE OF THEIRS, WE GET TO INVENT A PUNISHMENT FOR THE ENTIRE BOYS' CAMP TO DO.>
<BUT DON'T FORGET, IT GOES THE OTHER WAY, TOO. SO KEEP YOUR EYES AND EARS SHARP.>

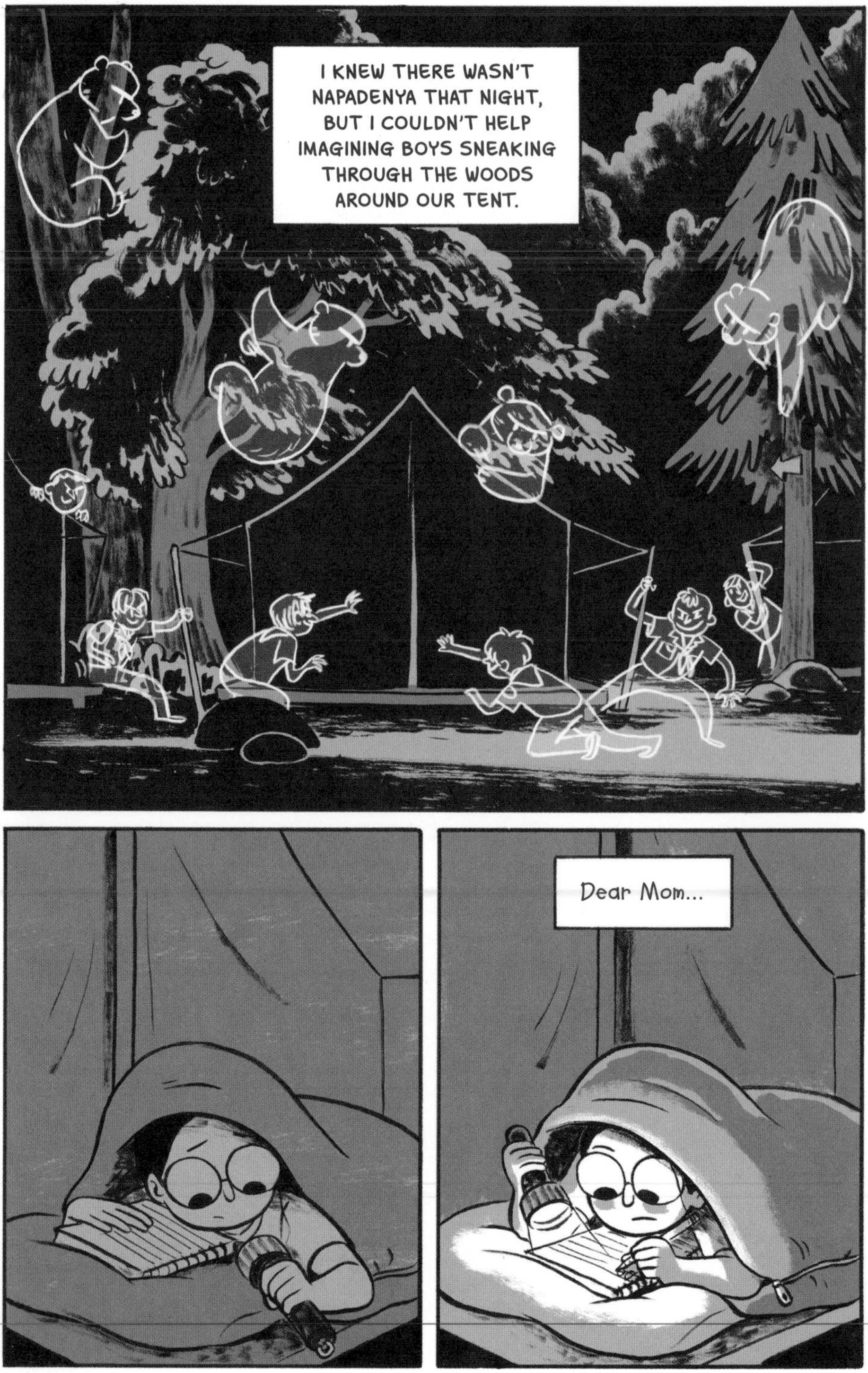
I KNEW THERE WASN'T NAPADENYA THAT NIGHT, BUT I COULDN'T HELP IMAGINING BOYS SNEAKING THROUGH THE WOODS AROUND OUR TENT.
Dear Mom...

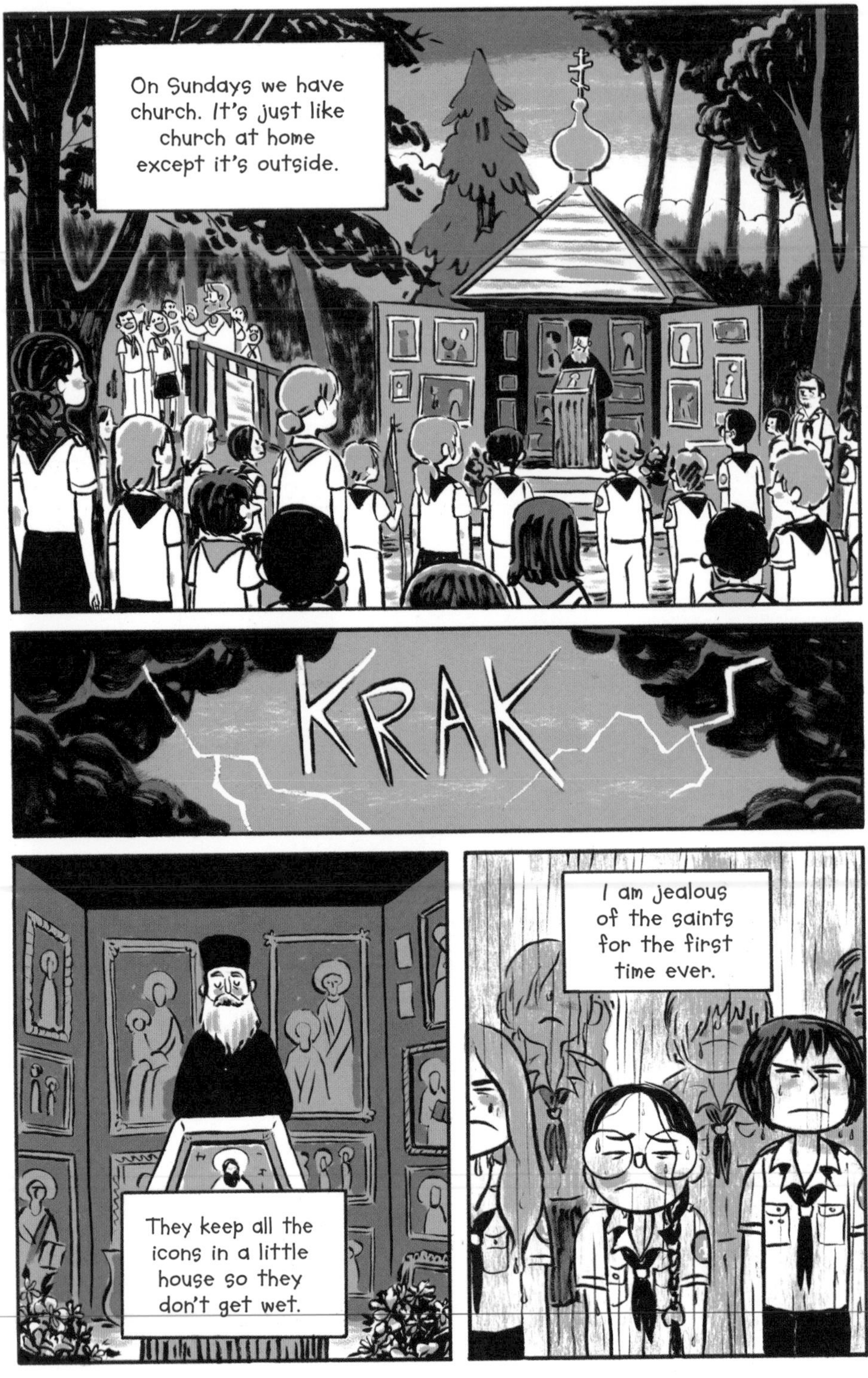
On Sundays we have church. It's just like church at home except it's outside.
KRAK
They keep all the icons in a little house so they don't get wet.
I am jealous of the saints for the first time ever.

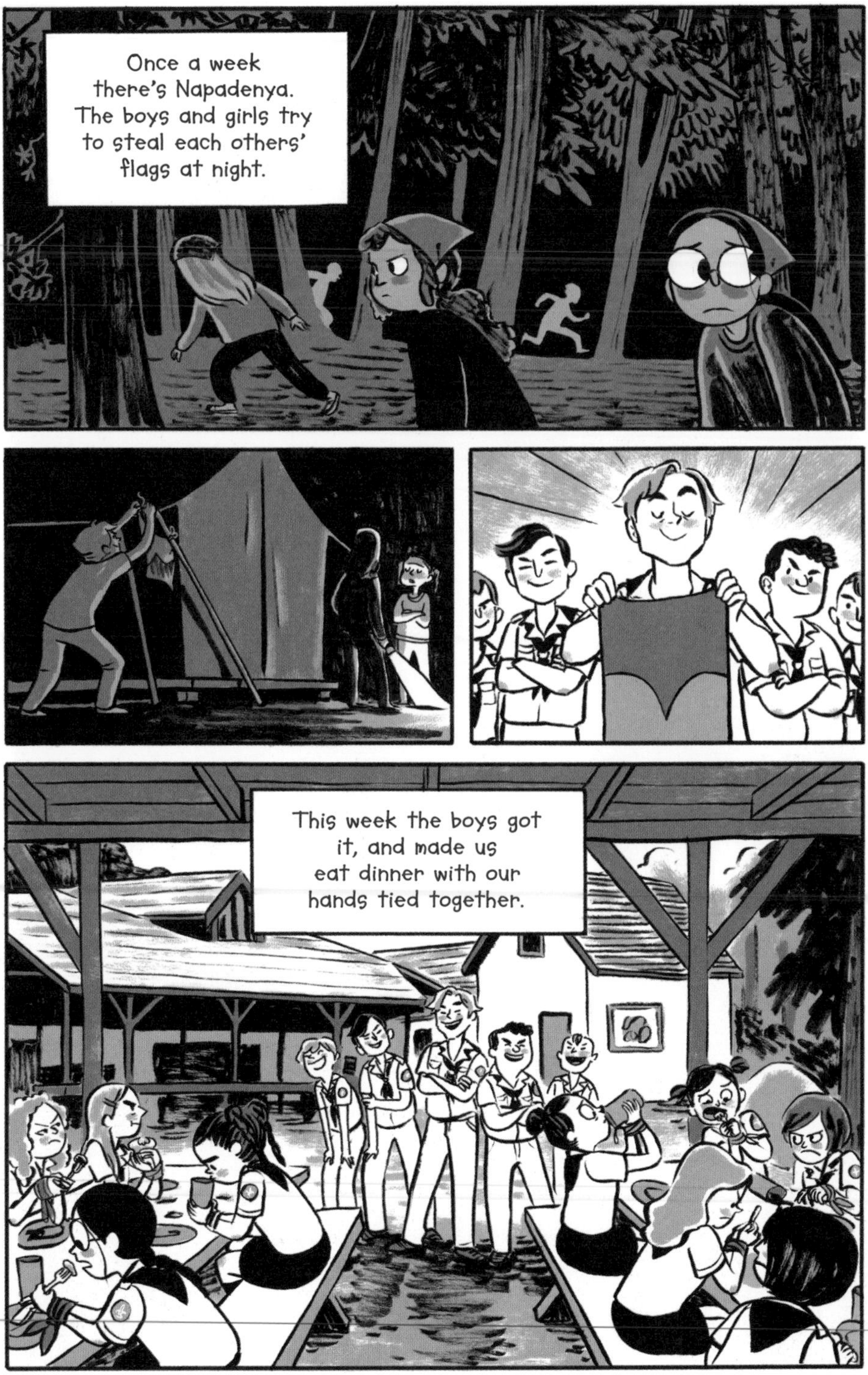
Once a week there's Napadenya. The boys and girls try to steal each others' flags at night.
This week the boys got it, and made us eat dinner with our hands tied together.

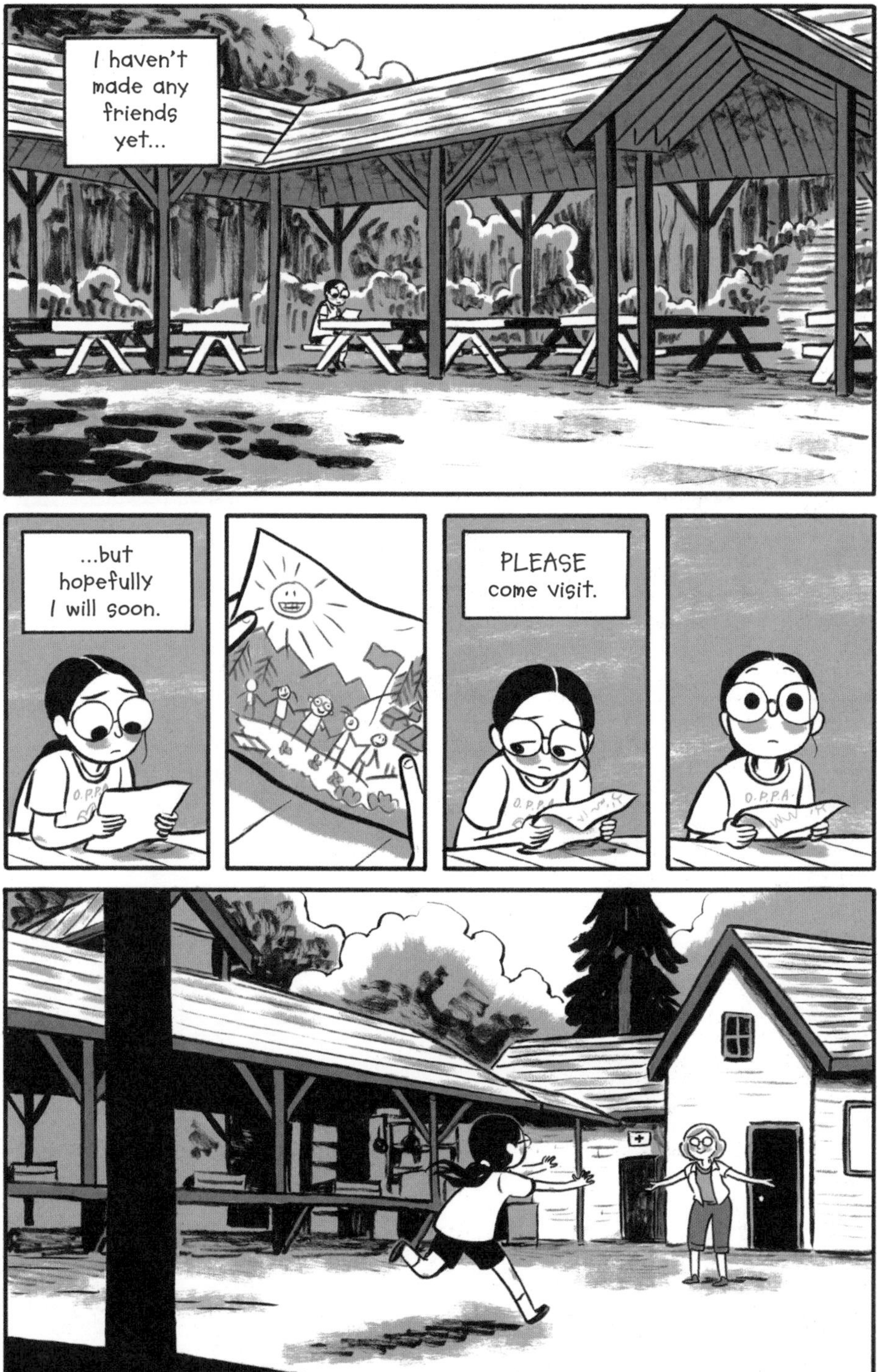
I haven't made any friends yet...
...but hopefully I will soon.
PLEASE come visit.

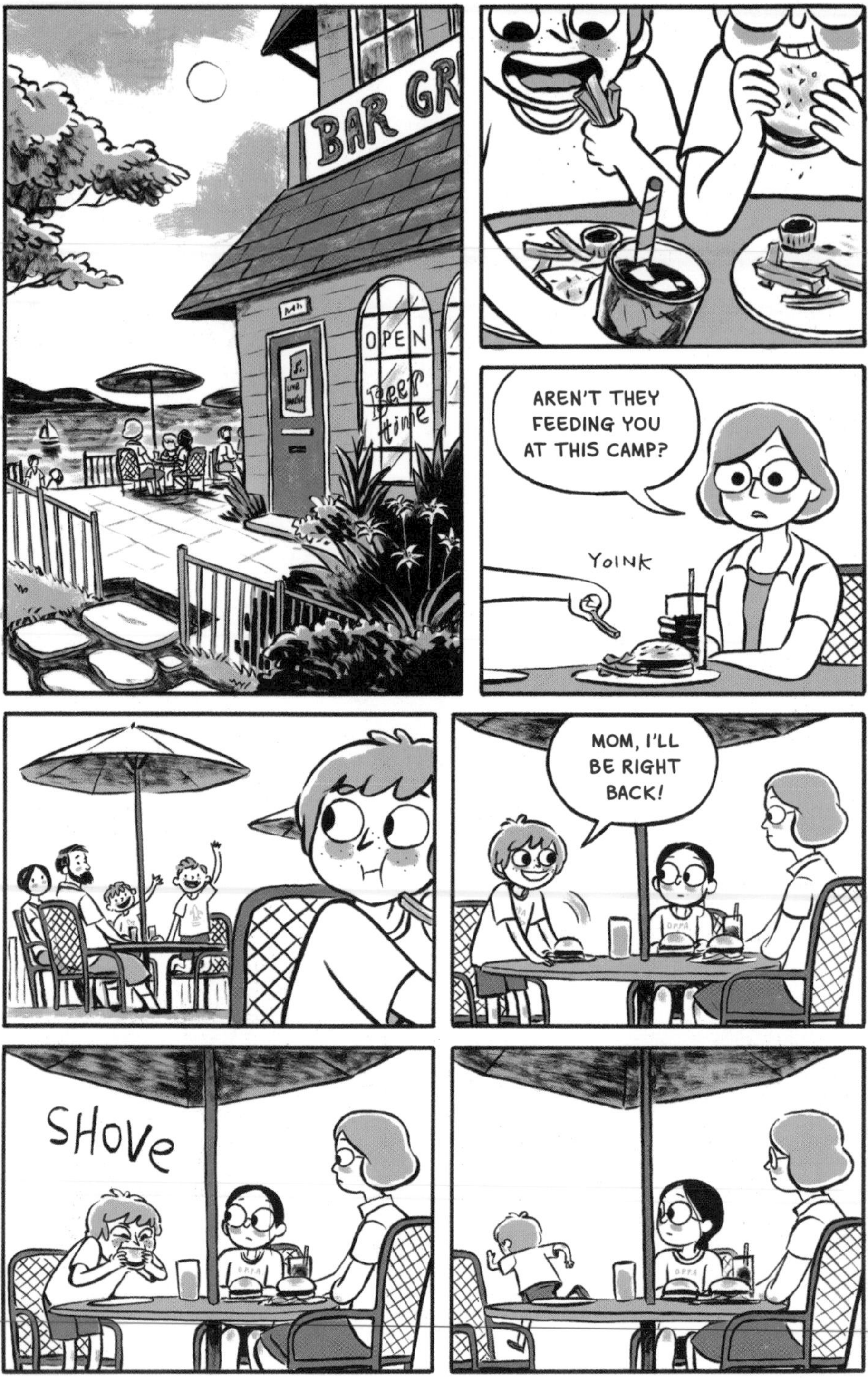
BAR GR
OPEN
Beer Home
AREN'T THEY FEEDING YOU AT THIS CAMP?
YOINK
MOM, I'LL BE RIGHT BACK!
SHOVE

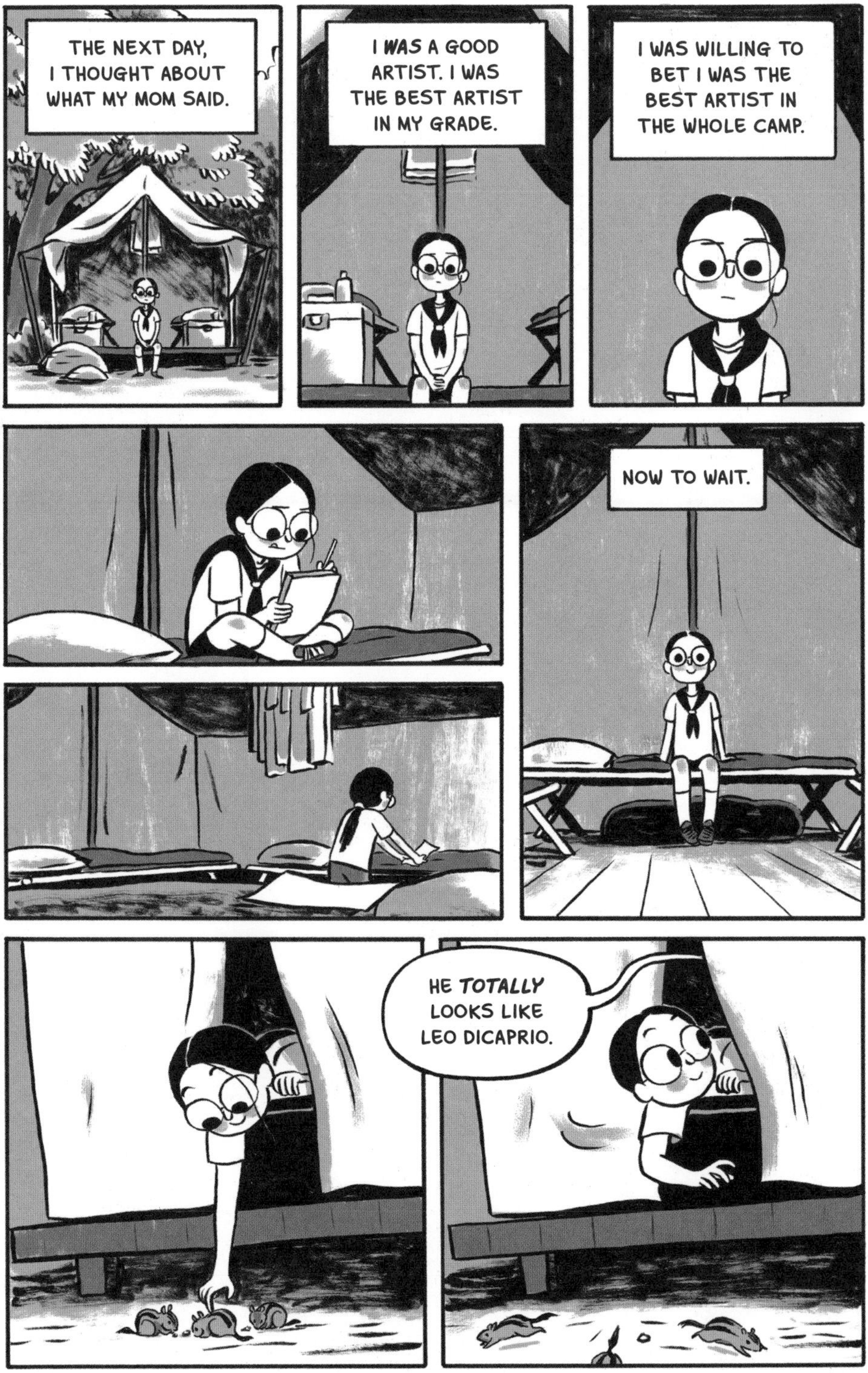
THE NEXT DAY, I THOUGHT ABOUT WHAT MY MOM SAID.
I *WAS* A GOOD ARTIST. I WAS THE BEST ARTIST IN MY GRADE.
I WAS WILLING TO BET I WAS THE BEST ARTIST IN THE WHOLE CAMP.
NOW TO WAIT.
HE *TOTALLY* LOOKS LIKE LEO DICAPRIO.

105

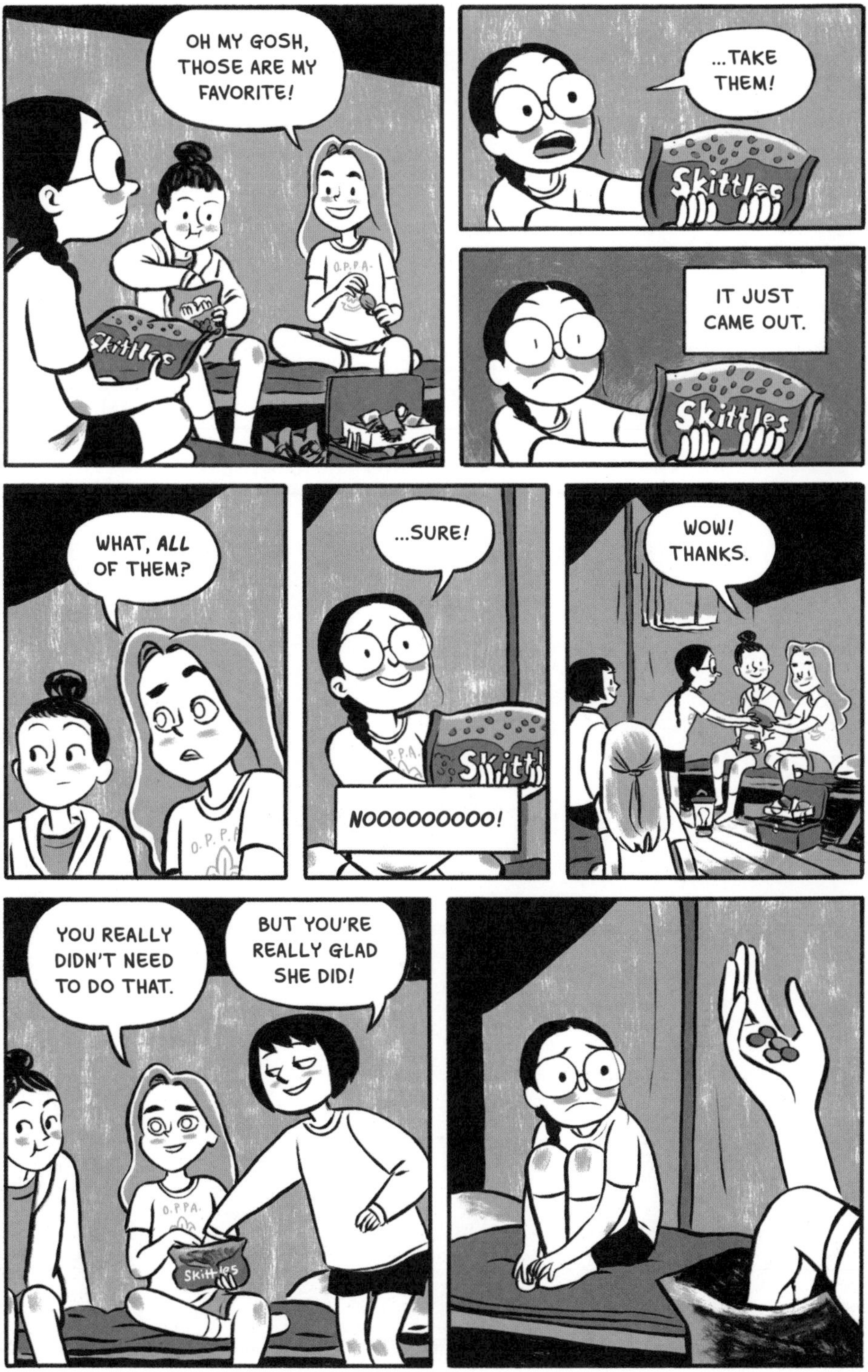
OH MY GOSH, THOSE ARE MY FAVORITE!
...TAKE THEM!
IT JUST CAME OUT.
WHAT, ALL OF THEM?
...SURE!
NOOOOOOOOO!
WOW! THANKS.
YOU REALLY DIDN'T NEED TO DO THAT.
BUT YOU'RE REALLY GLAD SHE DID!

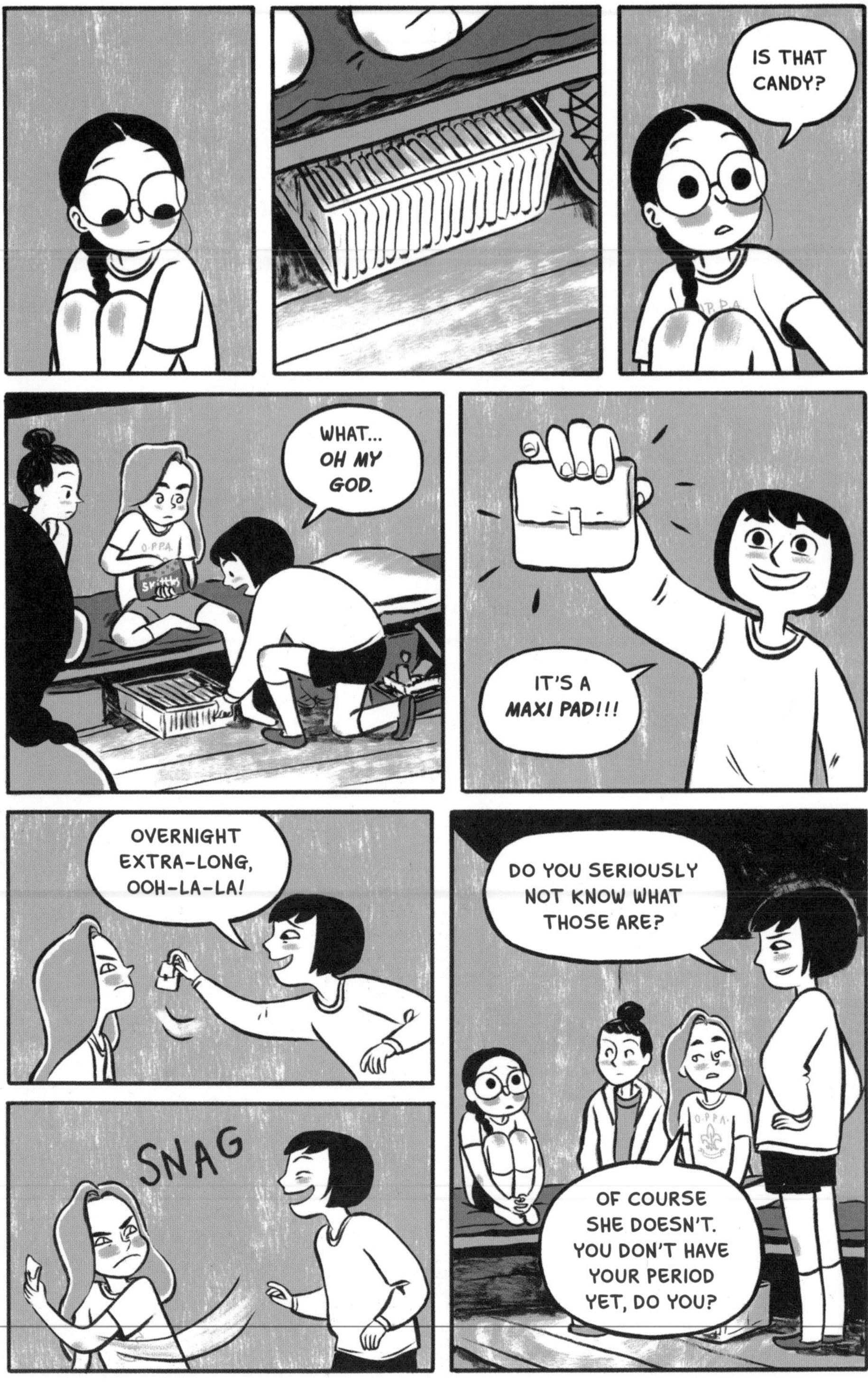
IS THAT CANDY?
WHAT... OH MY GOD.
IT'S A MAXI PAD!!!
OVERNIGHT EXTRA-LONG, OOH-LA-LA!
SNAG
DO YOU SERIOUSLY NOT KNOW WHAT THOSE ARE?
OF COURSE SHE DOESN'T. YOU DON'T HAVE YOUR PERIOD YET, DO YOU?

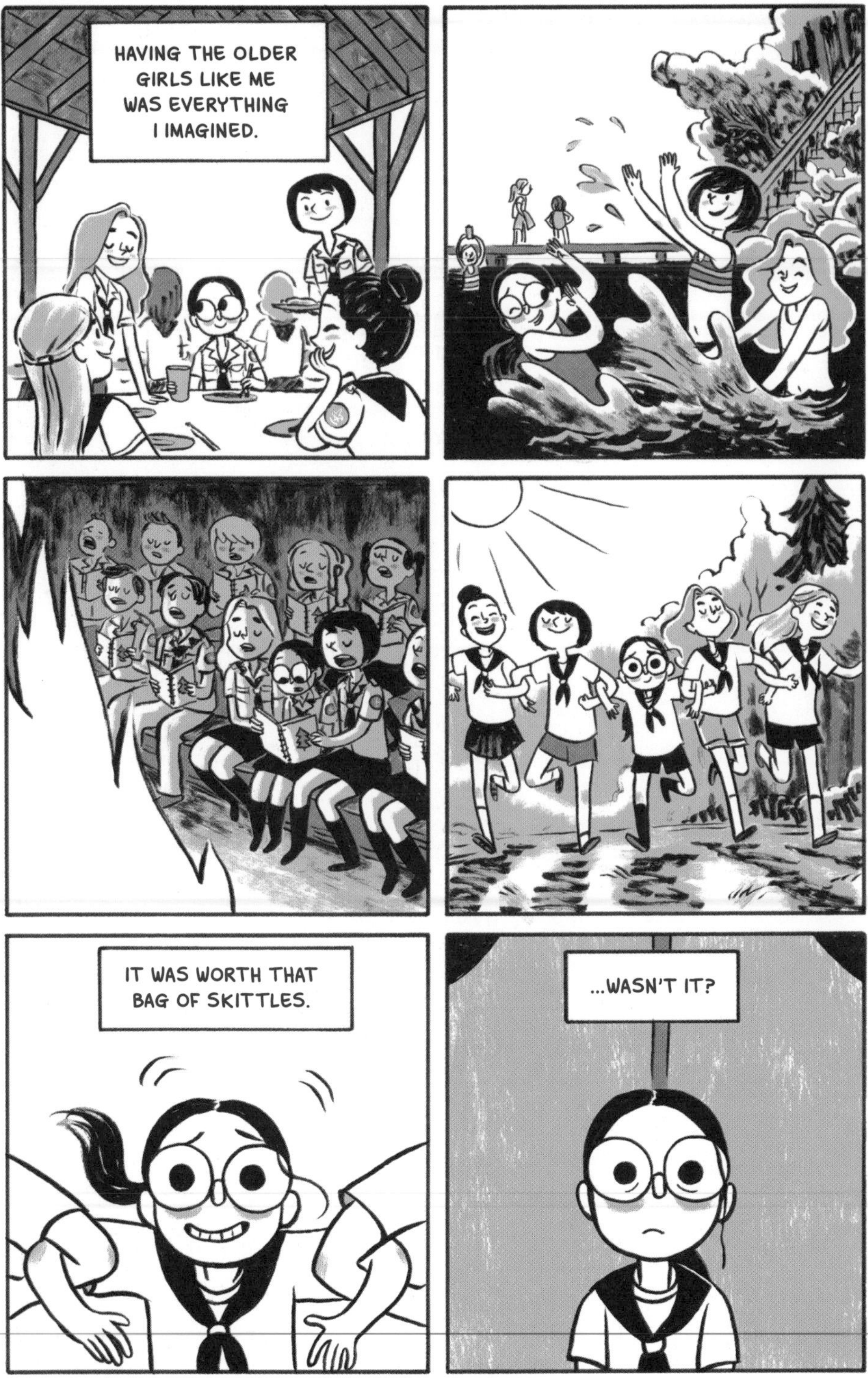
HAVING THE OLDER GIRLS LIKE ME WAS EVERYTHING I IMAGINED.
IT WAS WORTH THAT BAG OF SKITTLES.
...WASN'T IT?

119

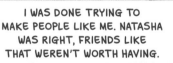

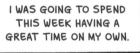

I WAS DONE TRYING TO MAKE PEOPLE LIKE ME. NATASHA WAS RIGHT, FRIENDS LIKE THAT WEREN'T WORTH HAVING.

I DIDN'T NEED THEM. I DIDN'T NEED ANYBODY.

I WAS GOING TO SPEND THIS WEEK HAVING A GREAT TIME ON MY OWN.

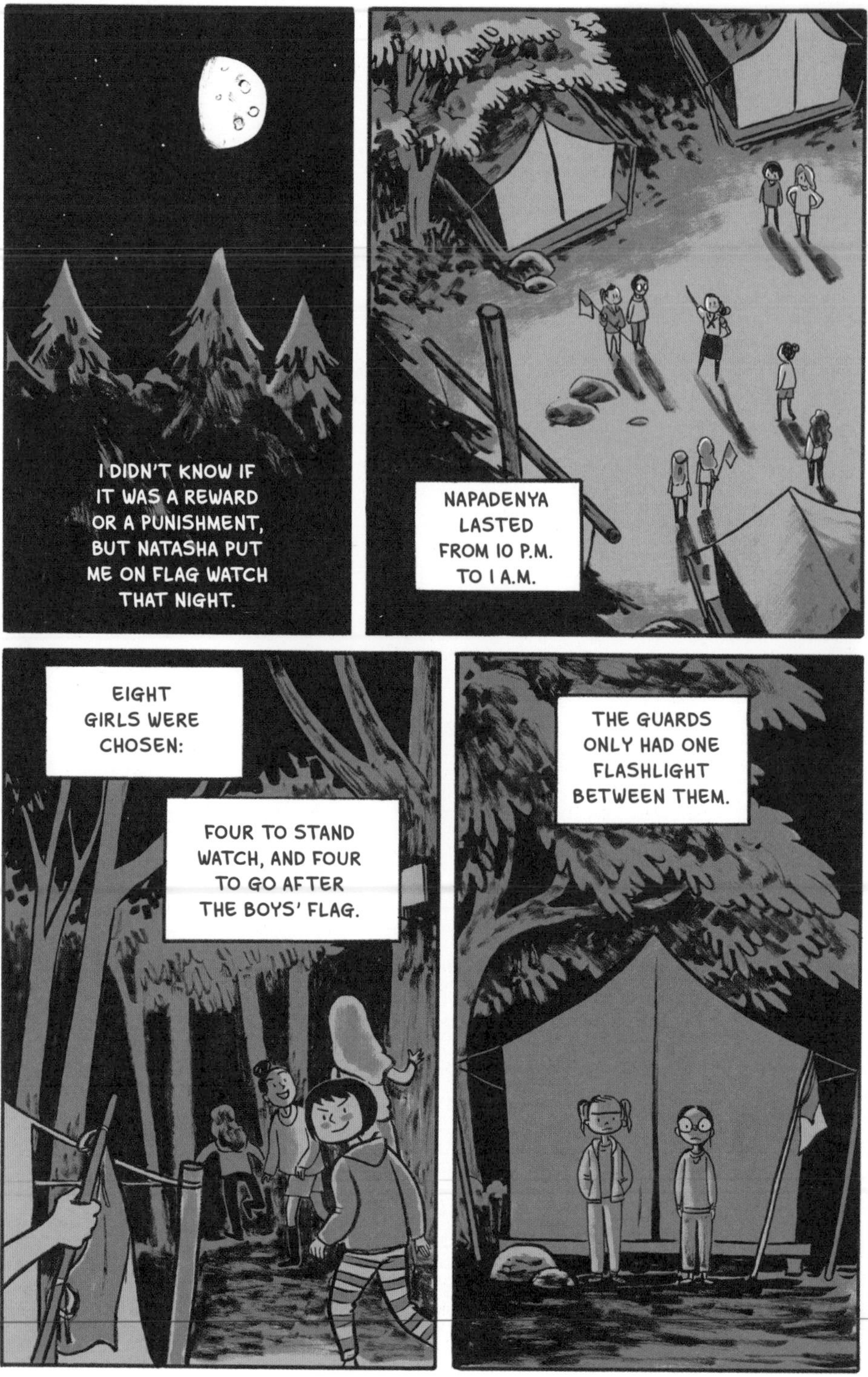
I DIDN'T KNOW IF IT WAS A REWARD OR A PUNISHMENT, BUT NATASHA PUT ME ON FLAG WATCH THAT NIGHT.
NAPADENYA LASTED FROM 10 P.M. TO 1 A.M.
EIGHT GIRLS WERE CHOSEN:
FOUR TO STAND WATCH, AND FOUR TO GO AFTER THE BOYS' FLAG.
THE GUARDS ONLY HAD ONE FLASHLIGHT BETWEEN THEM.

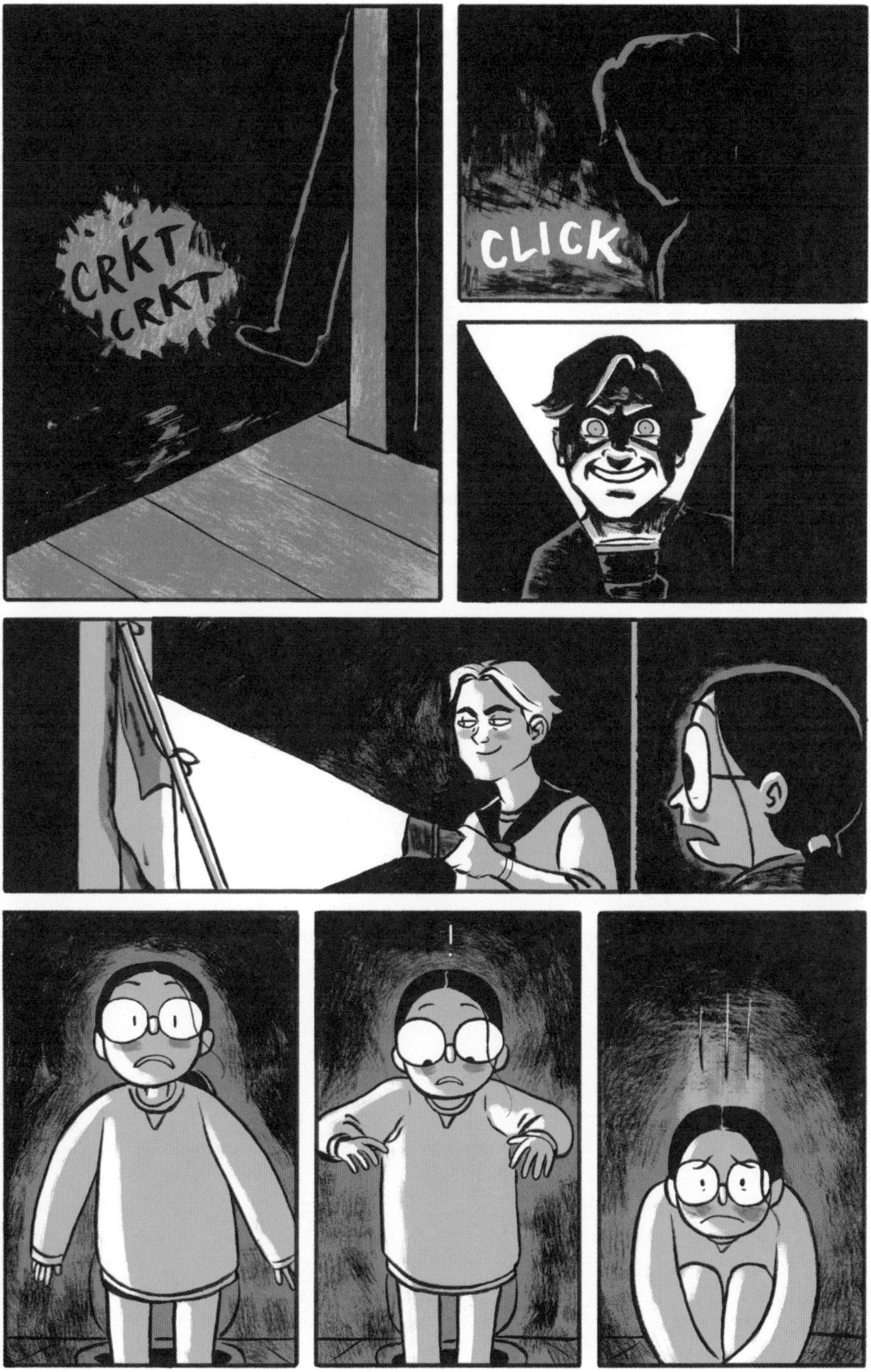
CRKT CRKT
CLICK
!

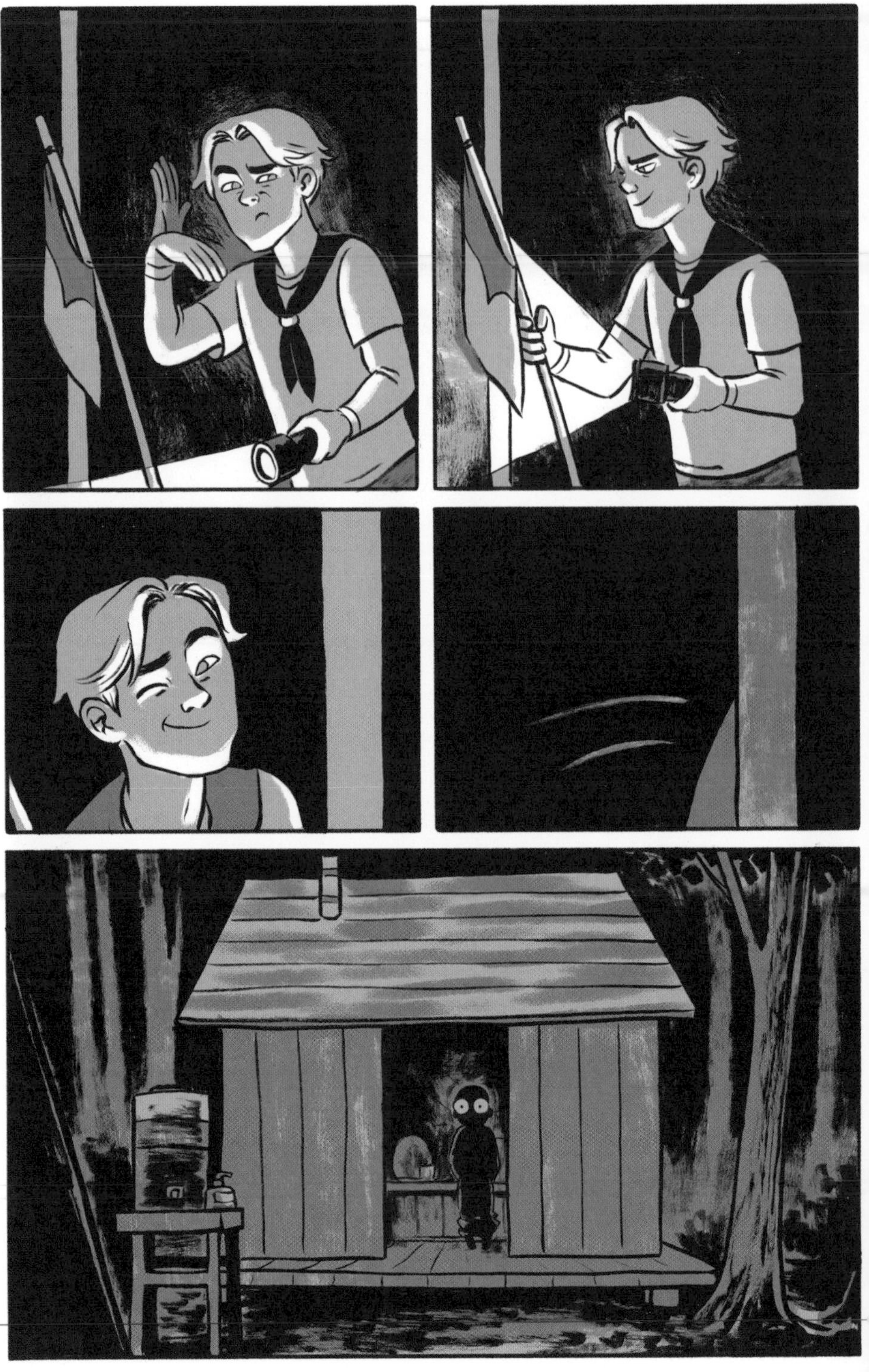

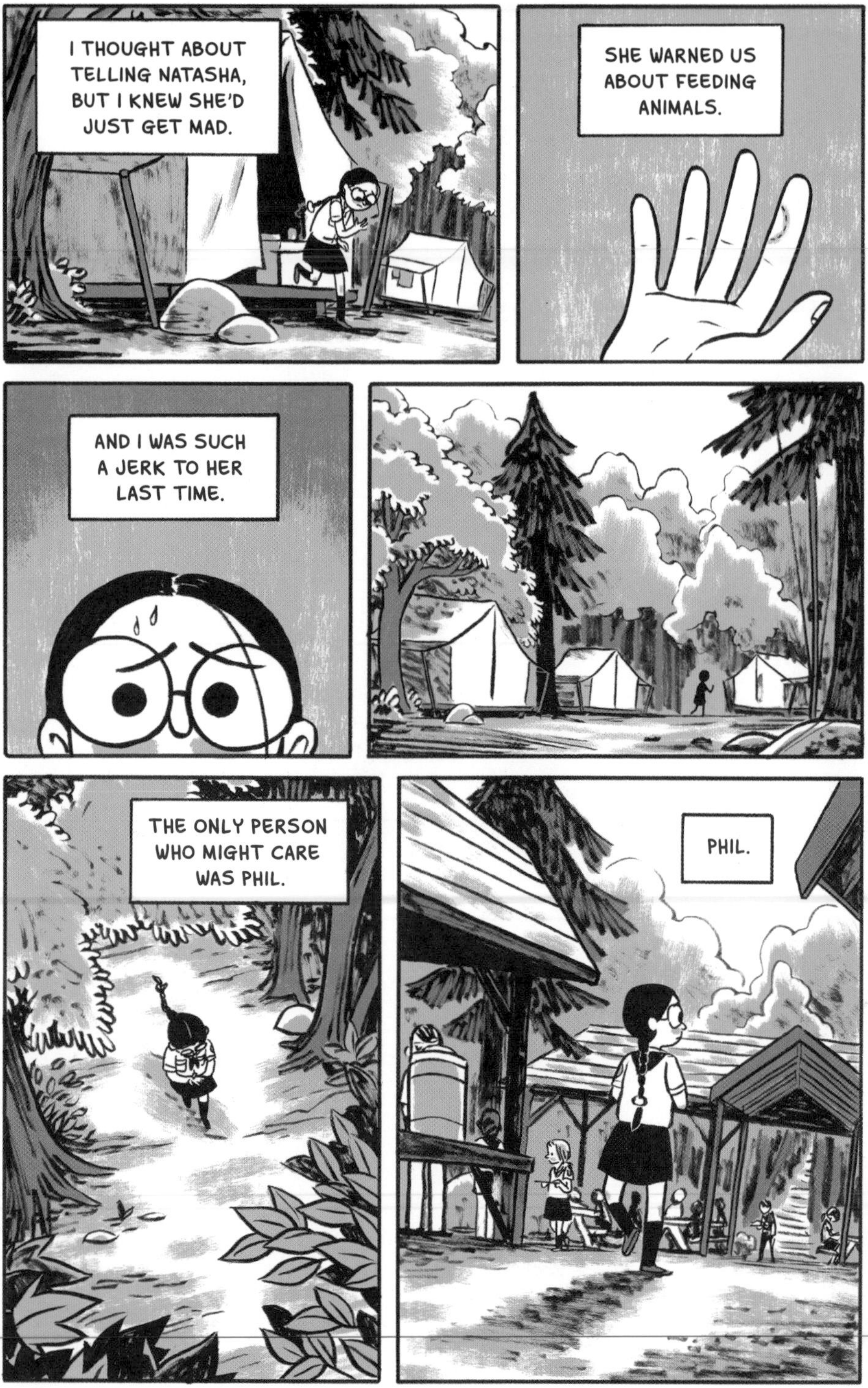
I THOUGHT ABOUT TELLING NATASHA, BUT I KNEW SHE'D JUST GET MAD.
SHE WARNED US ABOUT FEEDING ANIMALS.
AND I WAS SUCH A JERK TO HER LAST TIME.
THE ONLY PERSON WHO MIGHT CARE WAS PHIL.
PHIL.

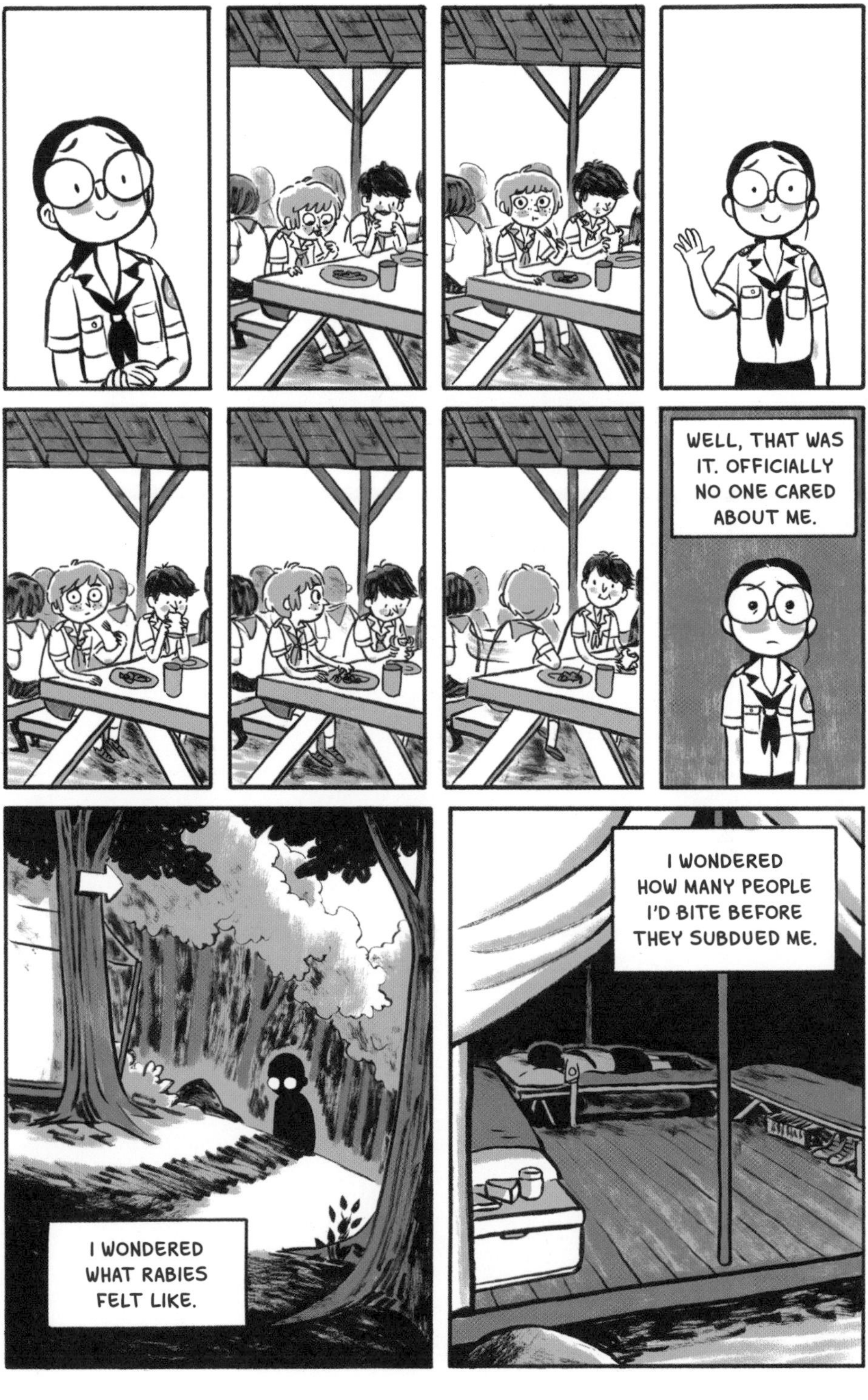
WELL, THAT WAS IT. OFFICIALLY NO ONE CARED ABOUT ME.
I WONDERED WHAT RABIES FELT LIKE.
I WONDERED HOW MANY PEOPLE I'D BITE BEFORE THEY SUBDUED ME.

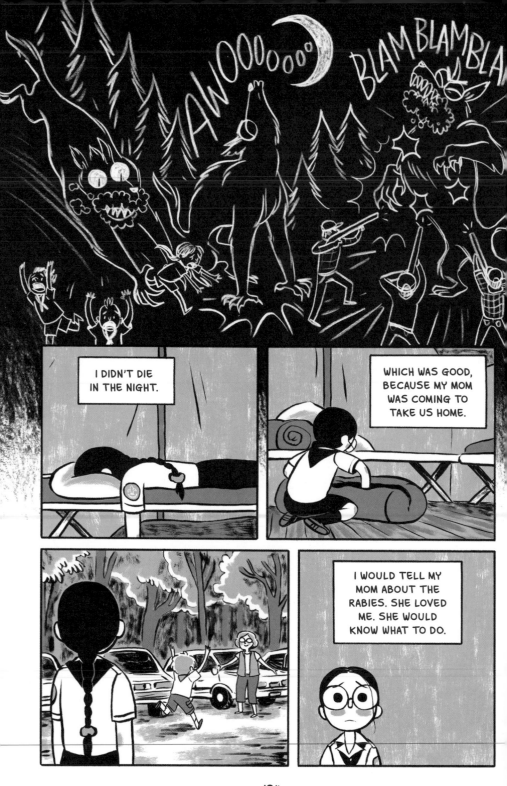

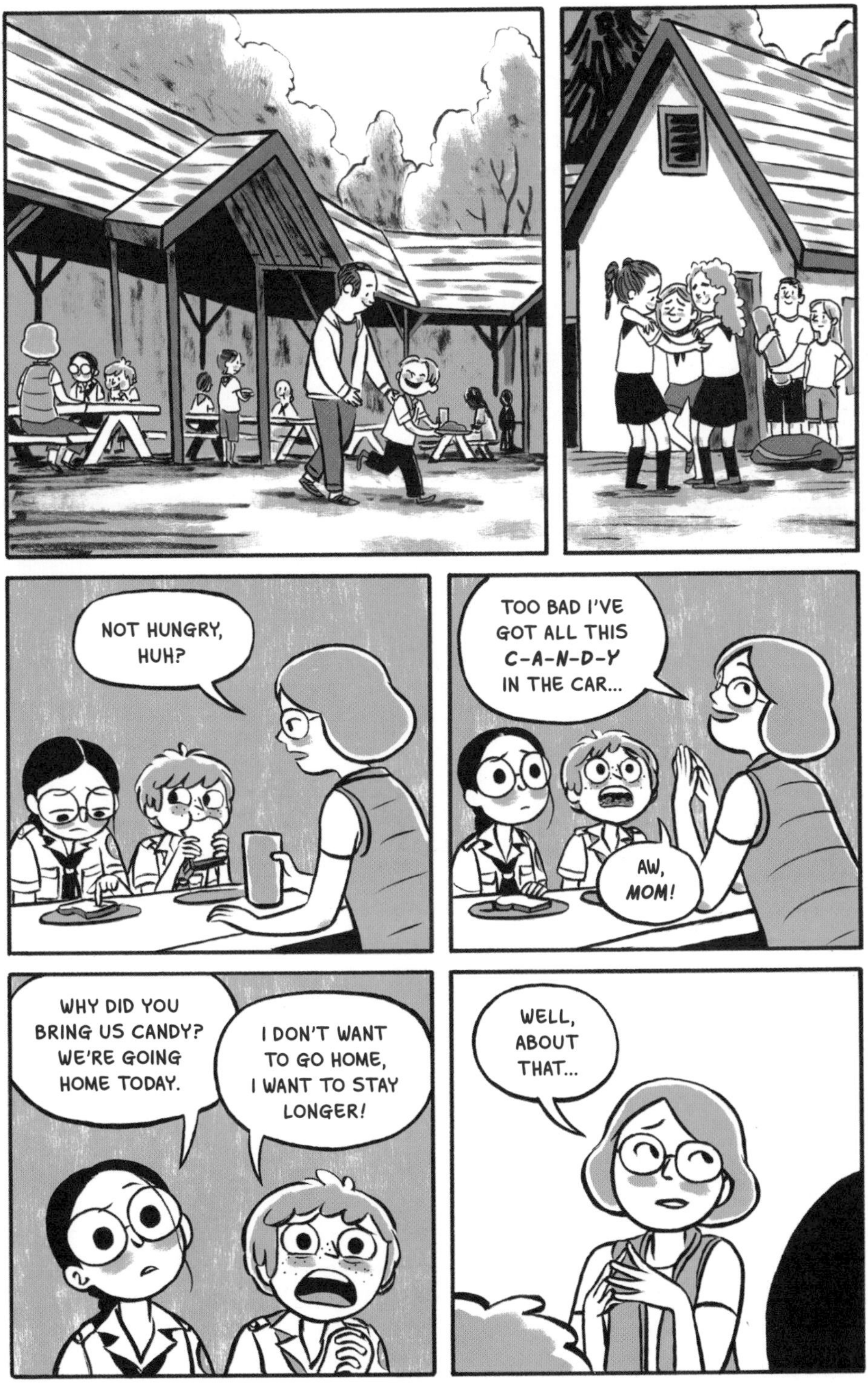
NOT HUNGRY, HUH?
TOO BAD I'VE GOT ALL THIS C-A-N-D-Y IN THE CAR...
AW, MOM!
WHY DID YOU BRING US CANDY? WE'RE GOING HOME TODAY.
I DON'T WANT TO GO HOME, I WANT TO STAY LONGER!
WELL, ABOUT THAT...

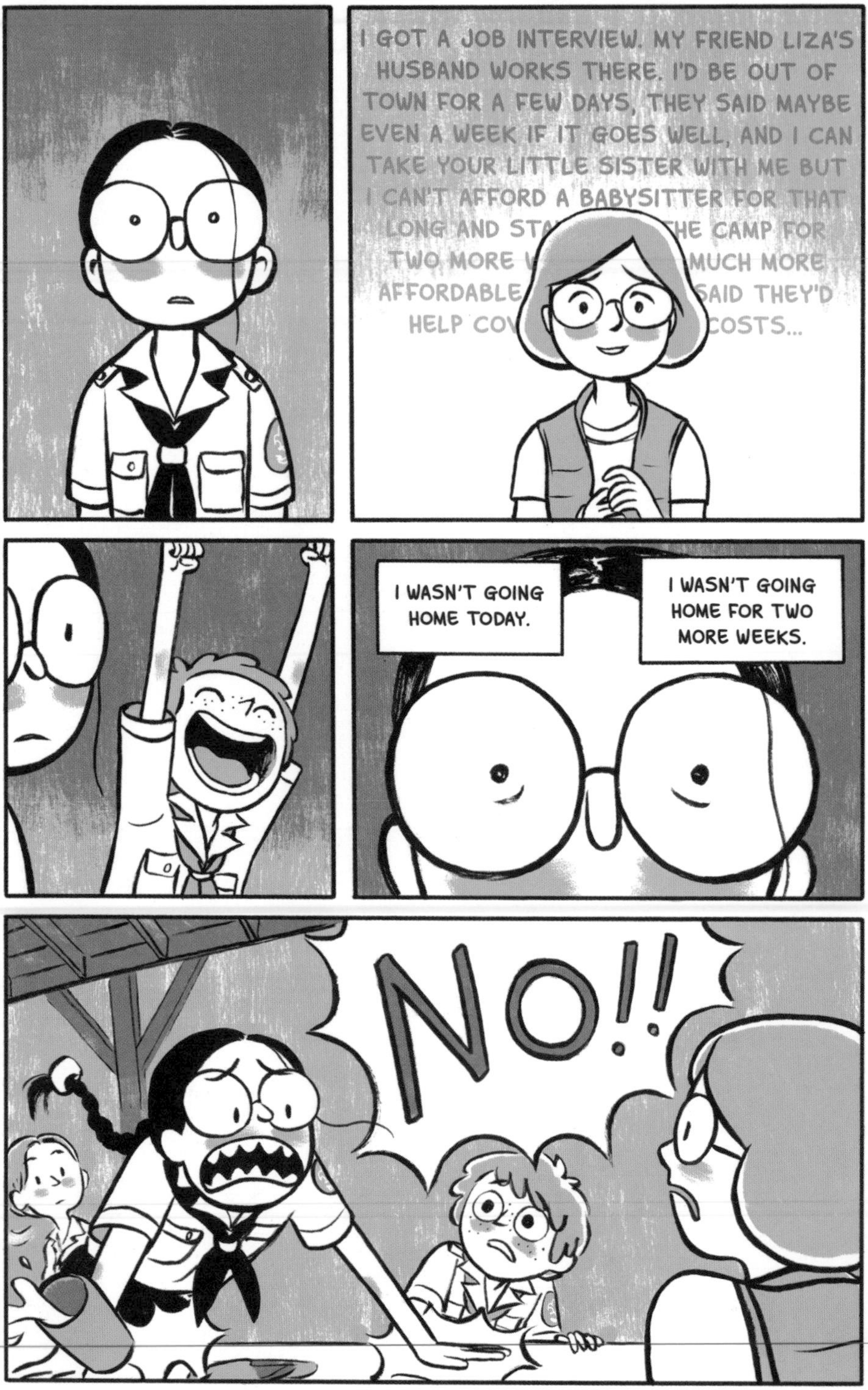
I GOT A JOB INTERVIEW. MY FRIEND LIZA'S HUSBAND WORKS THERE. I'D BE OUT OF TOWN FOR A FEW DAYS, THEY SAID MAYBE EVEN A WEEK IF IT GOES WELL, AND I CAN TAKE YOUR LITTLE SISTER WITH ME BUT I CAN'T AFFORD A BABYSITTER FOR THAT LONG AND STA
THE CAMP FOR
TWO MORE W
MUCH MORE
AFFORDABLE
SAID THEY'D
HELP CO
COSTS...
I WASN'T GOING HOME TODAY.
I WASN'T GOING HOME FOR TWO MORE WEEKS.
NO!!

137

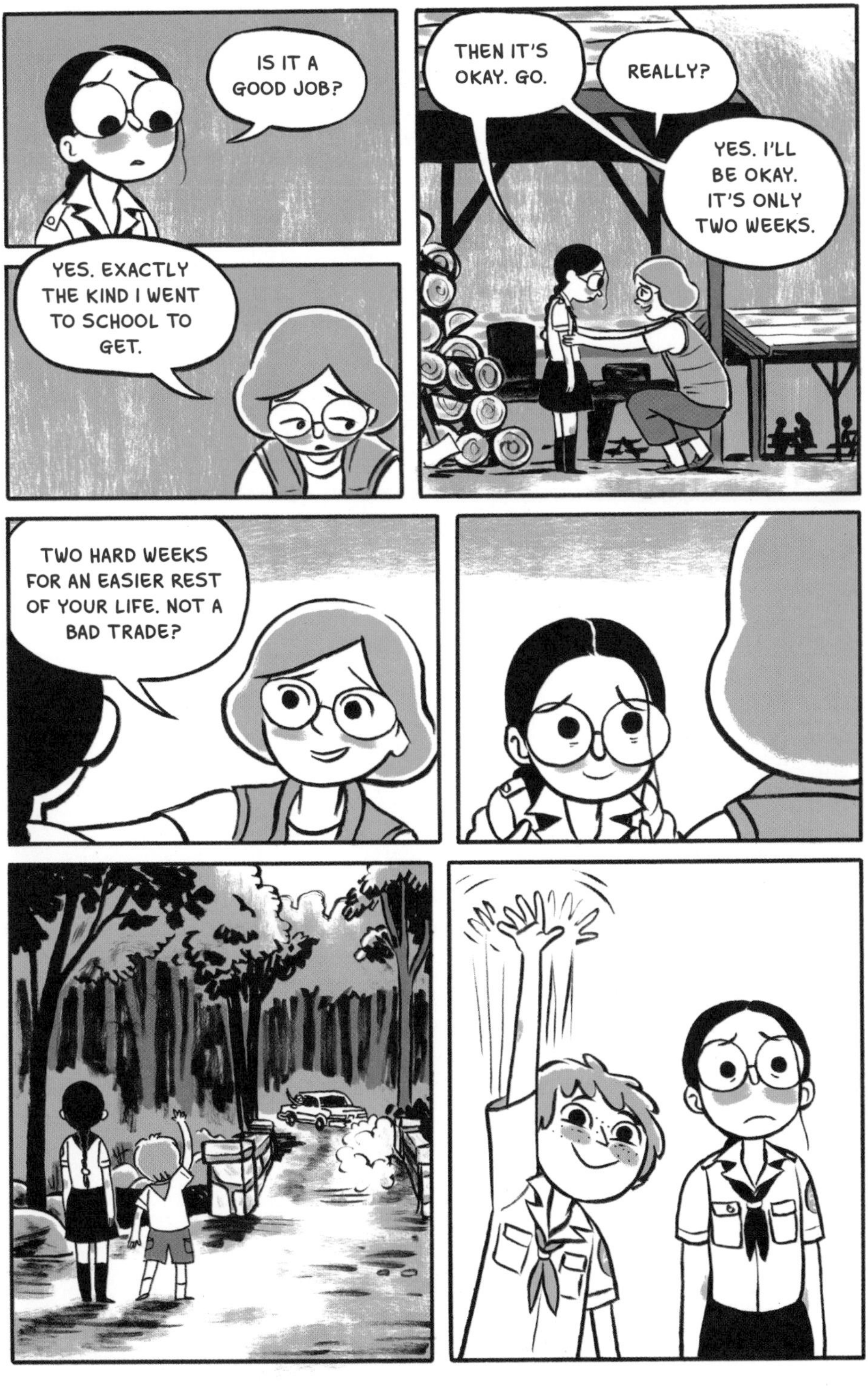
IS IT A GOOD JOB?
YES. EXACTLY THE KIND I WENT TO SCHOOL TO GET.
THEN IT'S OKAY. GO.
REALLY?
YES. I'LL BE OKAY. IT'S ONLY TWO WEEKS.
TWO HARD WEEKS FOR AN EASIER REST OF YOUR LIFE. NOT A BAD TRADE?

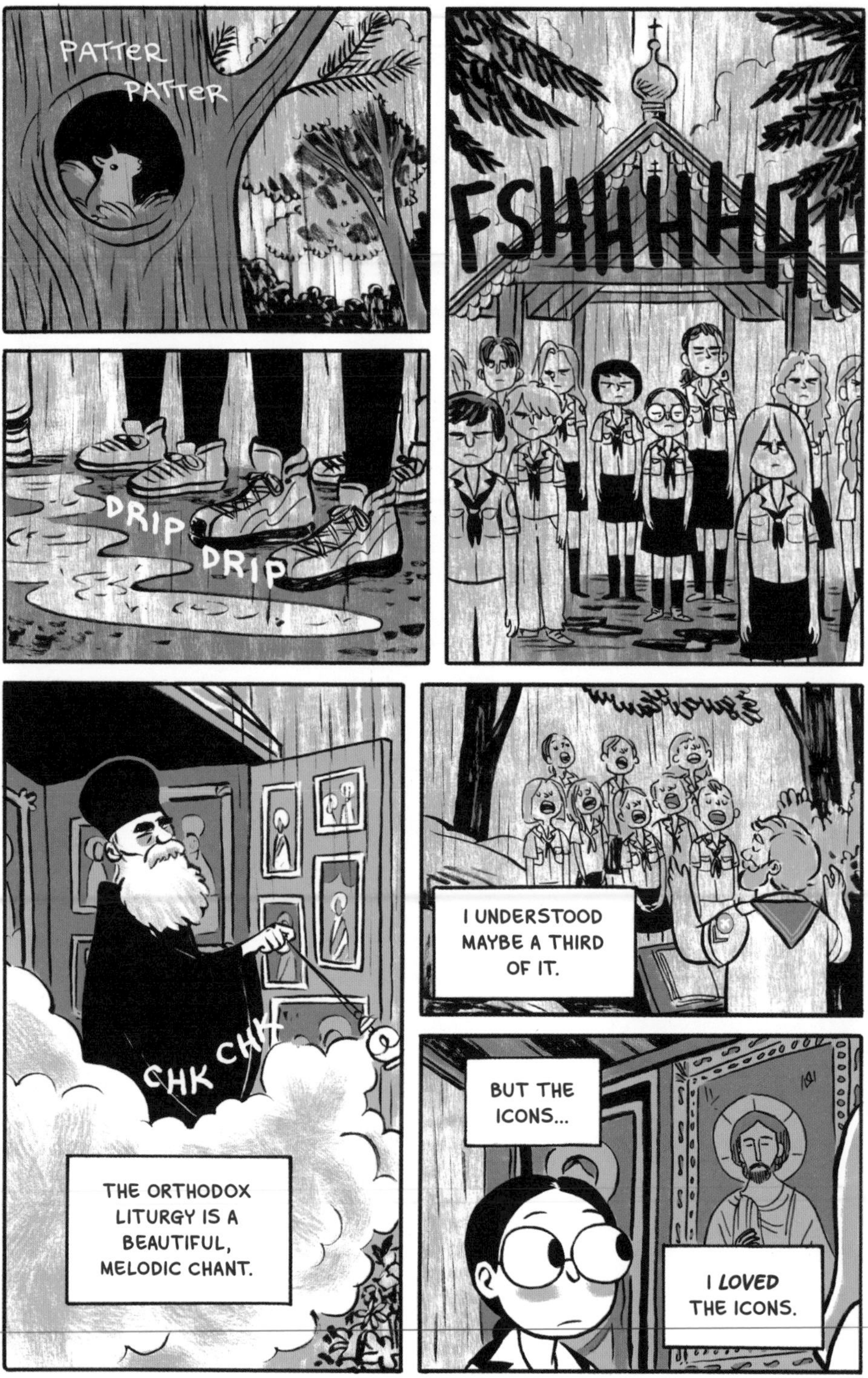
PATTER PATTER
FSHHHHH
DRIP DRIP
CHK CHK
THE ORTHODOX LITURGY IS A BEAUTIFUL, MELODIC CHANT.
I UNDERSTOOD MAYBE A THIRD OF IT.
BUT THE ICONS...
I *LOVED* THE ICONS.

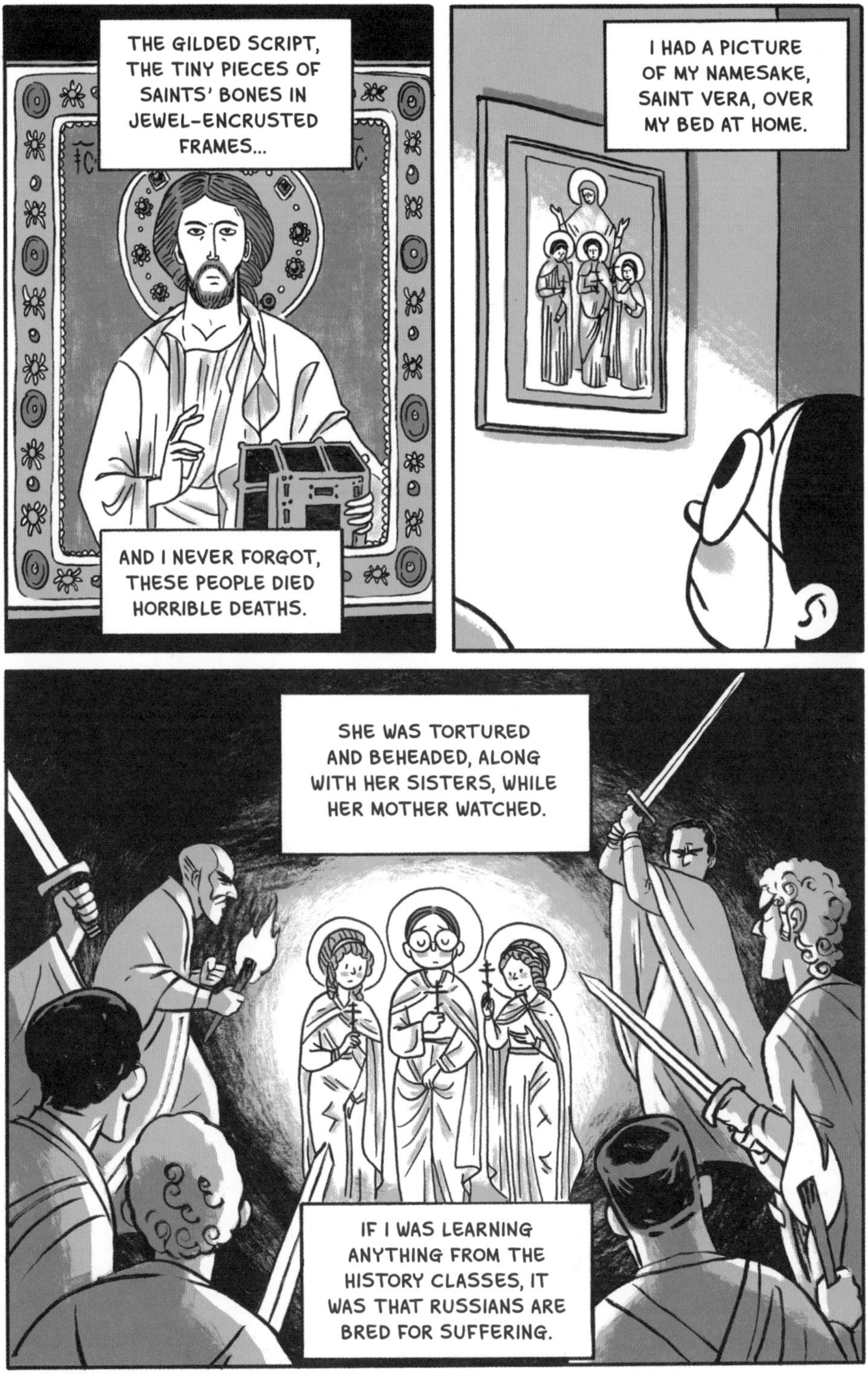
THE GILDED SCRIPT, THE TINY PIECES OF SAINTS' BONES IN JEWEL-ENCRUSTED FRAMES...
AND I NEVER FORGOT, THESE PEOPLE DIED HORRIBLE DEATHS.
I HAD A PICTURE OF MY NAMESAKE, SAINT VERA, OVER MY BED AT HOME.
SHE WAS TORTURED AND BEHEADED, ALONG WITH HER SISTERS, WHILE HER MOTHER WATCHED.
IF I WAS LEARNING ANYTHING FROM THE HISTORY CLASSES, IT WAS THAT RUSSIANS ARE BRED FOR SUFFERING.

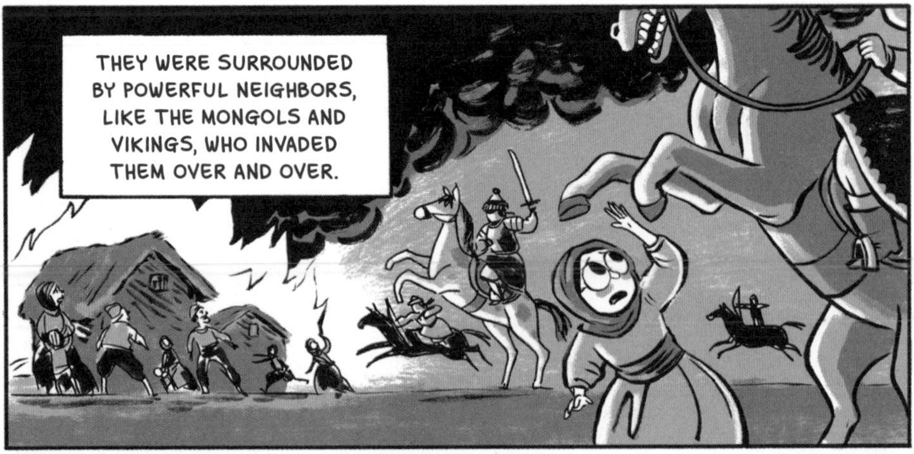
THEY WERE SURROUNDED BY POWERFUL NEIGHBORS, LIKE THE MONGOLS AND VIKINGS, WHO INVADED THEM OVER AND OVER.

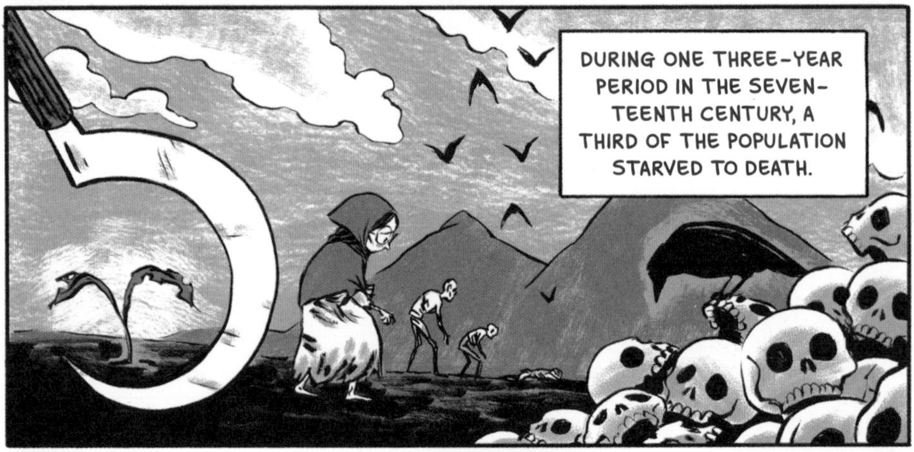
DURING ONE THREE-YEAR PERIOD IN THE SEVENTEENTH CENTURY, A THIRD OF THE POPULATION STARVED TO DEATH.

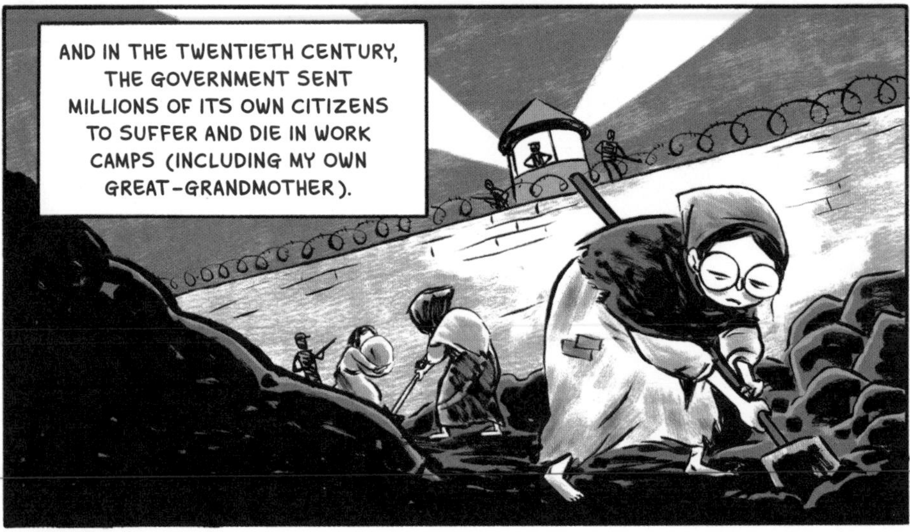
AND IN THE TWENTIETH CENTURY, THE GOVERNMENT SENT MILLIONS OF ITS OWN CITIZENS TO SUFFER AND DIE IN WORK CAMPS (INCLUDING MY OWN GREAT-GRANDMOTHER).

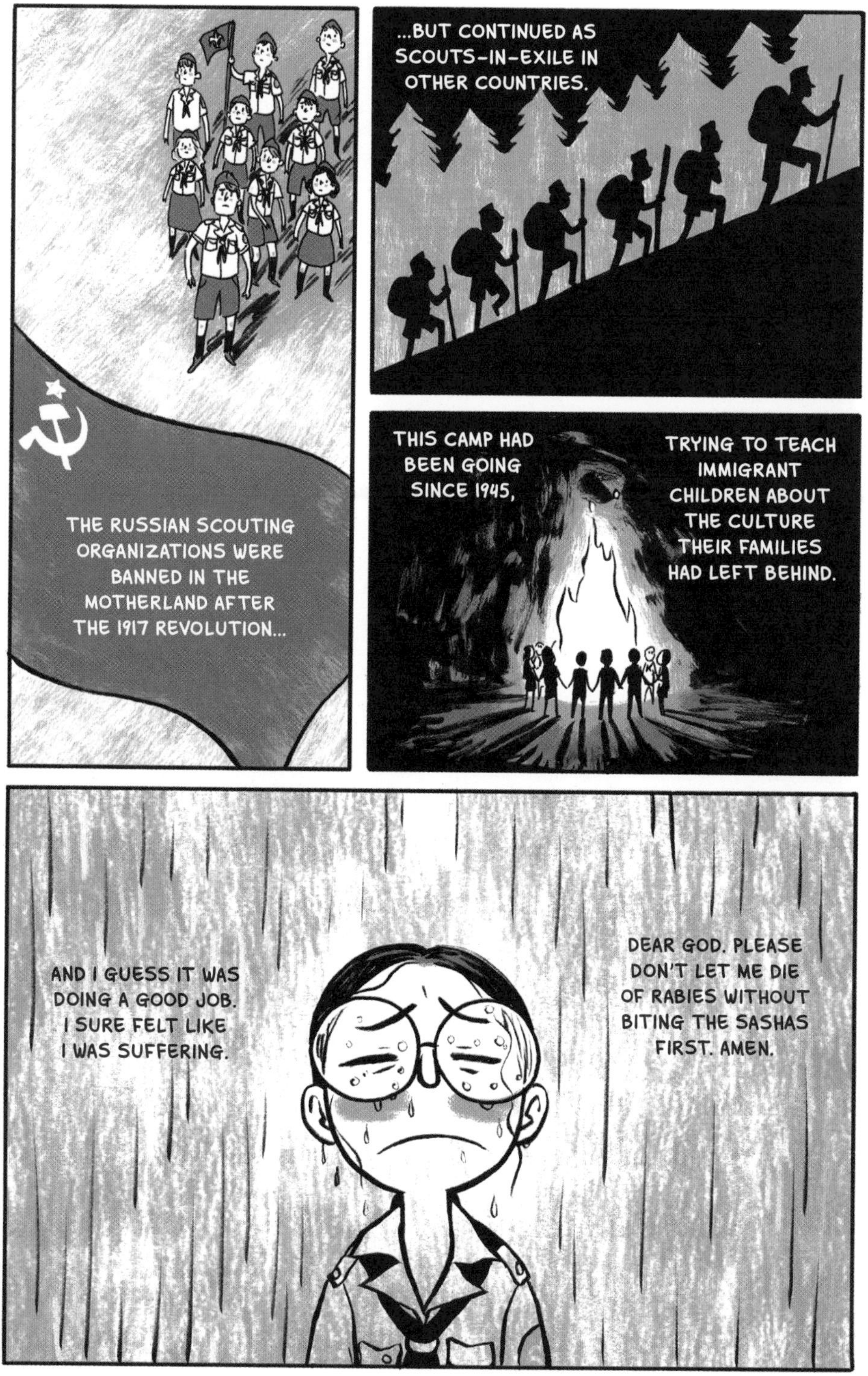
THE RUSSIAN SCOUTING ORGANIZATIONS WERE BANNED IN THE MOTHERLAND AFTER THE 1917 REVOLUTION...
...BUT CONTINUED AS SCOUTS-IN-EXILE IN OTHER COUNTRIES.
THIS CAMP HAD BEEN GOING SINCE 1945,
TRYING TO TEACH IMMIGRANT CHILDREN ABOUT THE CULTURE THEIR FAMILIES HAD LEFT BEHIND.
AND I GUESS IT WAS DOING A GOOD JOB. I SURE FELT LIKE I WAS SUFFERING.
DEAR GOD. PLEASE DON'T LET ME DIE OF RABIES WITHOUT BITING THE SASHAS FIRST. AMEN.

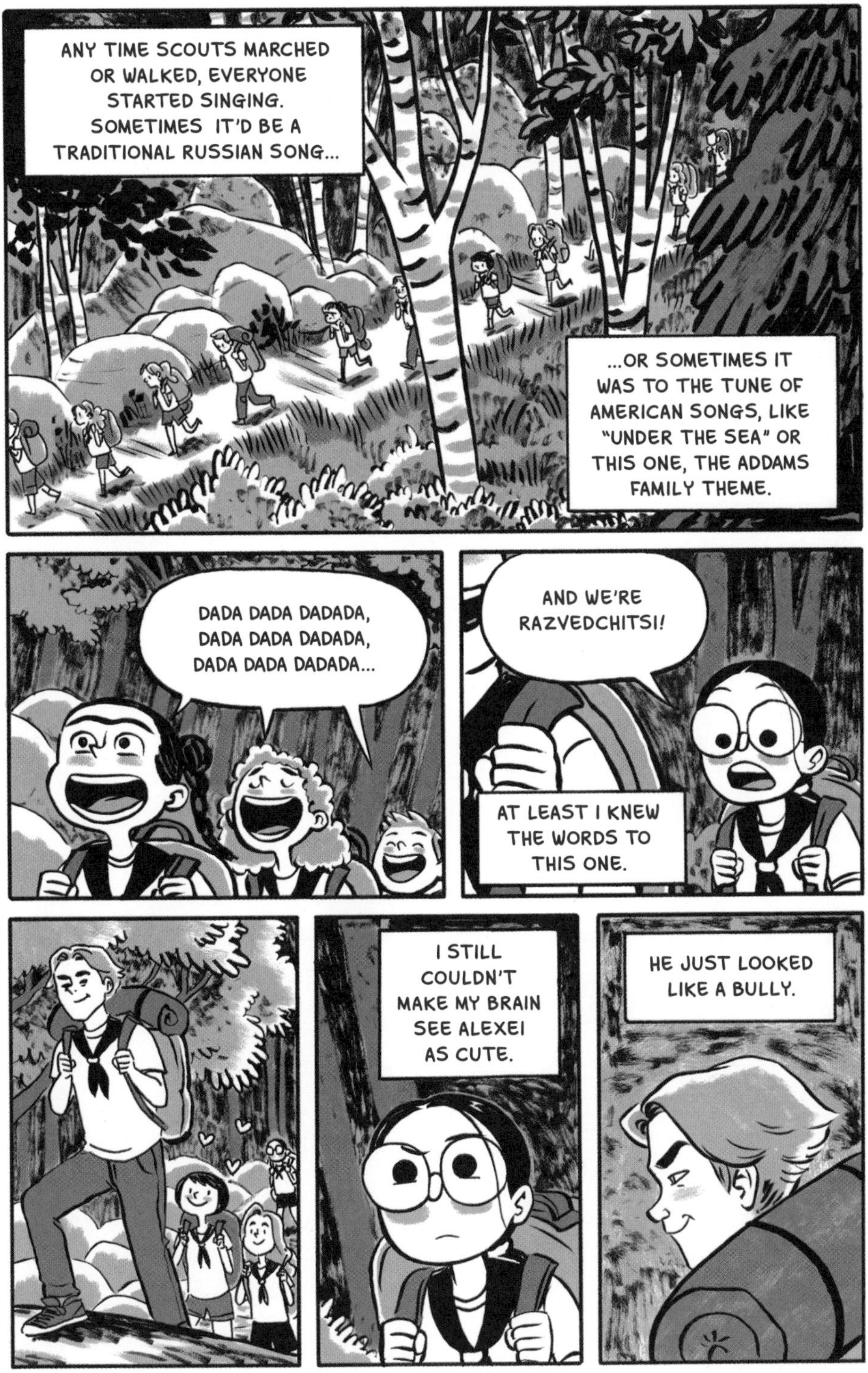
ANY TIME SCOUTS MARCHED OR WALKED, EVERYONE STARTED SINGING. SOMETIMES IT'D BE A TRADITIONAL RUSSIAN SONG...
...OR SOMETIMES IT WAS TO THE TUNE OF AMERICAN SONGS, LIKE "UNDER THE SEA" OR THIS ONE, THE ADDAMS FAMILY THEME.
DADA DADA DADADA, DADA DADA DADADA, DADA DADA DADADA...
AND WE'RE RAZVEDCHITSI!
AT LEAST I KNEW THE WORDS TO THIS ONE.
I STILL COULDN'T MAKE MY BRAIN SEE ALEXEI AS CUTE.
HE JUST LOOKED LIKE A BULLY.

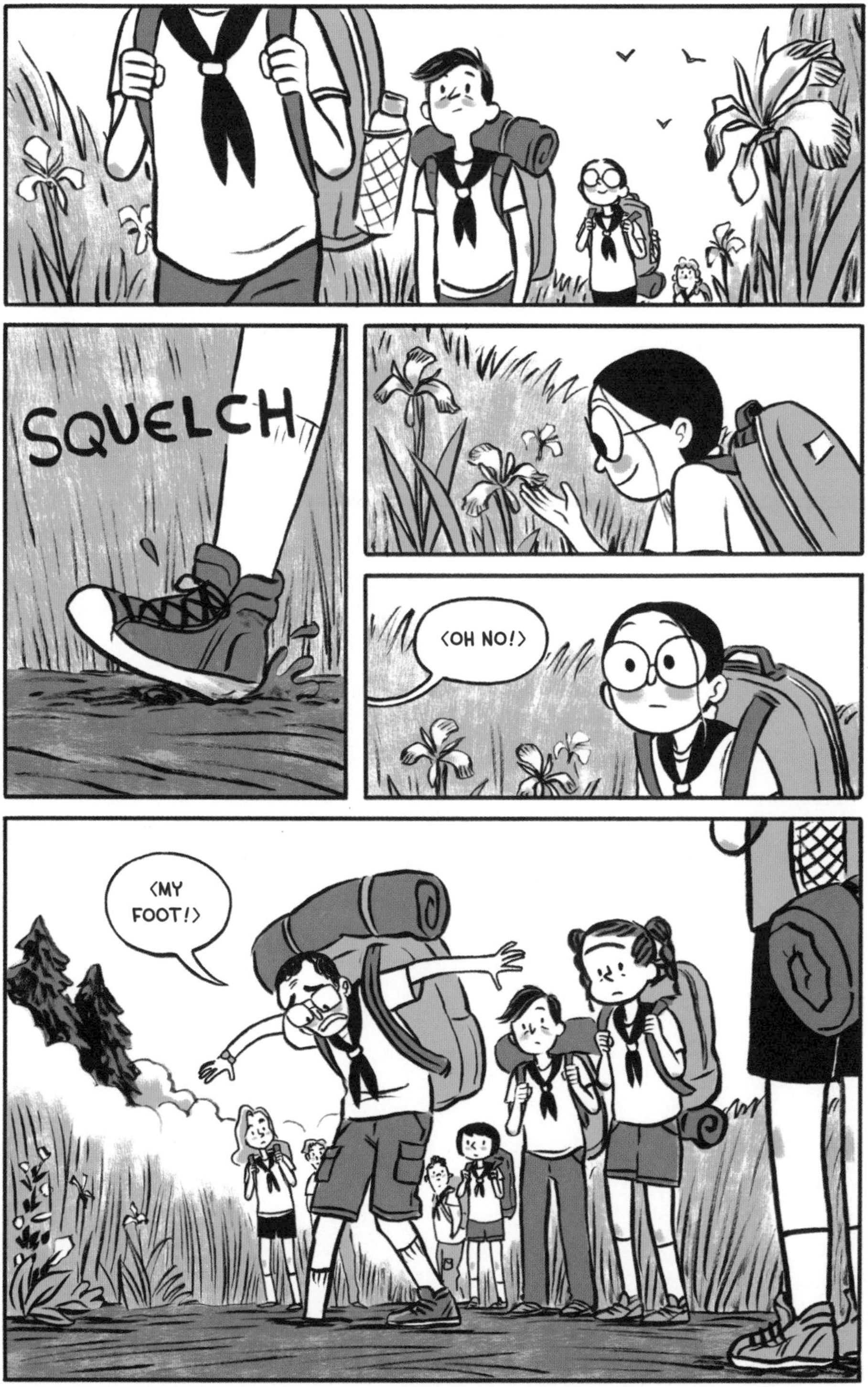
SQUELCH
<OH NO!>
<MY FOOT!>

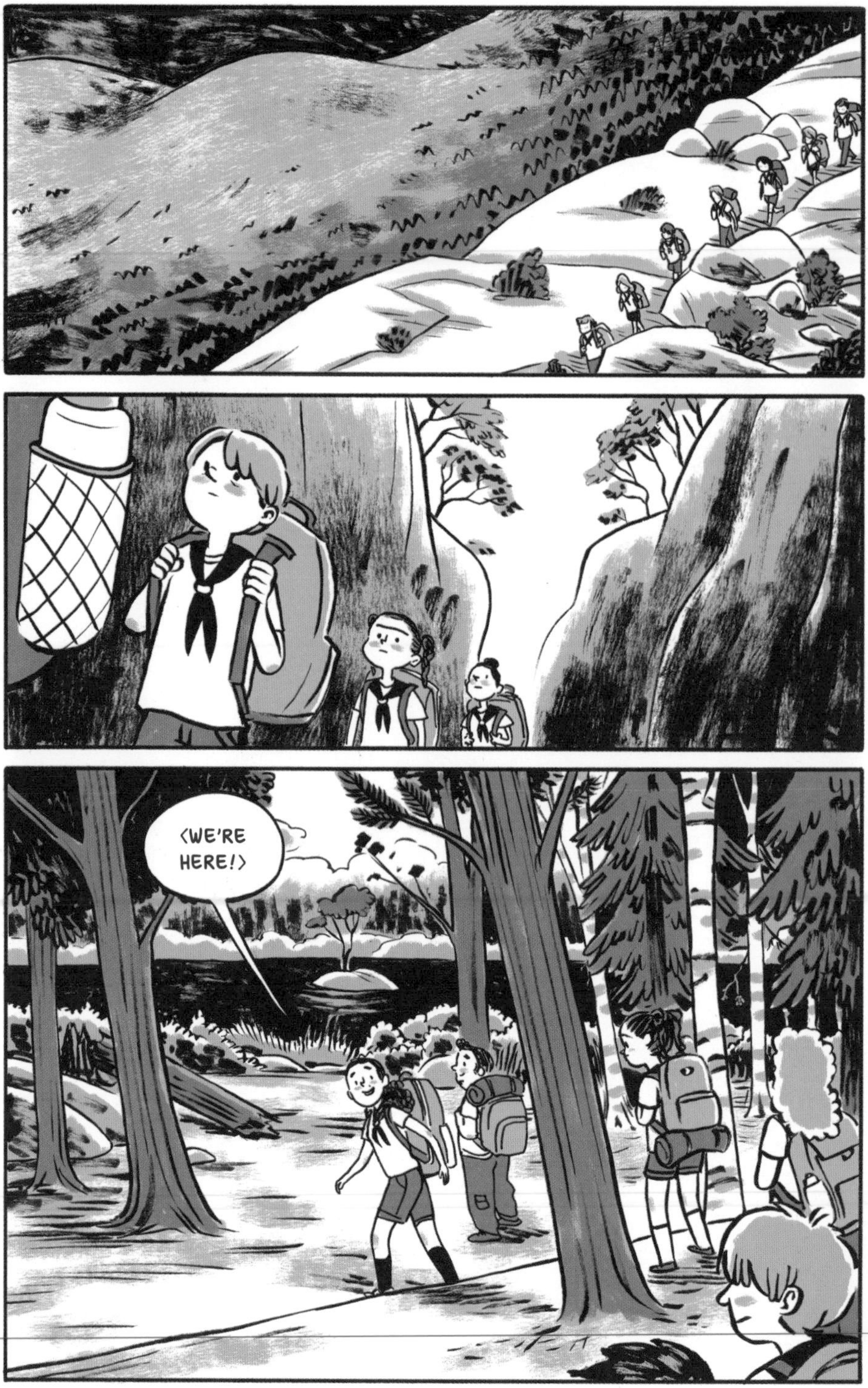
⟨WE'RE HERE!⟩

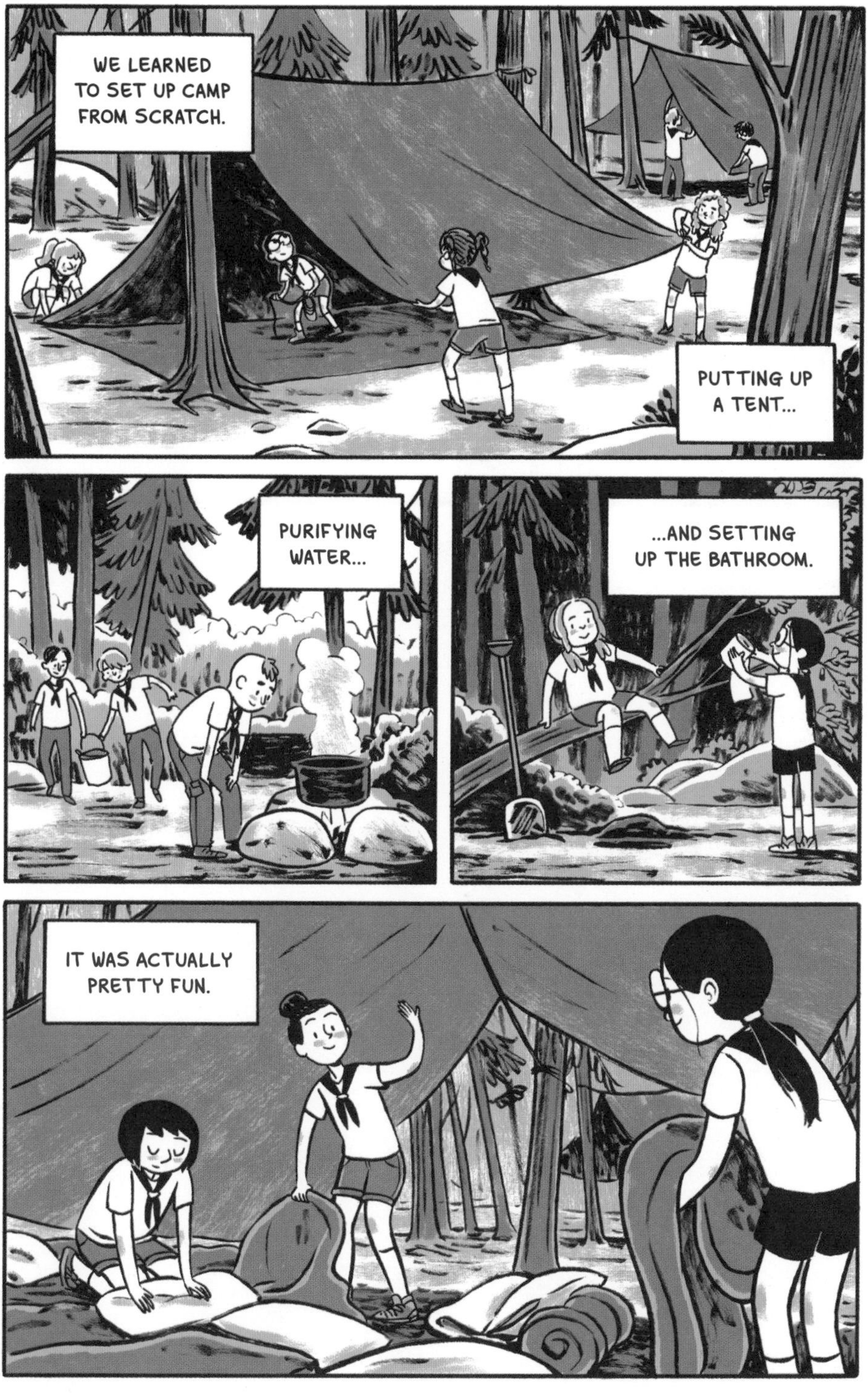
WE LEARNED TO SET UP CAMP FROM SCRATCH.
PUTTING UP A TENT...
PURIFYING WATER...
...AND SETTING UP THE BATHROOM.
IT WAS ACTUALLY PRETTY FUN.

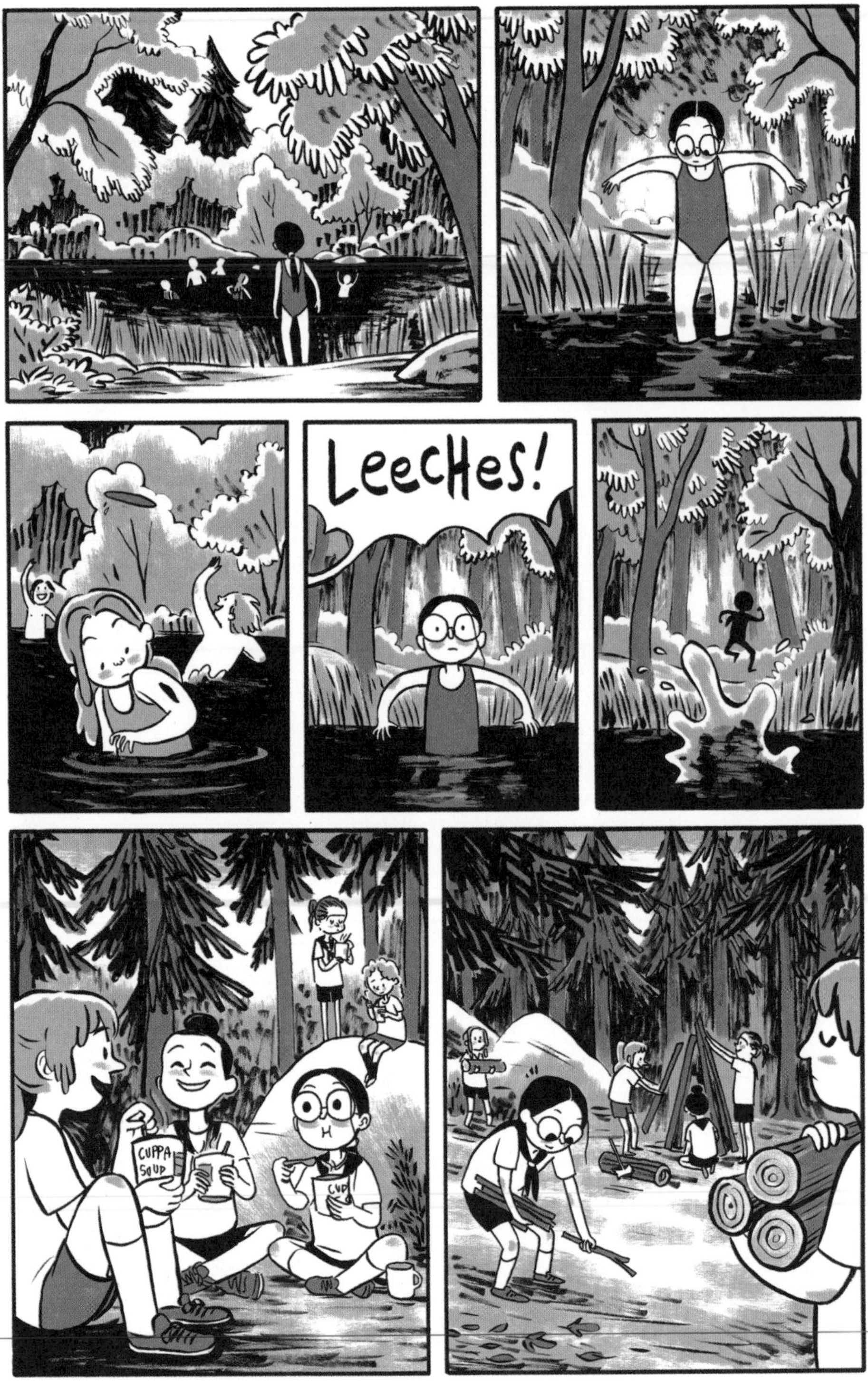
LEECHES!
CUPPA SOUP
CUP

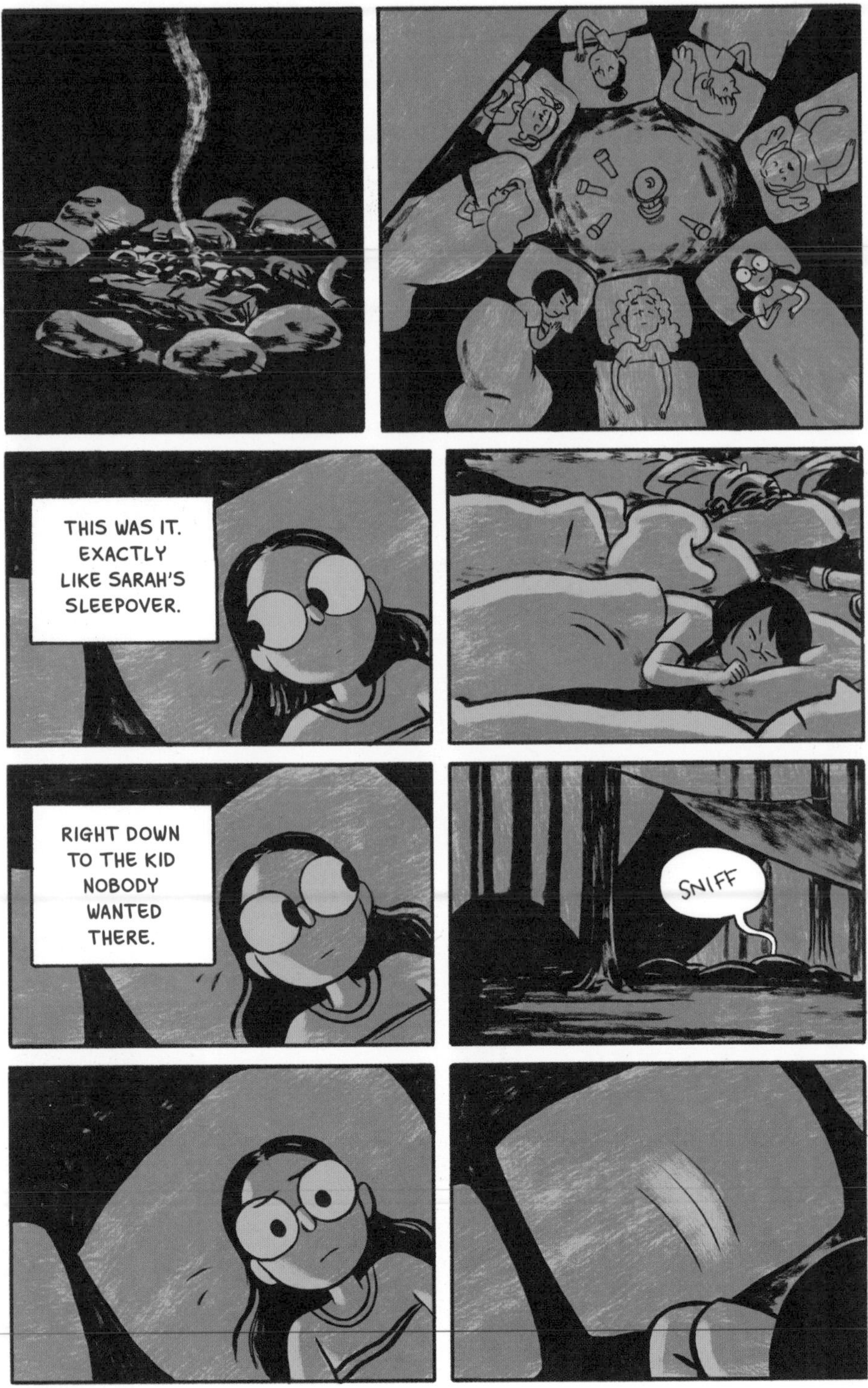
THIS WAS IT. EXACTLY LIKE SARAH'S SLEEPOVER.
RIGHT DOWN TO THE KID NOBODY WANTED THERE.
SNIFF

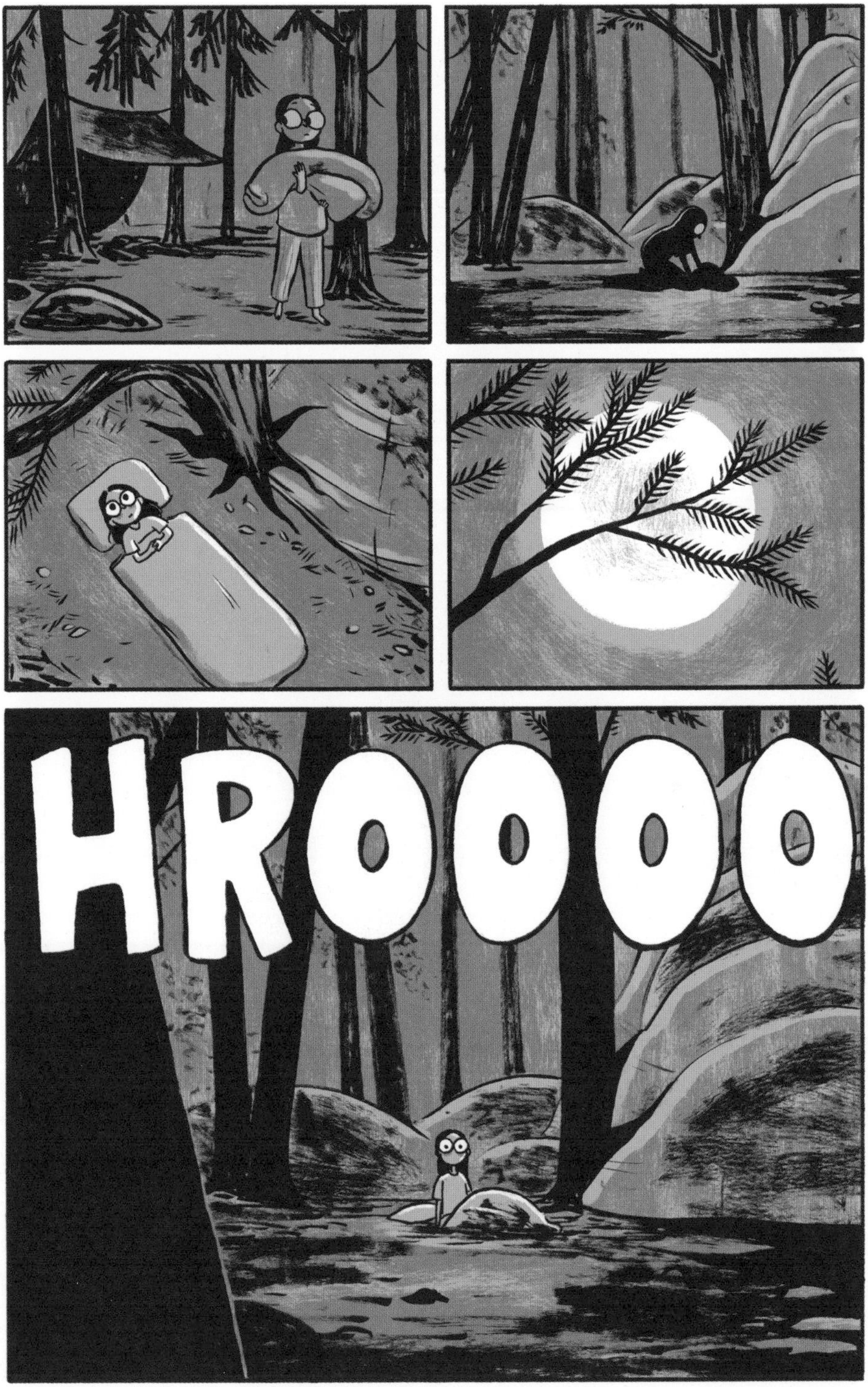
HROOOO

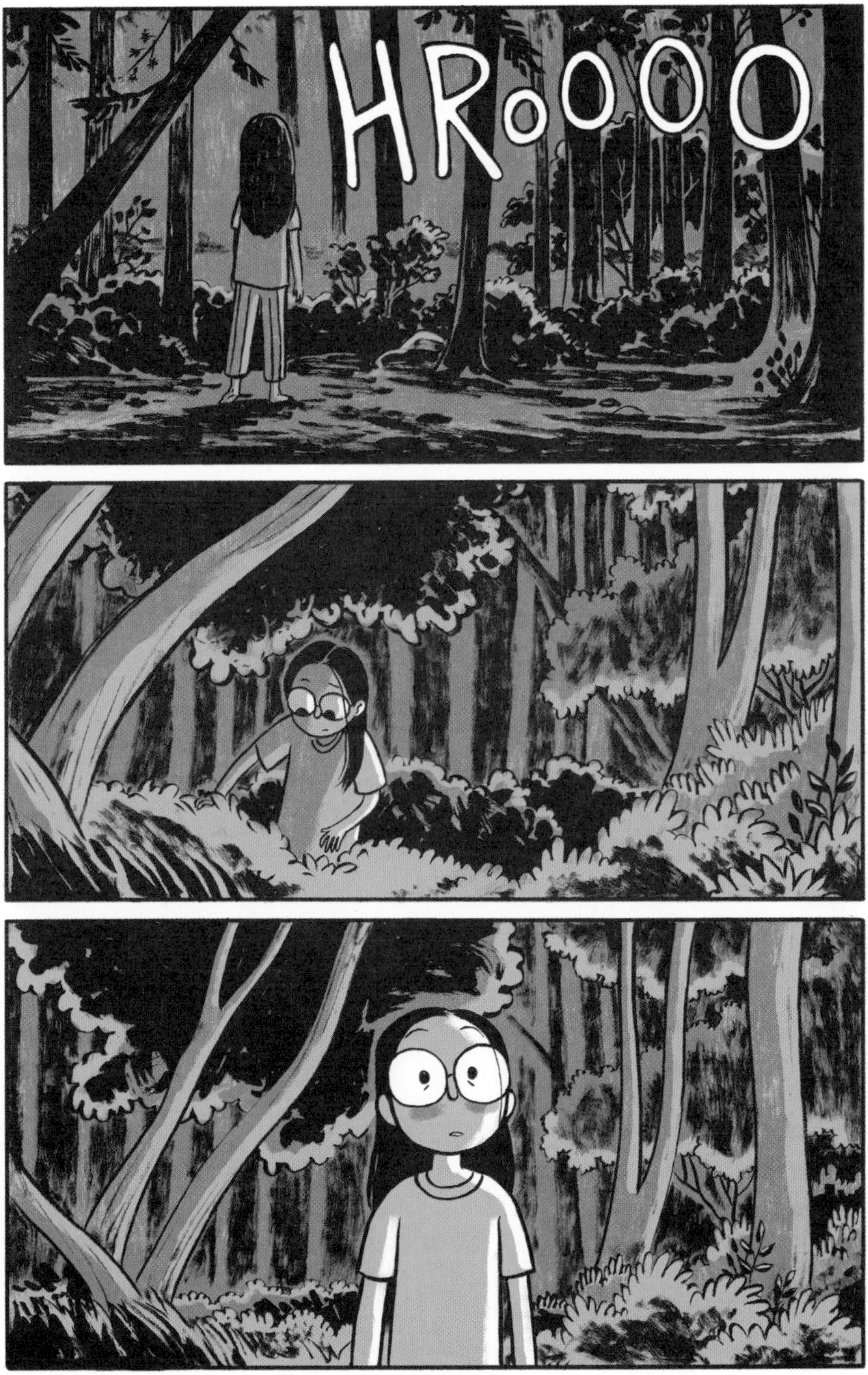
HROOOO

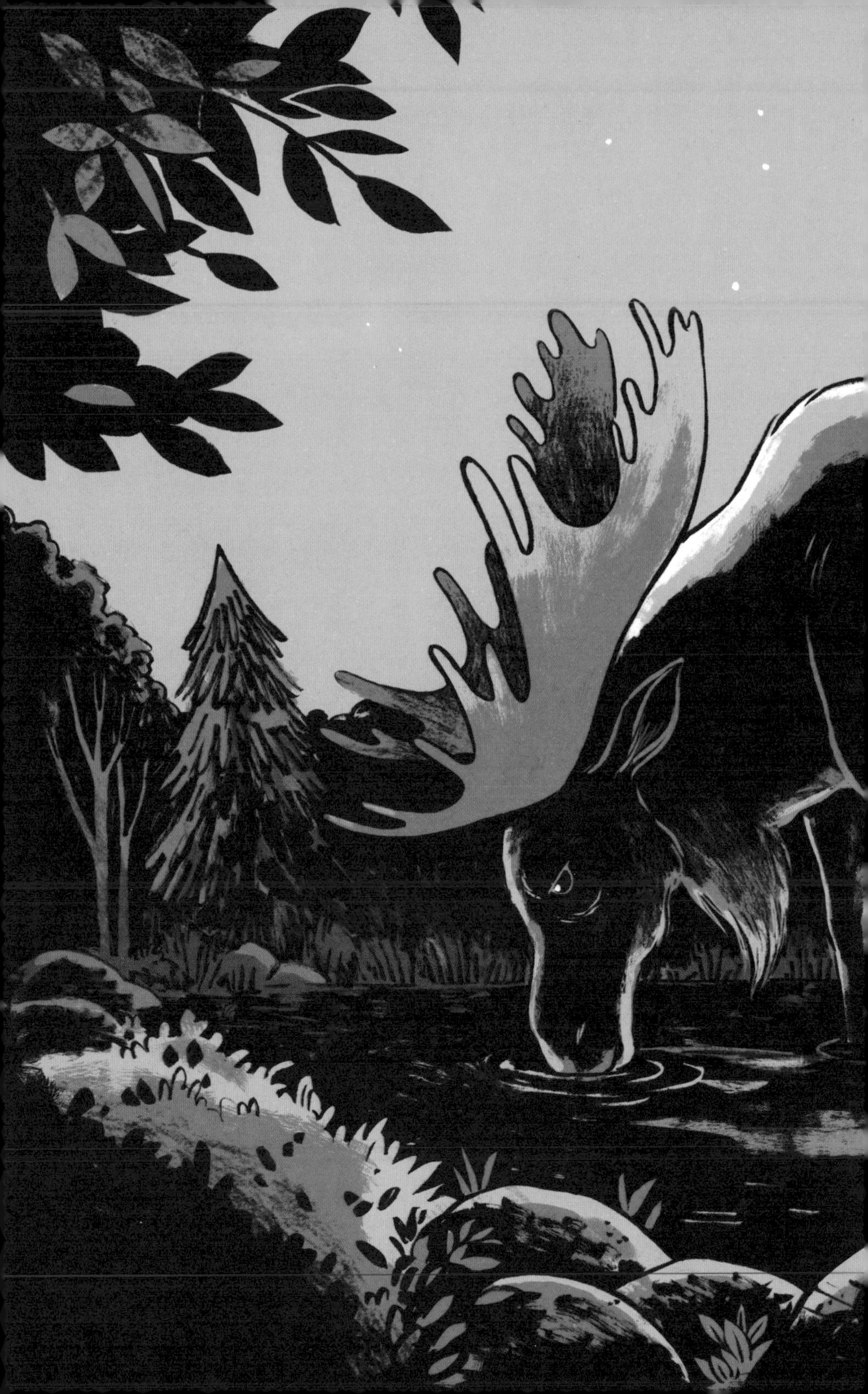

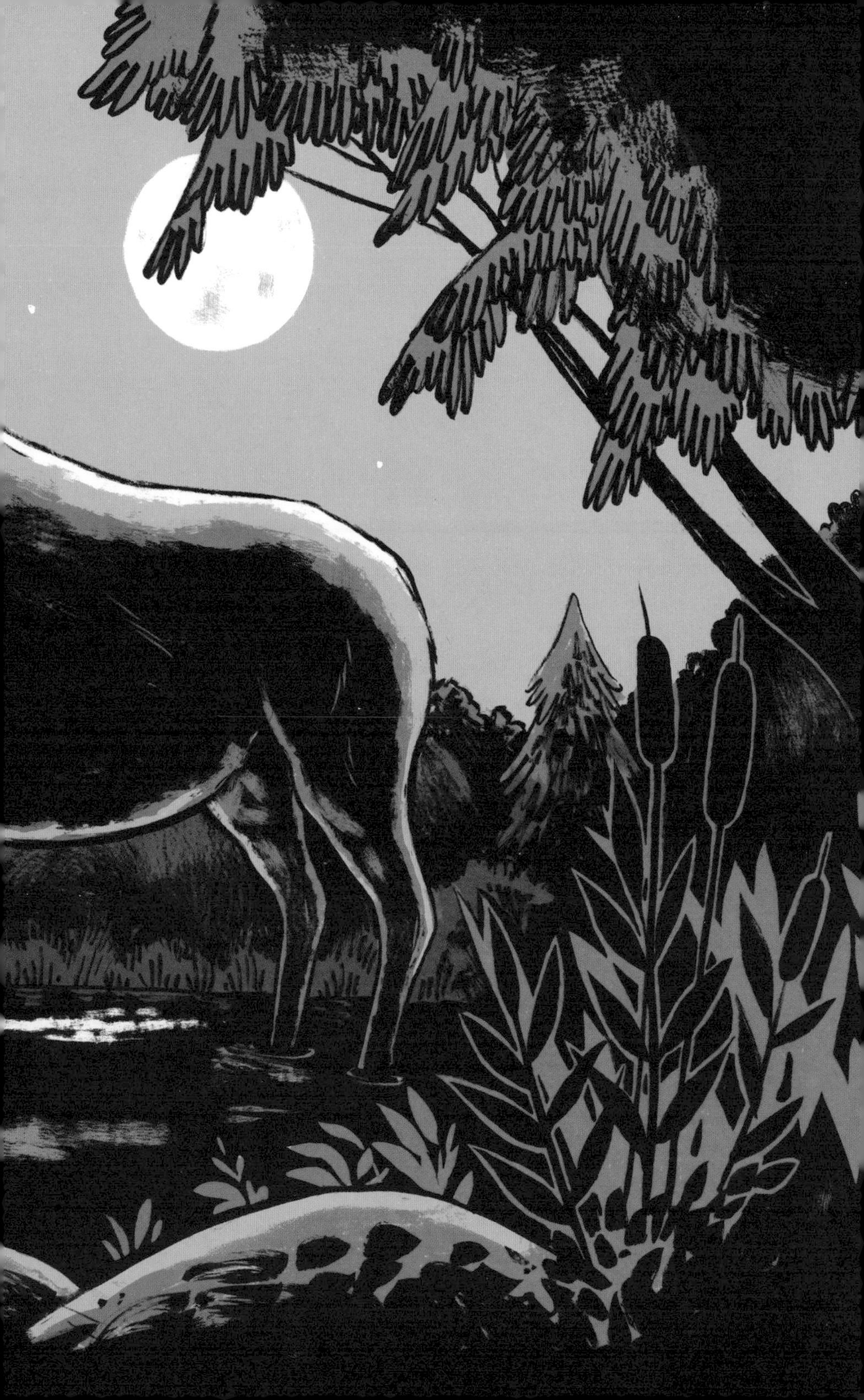

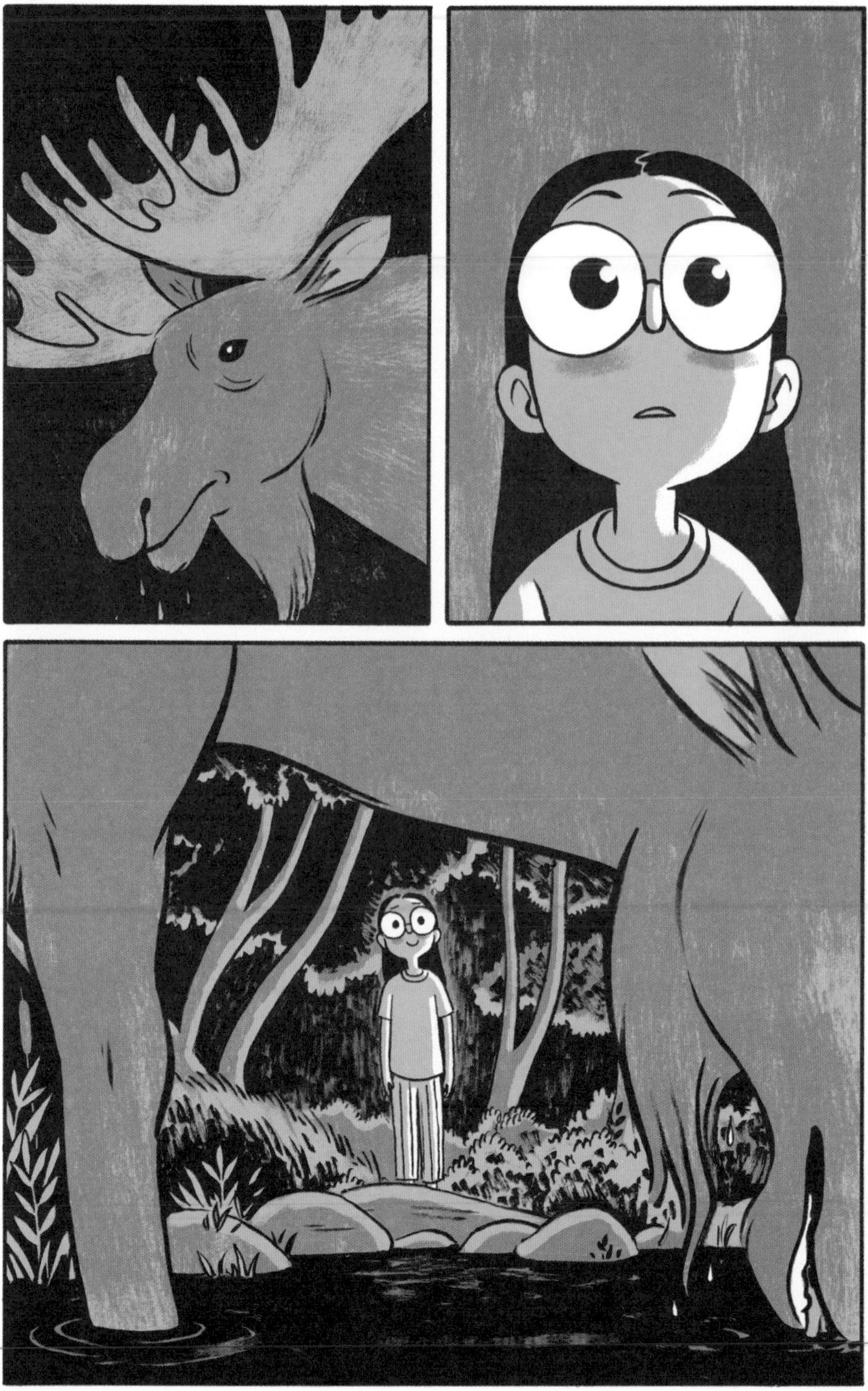

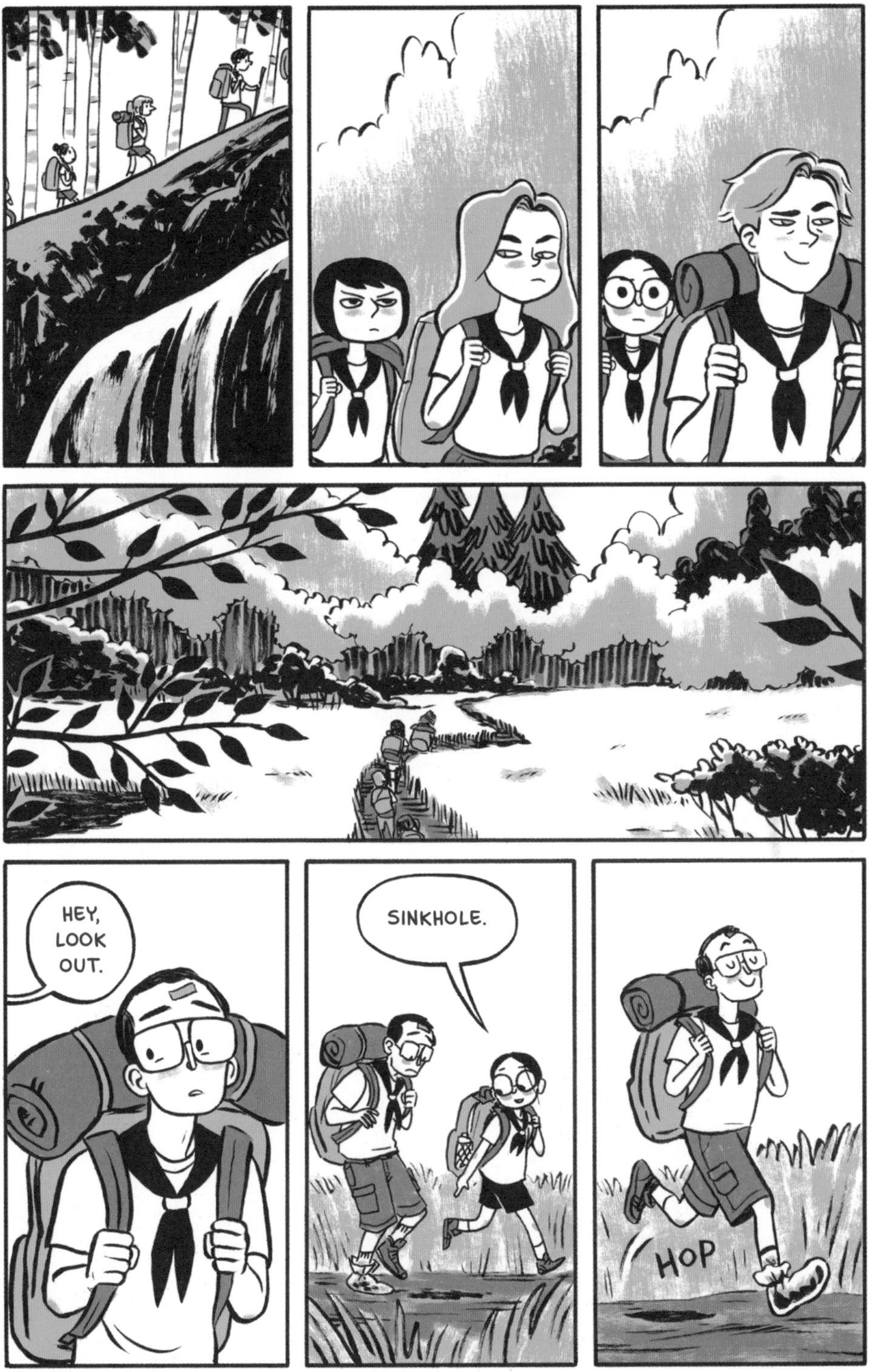
HEY, LOOK OUT.
SINKHOLE.
HOP

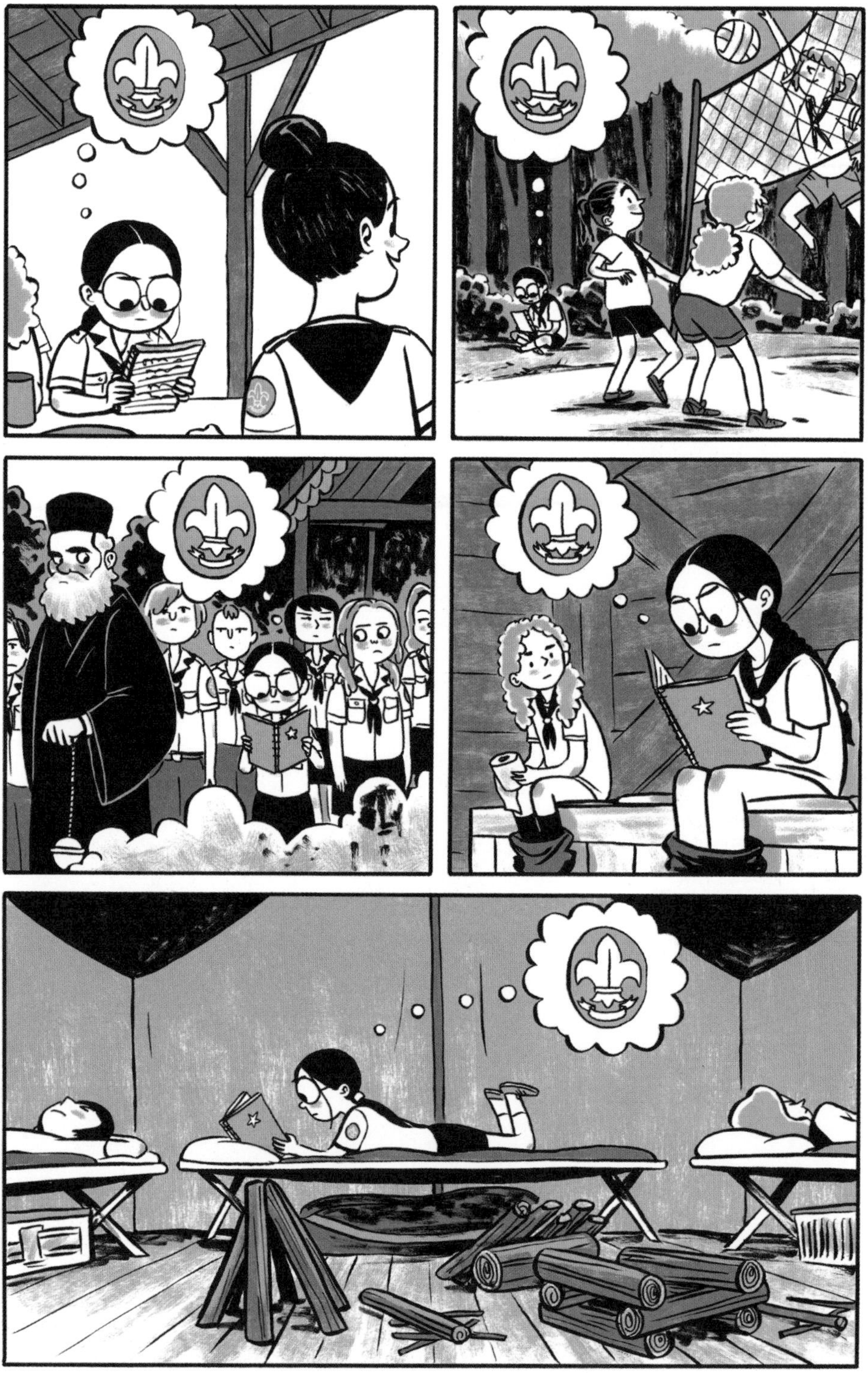

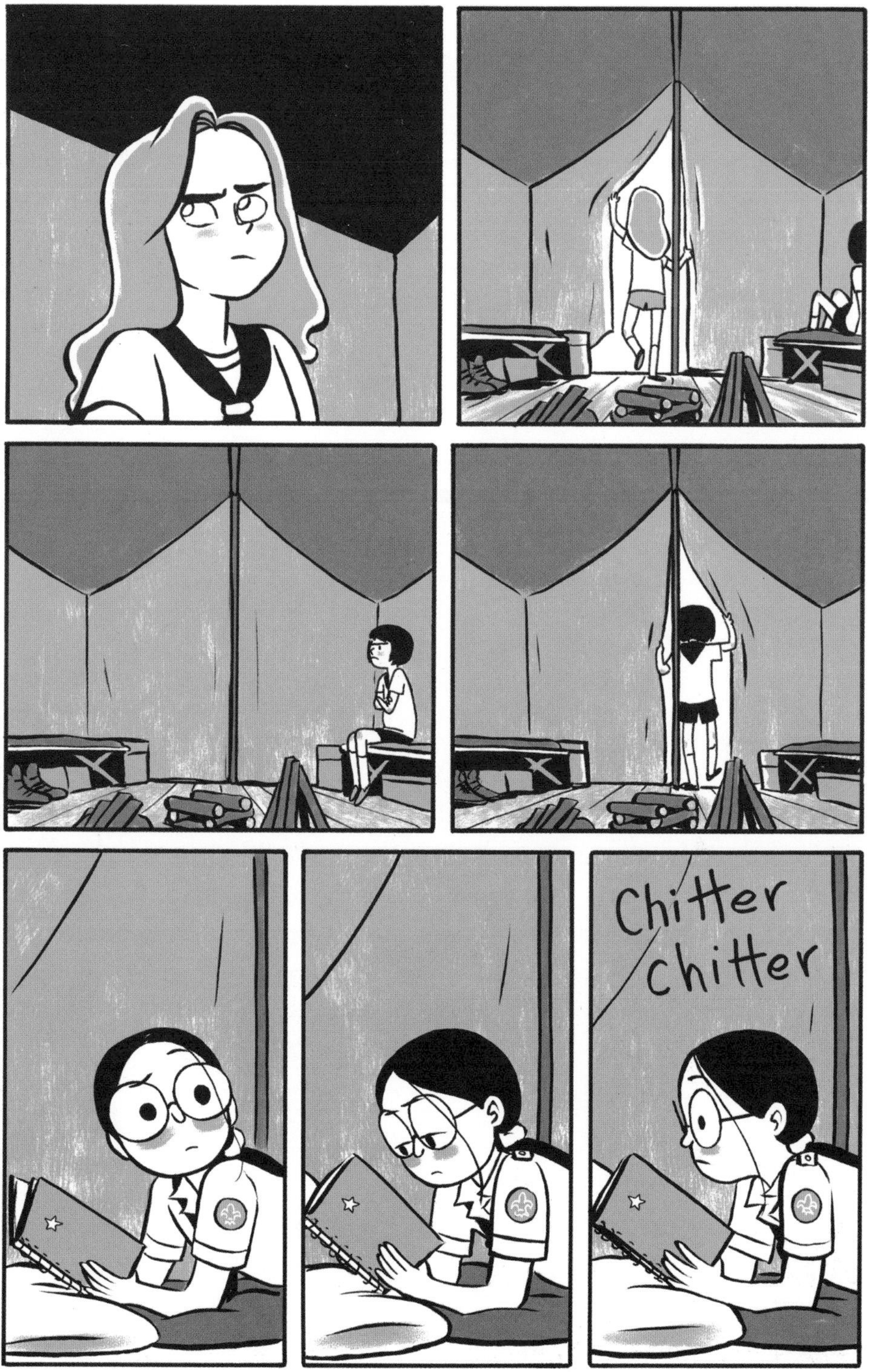
Chitter
chitter

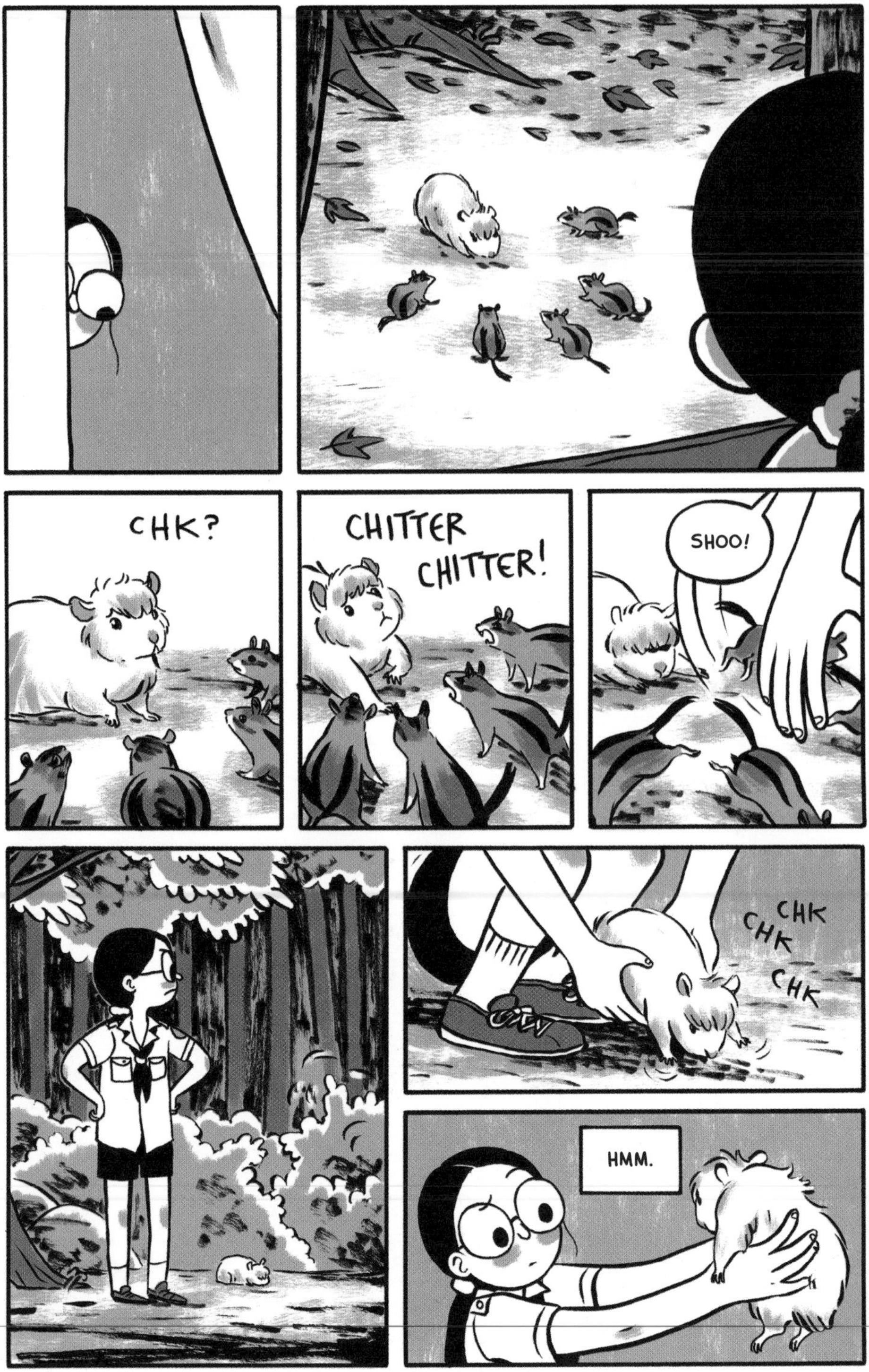
CHK?
CHITTER
CHITTER!
SHOO!
CHK
CHK
CHK
HMM.

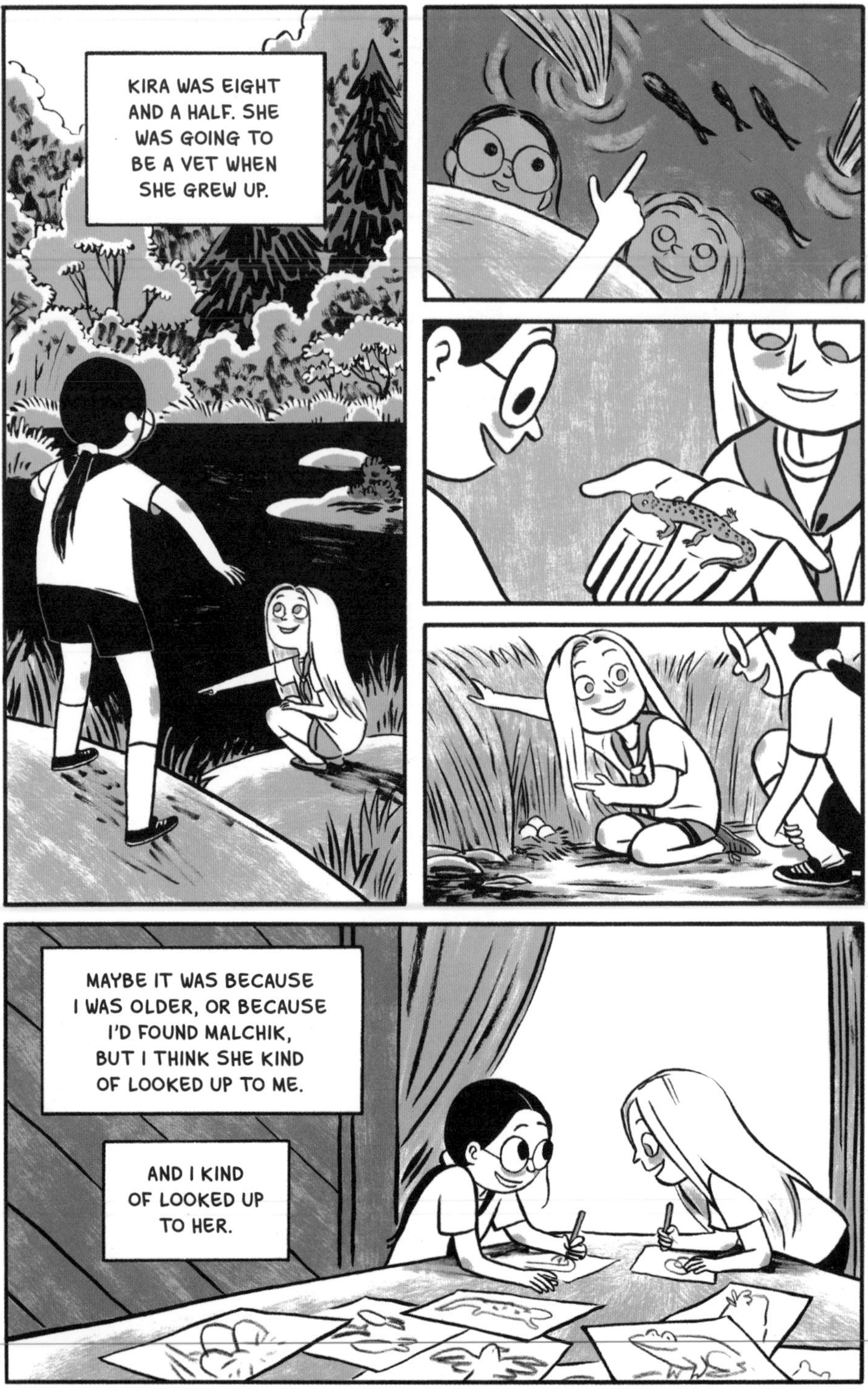
KIRA WAS EIGHT AND A HALF. SHE WAS GOING TO BE A VET WHEN SHE GREW UP.
MAYBE IT WAS BECAUSE I WAS OLDER, OR BECAUSE I'D FOUND MALCHIK, BUT I THINK SHE KIND OF LOOKED UP TO ME.
AND I KIND OF LOOKED UP TO HER.

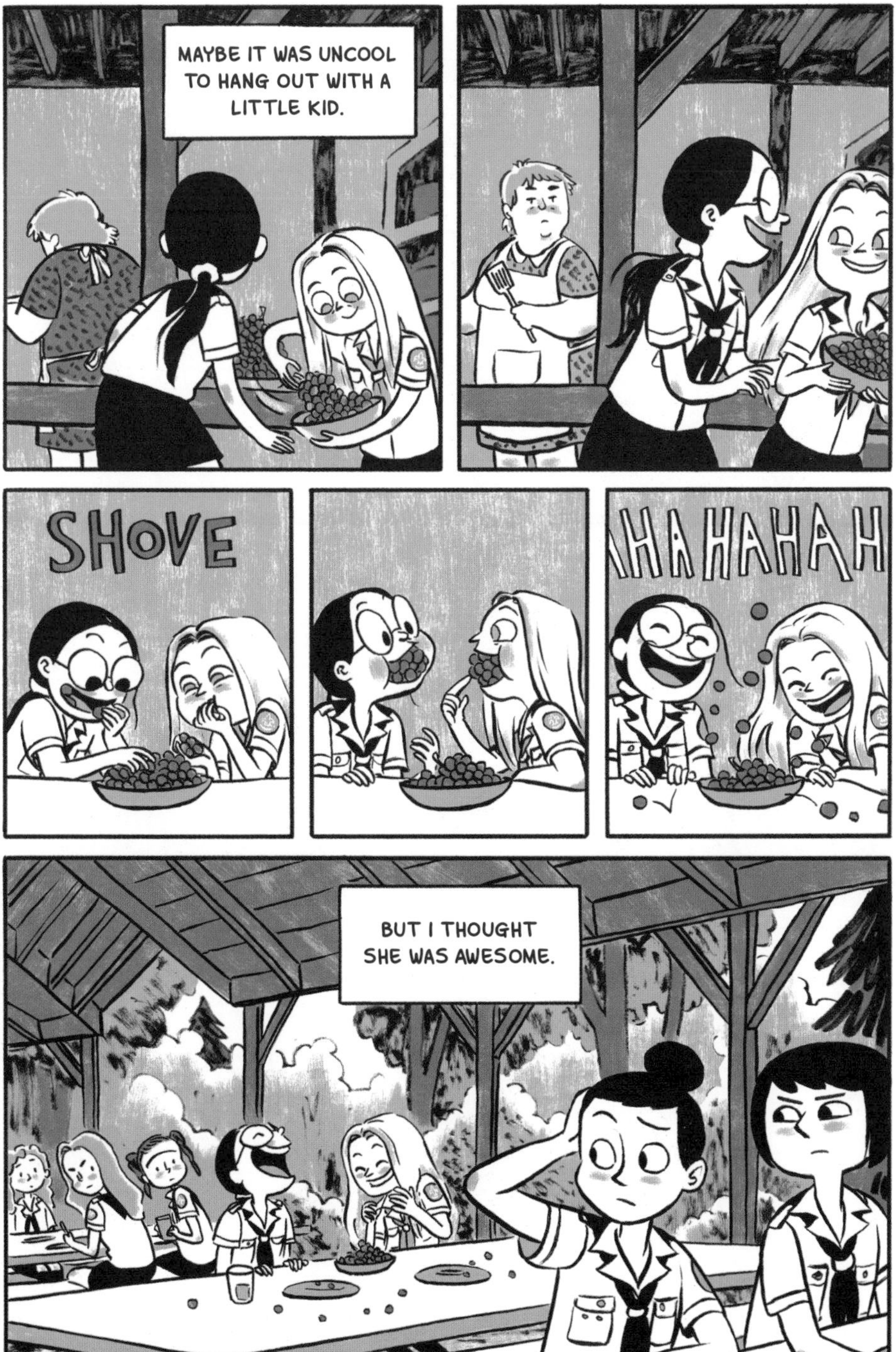
MAYBE IT WAS UNCOOL TO HANG OUT WITH A LITTLE KID.
SHOVE
HAHAHAH
BUT I THOUGHT SHE WAS AWESOME.

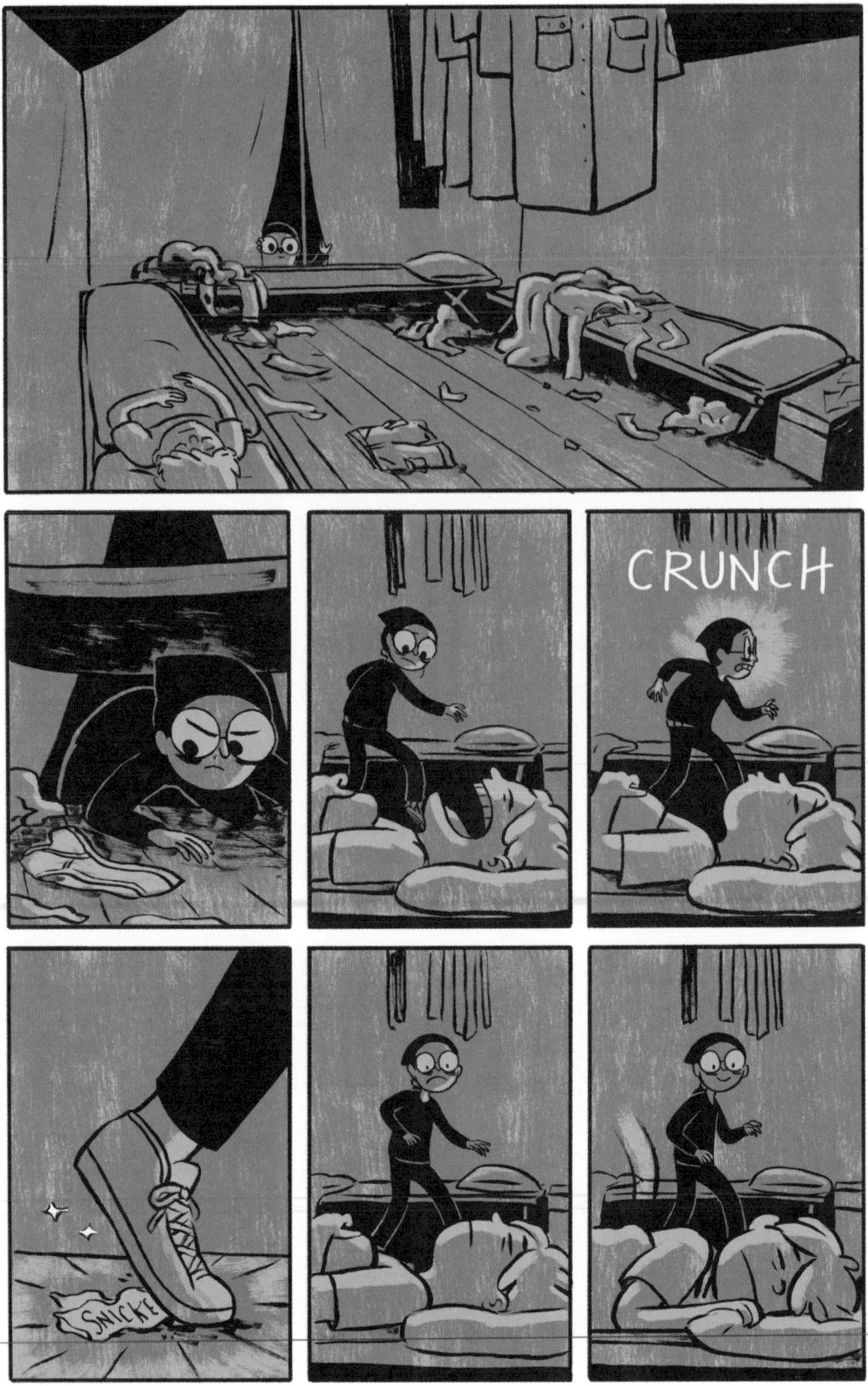
CRUNCH
SNICKE

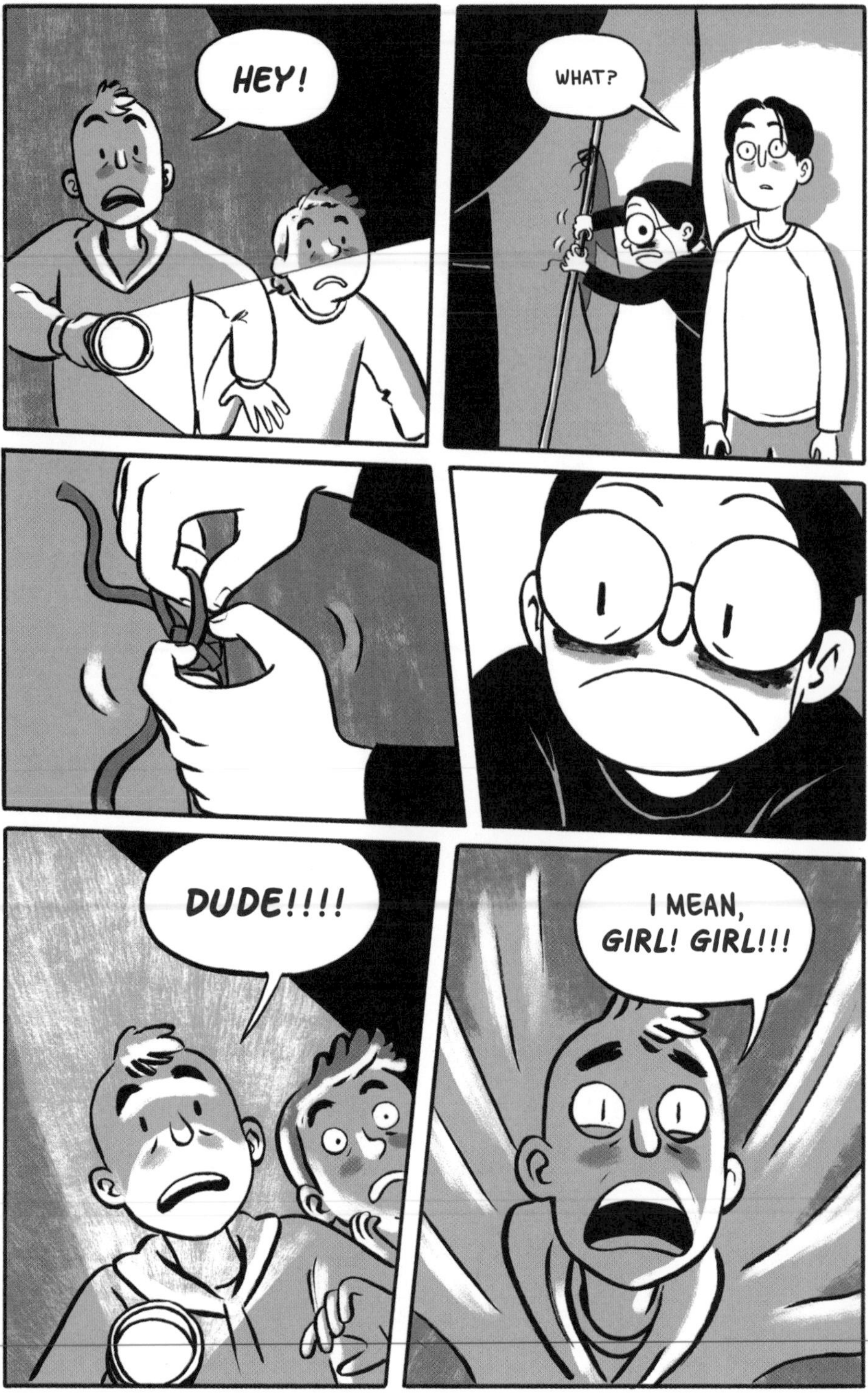
HEY!
WHAT?
DUDE!!!!
I MEAN,
GIRL! GIRL!!!

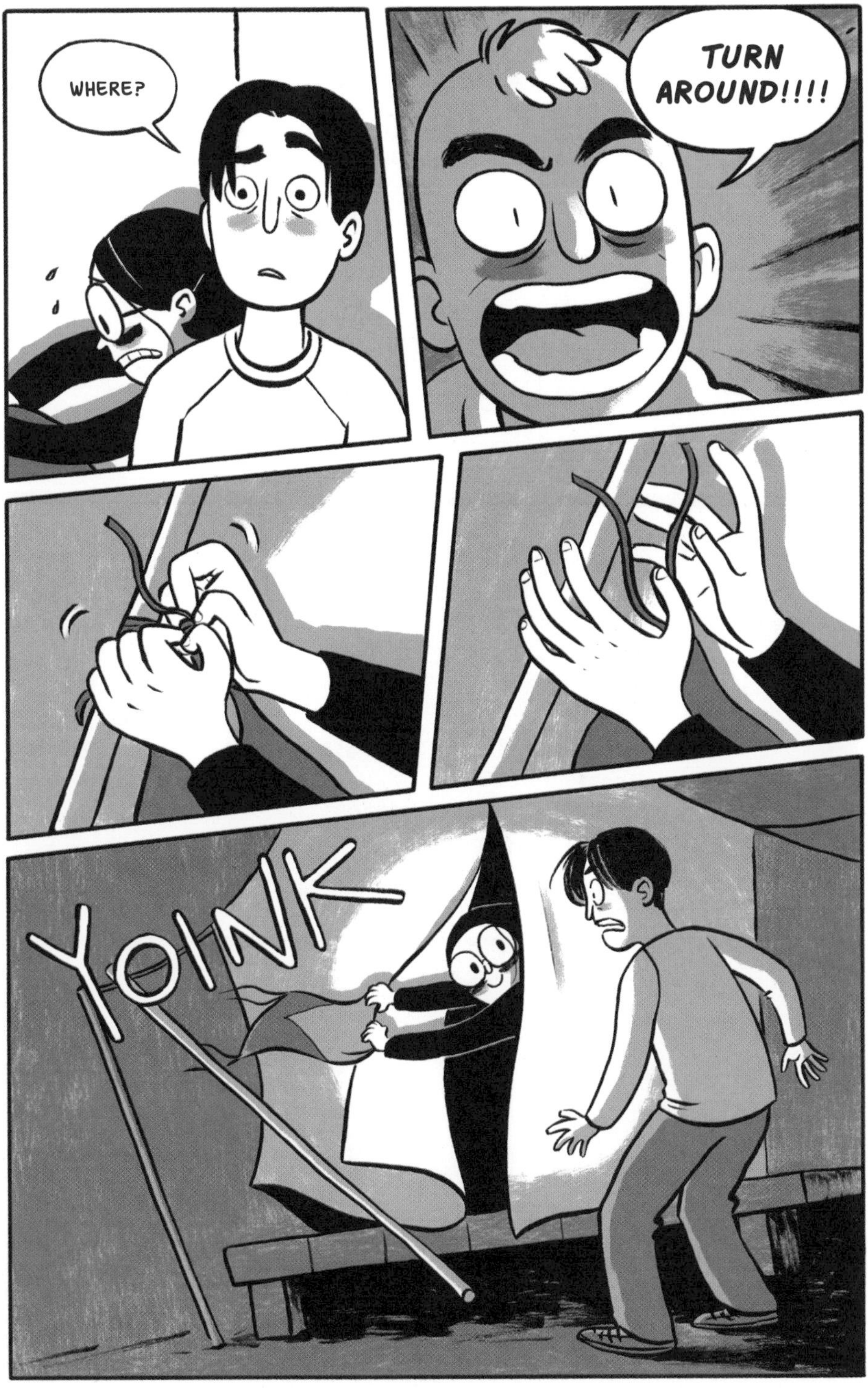
WHERE?
TURN AROUND!!!!
YOINK

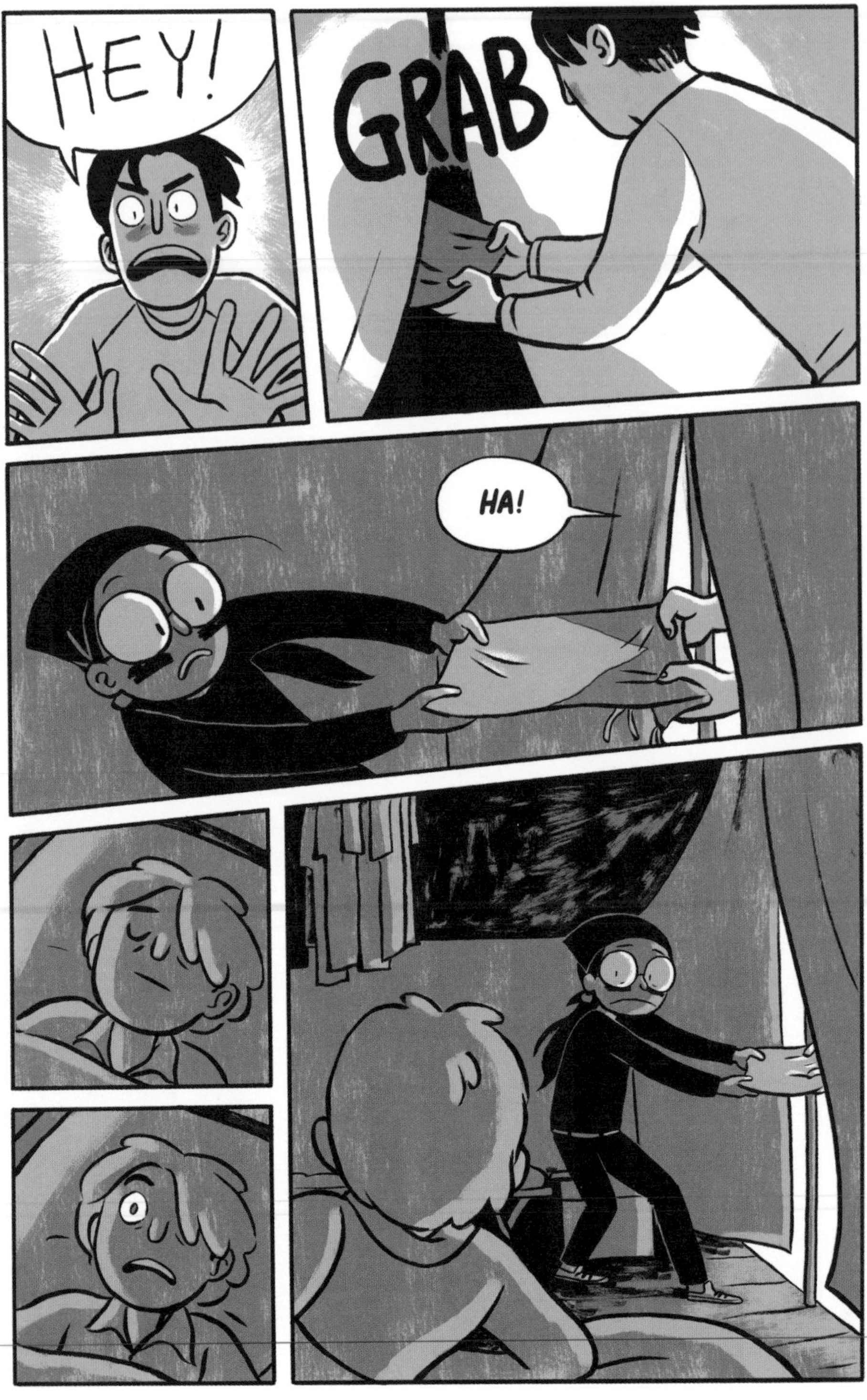
HEY!
GRAB
HA!

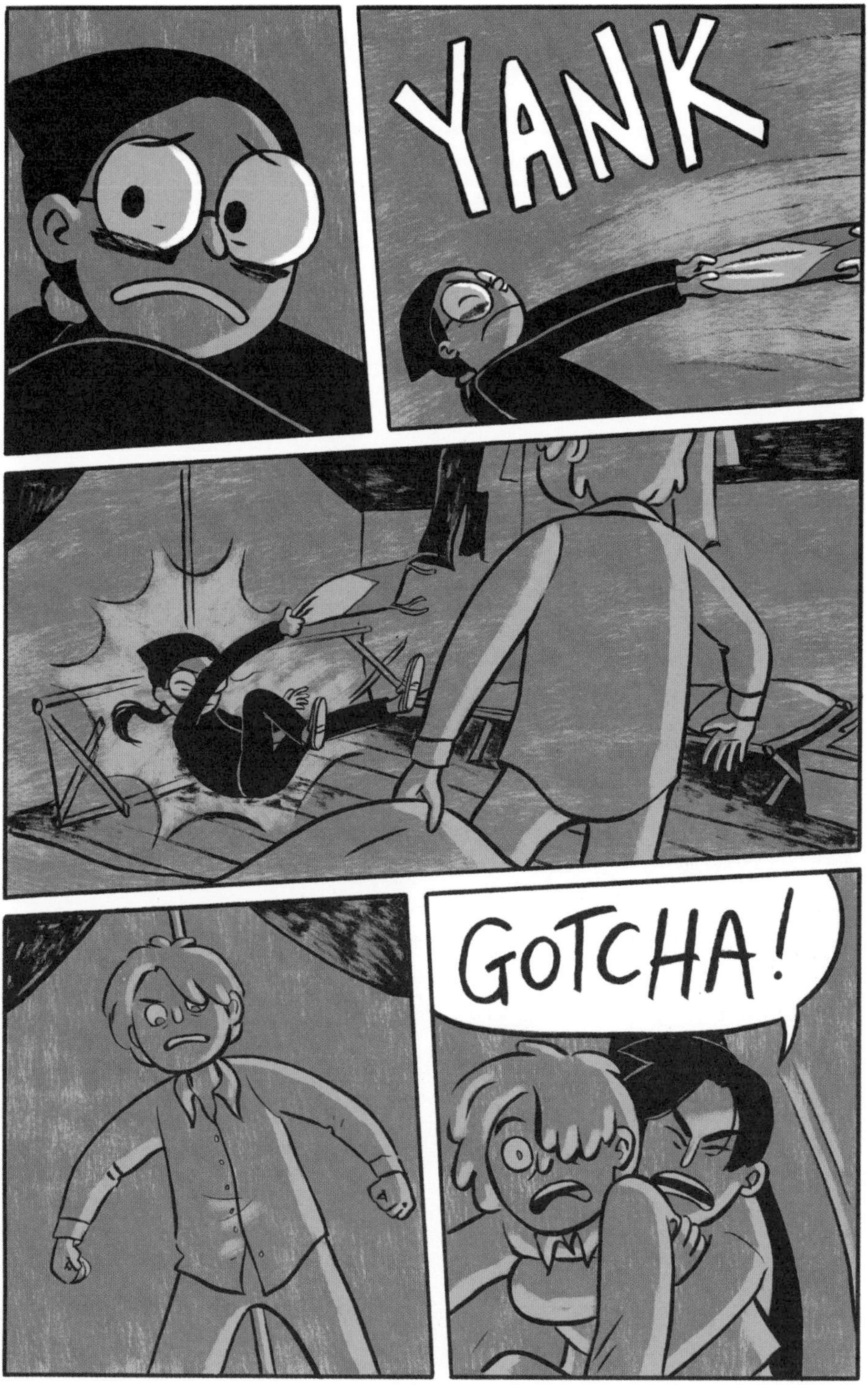
YANK
GOTCHA!

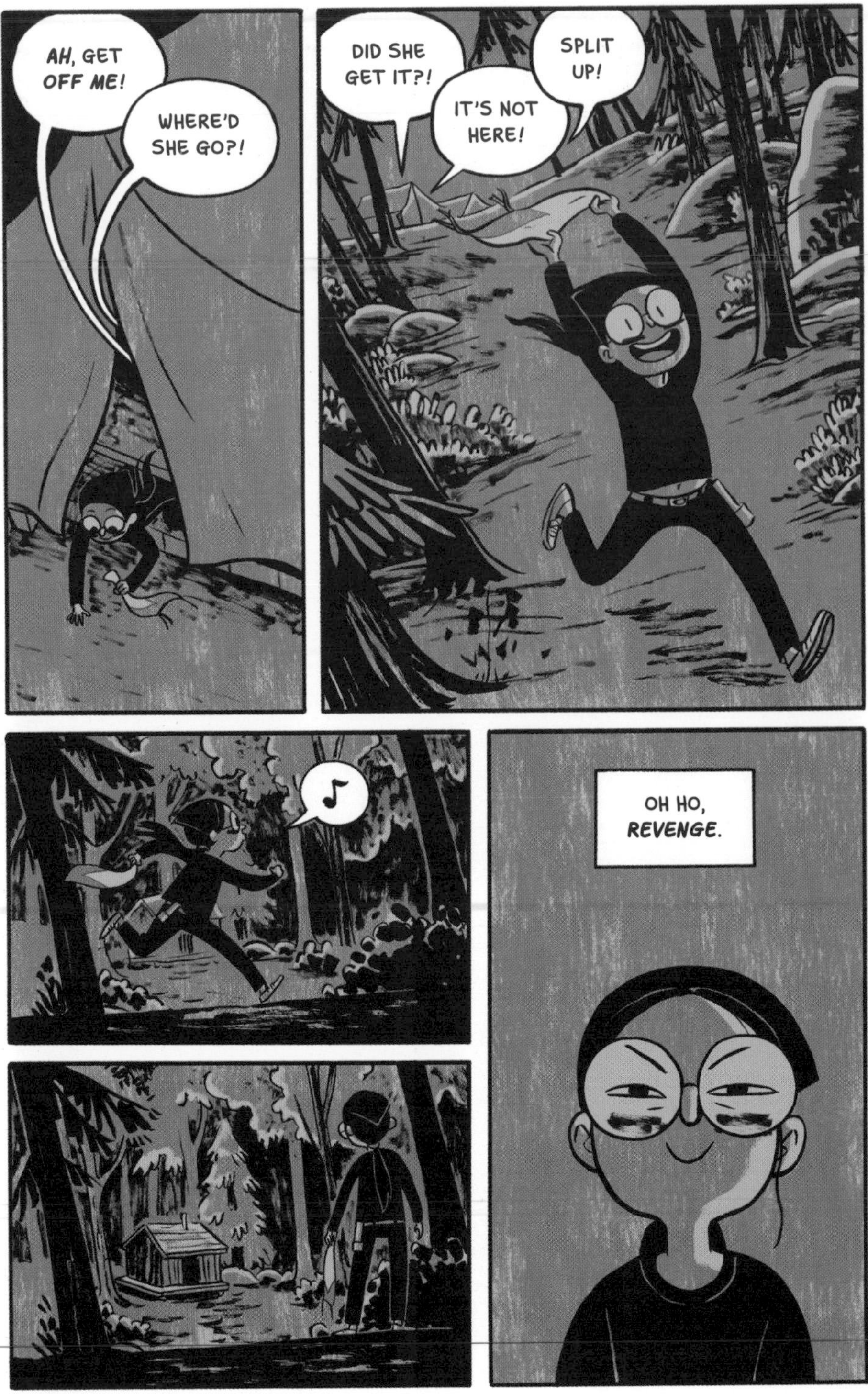
AH, GET OFF ME!
WHERE'D SHE GO?!
DID SHE GET IT?!
IT'S NOT HERE!
SPLIT UP!
♪
OH HO, REVENGE.

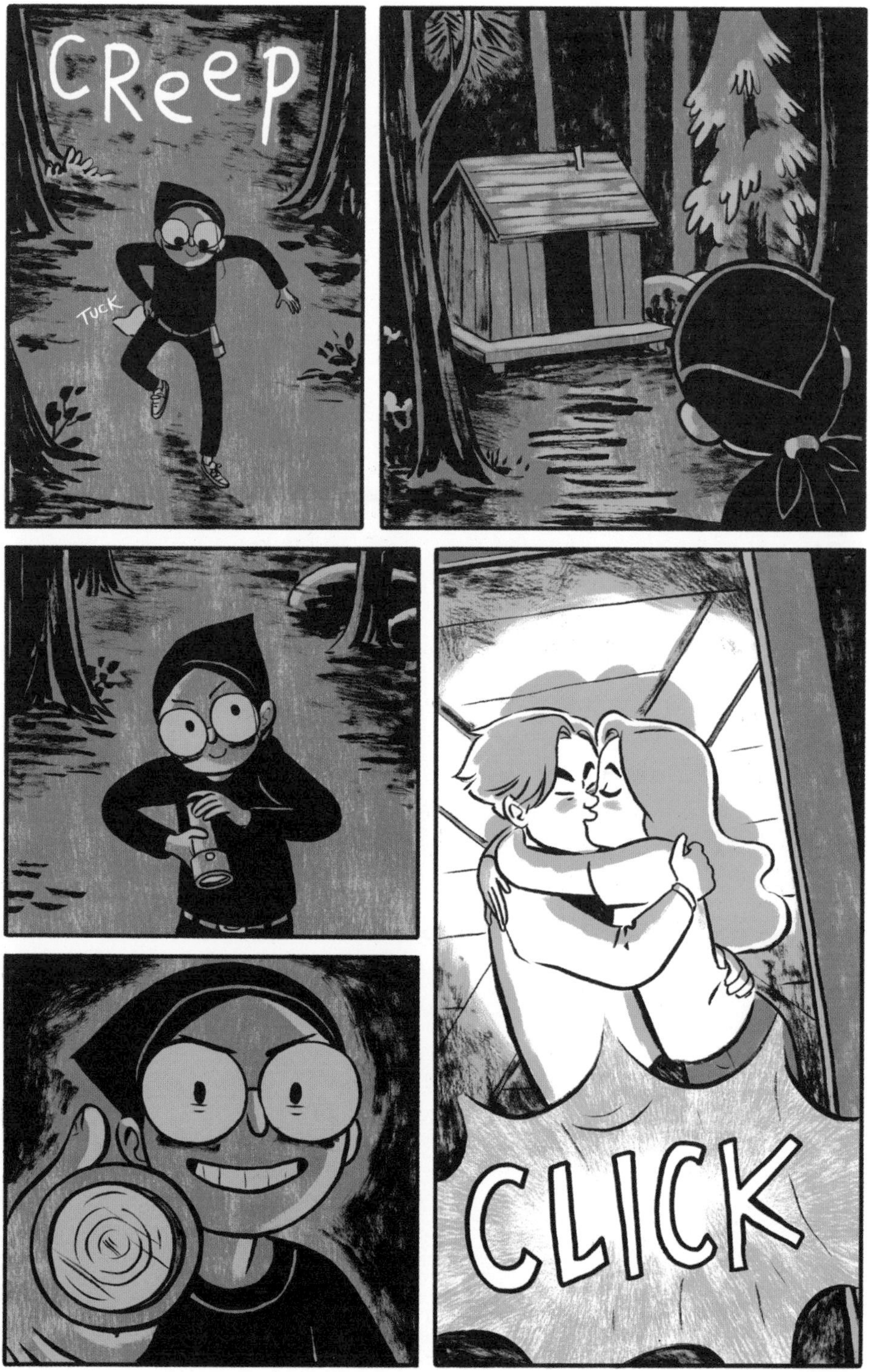
CREEP
TUCK
CLICK

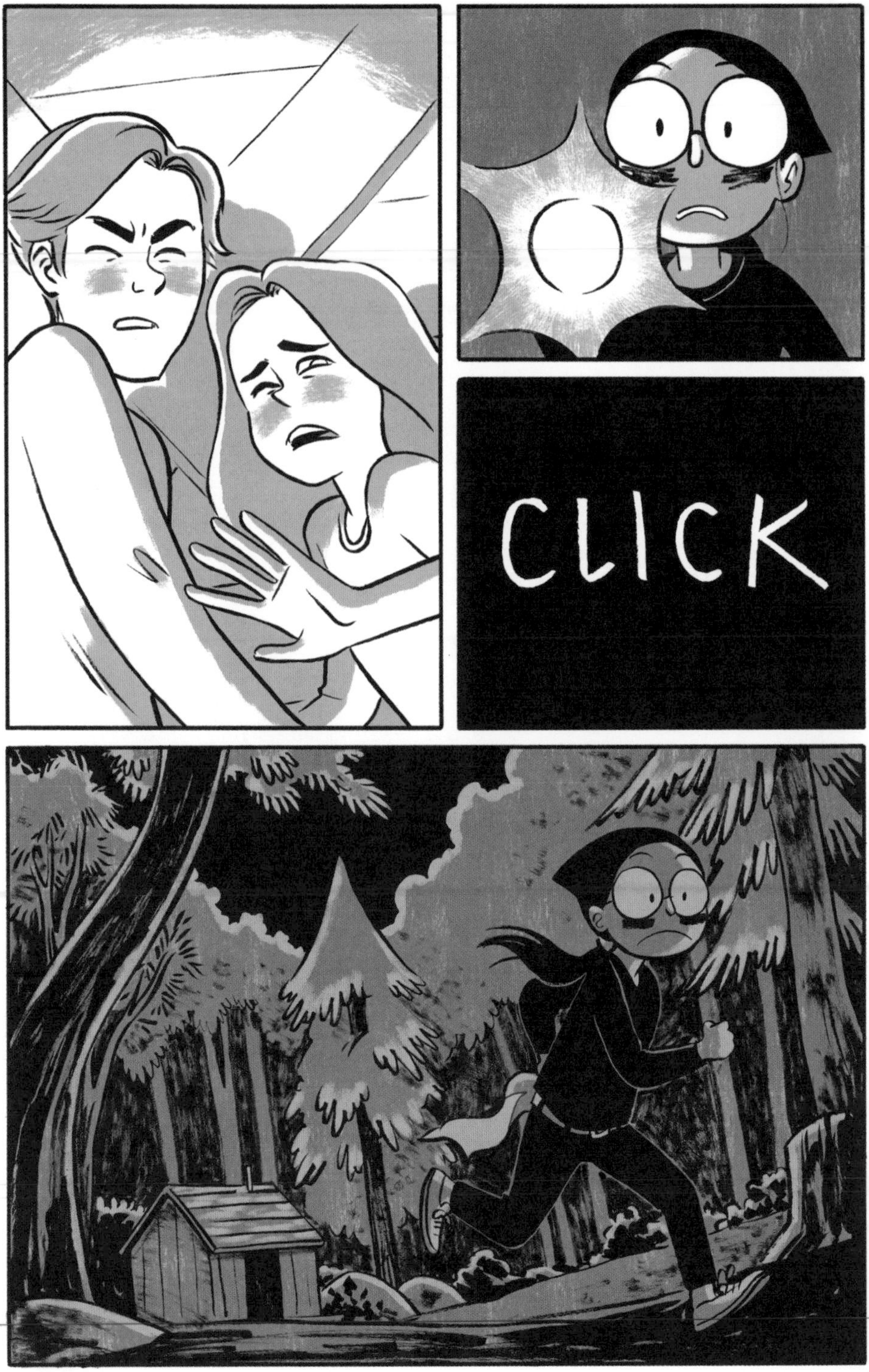
CLICK

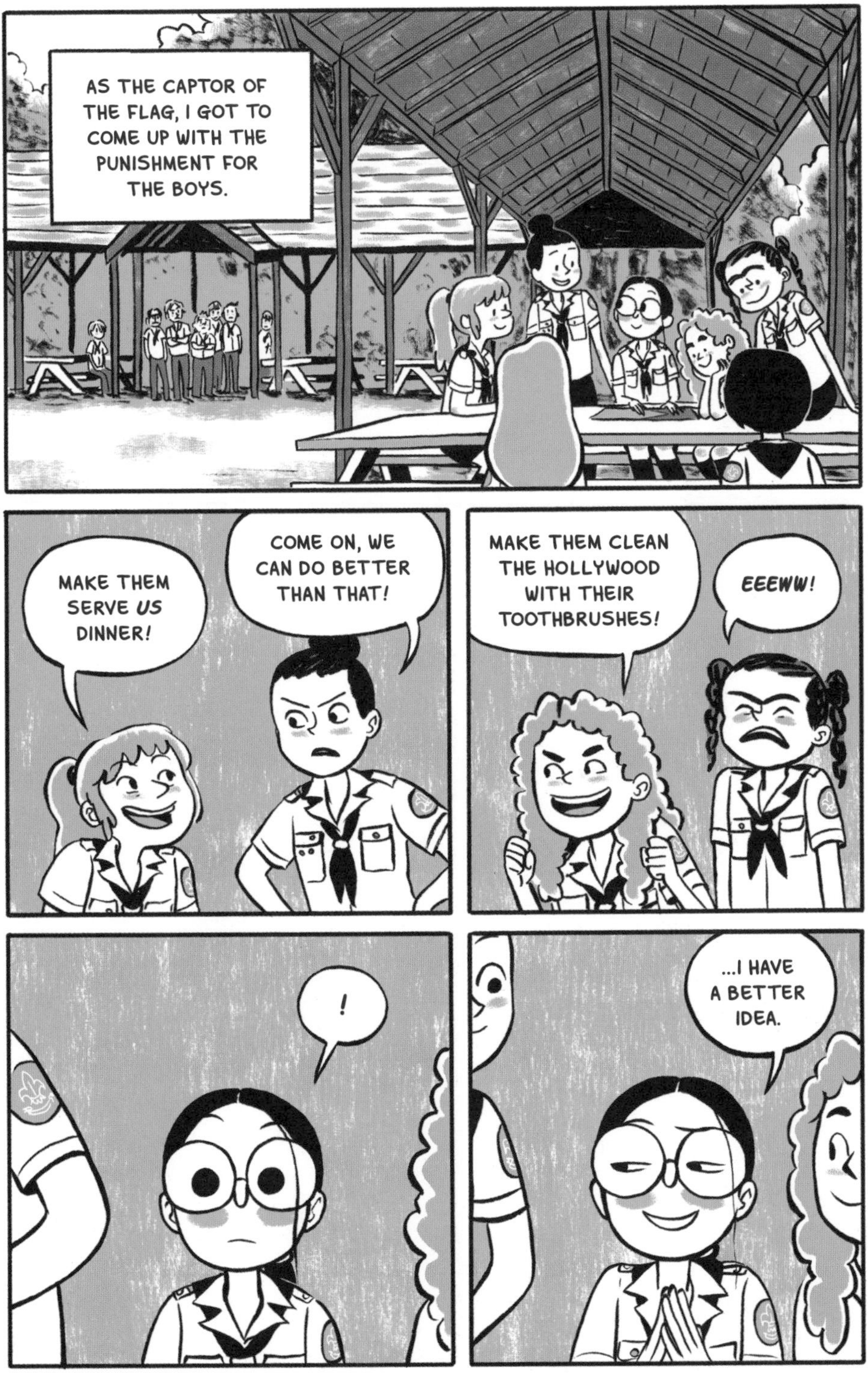
AS THE CAPTOR OF THE FLAG, I GOT TO COME UP WITH THE PUNISHMENT FOR THE BOYS.
MAKE THEM SERVE *US* DINNER!
COME ON, WE CAN DO BETTER THAN THAT!
MAKE THEM CLEAN THE HOLLYWOOD WITH THEIR TOOTHBRUSHES!
EEEWW!
!
...I HAVE A BETTER IDEA.

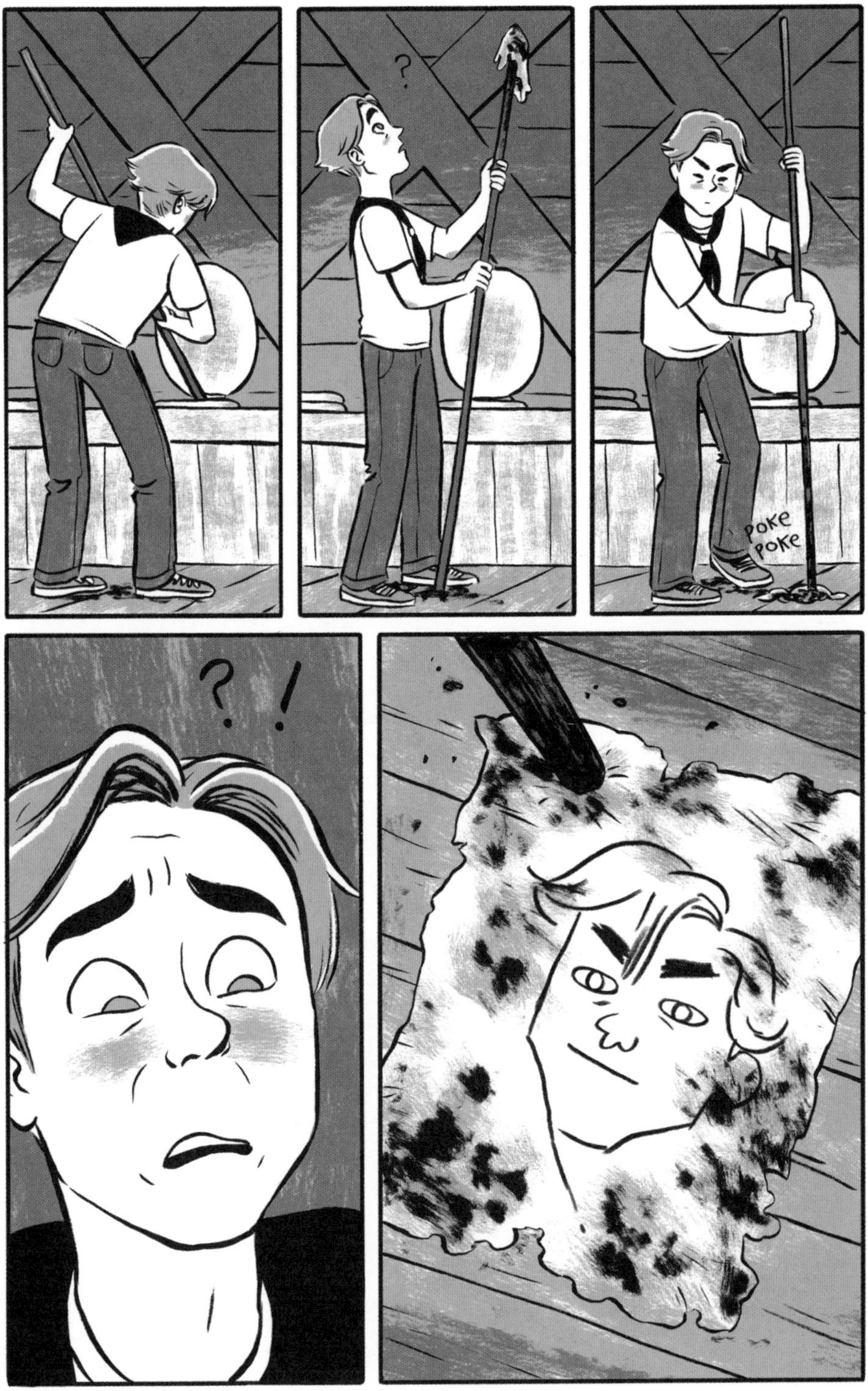
?
POKE
POKE
?!

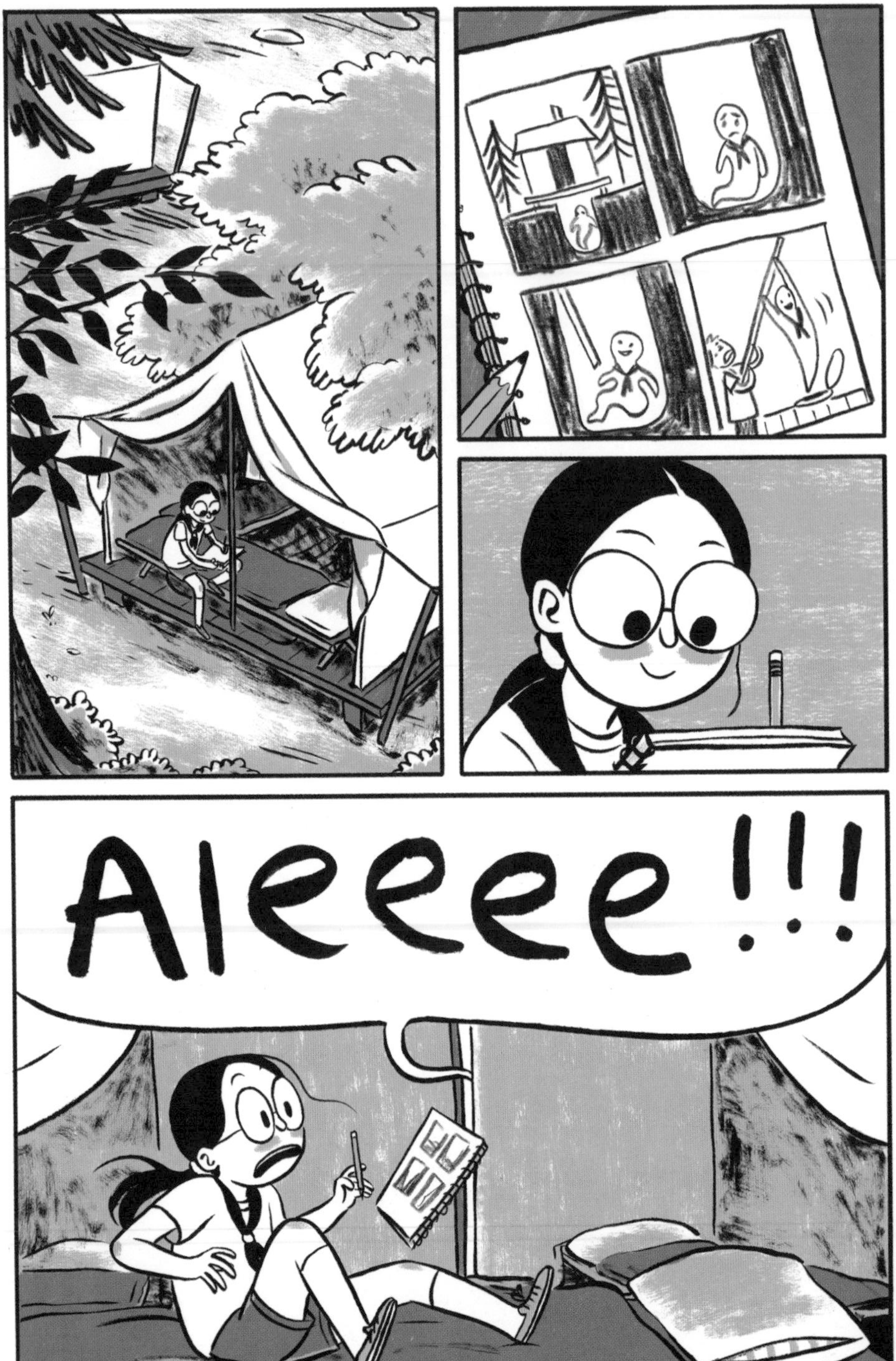
AIeeee!!!

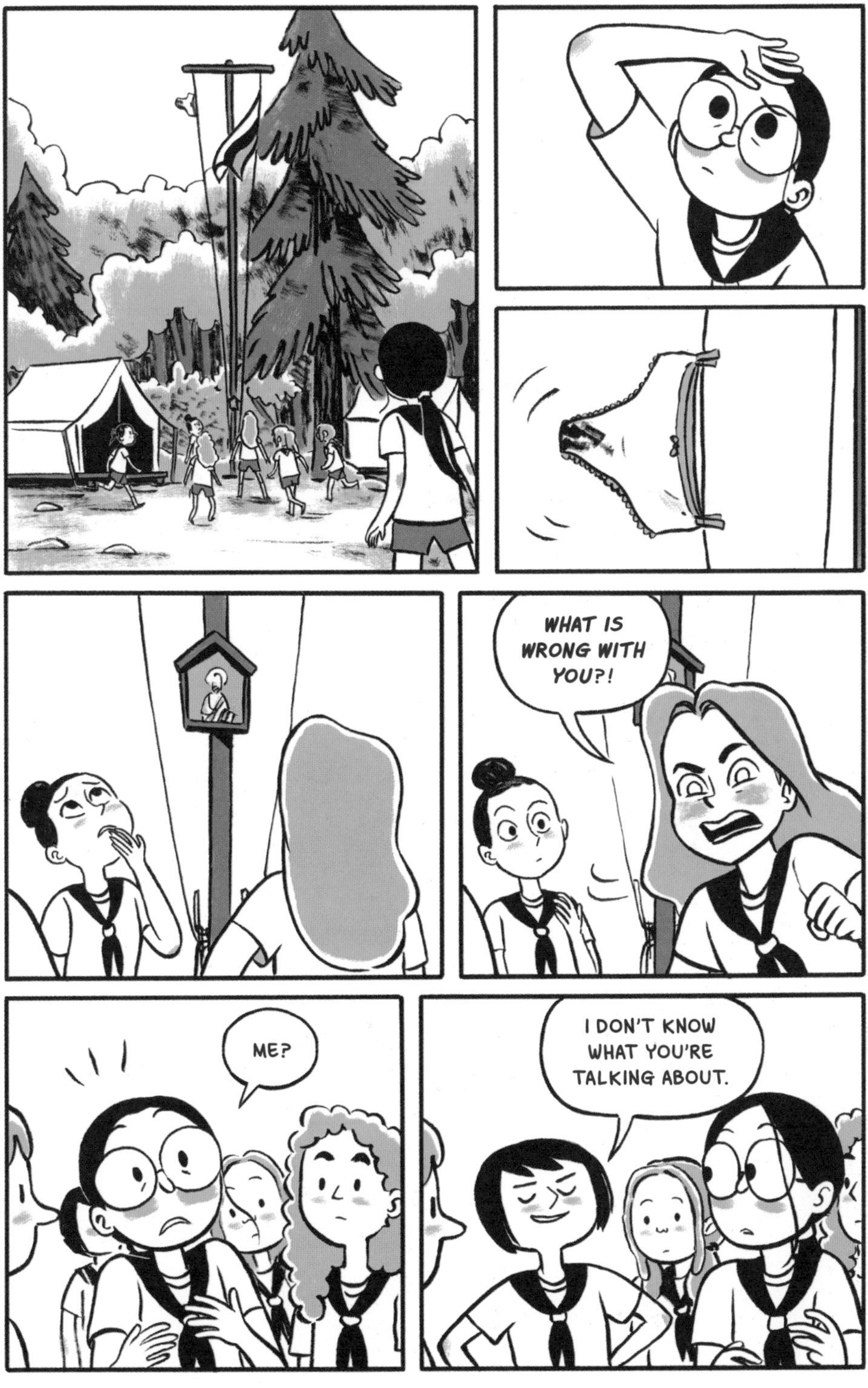
WHAT IS WRONG WITH YOU?!
ME?
I DON'T KNOW WHAT YOU'RE TALKING ABOUT.

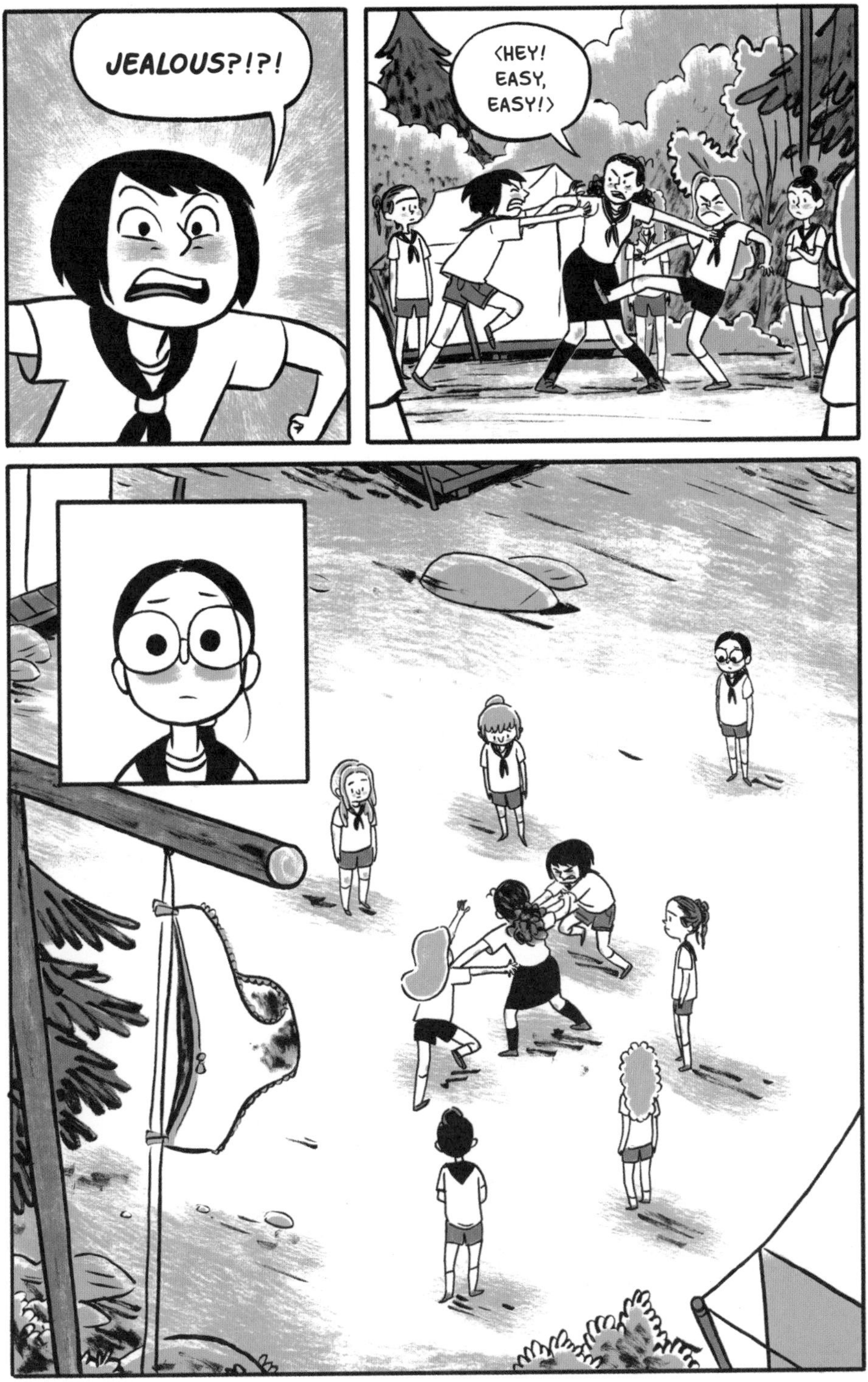
JEALOUS?!?!
<HEY! EASY, EASY!>

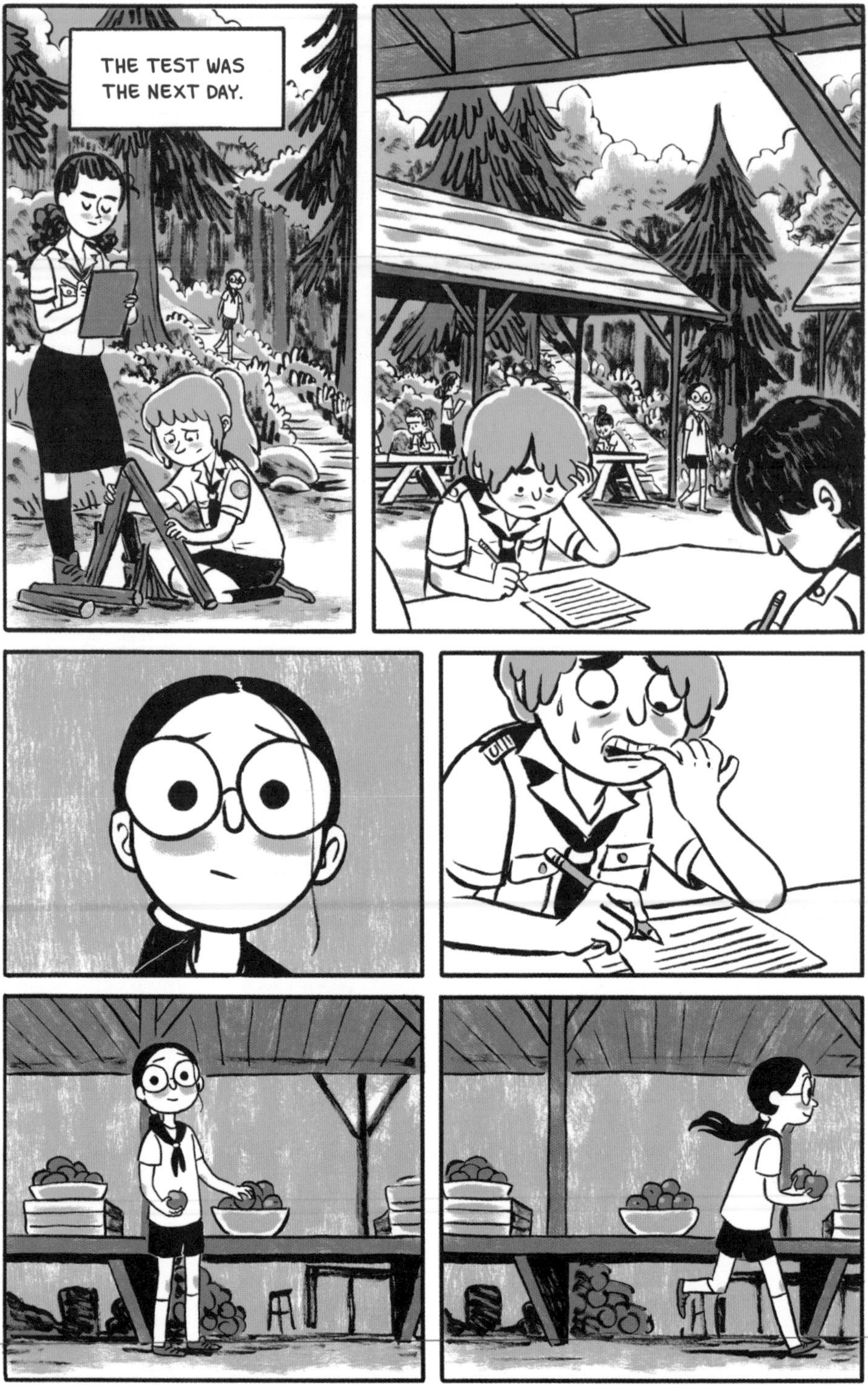
THE TEST WAS
THE NEXT DAY.

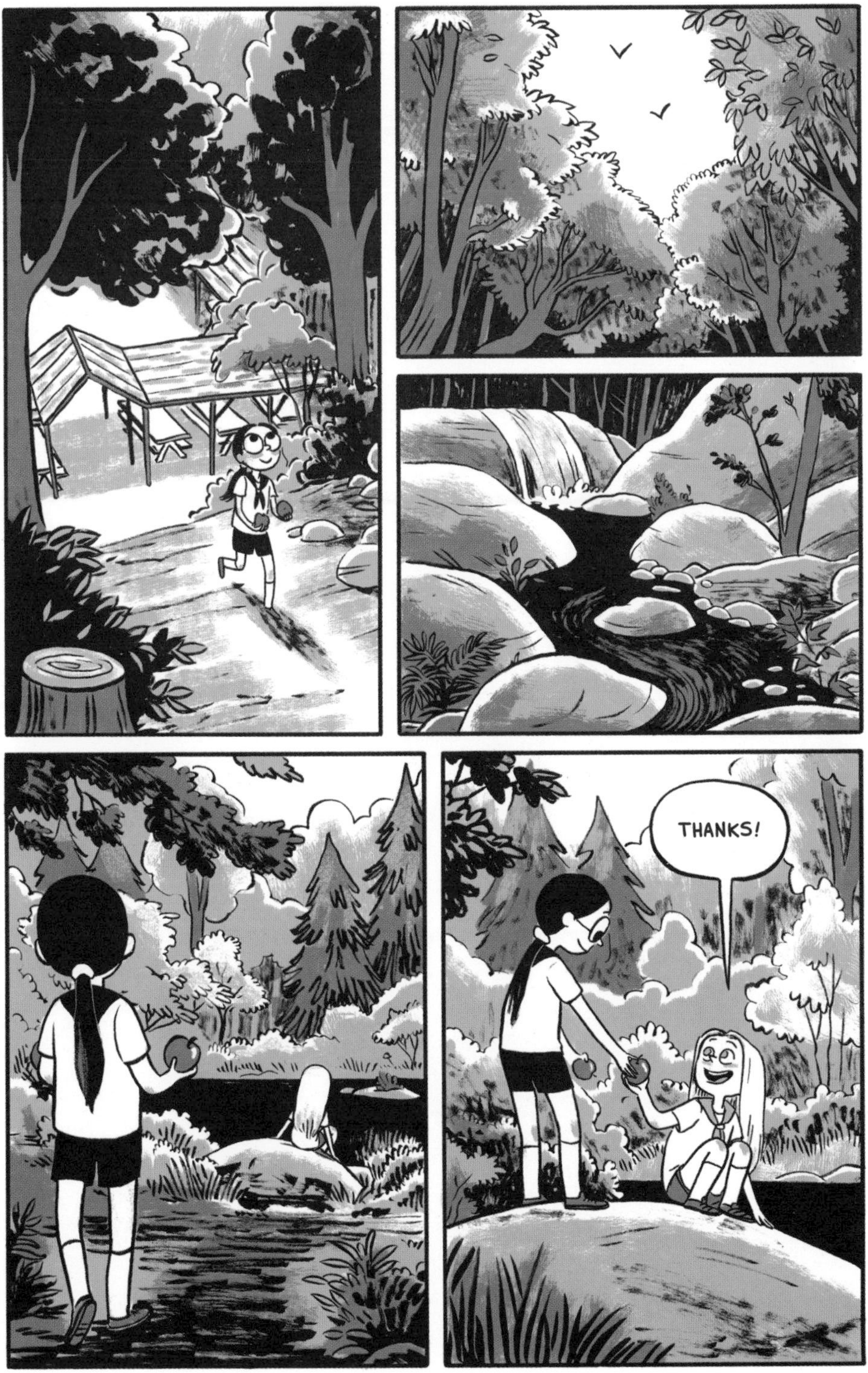
THANKS!

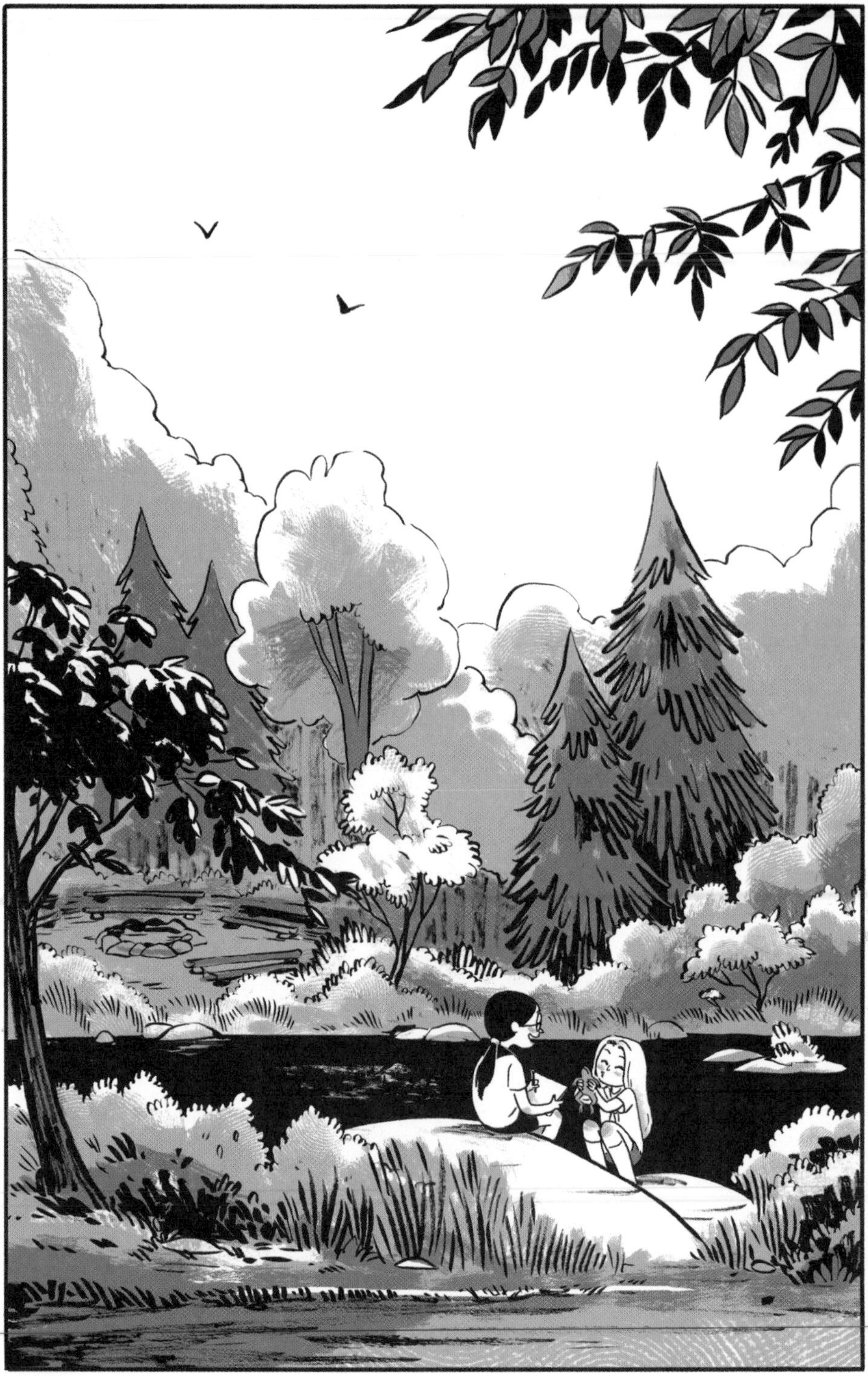

226

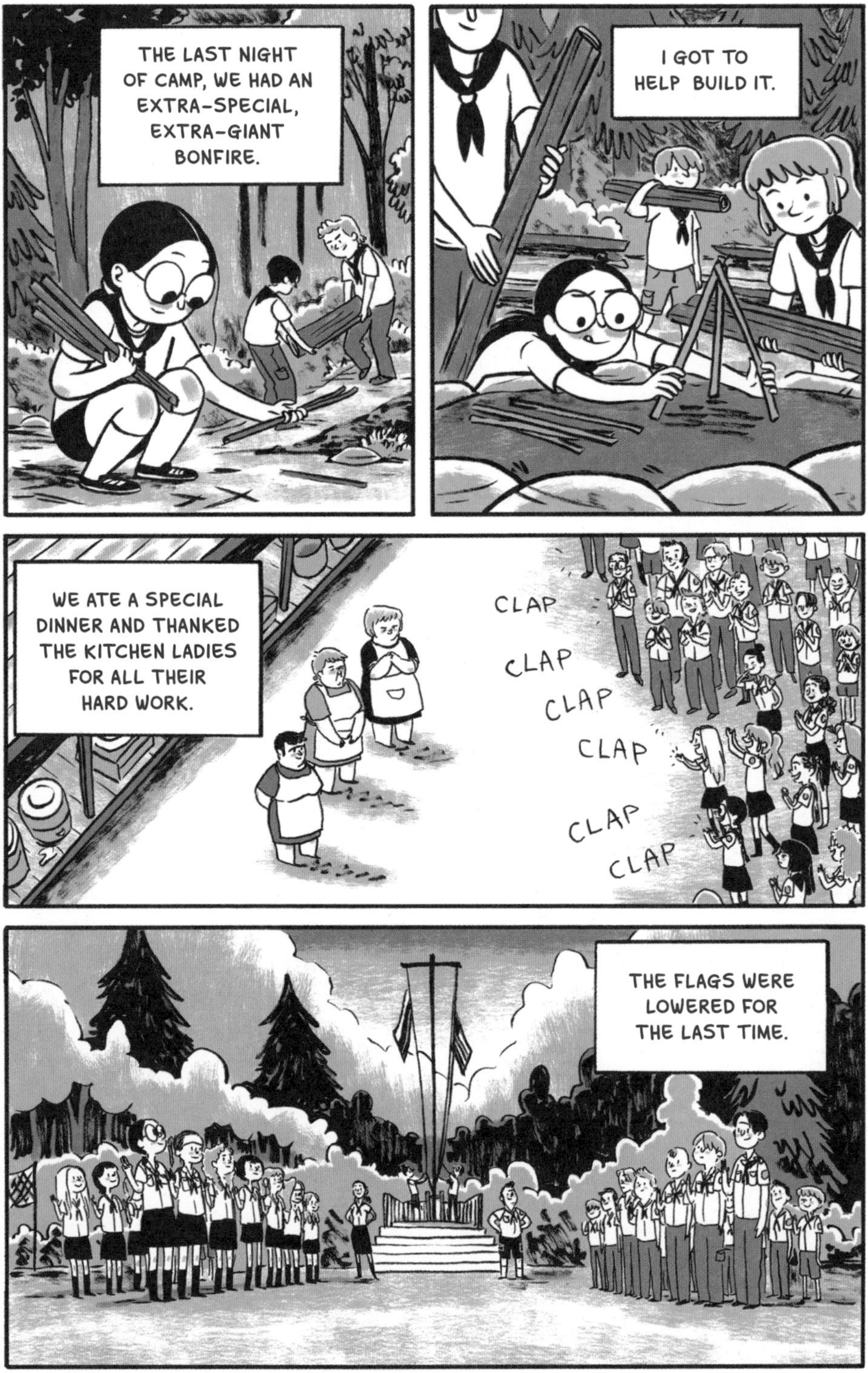
THE LAST NIGHT OF CAMP, WE HAD AN EXTRA-SPECIAL, EXTRA-GIANT BONFIRE.
I GOT TO HELP BUILD IT.
WE ATE A SPECIAL DINNER AND THANKED THE KITCHEN LADIES FOR ALL THEIR HARD WORK.
CLAP
CLAP
CLAP
CLAP
CLAP
CLAP
THE FLAGS WERE LOWERED FOR THE LAST TIME.

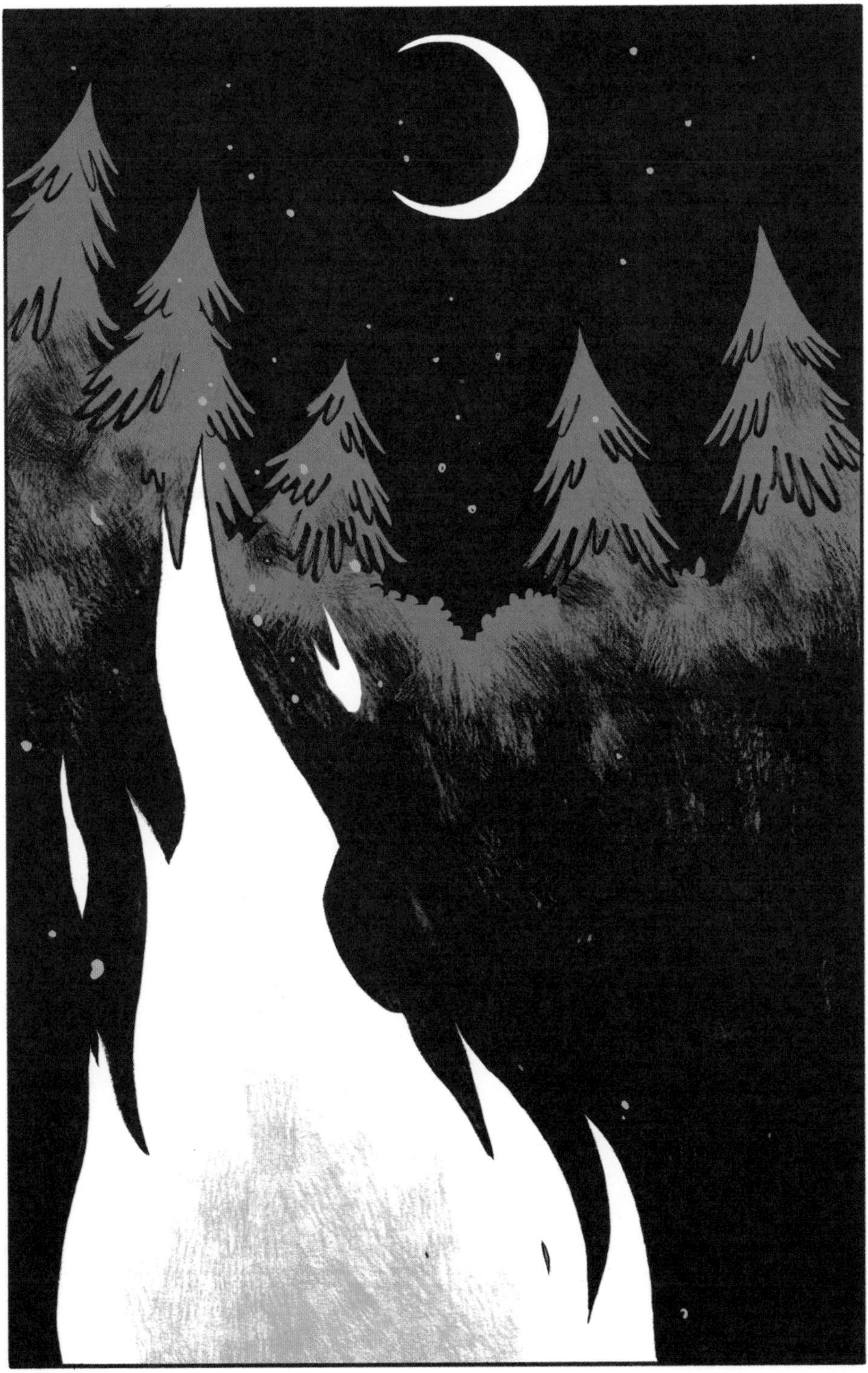

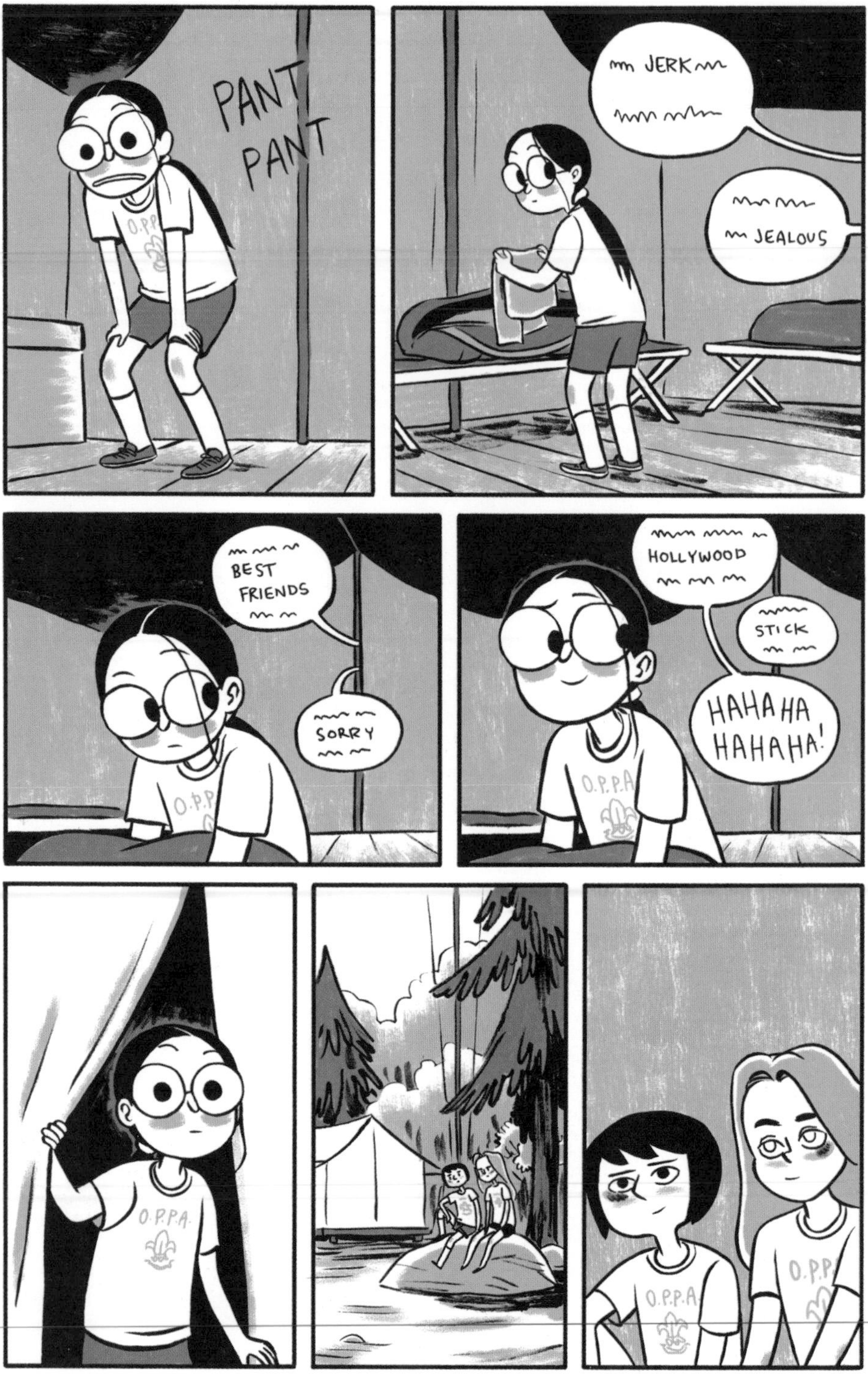
PANT PANT
JERK
JEALOUS
BEST FRIENDS
SORRY
HOLLYWOOD
STICK
HAHAHA HAHAHA!

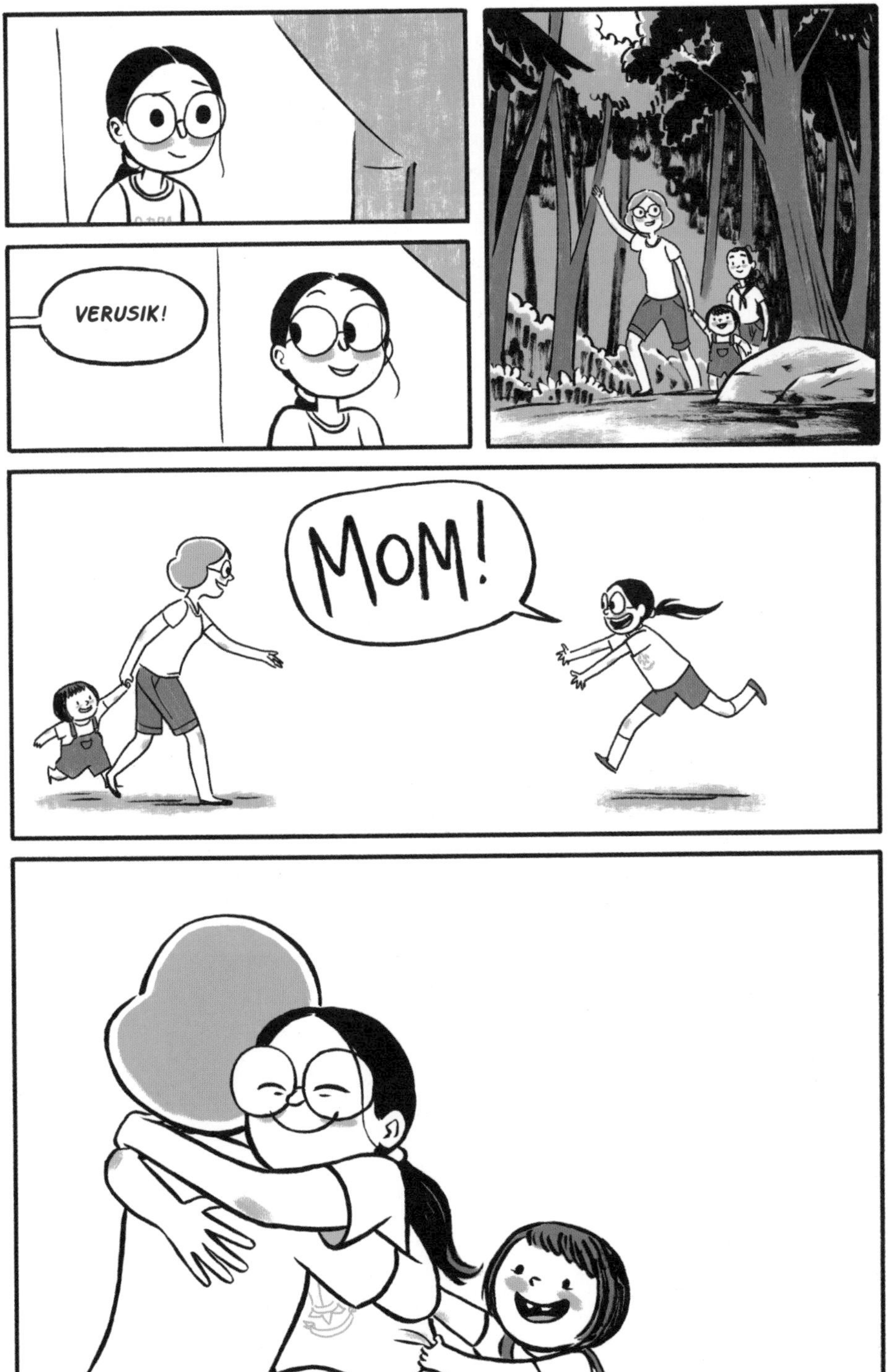
VERUSIK!
MOM!

243

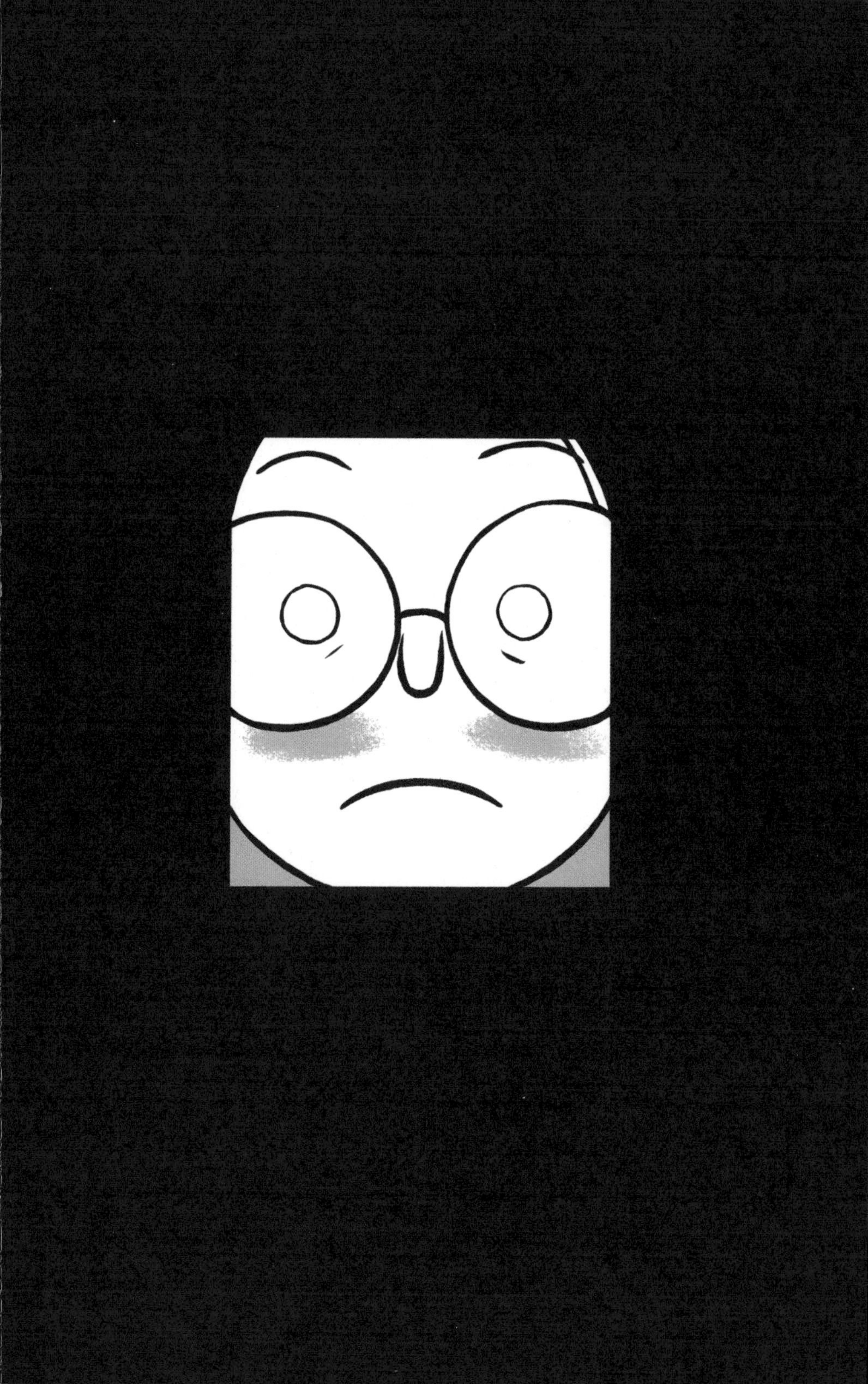

ПРИМЕЧАНИЯ АВТОРА*

*author's note

This book is a true story. And also made up.

Even if you could remember everything that happened during one month over twenty years ago, chances are it wouldn't make the best story. Days go by where nothing interesting happens. Then too much happens, but to the wrong people. Characters don't get their just desserts. It would be a bad book.

I actually spent two summers at camp (urgh), but consolidated the experience into one very eventful one. I wrote down all my memories in a big list, then grilled my siblings for THEIR memories. My mom dug up old letters and photos. I also interviewed Natasha, a former counselor who has been at camp much more recently than me. I even went to the camp myself, sneaking in during an open house to sketch and take photos. It was exactly as I remembered it, though they had added a door to the Hollywood and the campers were no longer washing their hair in the lake. (Thanks, Clean Water Act.)

I arranged those memories into what felt like a good story, changing names and locations to protect people's privacy and making up new characters. I really did have that awful sleepover party, and get bitten by a chipmunk. I didn't have an awesome counselor like Natasha, but I did have a great friend like Kira. I really did go off alone and hear a moose, but I never laid eyes on it. Gregor lost his boot in a mudhole, but I don't think he ever got justice. Books can be nicer than life sometimes.

Though some details changed a bit for dramatic purposes, the feelings are 100 percent true. I set out to write about a hard, lonely summer I had when I was a kid. It always took me a long time to make friends, and being dropped into a strange environment with older kids and giant horseflies didn't play to my strengths. Plenty of people love summer camp and look forward to it every year. Hooray for them, but I was not one of those people. I know I'm not alone in that experience, and this book will hopefully make some kids feel less alone, too.

Or you can just laugh at what a weenie I was.

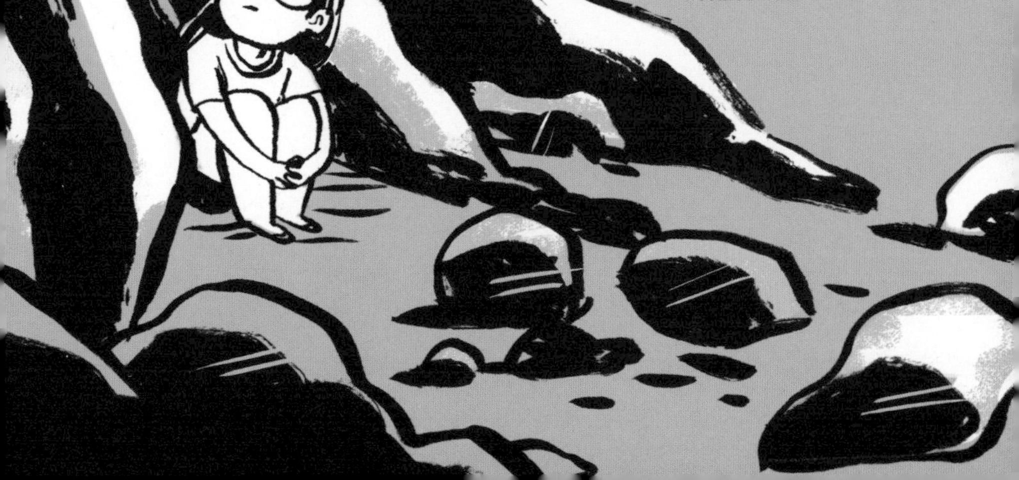

Dear Mom,

Hi. Camp is OK, but I really want to go home. For the first time I hate camp. All the people here are mean to me. Everyo[ne] has candy and they eat it in front of me. It is so hard to make a call because there is a line. There is no runni[ng] water in the whole camp, I swear. I cry almost every night. The people here are snobby and call me names. Last night at the KEPEP a girl called me the F-word because I stumbled in Russian, but had no accent or anything. When I told her I couldn't help it, she called me a liar. I almost cried in front of 45 people. I held it in. But at an overnight in the woods, I burst. I do it at night. We just had a fire drill. It sucked. I got a cramp. [A]ll I had for dinner was 2 spoo[ns] and cheese with garlic i[n] it. [...] a crappy camp game w[...] wake you up in the middle [...] and go to the boy's camp. T[hey woke] me up at 11:30 last night, [...] of sleep, and made me stand[...]

THIS IS AN ACTUAL LETTER I WROTE TO MY MOM FROM CAMP. THE ONE AT THE VERY BEGINNING OF THE BOOK WAS WRITTEN BY MY BROTHER, WHO IT TURNED OUT WASN'T ENJOYING HIMSELF AS MUCH AS I THOUGHT.

f camp without a flashlight. I didn't have enough $ batteries. The people here are nasty. I'm almost crying right now. I did something terrible too. I played a "joke", but I got into so much trouble. Can you please stop those darn installments? I really want to go home. I lost the automatic pencil, but I have one friend. She oil paints and draws too! Her name is KMPA. She's nice. Everyone here is mean. They have junk food and eat it without sharing. So, if I don't go home early, can you bring me a big bag of Skittles and one of ~~Starbursts~~ M&M'S? Pleze? I know you probably won't but at least take me home. I hate it here. Say hi to Masha. I send her my love and Geoffrey and his family, too.

Love,
(And homesick crying)
Vera

P.S. My stomach hurts every night. It does now, too.

СЛОВО БЛАГОДАРНОСТИ*

*words of thanks

Thanks to Mark Siegel and Judy Hansen for their wisdom, enthusiasm, and ferocious cheerleading. The invaluable eyes of the Story Trust made the book better each time they read it—thanks to Gene Luen Yang, Sam Bosma, Shelli Paroline, and Braden Lamb. Natasha Peavy was instrumental in helping refresh my memory of what camp was like twenty-two years ago, and even sent me photos of her uniform.

Alec Longstreth knocked it out of the park with his coloring, and I will owe him forever. The team at First Second put the book together with their customary aplomb.

Thanks to excellent buds Raina Telgemeier, Graham Annable, Tony Stacchi, Julian Nariño, and Brian Ormiston for their eyeballs, and to the gang on S.T. for their commiseration. Jeremy Spake loved this project from day one and wouldn't let me get down on it even for a second. Extra-special thanks to my family—Lyudmila, Philipp, and Masha—for merging their patchy recollections with mine and being such good sports. We all survived to tell the tale.

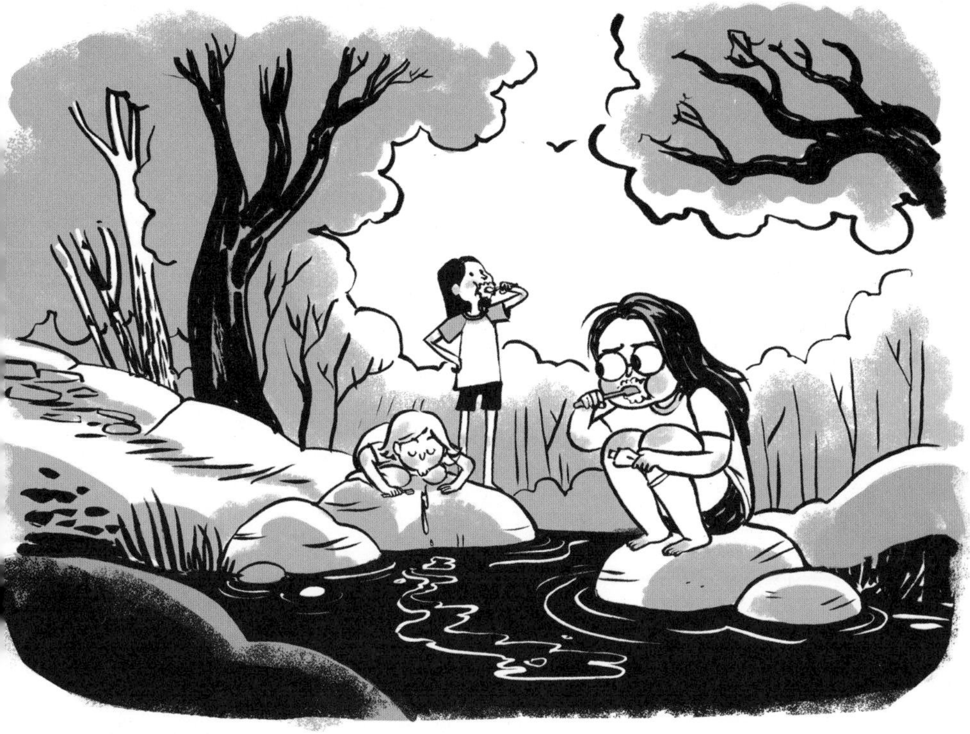

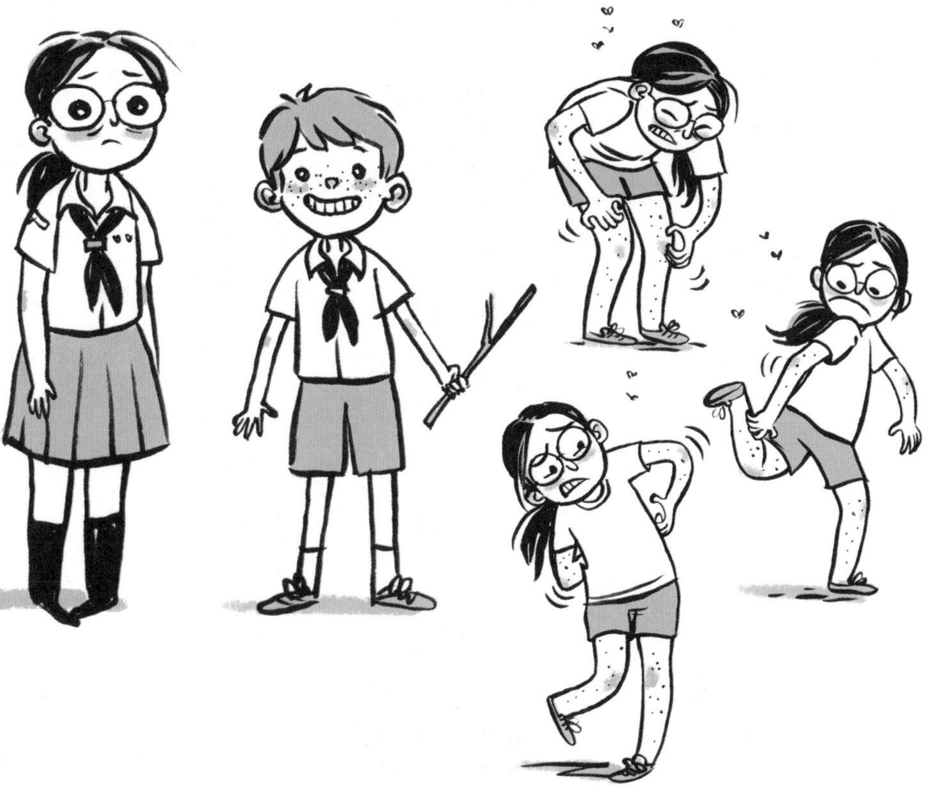

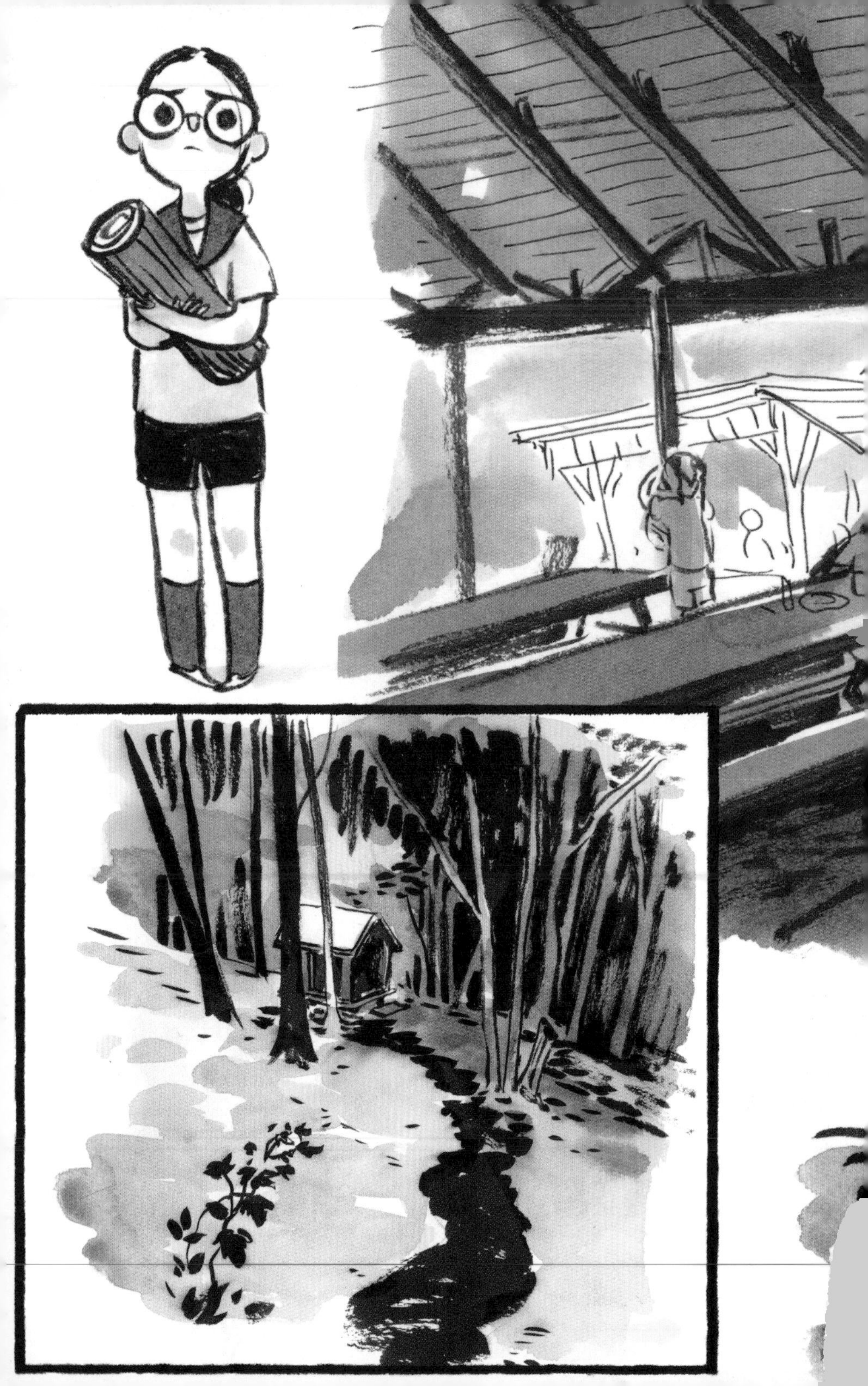

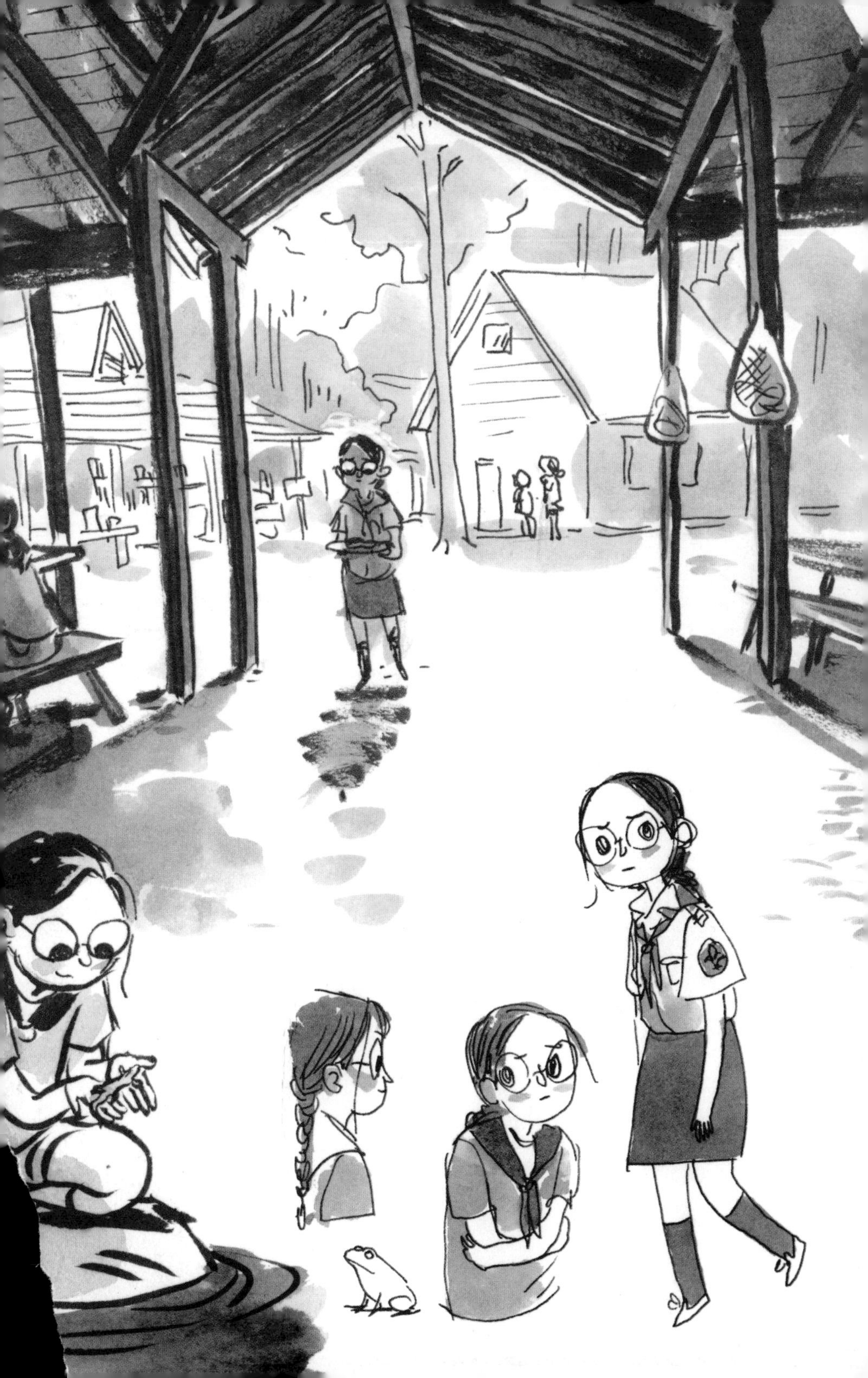

:01

First Second

COPYRIGHT © 2018 BY VERA BROSGOL

PUBLISHED BY FIRST SECOND
FIRST SECOND IS AN IMPRINT OF ROARING BROOK PRESS, A DIVISION
OF HOLTZBRINCK PUBLISHING HOLDINGS LIMITED PARTNERSHIP
175 FIFTH AVENUE, NEW YORK, NY 10010

ALL RIGHTS RESERVED

LIBRARY OF CONGRESS CONTROL NUMBER: 2017946145

HARDCOVER ISBN: 978-1-62672-444-0
PAPERBACK ISBN: 978-1-62672-445-7

OUR BOOKS MAY BE PURCHASED IN BULK FOR PROMOTIONAL, EDUCATIONAL, OR
BUSINESS USE. PLEASE CONTACT YOUR LOCAL BOOKSELLER OR THE MACMILLAN
CORPORATE AND PREMIUM SALES DEPARTMENT AT (800) 221-7945 EXT. 5442 OR
BY E-MAIL AT MACMILLANSPECIALMARKETS@MACMILLAN.COM.

FIRST EDITION, 2018
BOOK DESIGN BY DANIELLE CECCOLINI AND ROB STEEN
COLORS BY ALEC LONGSTRETH

PRINTED IN CHINA BY 1010 PRINTING INTERNATIONAL LIMITED, NORTH POINT, HONG KONG

PENCILLED DIGITALLY IN CLIP STUDIO PAINT. INKED WITH A BRUSH-PEN
ON BRISTOL BOARD AND COLORED DIGITALLY IN PHOTOSHOP.

PAPERBACK: 7 9 10 8 6
HARDBACK: 1 3 5 7 9 10 8 6 4 2

BY ART
WE LIVE